FLIGHT OF THE INTRUDER

"Extraordinary! Once you start reading, you won't want to stop!"
—Tom Clancy

"[Coonts's] gripping, first-person narration of aerial combat is the best I've ever read. Once begun, this book cannot be laid aside."
—*The Wall Street Journal*

"Kept me strapped in the cockpit of the author's imagination for a down-and-dirty novel."
—*St. Louis Post-Dispatch*

SAUCER

"A comic, feel-good SF adventure...[delivers] optimistic messages about humanity's ability to meet future challenges."
—*Kirkus Reviews*

"Tough to put down."
—*Publishers Weekly*

PRAISE FOR THE NOVELS OF
STEPHEN COONTS

LIARS & THIEVES

"Vintage Coonts...plenty of action and intrigue, with the added benefit of a new lead character."   —*Dallas Morning News*

"Excellent."   —*Publishers Weekly* (starred review)

LIBERTY

"Frighteningly realistic."   —*Maxim*

"Gripping...Coonts's naval background and his legal education bring considerable authority to the story, and the narrative is loaded with detailed information about terrorist networks, modern weaponry, and international intrigue...the action is slam-bang."   — *Publishers Weekly*

AMERICA

"The master of the techno-thriller spins a bone-chilling worst-case scenario involving international spies, military heroics, conniving politicians, devious agencies, a hijacked nuclear sub, lethal computer hackers, currency speculators, maniac moguls, and greedy mercenaries that rival Clancy for fiction-as-realism and Cussler for spirited action...[Coonts] never lets up with heart-racing jet/missile combat, suspenseful submarine maneu-vers, and doomsday scenarios that feel only too real, providing real food for thought in his dramatization of the missile-shield debate."   —*Publishers Weekly* (starred review)

MORE ...

"Fans of Coonts and his hero Grafton will love it. Great fun."
—*Library Journal*

"Coonts's action and the techno-talk are as gripping as ever."
—*Kirkus Reviews*

"Thrilling roller-coaster action. Give a hearty 'welcome back' to Admiral Jake Grafton."   —*The Philadelphia Inquirer*

HONG KONG

"Move over, Clancy, readers know they can count on Coonts."
—*Midwest Book Review*

"The author gives us superior suspense with a great cast of made-up characters…But the best thing about this book is Coonts's scenario for turning China into a democracy."
—Liz Smith, *New York Post*

"A high-octane blend of techno-wizardry [and] ultraviolence…[Coonts] skillfully captures the postmodern flavor of Hong Kong, where a cell phone is as apt as an AK-47 to be a revolutionary weapon."   —*USA Today*

"Entertaining…intriguing."   —*Booklist*

STEPHEN COONTS'

DEEP BLACK: JIHAD

JIHAD

**Written by Stephen Coonts
and Jim DeFelice**

St. Martin's Paperbacks

STEPHEN COONTS' DEEP BLACK: JIHAD

Copyright © 2007 by Stephen Coonts.

ISBN: 0-312-93699-0
EAN: 978-0-312-93699-0

Printed in the United States of America

St. Martin's Paperbacks edition / January 2007

St. Martin's Paperbacks are published by St. Martin's Press, 175 Fifth Avenue, New York, NY 10010.

10 9 8 7 6 5 4 3 2 1

CHAPTER I

THE LIGHT BLUE Mercedes came around the corner a bit too fast, tires squealing as the driver tucked around a tour bus parked near Istanbul's Grand Bazaar. Just then a cab spurted from the curb directly into the Mercedes' path. The Mercedes veered to the left, but the way was blocked by another bus; before the driver could veer back, two of his tires blew. The car plowed into the side of a small panel truck, striking it so hard that the truck's gas tank exploded with a gush of flames.

Or so it appeared from the Mercedes.

Most of the tourists and others nearby were too stunned to react, even to run away. But one devout woman who happened to be passing nearby saw the accident and rushed toward the flames, her long dress and chador fluttering in the wind as she ran. Dodging a vehicle that just slammed on its brakes, she ran to the Mercedes. As she reached it, a fireball rose from the tour bus, exploding above with a boom that shook the entire block.

"So far, so good," said Jeff Rockman, watching the disaster unfold on the large screen at the front of Desk Three's op center, commonly known as the Art Room.

"We have a considerable distance to go, Mr. Rockman," replied William Rubens, who as the number two man in the National Security Agency ran Desk Three, colloquially known as Deep Black. "Please direct your attention to Ms. DeFrancesca and keep your color commentary to yourself."

CHAPTER 2

LIA DEFRANCESCA THREW her hand against the window of the Mercedes, slamming what looked like a large cookie into the corner of the glass near the driver. She twisted her palm against the device and let go, jerking back as flames from the nearby bus erupted above her. The heat from the fireball drove her to her knees. There, she reached her right hand into her left sleeve and pulled out what looked like a fabric eyeglass case with a metallic nipple at the top. She rammed the nipple into the center of the cookie, which by then had drilled a hole through the glass window. Black smoke furled around her, so thick that Lia had trouble seeing the brown swatch at the side of the case she had to press. She worked her fingers across the canvas exterior, feeling for the button; when she found it, she pressed twice without feeling the click of the spring beneath her thumb. Finally a third touch solicited a loud *swoosh*, as the compressed gas in the canister inside the bag was released into the car through a hole drilled by the cookie. Still on her knees, Lia reached into her right sleeve and took a cell phone from its elastic holding spot. She flipped the phone open and punched the green button; rather than dialing a number, the phone sent a code to the car's master computer, unlocking the doors. By the time she got up, the device she'd placed on the window had already done its job: all four of the car's occupants were unconscious.

"The security team is out of the vehicles," said a voice in Lia's head. It belonged to Rockman, the runner back in the Art Room monitoring the mission. "You have thirty seconds."

Lia pulled the gas device from the window and kicked it under the car. Opening the rear passenger door, she removed a switchblade from her sleeve and hacked through the seatbelt of the passenger nearest her, then tucked her shoulder down and lifted him from the car. She'd just gotten him to the ground when a beefy set of fingers grabbed her right arm and threw her to the pavement.

CHAPTER 3

TOMMY KARR WINCED as his left leg was jammed toward his neck. The man looming over him began pummeling his back, pounding the muscles senseless. Without warning he grabbed Karr's head and pushed it to the side, first left then right, rocking back and forth with sharp jerks.

A beating had never felt so good.

"You like?" asked the *tellak,* a combination attendant, masseuse, and scrubber in the exclusive Turkish bath.

"Gave me goose bumps," said Karr.

"We move on when you're ready."

"Awesome." Karr rolled off the hot marble slab, letting his bones soak in the warmth from the steam. Then he went out through an archway opposite the one where he had come in. The *tellak* was waiting, a razor in his hand.

"I think I'll skip that, thanks," said Karr. The next stage of a traditional Turkish bath, *tozu*—the removal of hair from *all* parts of the body—was generally optional for foreigners, but the attendant looked disappointed as he put his blade away and led Karr through a set of columns to a shallow marble bath. There he poured water over the American and began rubbing his torso with a camel hair glove several grades rougher than coarse sandpaper, pulling dead skin and hair into his fist.

"Tickles," said Karr as he was flayed.

After he was buffed down, Karr was soaped with a cream that smelled like olive oil; he felt like a chicken being prepared for a barbecue. A rinse with ice-cold water followed. It took three large basins to properly baste the six-six American, whose muscles tingled with each splash.

Finally the *tellak* pronounced him finished by flapping a fresh towel in the air, wrapping it ceremoniously around Karr's midsection. As a final gesture, he gave Karr a long lecture in Turkish on the history of Turkish baths—they extended to the Romans, who had made their capital here in Istanbul in the sixth century—and their many health benefits. Since the American had no idea what the man was saying, he nodded as soberly as possible, given the circumstances. Only when he was properly educated did the *tellak* see fit to release him, pointing toward an archway beyond the columns.

These led to the *masak* or cold room, a lounge where bathers went to recover from the ordeal of coming clean. Karr's wooden clogs were two or three sizes too small, and he felt a bit like a ballet dancer in special shoes as he ambled into the room. The only other occupants were two middle-aged Turkish men sharing a *nargile*, a classic Turkish water pipe, smoking apple-scented tobacco. Karr smiled at them, giving his head a half bow. One of the men said something to the other, and they both laughed.

"Yup," said Karr, laughing himself. "Definitely my first time." He ran his fingers through his yellow hair. "Guess it shows, huh?"

The men looked at each other and laughed again. They were in their fifties, obviously well off or they wouldn't be here. They sat on a large couch covered with a cloth so thick it looked like a rug. A tray of dried apricots sat on a small table at the side, along with two glasses of *elma* or apple tea.

"Stuff in the pipe smells good," said Karr. "What is it? Ganja?"

"Eh?" asked one of the men.

"Dope. Pot." Karr put his fingers to his lips as if smoking a joint. The men remained confused. "Marijuana?"

"Oh, no, no, no," said the man on the left. "This is tobacco," he said, speaking in English. "Here—join us."

"Me?" Karr glanced around.

"Yes, yes, come, come. You're American?"

"Born and bred," said Karr. "You guys?"

The man turned and looked at his companion, then burst out laughing.

"We're Turkish," said the first man.

"Well, no, you just speak English real well," said Karr.

"English is the universal language," said the second man. "Come, sit with us, young fellow. Have a smoke. Very good."

The men moved over on the couch and Karr sat between them. He took a hit on the water pipe and immediately began to cough. This amused his new friends so much they nearly fell off the couch laughing. He did better with a second puff; the smoke had a soft, cool taste.

"Wow. Don't let the surgeon general taste that, huh? Get hooked right away." Karr laughed and sat back on the couch. "Name's Thomas Magnum. Dr. Magnum. I'm here for a conference. Great city."

"I am a doctor as well," said the man who had first spoken to him.

"More than a mere doctor," said his friend. "The head of neurology."

"I crack heads open to take a look," said the doctor. He laughed, then told Karr that he had trained for a while in the U.S., and had thought of living there for a while. But pleasures like his regular Tuesday and Thursday visits to the *hamam* brought him back.

An attendant came to ask if Karr would like any refreshments. He deferred to his hosts for advice; after conferring in Turkish, they recommended a glass of *ayran*.

"Okay," said Karr. "What is it?"

"Very healthy," said the doctor. "You will live to one hundred."

The attendant returned with a large glass of a white liquid that smelled like curdled cream. It turned out to be a salty yogurt drink that was clearly an acquired taste.

"Maybe some tea," he said, putting the glass back on the table.

Tears of laughter flowed from his companions' eyes. A small glass of tea appeared almost instantly. Karr took a sip, swished it around to get the salty yogurt taste from his mouth, then began to sneeze. The attendant reappeared with a small cloth—a handkerchief.

"Just what I needed. Thanks," said Karr, adding another of his meager store of Turkish phrases, "*teşekkür ederim.*" The words meant thank you, and were pronounced "teh-shek-kewr eh-deh-reem." Karr stumbled over the middle syllable in each word, and looked apologetically at his hosts.

"Did I get that right?" he asked. Then he covered his face as he sneezed.

The doctor corrected his pronunciation. Karr tried the phrase again, but once more had to sneeze. He excused himself—in English—rose and turned away to be polite.

It also made it easier to remove the small prosthetic tape at the roof of his mouth. He took the flat capsule and snapped it between his fingers, dividing the contents in the other men's tea cups, which were blocked from their view by his hulking back.

"Wow. Must be allergic to something." Karr held up his glass. "A toast, to Turkey and its great hospitality."

His hosts nodded, and raised their teas as well.

"Bottoms up," said Karr, draining his glass.

CHAPTER 4

CHARLIE DEAN TRIED not to react as the bodyguard grabbed Lia. As deliberately as he could, he pulled up the camera that hung around his neck as if to take a picture of the disaster in front of him. His fingers slowly manipulated the focusing ring, zeroing the crosshairs on the head of the man who had just grabbed his partner. The camera was linked to an automated sniper rifle hidden in a van parked nearby; when he pushed the autofocus button down, it locked the target, allowing the computer that guided the weapon to remember and track the head he'd zeroed in on for about ten meters.

He could hear Lia arguing with the man, her tone familiar despite the strange words in Egyptian Arabic she'd spent hours memorizing over the past few weeks.

She's okay, he told himself; just keep playing tourist. If he was going to work with her, if he was going to remain close to her—love her—he had to learn to hang back. That was the deal they made.

Not that he could ever be comfortable with it: his heart jumped when he saw the bodyguard pull her roughly to her feet.

"WHAT ARE YOU doing?" demanded Lia, speaking in Egyptian Arabic and then switching to English. "The men need attention and I am a nurse."

The first man ignored her. Another grabbed the sleeve of her long Muslim dress.

"Stay back, sister," said one of the bodyguards in Arabic. "We will attend to the wounded."

"I am a nurse, educated at Aga Khan University School of Nursing in Pakistan. That man in the back needs attention. Look at the cut on his head," she added, pointing.

"You're not from Pakistan," said the man. "Or here."

"I was born in Malaysia."

"You sound Egyptian."

"Where I have worked for ten years. Are we meant to argue here while your friend bleeds to death? Is that why God Himself directed me to walk down the block at the moment of this catastrophe?"

Smoke poured from the bus. The bodyguard who had thrown Lia down took the man she had pulled out and began dragging him away.

"No!" yelled Lia. She surged forward, pressing against the arm of the bodyguard holding her. "He may have a head injury. You will paralyze him! Careful!"

The man on the ground was Asad bin Taysr. Known in the West as "the Red Lion," he was the number three official in the al-Qaeda terrorist network. Traveling as a Syrian businessman, he had come to Istanbul for a meeting with other members of the terrorist network.

"*Hayir, hayir!*" screamed a man nearby, saying no in Turkish.

Lia turned in time to see another of the bodyguards pull a Beretta handgun from his holster and fire pointblank into the face of a driver whose car had stopped nearby. It was apparently a case of mistaken identity—the cabbie who had set up the accident was long gone—but it was too late for Lia or anyone else to do anything about it. The man's head flew back and his mouth opened, as if he were taking a last gulp of air before expiring.

The gunman turned and came toward her, gun pointed at her face. Lia stared at the barrel; Charlie Dean was nearby somewhere, but it seemed unlikely that he'd be able to do anything if the man with the gun decided to fire.

"Who are you?" he demanded in English.

"I am a nurse," she answered. "Your friend there needs attention or he will die. And you cannot drag him on the street like a bag of rice."

The man put the pistol a few inches from her forehead. "If he dies, so will you."

Lia scowled at him, then pushed herself from the other bodyguard's arm and knelt beside Asad.

"An ambulance," she said loudly. "An ambulance quickly, or he will join the Prophets in Paradise, all praise and honor to their souls."

"THE AMBULANCE IS two blocks away," Rockman told Dean. "You'd better get over to the hospital."

Dean didn't answer, watching as a police car pulled up. The officers ran over to the bodyguards standing over Lia as she pretended to minister to Asad. The guards had not bothered to holster their pistols. One of the policemen began shouting at them; Dean tensed, almost expecting a shootout. They'd rehearsed this operation more than two dozen times, but that was one contingency they hadn't thought of.

"Charlie, you there?"

"Relax, Rockman," said Dean.

One of the bodyguards raised his pistol and pointed it at the policeman. Dean glanced at Lia, kneeling a few feet away; she'd be sure to be hit in a crossfire.

A second and then a third police car drove up the street, followed by a fire engine, its siren blistering the air. The bodyguard who'd pointed the weapon at the policeman began telling him in English that someone had tried to murder his boss, a prominent Syrian diplomat.

"The lies just keep on comin'," said Rockman sarcastically. "Red Lion will be president of Syria next."

"You, back," barked someone to Dean's left.

He turned and found a plainclothes detective with his hand out, moving the onlookers back to the curb. Dean shuffled back to the sidewalk, deciding that it was indeed time to go— the hospital was only a few blocks away, but even with the bicycle it might take several minutes to weave through the traffic. Dr. Ramil would be wondering where he was.

But as Dean started for the corner, the plainclothes policeman caught up to him.

"The film," said the policeman in Turkish, grabbing him by the arm. "We need it for the investigation."

The policeman was considerably younger than Dean, but that was his only advantage; he had a potbelly, stood six inches shorter than Dean, and was already huffing from the few steps it had taken to catch up with him. But the last thing Dean needed at the moment was a confrontation.

"He's asking for the film in your camera," said the translator back in the Art Room. "Tell him you don't understand: *Anlamryoyrum.*"

You're a big help, Dean thought.

"This camera doesn't have film," Dean told the policeman in English. "Do you see? It's digital?"

The detective squinted. Dean guessed that like most Turks, the man could understand English, as long as it was spoken carefully, but felt more sure of himself in his native tongue.

"The camera doesn't use film," repeated Dean. He slipped his finger to the side, snapping open the compartment where the battery and memory card were kept. "I can give you this. Is this what you want?"

He pushed on the back of the small Memory Stick and removed it from the camera. It was blank, but the policeman had no way of knowing that.

"Film?" asked the cop.

"*Evet,*" said Dean, using one of the few Turkish words he'd been able to memorize. "Yes. Digital film."

He handed it to him. The policeman told him in heavily accented English that he could pick it up at the police station in two days. Then he waved him away, turning to find someone else who might have witnessed the accident.

"You have to work on your accent," said the translator as Dean hurried for the bike, chained to a post on the next street.

"I'll try and work that in," Dean replied, fumbling with the combination.

CHAPTER 5

THE SEDATIVE KARR had placed in the men's drinks was powerful, but the dose in the capsule had been designed for one
man, not two, and Karr wasn't sure it would completely knock
the doctor out. He hoped it would; the alternative plan
called for him to pop the physician while they changed. He
didn't want to do that, not because it was more complicated,
but because he didn't want to hurt the guy, who seemed a
congenial sort.

But the drug didn't seem to be working, even though the
doctor had drunk nearly the entire glass of tea. He picked up
the tube of the pipe, closing his eyes as he took a long breath.
Karr found himself staring at him when the doctor opened
his eyes.

"Have another puff," sad the doctor, passing him the pipe.

"Love to," lied Karr. The doctor's friend looked a little
tired at least.

"So what is your specialty?" asked the doctor.

"Pediatrics," said Karr. "But I was thinking I might get
into psychiatry."

"Psychiatry?"

"Yeah. Kind of like what you do, only from a different
angle."

Since he'd had to strip naked to get into the baths, Karr
was out of communication with the Art Room. A small implant in his skull functioned as an internal headphone, but the
real guts of the radio were sewn into his clothes and belt back
in a changing room. Without help from the Art Room, he

couldn't take the conversation too far or make it too specific; Karr knew a lot about a lot of things, but had always kept as far as possible from doctors and their craft.

"The brain—some things should be mysterious," said the Turkish doctor, taking the pipe.

"I think you're right," said Karr.

"The human organism—to be—it is not—a machine."

With the last word, the doctor's head edged backwards. Karr caught him and leaned him against the back of the seat. He turned and found the doctor's companion already passed out, head against the top of the cushion.

"I really want to thank you guys for the tobacco," said Karr, making them comfortable. "And the curdled milk."

He stood up. The attendant came over, staring at the men.

"Guess I bored them," Karr said, heading for his clothes.

CHAPTER 6

DR. SAED RAMIL SMILED at the head of internal medicine at Istanbul Medical University Center, nodding as Dr. Özdilick explained the small private hospital's elaborate computer system. Each resident at the hospital carried a wireless device that allowed him to see a patient's complete chart instantly. The devices could display X-rays and other scans as well, though it was generally more convenient to use one of the many larger screens littering the hallways and walls of the rooms.

"Impressive," said Ramil. He wondered where Charlie Dean was. He didn't need him for the procedure, but the op was good insurance if anything went wrong.

Not that it would.

Dr. Özdilick pulled up a pharmacological reference on one of the wall screens. Ramil, trying not to overplay his role as an interested foreign doctor, gave a restrained "mmm" in admiration.

"In your own specialties of neurology and trauma, we have all of the diagnostic tools one could wish," said his guide, jabbing a menu at the lower left of the large screen. The screen filled with icons indicating a number of programs. Ramil stared at them as if he were seeing them for the first time.

"You're frowning," said Dr. Özdilick.

"Oh, just trying to decipher these." Ramil feigned a smile. Instead of practicing the procedure umpteen times with the Desk Three people, he should have taken an acting course.

That was the tough part of this, wasn't it? Pretending to be someone else. The medical procedure he could do cold.

Any second, Red Lion would be wheeled through the doors downstairs and they could get to work. Then he'd relax. It would be like the old days, the *really* old days in Vietnam when he worked in the MASH unit. He'd be nervous until the snap of the gloves. Then something else would take over and the butterflies would disappear.

"Doctor?"

Ramil looked at his guide. "Might I have some water? I feel thirsty."

Dr. Özdilick led him a few yards down the hall to a large water cooler. Air bubbled up from the jug with a loud *kerklunk*. It tasted like cardboard in his mouth, but at least it was cold.

"There you are," said a quiet voice behind them.

Ramil turned and saw that Charlie Dean had finally arrived. Rather than reassuring him, it caused his stomach to turn—the operation was ready to begin.

"My colleague, Dr. Gomez from Madrid," Ramil told Dr. Özdilick.

"Yes, you introduced us yesterday. How was the session?"

"A little bit, eh, not interesting," said Dean. He spoke English with a Spanish accent that was more Mexico than Madrid, but few people in Turkey would know the difference.

Dr. Özdilick's pager gave a short beep.

"Excuse me," said the doctor, retreating a few steps down the hall to the open window of a nurse's station.

LIA ADJUSTED HER headpiece as the ambulance backed in toward the emergency room entrance of the Istanbul Medical University Center. The bodyguard who had shot the Turkish man was crouched near the door, watching the attendant who'd slapped an oxygen mask on Asad.

Even with the pure oxygen, the al-Qaeda operative seemed to be having trouble breathing. If Asad died, the whole operation would be a waste.

Even so, Lia would have relished seeing Asad choke to

death. In his mid-thirties, with the air of a humble and soft-spoken college professor, he'd been responsible for hundreds of deaths, and was in Istanbul to plan thousands more.

The ambulance doors opened and the bodyguard jumped out, surveying the area before letting the attendants take the stretcher out. Lia put her fingers on Asad's throat as if she were taking his pulse. She trotted alongside as the attendants pushed him inside, people backing out of the way to allow them to pass. She had a brief speech outlining his symptoms ready, but a nurse began immediately examining the patient as he was wheeled in, and before Lia could say anything, the woman had barked instructions for the hospital's neurologist to be called.

The attendants pushed the rolling stretcher toward a set of white curtains at the far end of the room. A nurse appeared and told Lia in Turkish that she was not permitted beyond the common area.

"I'm a nurse," Lia said, also using Turkish.

"I'm sorry—"

"No, she comes," insisted the bodyguard in English. Though his pistol was in his holster and out of sight, his voice was sharp enough that the nurse backed off and let Lia join them.

"They're just finding out that Dr. Kildare won't be joining the party," said Rockman over the Deep Black communications system. "They'll be calling our guy down any second."

"His pupils aren't responsive," Lia told the doctor who met them. The drug-induced symptom had an immediate effect: the doctor concluded that the patient probably had a concussion or an even more serious head injury.

"Explain that you are not Turkish and that's why you're using English," said Rockman, sounding like a play prompter when an actor went off script during rehearsal.

Lia, knowing it was unnecessary, ignored the voice in her head. She helped one of the nurses set up a blood pressure cuff. Asad's blood pressure had been low in the ambulance and was even lower now—a deviation from the script considerably more severe than Lia's dropped line.

"We need the neurologist very quickly," the young doctor told one of the nurses. "And get Dr. Kayseri, the trauma expert."

DEAN WATCHED RAMIL stare up at the ceiling as Dr. Özdilick explained the situation. A prominent visitor, a businessman from Syria, had been involved in a car accident and had an unknown head injury. The hospital's chief trauma expert had not answered his home phone, and their neurologist was on his break at a local Turkish bath; it might be a half hour or more before either arrived.

"Of course we must help," said Ramil, glancing at Dean. "Where is the emergency room?"

"This way," said Dr. Özdilick, nodding gratefully. He started toward the elevator.

"Lia's downstairs in the emergency room," said Rockman from the Art Room as Dean got into the elevator. "Everything's going great."

THE ELEVATOR STOPPED but the door didn't open right away. Ramil's stomach lurched. For a half second he was sure the elevator had malfunctioned and they were trapped here.

To be tripped up by a ridiculous mechanical failure . . .

The door sprung open. People rushed at them. Ramil followed Dr. Özdilick down the hall. It was all very familiar—they'd constructed a set just like this in an abandoned warehouse near Baltimore.

"We can wash up here," said Dr. Özdilick, gesturing to the left. "I'll find you a coat."

During the rehearsals, Ramil had bantered with the actor playing Özdilick, saying things like, "Do you arrange these emergencies for all your guests?" or, "Cutting down on staff costs by using visitors?" But he couldn't find the words now. His stomach roiling, he wanted to fast forward everything, just get the knife into his hand, relax, focus on what he was doing.

Ramil glanced back at Dean. The Deep Black op wore the expression he always wore: stoic watchfulness. For some men, such an expression masked deep fear, but in Dean's case it was an expression of who he was. From what Ramil knew of him, Dean never felt fear, or even butterflies in his stomach.

Ramil scrubbed his hands at the sink so thoroughly even the old doctor who had supervised his first residency would have been pleased. Dr. Özdilick had found white physician's coats for him and Dean; Dean's looked a size too small, but Ramil's was a perfect fit.

"This way, doctors," said Dr. Özdilick.

A door swung open at the end of the corridor and Ramil caught a glimpse of daylight from the windows in the clinic beyond. His colon twisted ever tighter as he followed Dr. Özdilick down a corridor of examining spaces formed by curtains suspended from the ceiling. One flew open abruptly; Ramil jumped back as a man with a stubble beard and an ill-fitting suit loomed in the middle of the passage. He had a gun in his hand, and he pointed it at Dr. Özdilick.

"Help him," demanded the man. "In the name of God, help him. He is dying."

CHAPTER 7

WILLIAM RUBENS LOOKED up at the large screen at the front of the Art Room, watching the feed from one of the security cameras in the Istanbul hospital. If there was a commercial computer system in the world that Rubens' team of computer specialists couldn't break into, they hadn't found it yet. Conveniently for Desk Three, the hospital's security videos shared the same mainframe that housed its impressive—though not entirely secure—patient information system, where Asad's vital signs were just now being recorded by a special set of instruments.

Contrary to the calculations of the experts who'd said the accident wouldn't produce any real injuries, the driver of Asad bin Taysr's car had suffered a compound leg fracture, but otherwise everything was proceeding smoothly. Lia had indicated that Asad had been stunned but not hurt, exactly as planned. Now, however, Rubens realized that the terror leader's blood pressure numbers were not what they had expected. He walked up the wide steps at the center of the Art Room to a set of consoles where an NSA doctor was monitoring the situation, standing by to give the team advice if needed.

"Asad's blood pressure—is it wrong?" he asked.

"It's low," said the doctor. "It's the opposite of what was supposed to happen from the drugs Lia gave him. Perhaps it's a reaction to the knockout gas."

"I see."

"If it's a reaction, I wouldn't want to give him any more anesthetic. It might kill him."

"On the other hand, he may really have a severe head injury requiring surgery," said Rubens.

"Yes, that's the problem."

CHAPTER 8

LIA SAW DR. RAMIL freeze as the bodyguard demanded that he save Asad. His face paled and his eyes seemed to push back in their sockets. He was the perfect picture of fear.

"Brother," she whispered in her Egyptian Arabic, tugging at the bodyguard's shoulder. "The gun may not be a good idea here. The doctors are not used to being threatened. If they are nervous, they may not be able to do their job."

The man turned and glared down at her.

"And someone who sees it might call the police," added Lia.

Something flickered in the bodyguard's eyes—hate, she thought, though she wasn't sure whether it was toward her or the police.

"I will be nearby," the bodyguard told her. Lia needed the translator's help to untangle his quick Syrian tongue. "If they do the slightest harm to him, scream, and I will run and send them to hell where they belong."

DEAN NUDGED RAMIL into the curtained cubicle. The emergency room physician gave Dean and Ramil a quick read of the patient's vital signs and condition: shallow head wound, unconscious, low blood pressure.

"There are other patients arriving," said the doctor. "Can you take him?"

"Of course," said Ramil smoothly.

Dean took a small penlight from a nearby tray and checked for a concussion. The pupils were nonreactive; Dean gave a loud "hmmmm."

"Mr. Dean, there appears to be a problem with the patient's blood pressure," said the specialist back in the Art Room. "There's a chance it may be a reaction to the drugs. His heart beat also seems irregular. You'll want to make sure Dr. Ramil makes a note of it."

Dean glanced up at Ramil, who was just checking Asad's eyes with a borrowed penlight.

"Can we have skull films?" Dean asked. "We should get them right away. If there's a hematoma—"

"I would strongly recommend a CT scan," said Ramil. "As a precaution."

"Yes, by all means," said Dr. Özdilick.

"Blood pressure is low," said Dean.

"Is it?" said Ramil, bending over Asad.

RAMIL HAD ALREADY seen the blood pressure, but he pretended now to notice it for the first time. He was not a neurologist, but he had extensive experience with trauma patients, and he knew that this was not only unexpected but a bad sign. It might mean not only that Asad had really been injured in the accident, contrary to expectations, but that the injury was life threatening.

On the other hand, there were no obvious signs of cranial swelling. There was no obstruction to his airways and he was breathing normally. His temperature was fine.

If anything, the drugs that Asad had been given should have raised his blood pressure slightly. So was this a reaction to them?

They had planned to check for a hematoma. It was part of the standard medical procedure for a potentially serious head injury. And since the bug could be spotted on a scan, the films taken before the implant could be substituted in the hospital's high-tech system later on if Asad was kept overnight for observation. Now, though, they had to take the scan to really rule out a head injury.

In layman's terms, a hematoma was a pool of blood that leaked into a place where it shouldn't be; it had to be removed or a patient might die from the injury. If this was the case, the low blood pressure would cause the brain to receive less oxygen. At the same time, the arteries in the brain would attempt to overcome the flow restriction and dilate, increasing blood flow and amplifying the injury. The result would be fatal unless Ramil operated immediately to relieve the pressure.

He could do that. He hadn't expected to, but he could.

Then again, the patient didn't have any of the other symptoms Ramil would expect to accompany that sort of head injury. This might be a reaction to the drugs he'd been given.

Something which also could be fatal.

"We need to insure positive ventilation," said Ramil. "Is there an anesthesiologist?"

"He's been paged," said the nurse.

"We can't wait. We need an intravenous, and we'll want to ventilate," Ramil told the nurse, adding that she should prepare doses of morphine and fentanyl, and to have ephedrine on hand.

Ephedrine especially, he thought, but he had to play it as someone who didn't know what was going on would.

"Pressure dropped a little," said Dean. He wasn't looking at the instruments, and Ramil realized he had probably been prompted by the medical expert back in the Art Room.

"Six milligrams of ephedrine," said Ramil.

He caught Dean looking at him as he waited for the hypo.

"He'll be all right," said Ramil.

CHAPTER 9

"TOMMY, YOU'RE STILL at the bath? You have to get over to the hospital and back those guys up."

"Rockman, you're a worry wart, you know that?" Tommy Karr blinked as he stepped into the sunlight. After the damp, heavy air of the bath, the cool breeze felt bracing. He turned left, then right, getting his bearings. He was four blocks from the hospital and the rental car he'd left there, but none of the streets in this section of Istanbul ran in a straight line. His sense of direction seemed to have been scraped off with the dead skin and hair in the camel's hair mitt. Finally he decided he was supposed to go right, and set out.

"The messenger reported the doctor was sleeping and wouldn't wake up five minutes ago," said Rockman. "What have you been doing?"

"Getting dressed. Paying the bill. What have you been doing? Where's Sandy?"

"I'm going to run all three of you since you're all supposed to be at the hospital," said Rockman.

"I'm still on the line if you need me, Tommy," said Sandy Chafetz.

"Ooo, a *ménage à trois*."

"You're in a goofy mood," said Chafetz.

"I think the doc had something extra in his tobacco," said Karr.

CHAPTER 10

"CT IS CLEAN," the doctor in the Art Room told Dean. He sounded both relieved and surprised. "Great. It was just a reaction to the drugs."

Dr. Ramil, across from Dean, stood at the computer screen, waiting for the image to appear. Also sometimes called a CAT scan, the computed tomography or CT device was a special X-ray machine that took pictures of the skull from different angles. It showed a cross section of the head and could detect bleeding and soft tissue injuries much better than regular X-rays. To Dean, who'd briefly owned a pair of laundromats in Arizona, it looked like a large front-loading washing machine.

"He does not seem to have a hematoma," said Ramil. "Would you doctors care to have a look?"

Dean gestured to Dr. Özdilick, letting him go ahead. The scan showed a large clump of gray in the middle of the skull, with the different areas of the brain shaded like a black and white satellite photo of mountains. Had there been any bleeding, it would have shown up as a bright spot, pushing the brain toward the other side of the skull.

"I will address the superficial wounds myself," said Ramil. "Can I work across the hall?"

"Absolutely," said Dr. Özdilick. "Thank you for this."

Dean glanced at Lia as they walked with the gurney back to one of the curtained cubicles.

"Where's the bodyguard?" he asked in a whisper.

"Outside."

"Trouble with him?"

"Not yet," she said, eyes still fixed on the hallway.

RAMIL BEGAN THE way he began all operations, big or small: he held his hands out in supplication and prayed that Allah would guide him.

When was done, he reached to the tray of instruments, chose a scalpel and a pincers. Examining the wound, he slipped the scalpel into the edge and gently cut a deeper flap. He glanced over at Dean, made sure he was watching the entrance to the cubicle, then removed the plastic vial with the bug implant from beneath his gown.

Sweat poured down his forehead. Ramil snapped the end of the vial with the pincers and removed the device, holding it gently in the tool's claws. Roughly the size of two matchsticks, the bug was a small radio that could broadcast its signal roughly two miles, far enough to be picked up by a booster unit and transmitted back to NSA headquarters at Fort Meade, Maryland. Once inserted, it would turn al-Qaeda's number three man into the most important—and unknowing—informer the West had ever had.

Ramil made sure the bug was oriented properly before pushing it into the slot he'd cut behind Red Lion's ear, making a small flap beneath the occipital belly of the occipitofrontalis muscle.

What a work of wonder the human body was, he thought, folding the skin over; the intricate handiwork of God was displayed in the tiniest piece of us.

"Mr. Dean," he said, looking up. "It's ready to be tested."

DEAN TOOK A small handheld computer from his pocket and placed his thumb over the reader at the base. When the screen snapped on, he held the unit up and softly spoke his name. Then he tapped the menu at the top and selected "Jawbreaker" from the choices.

The screen filled with colorful little balls. A casual observer familiar with handheld computers would think the program was the popular game that came standard with many of the machines. But it was really a "skin" for a program designed to test the transmitting strength of the device Ramil had just implanted.

Dean tapped the ball at the lower left corner. The unit blinked; all of the balls on the screen flashed blue, then returned to a random arrangement of red, yellow, green and purple.

"I'm ready," he told Rockman.

"Good, Charlie. The hallway's clear. Turn on the booster unit so we can run the tests here as well."

"Yeah," said Dean. He took what looked like a small camera from his pocket and pushed one of the control buttons, waiting for the light to flash. When it did, he slipped it back into his pants.

Sweat poured from Ramil's forehead.

"I'm going down the hall," Dean told him.

"Go, Charlie," said Lia. "It's under control."

Dean walked toward the room where they'd gone for the scan; there was a restroom there where he could repeat the test without anyone watching. Dr. Özdilick came out of the cubicle just before the hallway, nearly bumping into him.

"Your patient?"

"Dr. Ramil says he's fine," said Dean.

"Very good." Dr. Özdilick started in that direction.

"Doctor," said Dean to stall him. "The restroom—is there a staff restroom nearby?"

"Just around the corner." Özdilick seemed puzzled, and Dean realized that he had inadvertently dropped his Spanish accent.

"Is there a lounge nearby?" he said in quick Spanish before repeating it in slower—and lightly accented—English. "To get something to eat? I'm afraid I'm a little hungry."

Dr. Özdilick gave him directions to the staff cafeteria. He smiled, but Dean couldn't tell whether he'd covered his mistake or not.

"DR. ÖZDILICK IS COMING toward you, Lia," Rockman warned. "Charlie's talking to him at the end of the corridor."

"Someone's coming," Lia told Ramil. "You'll have to suture the wounds."

"Lia, the test isn't complete," said Rockman.

Lia ignored him. Clearly they weren't going to have a chance to slip the backup transmitter in now anyway.

Ramil blinked at her.

"Do you need me to do it?" she asked.

"No. But are the tests done?"

"Forget the tests," said Lia. She started toward the suture tray but Ramil waved her away.

"A few steps away," warned Rockman. "It's Dr. Özdilick."

"I got it," Lia told Ramil. "Take care of Özdilick."

"I have to do this. He's my patient."

"Just talk to Özdilick."

"Thank you, nurse," snapped Ramil dismissively.

Lia just barely kept herself from smacking him. She stepped back just as Özdilick entered.

"How's the patient?" Özdilick asked, pulling the curtain closed behind him.

"Very good," said Ramil without looking up as he closed the wound.

"Still out of it?"

"He stirred a bit," said Ramil.

"Were you worried about the low blood pressure?"

Lia saw something flicker in Ramil's eyes, but the doctor recovered, saying that it had thrown him as well, but the CT had shown there was nothing wrong.

"I don't like the fact that he is still unconscious," said Özdilick.

"No. But the CT was quite clear."

"Perhaps we should do another with contrast. Or an MRI."

"Well, if it is necessary," said Ramil. "Perhaps you'll want to call in your own man."

"I have. He hasn't answered his pager."

"A different specialist then. A second opinion is always welcome."

"What the hell is he doing?" Rockman asked Lia. "That's not in the script."

No kidding, Lia thought. But she wasn't in any position to object. The Turkish doctor agreed that it would not hurt to have another consult, and then left the cubicle.

"Why did you tell him to do that?" hissed Lia after he left.

"It's what I would do. He's worried."

"The scan will find the device."

"We can control the appearance of the MRI if necessary," said Ramil. "But the machine is located in a separate building and the experts who run it are not at the hospital today. Inserting the dye is time consuming and, given the patient's present symptoms, I doubt anyone would recommend it. The drug you gave him should wear off in a few minutes."

Before she could tell Ramil not to count on it, their patient groaned loudly and opened his eyes.

"HOW'S THE SIGNAL?" Dean asked Rockman.

"Diagnostics are fine. We're picking him up outside from the cars as well. The buggee has been successfully buggered." Rockman laughed, as if this were the funniest joke in the world.

"We'll wrap up and get out of here," said Dean, in no mood for laughs.

"The bodyguard is coming back into the building," said Rockman, seriously again. "Two more men are with him."

"They police?"

"No. The police seem a little disorganized."

"Haven't they found the guy Red Lion's bodyguards shot?"

"The bodyguards hustled the body away. They don't know there's a crime yet."

Dean slid the small computer into his pocket, then reached to the small Walther pistol secreted at the small of his back, just making sure it was there before going back toward Lia and Ramil.

THE CURTAIN FLEW open with such force that Ramil jerked back. The bodyguard lurched toward him, then veered away, surprised to see Asad sitting up on the bed.

"You're ready?" said the bodyguard in Arabic.

The terror leader didn't answer.

"He should stay overnight," said Ramil, pointing to Asad. "We did a scan, and we're confident that there is no hematoma. Still, he was unconscious for a while, and given a concussion of this type—"

"He has to come now."

"He's not ready," said Ramil so forcefully that the bodyguard backed off.

"I will go now, Doctor," said Asad, his voice very soft.

"You have had quite a sharp blow to the head," Ramil told him. "You should rest."

Asad started to get up. The bodyguard hesitated, but then helped. The two men whispered together, the bodyguard trying to persuade him that the doctor's advice should be heeded, but Asad insisted.

"You must take something for the pain," said Ramil. "Aspirin would be best. But if it is stronger, here is a prescription."

"I don't feel much pain, praise be to Allah." Asad took a faltering step.

"There will be a ringing in your ears, and pressure, sensitivity to light," added Ramil, describing the aftereffects of the drugs he had been given rather than a concussion.

"The sutures should be removed in about a week. If there is bleeding or more pain—here." Ramil took a card from his pocket and folded the prescription around it. "Call this number. This is an office in Istanbul, the best clinic. They will call me."

It's over, Ramil thought to himself. Don't say anything more.

CHAPTER 11

THE SHIP LOOMED out of the Lake Erie fog, its prow knifing toward the shore like a warrior's scimitar. The lights from the nearby docks and the highway above bathed the oil tanker in a finicky, flickering yellow, and Kenan Conkel saw that the bow was flecked red—blood, thought the young man, staring at the ship as it made its way slowly south of Detroit. It was late; Conkel had lost track of time and knew he should not linger here, knew he should rush to the small house a few blocks off the water where he had rented a room. But he stood staring at the ship, watching as the cloud wisps seemed to battle with the light, pushing and then yielding, obscuring and then revealing.

The struggle between darkness and light was one he well understood. Wind whipped off the lake, howling in his ear, reminding him: *Allahu Akbar, Allahu Akbar*—God is Greater. God is Greater.

Kenan stared at the ship, picturing its bridge. He could see it in his mind, the navigation gear, the lights looping over the console, the radio, even the fire alarm and auxiliary lights. It might be slightly different aboard this ship, but it would take only a few moments to orient himself. Kenan had always been a quick study, "a bright kid," as his teachers said, though usually they followed it with a remark along the lines of, "when he wants to be."

They were right. It was only when he found Allah and surrendered to the will of the God of Abraham and the Prophets that Kenan reached his potential. He'd done better at the advanced training class for bridge supervisory skills than seamen twice his age, even though he had spent less than a month on ships before then, most of that as an observer.

What a wonderful explosion a ship this size would make if it were stuffed with explosives. What a glorious statement of devotion to God.

And the explosion of the ship would be only the start of it.

Not this ship, thought Kenan. He did not know for certain, of course, but he had hints that the operation would be conducted far to the south. Nor did he know when—though again, he sensed it would be very, very soon.

And he did not know the target, but surely its destruction would humiliate the People of Hell.

One of them was watching him now. Kenan turned and began walking in the direction of his house, moving to the side of the walk where the streetlamps were strongest. He leaned forward against the wind, quickening his pace.

But he was too late.

"Yo, white boy!"

Kenan ignored the shout, and then the footsteps behind him.

"I'm talking to *you*."

The man behind him grabbed his arm and spun him around.

"What are you doing here?" demanded the man. He was black, about his age, but at least twice his weight and a half foot taller.

"I was coming from the *masjid*," said Kenan.

"Masjid? Whus that?"

"Mosque."

"Mosque? You Muslim?"

Kenan nodded.

"I thought only brothers were Muslim."

"God spoke to me and—"

"Never mind that shit. Gimme your money." The man pulled out a gun.

Kenan had only a few dollars in his wallet, but he was reluctant to part with it. There wasn't much he could do, though—he took it out slowly.

"Throw it to me, punk," said the thief.

Kenan tossed it. The man took his eye off him for a moment and Kenan thought of jumping at him, but he hesitated too long; the man grabbed the wallet and waved it at him. "Start walking."

"Are you Muslim, too?" asked Kenan.

"Walk."

"I need my driver's license." The license, an Illinois fake, was one of three Kenan possessed, but he had been warned against losing any of them because they could potentially expose the source.

"Driver's license." The robber spit. He opened the wallet, pulled out the few bills, then rifled through the compartments quickly. "This all you got? Twelve bucks? No credit cards?"

Kenan shook his head.

Angry, the thief threw the wallet into the lake. Then he pointed his gun at Kenan's chest.

"There is no God but God," muttered Kenan, determined to make his last act on earth one of devotion.

"Jackass," said the robber. He stuffed the gun into his pocket. "You follow me, I'll kill your white ass."

Kenan watched silently as the man walked away. Rage boiled inside him. He took one tentative step, but as he did the man looked over his shoulder and Kenan's resolve wilted. He heard the man laugh as he walked away.

Yes, laugh, thought Kenan as tears streamed from his eyes. Let all the Devil People laugh. Soon, they'd see what the Followers of God were capable of.

CHAPTER 12

TOMMY KARR SLIPPED his thumb behind the plastic backing of the tracking device, pushing off the protective cover to reveal the stickum. He reached his hand in under the air deflector at the rear of the Toyota SUV, sticking the tracker against the plastic surface. As he turned around, a police car drove up to the entrance ramp to the hospital and stopped near the door.

"Looks like the police have finally taken an interest in our friend," said Karr, walking back to the rental car, which was parked strategically near the driveway on the street. "How are Dean and Lia doing?"

"They're okay," said Rockman. "Asad should be on his way out. It would be better if the police didn't stop him."

"Sorry, Rockman. There's no little old ladies to rob, so I guess I can't create a diversion."

Karr was just opening the door to the car when an SUV similar to the one he'd just attached the homing device to drove up toward the emergency room.

"It's the other bodyguard vehicle," said Rockman, who was watching via a video "bug" on the grille of the rental.

Karr turned abruptly and started up the drive. As he did, he reached into his pocket and pulled out a small brown envelope. Gently pressing the sides together, he shuffled out a second tracking device. It looked like a large button, with a gray ring around a brown center.

"Tommy, where are you going?" asked Rockman.

Karr folded his arms at his chest, holding the tracker in his right fist. The SUV had stopped across from the one he'd just tagged; two men jumped out and went inside. Karr walked around to the driver's side and knocked on the window.

"'Scuse me," said Karr. He put his right hand on top of the SUV, slipping the tracking device under the roof rack. "I'm a little lost and I was looking for Sultanahmet Square?"

The man answered by aiming a Beretta at his face.

"Whoa—probably not around here, huh?" Karr took a couple of steps backwards, then trotted sideways down the driveway. He didn't figure that the bodyguard would be stupid enough to shoot him if he didn't have to—but you never could tell. Syrians weren't noted for common sense.

"What are you doing?" said Rockman.

"Just playing the ugly American," said Karr, ducking around the corner. They'd parked two other cars nearby, and Karr decided to walk to the red Volkswagen on the nearby side street, making it less likely that the driver would spot him. Between the tracking devices and the bug implant, which could be tracked using triangulation, it was unnecessary for him to stay very close to Asad as he trailed the terrorist to his lair.

"Tommy, Red Lion's coming out. Get ready to follow him."

"Ya think?" laughed Karr, getting into the car.

CHAPTER 13

THE PAIN CAME in waves, shaking Asad bin Taysr's head from the inside, as if his brain were pounding against his skull, trying to escape. The doctor had said something about pain killers, and while Asad wouldn't ordinarily trust an Egyptian—they were as a rule decadent, corrupted by their proximity to the Jews—the man had seemed to know what he was talking about, accurately describing how the pain would feel.

He was lucky to have escaped so easily. God had delivered him from calamity, from the Devil himself, to preserve his mission. In a few days, Asad bin Taysr would lead Islam to the next stage in its historical battle with the demonic West. His blows would strike at the heart of the western economies, sweeping away the foundation of their oppression against Islam. The strikes would not be as symbolic as the glorious raid on the World Trade Center and Pentagon in America on 9/11, peace be with the souls of the brave martyrs who had carried it out. But it would be more devastating. Their economies would crumble.

"Find out what this medication is." Asad handed over the prescription to Abd Katib, the chief of his bodyguards. "And get me some."

"Yes, sheik. It will be done."

"The others?"

"The driver is still in the hospital. He broke his leg and his face was burned by the air bag."

The driver had joined them in southern Turkey; though a Saudi who had been recommended by a trusted associate,

Asad did not know him well enough to gauge how far he could be trusted.

"He is a liability in the hospital," said Asad.

"That will be taken care of before the sun goes down."

"His widow will be told that he was a martyr. He was a soldier of God, and peace be upon him."

CHAPTER 14

"THEY WANT TO kill the driver," Marie Telach said, pushing the microphone of her headset away from her face. "What do you want to do?"

Rubens stared at the screen, which showed the feed from Tommy Karr's Volkswagen as he drove through the streets of Istanbul. It had been many years since Rubens was in Turkey, but at least from what he saw on the screen, little had changed. Past and present bumped up against each other in a dusty jumble. Minarets rose over cascades of domes, but what drew the eye were the billboards for credit cards and Western cigarettes.

"How long has the driver been with Asad?" asked Rubens.

"He met Asad and the bodyguards just over the Syrian border. The CIA has nothing on him, not even a name."

This didn't mean that the man was unimportant. The CIA was notorious for its ignorance.

"If he's to be of any use, he would need to see that they wanted to kill him," Rubens told Telach.

"That'll be tricky. We'll need to use the backup teams."

The Red Lion operation was a Desk Three venture, but the Deep Black field team was too small to insure success in the event something went wrong. Several teams of backup surveillance people and resources like small boats and planes were scattered around the Istanbul area. Coordinated by the Art Room, the individual units had limited knowledge of the operation to help insure secrecy. Security was so great that the CIA agents and paramilitaries on standby had not participated in the extensive rehearsals.

"Where are our operatives now?" Rubens asked Telach.

"Tommy and Dean are in separate cars, tracking Asad," said Telach. "We assume they're en route to a safe house."

"Lia?"

"Just picked up Dr. Ramil and is heading to his hotel."

"If the others don't need her, have her arrange to meet one of the CIA teams near the hospital. You can see the driver's room through the security network?"

"Yes."

"Lia should plan something to snatch the driver—but the danger he is in has to be clear."

CHAPTER 15

LIA HAD THE cab stop at the Four Seasons, a deluxe hotel in the Sultanahmet area of old Istanbul, the center of the city's main tourist attractions. She paid the driver, rounding up the tip to the next whole lira, then joined Ramil on the sidewalk. The doctor seemed spent, his face white and drawn.

"You all right?" she asked.

"Tired. Did you change my hotel?"

"We're going to walk around this way," said Lia, pointing to the right. "I want to make sure the hotel isn't being watched before we go in."

"Uh-huh."

They walked down the cobblestone street, turning up the hill in the direction of the Blue Mosque. The stones were not as old as they seemed; the area was booming because of the tourist trade, and the road had recently been torn up and resurfaced. Middle-aged men watched them from the sidewalk near their stores. Had they looked more like rich tourists, the men would have approached and hawked rugs or a nearby restaurant, but Ramil's Egyptian face and Lia's heavy dress signaled they weren't worth the effort.

Watching tourists was a favorite pastime in this part of Istanbul, but as they circled the block Lia didn't spot anyone who looked like they were interested in anything other than selling them a rug. In the meantime, Sandy Chafetz checked the feed from the video bugs they'd planted in the hotel and told her everything was quiet.

The Sari Oteli had been built as a townhouse by a member

of the sultan's entourage sometime in the seventeenth century. Rebuilt at the end of the twentieth, it had the air of a country inn rather than a big city hotel. The woman at the desk greeted Ramil warmly, remembering the cover story he had told her that he was a doctor.

"My friend is a nurse I met at the conference," said Ramil. "She's going to help me with some notes."

Lia rolled her eyes.

"You made it sound like you picked me up," she told him after scanning the room to make sure there were no bugs.

"I don't think she thought that." Ramil collapsed back on the bed.

Lia retrieved the suitcase of spare clothes she'd left in the closet. Sweating like a pig under the heavy Islamic dress, she jumped into the shower before changing into Western clothes, a long skirt and knit sweater baggy enough to hide one of her guns as well as a satphone and her handheld PDA.

Ramil was snoring on the bed when she came out. Lia checked the video feeds, then sat on the other bed to check in with the Art Room.

"How's the doc?" asked Chafetz.

"Out cold. Where are Dean and Karr?" Lia asked.

"They're trailing Asad," said Telach, coming on the line. "Listen, we want you go back near the hospital."

"Why?"

"We want to put together an operation to snatch Red Lion's driver. The al-Qaeda people are going to kill him. We heard Asad okay the plan."

"So?"

"Lia, I'm not in the mood. Get back over there right away. Dr. Ramil can go back to the hospital to set up a review of his patient."

"Ramil's going nowhere," said Lia. "He's out cold. Besides, he's supposed to be able to take care of himself, isn't he? He doesn't need me watching him."

"Fine." There was a pop on the line as the Art Room supervisor switched out of Lia's channel.

CHAPTER 16

KARR TURNED ONTO Kennedy Caddesi, the highway that circled old Istanbul, and drove along the Sea of Marmara, the
large body of water connecting the Mediterranean with the
Black Sea. He passed a large marina of pleasure boats and
turned off to the left, circling toward the water. Both SUVs
were about a half mile dead ahead.

"Hey, Charlie, you hearing me?" he asked Dean.

"I'm here."

"I'm off the Kennedy road, near the water. Why don't you
go on ahead in case they get back on?"

"They're probably going to take a boat."

"Yeah, that's what I figure."

If Asad went out in a boat, Karr would launch a Crow—a
small robot aircraft that looked like the bird it was named for.
The Crow would stay near the al-Qaeda leader until Karr
arranged for a boat to pick him or Dean up. They had four
small vessels in the waters nearby, all operated by contracted
paramilitaries who had no knowledge of the overall mission.

The PDA he was using to plot the SUV's positions beeped,
then beeped again, indicating that the vehicles had stopped.
According to the map, they were on the other side of the highway, away from the water.

"Yo, Rockman—what are these dudes talking about?" Karr
asked. "They going for a boat or what?"

"Buggee isn't talking, Tommy. They're just sitting there."

"Tommy, how close are you to Red Lion?" asked Marie
Telach.

"Quarter of a mile, little more. Right?"

"We're worried that we're not hearing anything. It's possible something is interfering with the signal."

"Yeah, I was thinking that myself. I'll take a walk with one of the boosters and see if that helps."

He pulled the car forward, leaving just enough space for someone else to get by. Then he grabbed his backpack and got out, pulling on a baseball cap and a pair of sunglasses. He'd just reached the highway when Rockman warned him that the cars were moving again. It was too late to turn around without seeming suspicious, so Karr continued walking, thumb curled in the backpack's strap.

"Bug's working," said Rockman. "They're just following some sort of prearranged plan."

"Great," said Karr. "Then you'll hear them shoot me."

Neither of the SUVs slowed down as they passed. Karr continued past the spot where they had stopped, figuring the second car might have dropped off someone to watch for a trail.

"Coming your way, Charlie," he said. "I'll catch up in a bit."

TRAFFIC WAS LIGHT, and Dean had no trouble pulling out about a half a mile ahead of the SUVs, protected from sight by a bend in the road. He drove slowly enough that they passed him within a few minutes. Dean waited until they were nearly out of sight to pick up his pace. A *dulmus*—a minivan used as a local bus—pulled onto the road between them and Dean had to slow down again. He was just thinking he might pass the bus when one of the SUVs turned off the highway, once more heading toward the city.

"Tommy, you in your car?"

"About five minutes away. I thought they might have dropped someone off but I can't see him."

"They split up. Asad's in the truck that got off the highway. I'm going to stick with him."

"Gotcha."

Dean followed the SUV into a residential area. A few minutes later, he passed the vehicle, which had parked in front of a three-story house. The bottom of the house was made of narrow gray bricks, which gave way about the middle of the second story to dark black clapboard.

"You got him," said Rockman. "The buggee's inside." He chortled a bit, in love with his earlier joke about the buggee getting buggered. "Looks like the other SUV is circling around and headed in your direction. He's at least ten minutes away. Tommy's on his tail."

"Great," said Dean, continuing down the street so he could find a place to park.

"BEST PLACE TO put the receiving unit is this tree behind the house," said Karr, jabbing his finger at the picture in the screen of the PDA.

"Too close," said Dean. "You can see it from the top floor of the house."

They were three blocks away, sitting beneath the pink umbrella of a small cafe. Small was the operative word— there was only one table, and they were the only customers. Karr had launched the Crow, allowing them to view the neighborhood.

"I could land the Crow in the tree and we could get it," said Karr. "Claim it's a kite."

Dean took the PDA and looked at the image from the small, unmanned aircraft. The robot plane flew a random pattern, and looked so much like a real bird that Dean had mistaken a real one for the robot soon after Karr launched it.

"This house here is above them," said Dean, pointing to a smooth white building two doors away. Even though it appeared to be only two stories, its roof was higher and flat. "We could climb up the vine at the back and stick the unit in the gutter. No one'll find it."

"That vine will never hold me. We need Lia."

"Lia's not around," said Dean. "Stay here."

THE VINE GAVE way as soon as Dean pulled at it. He threw it to the ground and stepped back, looking for another way up. A large metal garbage can nearby would give him a decent boost if he dragged it over; he could push it over to the side and grab onto the metal conduit protecting the power line and pull himself up—assuming it didn't give way under his weight. But the spot there was exposed; while he hadn't seen anyone yet, he'd be in easy view from any of the neighboring houses.

Dean took another two steps back and bumped into something that moved. He swirled around, bowling over a boy six or seven years old. The kid's soccer ball bounced from his hands, rolling away.

"Sorry," said Dean. "*Affedersiniz,*" he added immediately, remembering the Turkish word for *excuse me*. He grabbed the ball and held it out to the boy, who was seven or eight.

The kid leaned forward, tilting his head—and then with a quick flick of his hand swatted it from Dean's palm. He jumped up in time to rebound it off the top of his knee, settling it down on the ground with a grin.

"Pretty good, kid," said Dean. The translator gave Dean the phrase in Turkish, but Dean didn't have time to use it—the boy kicked the ball to Dean, who caught it as if it were an American football.

"How high can you kick it?" Dean asked the kid.

"I can kick higher than the house," said the boy, his English perfect.

"What are you doing, Charlie?" Rockman asked.

Dean pulled a ten-lira note from his pocket and showed it to the boy. "Yours if you get the ball on the roof."

He made it on the first try. Dean pulled the garbage can over; as he climbed on top of it the boy reappeared on the edge of the roof above him, laughing.

"How'd you do that, you little monkey?" asked Dean. He grabbed hold of the pipe and pulled himself to the top of the roof. The kid was waiting, ball under his arm, smiling.

Dean dug into his pocket and took out a bill.

"You wanna play soccer, mister?"

"You'd whip me ten ways to Sunday," Dean told the boy. "Thanks, though."

The kid gave him a forced little smile, then popped the

ball upwards off his head. It shot up about five feet; he headed it again. Dean's heart leapt as the boy tottered near the edge of the roof. But he recovered his balance, tapped the ball upwards, then dropped and climbed down the side, landing on the ground just as the ball completed its third bounce in front of his feet.

Dean planted the booster device between a gap in the bricks that formed a crown on the front part of the roof.

"Working," said Rockman. "Much better signal."

"I'm going to kick the ball around with this kid a bit before I go back to the car," Dean said, starting down. "For cover."

"Since when are you nice to kids?" Rockman asked.

"I'm always nice to kids."

CHAPTER 17

WILLIAM RUBENS WAS due at the White House at noon to brief the new national security advisor on the operation. With things running well, he decided to leave Crypto City early enough to stop and visit the *old* national security advisor, his friend and one-time teacher, George Hadash. But as he approached Hadash's hospital room, he was suddenly filled with dread; it was only out of a sense of loyalty and duty that he forced himself to continue down the corridor. Two days before, Hadash had undergone an operation to remove a brain tumor. The doctors had pronounced the operation a great success, but Rubens, visiting him a few hours later, had a completely different impression.

"Come," said Hadash when he knocked on the door. Rubens was pleasantly surprised to find him sitting up in bed, the newest issue of *Foreign Affairs* in his hands. A pile of books sat on the bed next to him; two laptops sat on the rolling tray to the left.

"William! How are you?" said Hadash, his voice as strong as ever.

"I believe the question is how are you?" said Rubens. He shook Hadash's hand—a good grip, though a little cold—and looked for a chair to sit down in. The nearest one was covered with books: all on the Civil War, Rubens noted as he piled them on the floor.

"Have you read this?" Hadash held up the *Foreign Affairs*. "McNally on Russia?"

Before Rubens could answer—he had read a few paragraphs and then moved on in disgust—Hadash launched into a lengthy and devastating critique, punctuated several times by the phrase "and people in Congress talk *seriously* of McNally as the next secretary of state."

"A comment on the ability of Congress, surely," said Rubens when the former national security advisor finally paused for a breath.

Hadash burst out laughing.

"You're doing much better than the other day," said Rubens. "When will you be out?"

"When they've grown tired of poking me. I have another MRI session scheduled for this afternoon. They promise a date then."

Rubens nodded.

"Do you think about death, William?"

"I don't," Rubens answered honestly. "But I don't think you're going to die."

"Eventually we all do," said Hadash. "I'm ready, if it comes to that."

Death seemed an impossible thing to be ready for. Rubens changed the subject, asking what Hadash was doing with all the Civil War books.

"I have been thinking of General Lee and McClellan. An interesting pair, symbols of their age," said Hadash. "Brilliant, yet both deeply flawed."

McClellan, commander of the Army of the Potomac, had faced off against the Confederate Robert E. Lee in the first half of the war; Rubens knew enough Civil War history to realize that most historians regarded him as a poor military leader. But Lee's flaws were less known, at least to him.

"He overextended his army," Hadash quickly explained. "You see, the critical difference—well, look at George Washington during the Revolution. The turning point of the war comes after the British take New York and the Revolution doesn't collapse. General Washington realizes what sort of war he's fighting. All he has to do is survive. Lee missed that."

"I doubt Lincoln would have settled for that," said Rubens.

Hadash smiled. He relished well-reasoned arguments and was just revving up. "True. Lincoln was not King George. But there were elections to contend with. Lincoln might not have been there had events gone differently."

Hadash charged into a short lecture on McClellan, laying out how he would have sued for peace had he won the election. There was a glint in his eye that Rubens realized meant he was purposely overstating his case.

This was an excellent sign, Rubens thought; Hadash was clearly on the mend.

"I'd like to hear more, but I'm afraid I'm due at a meeting," said Rubens finally. "I'll call you tonight, to see how your scan went."

"Yes, very good. And we'll talk about Grant," added Hadash.

"I'm afraid I know relatively little about him and the war in general."

"Then I'll have the advantage."

CHAPTER 18

ASAD'S DRIVER HAD been placed in a room with three other patients on the third floor of the hospital, next to an emergency staircase and only a few yards from the elevators; snatching him would not be difficult. But that meant the men coming for him would have an easy time as well.

One of the patients in the room was suffering from the advanced stages of Alzheimer's disease. Posing as an acquaintance of the man's daughter—her name and address were in his file, easily accessed by the Art Room—Lia went up and surveyed the room. The driver lay in the second bed from the door, knocked out by the drugs they'd given him to ease the pain of his burns. Lia placed a video bug and an eavesdropping "fly" inside the room and in the hallway, making up for a gap in the hospital's video security system that failed to completely cover the hallway down from the nurse's station.

"Easiest thing to do is to take him down the stairs, slap him in a wheelchair and roll him out the front door," she told Rockman as she descended in the elevator. "Can you kill the alarms on the staircase?"

"Not a problem. We have two CIA paras in a car outside."

"Para" was short for paramilitary officers, CIA operatives specially trained for covert military mission.

"Describe their car."

Lia left the hospital through a side exit and circled around the block, coming up on them from behind. Unlike some of the CIA people she'd worked with, these ops were smart enough to be out of the car, watching their backs. Still, they were ridiculously easy to spot, wearing mirrored sunglasses and identical black baseball caps, seemingly oblivious to the evening shoppers passing nearby. Lia pulled a guidebook from her pocket and strolled down the block; as she got close to them, she flipped open the book and turned to one of the men.

"Can you help me with directions?" she said in a loud voice. "I was looking for the tram line."

"Lia?"

The voice took her by surprise. She looked into the CIA officer's face, staring past the sunglasses. Never in a million years would she have expected to see the face behind them, and even as she stared at them she told herself it must be a mistake, must be some trick of her unconscious.

But the voice was definitely his.

"I believe you have to go up about three blocks," said the man, shaking off his own surprise. "And I think it's that way."

He pointed to the left, down the street.

"Could you show me?" Lia asked, regaining her composure.

"Love to."

"Lose the hat and glasses," she said, starting down the block.

"You haven't changed at all," replied the CIA officer.

CHAPTER 19

BLOOD LAPPED AT Ramil's feet, surging from the floor. The young man the doctor was supposed to operate on lay on the table in front of him. The kid's skull was misshapen, too large, too shot up. How could he save this boy? There was so much metal his knife couldn't even find flesh to cut.

The ceiling of the tent fluttered with the wind, then flew off. The lights they'd put up to help him with the surgery shot upwards, captured by the gale.

God help me. Help this kid—I can't save him. Please help me.

The wind settled. The tent, which had been sweltering despite the massive air conditioner at the side, instantly cooled. Ramil bent over his patient and realized that the wounds, though numerous, were not impossible to deal with; it was a matter of taking them in order, working steadily. He didn't have to rush. All he had to do was be precise.

I've saved him. Allah saved him.

Intense white light filled the tent.

Ramil woke with a start. He felt as if his lungs were filled with ice, incredible coldness emanating from inside his body. Disoriented, he stared around the shadows of the room, not knowing where he was.

Istanbul, Turkey. For Desk Three.

Yes.

He was still in his dress clothes, still wearing shoes. The clock next to his bed said it was just after seven. Ramil remembered coming back with Lia, collapsing on the bed.

He should check in via satphone. Then maybe get something to eat, though that meant leaving the hotel. The Sari Oteli served only breakfast, and drinks on the roof terrace.

Ramil stared at the shaft of dim light that fell across the extra bed beside him. The dream hadn't really been a dream, or rather, it was a dream based on something that had really happened, an experience as a young surgeon in Vietnam. The wind wasn't there, or the light, but the core—the panic and the dread, the prayer, the calm that followed, the success especially—those had truly happened.

He hadn't thought of it in a long time.

Why not?

"I just haven't," he said aloud, answering the thought as if someone had spoken to him.

He looked at the phone, then pushed the buttons to call the Art Room.

"This is Ramil," he said.

There was a slight pause while a security system confirmed his voice pattern. Then Marie Telach came on the line.

"Doctor, how are you?"

"I thought I'd check in. I've had a nap." Ramil got up from the bed, walking across the small room. "I think I'll have a shower and then go and get something to eat. There's a hotel across the way with a restaurant. I'll probably eat there."

"Good."

"My patient?"

"He's fine. I'll call you if we need you. In the meantime, just relax and play tourist."

"Yes," said Ramil absently, thinking back to the dream. He had saved that young man. Why hadn't he thought about it? It was a triumph, a real achievement, saving a life. He'd saved many in Vietnam.

With God's help.

He hadn't done much of importance since. Teaching and consulting and the work with the NSA for nearly two decades now, boring work mostly, giving advice on stocking first aid stations and standing by for emergencies that never occurred.

This was by far the most interesting assignment he'd had. But even this wasn't as important as saving a life.

Wasn't it, though? It would save many lives, potentially.

"Doctor, are you still there?" asked Telach.

"Yes, I'm sorry. My blood sugar, I think, is probably low. I'd best get something to eat."

CHAPTER 20

LIA BIT THE side of her cheek as she helped Terrence Pinchon roll up his pants beneath the hospital gown. Touching him like this, even like this, shot a wave of barely controllable emotion through her. She fought against the shudder, gritted her teeth together to avoid reacting to her old lover, to the man she'd given up for dead three years before.

"Remember: Don't do anything until I'm in the room," she told him. "Wait to hit him with the syringe; he has to *see* that these guys are after him."

"That's taking a risk, isn't it?"

"Just do what I say. You have the .22?"

Pinchon patted the pistol in his lap, which had a silencer.

"We use the .22s, not the heavy artillery," Lia added. "The Glock is only for emergencies."

"Aye, aye, Captain Bligh." He winked at her. "Like being on top?"

"Just do what I say."

"Always."

Lia glanced at the other CIA paramilitary, John Reisler. Reisler wore a long lab coat that made his MP5 submachine gun less conspicuous. Lia was dressed as a nurse, wearing a long white dress; she had added a stethoscope and a nameplate she had found at the nurse's station on floor two.

"Ready?" Lia asked.

Reisler nodded and adjusted the earbud for his radio. The radio was tied into his satellite phone, and through that connected to the Deep Black system; the signal would go halfway around the world even though the team members were almost nearly next to each other.

"Coast is clear, Lia," said Rockman, monitoring the hospital security system as well as the flies Lia had planted. "The only nurse on duty is at the other end of the hall."

Lia pried open the door, waited a second, then stepped into the hallway. She walked briskly to the nurses' station and retrieved a wheelchair. Twirling it around, she headed back toward Pinchon, who was standing near the stairway in his hospital gown. He looked like a ghost in the dim light.

"You've gained weight," she whispered after she started to push him in the wheelchair.

"Too much easy living."

"I thought you were dead."

"Death's overrated." He tilted his head back slightly. "We working here or what?"

"This doesn't seem to be right," Lia said aloud, using Turkish supplied by the Art Room translator as she entered the room. "I'll be back in a few minutes."

"Nurse," said one of the men as she started to leave. "I have not had my shot tonight."

"Don't worry. You're next," said Lia in Turkish. What she lost in pronunciation she more than made up for with her eyes; the man flushed and she was sure that his pulse must have doubled.

"Our guests are here," said Rockman. "Just pulling up outside."

Lia walked back to the stairway door, knocked twice quickly, then leaned against the crash bar and eased it open. Reisler was waiting—his MP5 pointed at her chest.

"You don't trust my knock?"

"Maybe there was somebody behind you," he said.

Lia took the pistols she'd prepared earlier, a pair of .22-caliber Ruger Mark IIs equipped with silencers.

"Three of them, coming up in the elevator," Rockman told her. "They went straight past the front desk. I'll tell you when they're on the floor."

Lia turned to Reisler. "Ready?"

"Yeah." He raised the submachine gun. "How do you know Pinchon?"

"We were in the army together. Delta."

"On your floor," said Rockman. "They have pistols, down at the side. One's hanging back, trailing them toward the room and facing the elevator."

"Terry, they should be just about at the door," said Lia. "Grunt, and I'll take the guard."

Lia listened for Pinchon's groan. Instead, she heard the sharp bark of a rifle from down the hall.

CHAPTER 21

WITH ASAD BEDDED down for the night, Dean and Karr flipped a coin to see who got the first shift, staying nearby in case something happened.

Dean won. But rather than going off to sleep, he volunteered to back up Lia and the CIA people at the hospital.

He'd just found the terrorists' car when Rockman warned him that shots had been fired inside. Stifling the impulse to run inside and help Lia, he drove past the car, pulling into a parking spot a short distance away.

"One guy, watching the driveway to the hospital," he told the Art Room.

"All right. Stick with the game plan. Stay back," said Rockman. "Let's not make any unnecessary fuss."

Dean rolled down the window and slid a video bug on the mirror to give the Art Room a view of what was going on. Then he leaned back in the seat, calmly waiting as directed.

For all of five seconds. Then Dean reached below the seat, pulled out his silenced .22, and went for a walk.

CHAPTER 22

LIA SLAMMED HER elbow against the crash bar, pushing the door open as she threw herself into the hall. It took her only two seconds to sight her gun and fire—but that was at least a second and a half too long, for it allowed the terrorist to point his AK-47 in her direction and fire. His bullets flew high; Lia's did not. Two struck him square in the forehead, the small-caliber bullets punching through his skull and sending him to the ground.

Reisler rolled into the hallway behind her.

"I got them," said Pinchon.

Lia glanced in the doorway, saw two bodies on the floor, and raced to the elevator, jamming the button to bring the car to their floor.

"Security people are heading for the stairs," said Rockman. "They don't know yet where the gunfire was. Your nurse is coming back—up the corridor at the left side of the station."

"Pinchon, bring him to the elevator," said Lia, moving to the corner of the hallway. "Hit him with the Demerol and make sure he's out."

Lia saw the nurse running toward her in the corner mirror at the ceiling. She put her gun in her left hand, watching the woman with one eye and glancing down the hallway with the other. As the woman came around the corner, Lia threw her body around and kicked out the nurse's legs. Then she leapt over her and smacked the back of the head, knocking her out.

"I'm sorry," Lia said, making sure the woman was out.

The fire alarm began to sound.

"Security people are checking each floor," said Rockman. "You have about three minutes, maybe a little more."

The elevator was just arriving. Pinchon emerged from the room with Asad's driver in his wheelchair. He sprinted down the hall with Reisler in pursuit. An old man appeared in the doorway of one of the rooms; Lia raised her pistol and shooed him back inside.

"Go! Go!" yelled Reisler.

Pinchon barreled into the elevator. Lia reached into the one next to them and released it. She bumped Reisler getting into the car with Pinchon. The doors closed. It seemed to take forever before the car started downward.

"Get the gown off!" Lia barked at Pinchon. "Go, come on."

Pinchon was already fumbling with his clothes. Lia grabbed at the collar and helped, buttons popping as she pulled.

There was blood on the wheels. Lia took the gown and started sopping it up.

"Let me," said Pinchon, dropping to his knees next to her. "You hide the guns."

"There are two security people in the lobby," warned Rockman. "They're looking at the elevators now."

Lia glanced at the panel. They'd just passed the second floor.

THE DRIVER OF the Mercedes tapped nervously on the side of the door, keeping time to a song Dean couldn't hear. Dean walked past him, making sure he was alone in the sedan.

"Charlie, they're in the elevator," said Rockman. "They need you—fast."

"On my way," said Dean, turning around. He walked to the Mercedes and rapped on the car window.

The driver glared at him, then reached for the door. The bodyguard had his pistol in his hand, but before he could even point it in the American's direction, Dean put a bullet an inch and a half above his nose.

• • •

LIA STOOD BEHIND Reisler and the wheelchair, holding the .22 down at her side as the doors to the elevator opened.

"Here we are now, almost home," she said in Turkish, mimicking the translator's accent as closely as possible as they started from the elevator. The security people glanced at her, then at the "patient" in the wheelchair. Lia saw from their eyes that they sensed something wasn't right, but they weren't quite sure what it was. She flicked her left hand behind her, keeping the pistol hidden.

"*Dur!*" said one of the guards. "Stop!"

In the next second, something exploded in the elevator—the small flash-bang grenade Lia had tossed a second before. Everyone dropped to the floor—except Lia, Reisler, and Pinchon, who began running for the door. Lia dropped two more small grenades—they were about the side of cigarette lighters—and a second loud explosion and bright flash rocked the lobby. Smoke spewed behind them.

Through the door, Lia turned to her left and started to run. A horn sounded to her right. She turned, and saw a Mercedes.

Charlie.

Charlie!

CHAPTER 23

ISTANBUL LAY AT the intersection of two continents; historically it was the crossroads of several great civilizations. For Tommy Karr, this meant one thing: great food.

And lots of it. He began with a plate of *mezes* or appetizers, a mixed bag of exotic salads, minced vegetables, and brightly colored dips. Eggplant, yogurt, and olives reappeared in various combinations, accented with strange spices and little green curlicues he assumed were herbs. He couldn't identify a single dish, but that only added to the adventure. He wolfed them down with the help of a triangular piece of pita-like flat bread, whetting his appetite for the main course: grilled *palamut,* a local fish specialty. A silvery pair arrived with their heads poking up from the center of the plate, eyeballing him like the evil eye charms available on the nearby street corner.

"Almost seems a shame to bother them, huh?" Karr said to the waiter, picking up his fork. "Maybe I'll just eat around them."

"Tommy, can you talk?" asked Sandy Chafetz from the Art Room.

Karr waited for the server to leave, then prodded one of the fish. "You're sure you're dead, right? If I talk to you, will you answer?"

"Two cars have pulled up a block from Asad's safe house," said Chafetz. "Can you check them out?"

"On my way." Karr rose, digging into his pocket for some Turkish bills.

The waiter came over immediately.

"I'm afraid I just realized I have another appointment and I'm a little late," said Karr. "Think I could get the fish to go?"

CHAPTER 24

ASAD BIN TAYSR welcomed Marid Dabir with a hearty hug, taking his arm to lead him into the small room where they could sit alone. It was his practice to show people he despised as much kindness as possible. It kept them off balance.

"I heard that you were injured," Dabir said, gesturing at the bandage on Asad's head. "I feared our meeting would be delayed."

"It's of no consequence. An unfortunate mishap."

Asad offered his guest some of the water he had been drinking, along with a plate of Syrian figs. They sat next to each other on the couch in the Turk's small room.

"It has been a long time," Asad told his visitor. "Quite long."

"Not of my own choosing."

"The Sheik sends his blessings."

Others might honor Asad by calling him "sheik," but there was only one man in the world Asad would refer to by that name. Dabir knew instantly that he was referring to Osama bin Laden, and bowed his head.

Such a show, thought Asad. As if the man had no vanity or ambitions. But he wasn't fooled.

Three years before, Marid Dabir had been as close to bin Laden as Asad. But Dabir's ambitions to succeed the great leader had caused so much division among the al-Qaeda followers that finally the Sheik had given him tasks far from the leadership circle in Pakistan. Dabir, stubborn as always, went on his own initiative to Europe, settling in Germany and starting his own organization there. In doing so, he ignored the networks others had already established. It was rumored that he had done this elsewhere as well, though Germany was where he was based.

And now he was back in the Sheik's good graces, an important part of the plan for the second offensive against the West. Asad regarded him as a dangerous enemy still, but even a demon could be useful in the campaign against the followers of the devil.

"You are prepared?" Asad asked.

Dabir nodded.

"Good." Asad excused himself and left the room, walking to the room he had been given as a bedroom. He retrieved a small Koran from his cloth bag and went back to the room.

In his absence, Dabir had eaten all of the fruit. Asad pretended not to notice. He handed him the holy book.

"God is powerful," said Asad. Then, seeing no need to prolong the meeting, added, "I seem to be a little tired."

Dabir nodded. "Until we meet."

"May it be in paradise."

They kissed each others' cheeks and took their leave so warmly, even a careful observer might have thought they were the greatest of friends.

CHAPTER 25

RUBENS TOOK THE phone with him as he walked across the secure communications center in the White House basement, listening as Telach told him about what had happened at the hospital.

"The Istanbul police seem to think it was retaliation for the accident," continued Telach. "There's a lot of smuggling activity through the port, and with the Russian mob involved, the rumors are already flying. We've sent an anonymous e-mail to one of the papers to help the theory along."

"Very good," said Rubens. "And the driver?"

"On his way to the airport. Asad is meeting with someone right now," added the Art Room supervisor. "Hold on."

Rubens checked his watch; he was due upstairs to talk to Donna Bing, the new national security advisor, in five minutes, which meant that he was already late. But this was worth being late for. They'd been planning the Red Lion operation for just over two years, ever since the bugging device was successfully tested. Picking the right subject, getting the president's approval—a lot of hard work was about to pay off.

But not necessarily right away.

"He's leaving. He said nothing."

"Nothing?"

Telach turned him over to one of the Arab translators, who said that both men sounded as if they had come from Yemen or Saudi Arabia. Their conversation had consisted entirely of greetings and stock religious phrases.

"Who was the other man?" Rubens asked Telach.

"We're not sure yet."

"Have Mr. Karr follow him."

"He's already on it."

RUBENS HATED LUNCH meetings for any number of reasons, starting with the fact that it was difficult to discuss matters of state with the deserved gravitas while wiping mayonnaise from one's chin. He especially hated "working lunch meetings," a euphemism for a gobbled sandwich at the desk of an overworked superior. In his opinion, the only tangible result was heartburn.

But Donna Bing was the doyenne of working lunch meetings; Rubens had been down to see the new national security advisor twice in the three weeks since she had taken over the job, and each time he'd been forced to share a roast beef sandwich in her office. Today Bing showed her bold side—she ordered her sandwich with Russian dressing. Rubens had his dry, as usual.

He gave her the latest on Red Lion, including the fact that they had taken his driver. Bing blanched so severely when Rubens mentioned that the terrorists who had come to kill the man had themselves been killed that he quickly added the Turks had started the fracas by firing automatic rifles.

"This could be an incident if our role is discovered," said Bing.

"I don't believe that's likely," said Rubens stiffly.

"You're ready to take Red Lion at the end of the meetings?"

"Absolutely." A Gulfstream jet was sitting at the airport in Istanbul; once captured, the terrorist leader would be flown to Diego Garcia, an isolated Navy base in the South Pacific, for interrogation.

"Thank you for the update," said Bing. "The president is very interested in the project."

"I had been under the impression that I would brief him as well," said Rubens.

"Oh?" Bing managed to mix a tone of genuine surprise with

the hint of haughty disdain in her voice—quite an achievement in one syllable. "Well, I don't believe that it's really necessary for you to waste your time waiting for the president. And of course the president's agenda is chock-full these days."

The real waste of time, Rubens thought, was coming down to Washington to deliver a five-minute progress report that could have been just as easily conveyed in a phone call, if not an e-mail. But time or convenience wasn't what was at stake here—nor, really, was the operation, not at all.

"I believe the president prefers to be briefed in person on sensitive matters," said Rubens.

"I don't know that that's necessary at this point," said Bing. She reached down and took a bite of her sandwich, dribbling dressing on her chin. "And as it happens, the president is not in the Oval Office this afternoon; he's lunching with the vice president and the Senate majority leader. That meeting has been arranged for some time."

In other words, Rubens had been summoned here at *precisely* the time the president would be away.

"There is another matter I'd like to discuss with you at some point," said Bing. "Of a more philosophical nature. Desk Three is, for all intents and purposes, a reincarnation of several CIA operations established at the NSA's behest during the Cold War, and given that—"

"That's not precisely correct," said Rubens.

"Oh? I did get that impression from the briefing papers and the background memoranda establishing it."

"The key is the melding of the technology with the field operatives," said Rubens, realizing what was going on. "As for the mission set, it goes beyond the so-called black bag operations common to ZR/RIFLE—"

"I'm not referring to the mission set, but to organizational arrangements and missions."

"That debate was conducted at the beginning of the administration."

"Perhaps it is time to revisit it."

It had been an admirable performance really, not especially subtle yet couched in just enough ambivalence to give plausible denial that it wasn't what it surely must be: a play to cut Rubens' role in the administration. Bing would start by cutting off his access to the president—under Hadash he'd had almost unlimited access—and would finish by giving Desk Three to the CIA, limiting the National Security Agency to a strictly secondary role in the intelligence community.

It was also a move meant to establish her as a major player in the administration. She needed a scalp on her belt and had decided that his would best serve her purposes.

"As national security advisor, it's certainly your prerogative to open or close any debate," said Rubens, rising. "I hope you'll keep me informed."

"Naturally," said Bing. She extended her hand; Rubens shook it, not realizing until too late that it was greasy with dressing.

CHAPTER 26

DEAN DROVE TOWARD the Yenikapi ferry terminal where they had a backup car they could swap into. According to the Art Room, the Istanbul police had not yet arrived at the hospital, so there was no need to rush. The driver was in the backseat, sandwiched between Lia and John Reisler; the other CIA agent, Terrence Pinchon, was next to Dean in the front.

"We're going to need some more Demerol," Lia said, leaning over the front seat. "He's stirring."

"He ought to be down for the count."

"Tell me about it."

"We'll change cars first, then we'll swing back and get one of the kits. You guys are taking him to Bayindr," Dean added. "You think you can do that by yourselves?"

"We can handle it," said Pinchon.

"I'm only asking if you need backup," Dean told him. "Don't get insulted. Bayindr's a good drive from here."

They were using the operation's backup plane; the Gulfstream for Asad had to stay in Istanbul just in case anything went wrong.

"I've done renditions before," said Pinchon, using the CIA term for operations to snatch terrorists and "render" them elsewhere, generally to another country for justice. "Just like old times, huh, Lia?" added the para. "Except the body count's higher. Guess you don't have a colonel screaming up your backside, huh?"

"You were in the army together?" Dean asked.

"More or less," said Lia.

"You ever hear that slogan, 'Army of One'?" said Pinchon. "Lia kind of took it to heart."

"Still does," said Dean.

LIA CHECKED THE terrorist's wrists, which were cinched in his lap, making sure they were tight. His lower right leg was in a cast that ran from his ankle to his knee, covering the area of the fracture. He groaned as she pushed him back into the seat.

"You gave him the whole hypo?" Lia asked Reisler. "He's coming to already."

"Whole shot, yeah."

Lia didn't think that was possible, but there was no use arguing.

"So who is he?" asked Pinchon.

"Abul Hazanwi, Red Lion's driver," said Lia. "We want him alive. He may talk."

"Right."

"He's a source. He has to stay alive," repeated Lia. "You hear that, Terry?"

"Hey, loud and clear."

Lia wanted to ask him how he had survived Kyrgyzstan. She wanted to ask many other things as well, starting with why he'd let her think he was dead. But she couldn't—she didn't dare—ask anything. She already knew she wouldn't like the answers.

"Our swap car is a blue BMW, in the corner of the lot," Dean told them. "I'm going to go past once, drop someone off on foot. They check the lot. When they give the high sign, we come back and we'll make the swap."

"Drop me," said Lia.

"Fine."

And then there was Charlie.

What about Charlie? She loved him. Loved him with a deep ache.

But she'd loved Pinchon more, hadn't she?

She had.

"Drop me right here," said Lia. "I can walk past."

Dean pulled to the side.

"Hey," he said, turning to her as she started to get out.

"Yeah?"

"You got your gun?"

Lia held it up.

"You all right?" Dean stared at her, his eyes trying to penetrate her skull, figure out what she was thinking.

"I'm fine, Charlie Dean," she told him, slamming the door.

CHAPTER 27

KARR PLANTED TRACKING bugs on the cars belonging to Asad's visitors, then walked down the street and around the corner to a block populated by small stores. With the exception of a restaurant on the corner, all were closed, but he wasn't here to shop. Three motorbikes were parked at the side of a bicycle repair shop; Karr went to the one at the far end, got on, and backed away from the curb. The engine hummed to life, strong and steady.

"He's coming out now, Tommy," said Rockman. "Don't get too close."

"Why would I do that?" said Karr, gunning the bike to life.

CHAPTER 28

DEAN SWUNG OUT of the parking lot and headed down the road, waiting for Lia to report back. When she told him it was clear, he pulled into a crowded gas station and made a U-turn, heading back to the lot. Dean decided that he would drive the Mercedes back toward Istanbul before abandoning it, just in case someone connected the two cars.

"Beemer, huh?" said Pinchon as he drew up next to the BMW. "You guys really know how to live it up."

Dean remained silent. Something about Pinchon rubbed him the wrong way.

"I'll tell you where to pick me up," Dean told Lia as they hustled the terrorist into the other car. "I don't want to leave the Mercedes here."

He drove about two miles on the highway back toward the city before finding a parking lot where the Mercedes wouldn't stand out. Lia met him up on the highway; he got into the back, sliding next to the prisoner and Reisler.

"Stuffy in here," said Pinchon, rolling down the window. The breeze hit Dean full in the face as Lia picked up speed.

"Do me a favor and roll that back up, would you?" Dean asked.

Pinchon smirked—Dean could see it in the passenger-side mirror—and raised the window about an inch.

"So what are we doing?" Reisler asked.

"We're going to get a sedative to make sure he sleeps through the night," said Dean. "We have a cache of gear about a half hour outside of the city in the direction you're going.

You can leave Lia and me there. You drive to Bayindr. There'll be a team to meet you there tonight. You know how to get there?"

"We'll find it," said Pinchon.

"I'd put him in the trunk if I were you," said Dean.

"You gonna tell me how to wipe my ass, too?"

Dean leaned forward, then, in a sudden motion that he could barely control, swung his arm around the headrest and grabbed Pinchon by the neck, pressing his fingers hard against the side of his throat.

"I asked you to *raise* the window."

Only when the window was all the way up did Dean let go. No one spoke after that.

LIA PULLED UP next to the white Toyota Corolla, dust and ash flying up from the small lot. Dean got out and walked around the car, scanning the nearby building to make sure it was empty. Her heart clutched when he jumped over the guardrail behind the Corolla's trunk; there was only a narrow concrete ledge there before a sheer drop of twenty or thirty feet into the surf below.

"Let's get al-Qaeda here in the back," said Pinchon, getting out.

Lia popped the trunk, then watched through the side mirror as the two CIA agents pulled the prisoner out. Either Pinchon had not given him all of the dope, or the dose was somehow bad, because the terrorist was clearly conscious.

"Is the Arabic translator on the line?" she asked Rockman, who was listening to her in the Art Room. "Haznawi just came to and he's talking."

"She's here."

"He's asking what we're doing," said Reisler.

"What are we doing?" said Pinchon in English outside the car. "We're saving you from your friends, raghead."

As Lia threw open her door, Reisler started to explain in Egyptian Arabic that Haznawi's al-Qaeda companions had tried to kill him at the hospital.

"You're safe now," said Reisler. "Very safe."

Haznawi responded by launching himself headfirst over the nearby guardrail.

DEAN DIDN'T REALIZE what had happened until he heard Lia curse. He turned in time to see their prisoner tumbling over the rocks and then falling into the water head first. Reaching back into the trunk, he grabbed one of the nylon ropes, planning to lower himself down to the water. As he straightened, three shots rang out. At least one hit the prisoner; his body bobbed backwards, disappearing for a moment before resurfacing face down. Even in the dim light Dean could tell he was dead.

"What the hell did you do that for?" Dean shouted.

"What, I'm supposed to let him get away?" said Pinchon.

"He had a cast on his leg and his hands were bound. How far could he have gone before I grabbed him?"

"I didn't think you'd make it, old man."

"Get him," said Dean.

"He's your prize. You get him."

"Get him. Then find your own way home."

"We can't just leave them here, Charlie," said Lia as Dean stomped back to the BMW.

Rockman was practically yelling in his head, asking what was going on.

"The al-Qaeda driver is dead," Dean told him. "I'll get back to you."

"Charlie—"

"I can't explain now." Dean snapped the com system off.

"Take the Toyota," Dean told Reisler, who had a stunned look on his face. He pointed to the car, which was parked a short distance away. It was one of their backups. "Key's in a case under the driver's side.

"I'm sorry."

"Yeah."

Lia ran to Dean as he strode toward the BMW.

"Charlie, we can't go like this."

"Are you driving or am I?"

"I'll drive," she told him finally, getting into the car.

• • •

LIA DROVE ACROSS to the Beyoğlu section of Istanbul, parking near a jazz place they'd gone to during their orientation stay a few weeks before. She turned off the engine, then reached to the back of her belt, making sure her com system was still off.

"What are we going to tell Telach?" she asked Dean.

"What do you mean? We tell her what happened."

"I don't know, Charlie."

"They heard the whole thing, Lia."

"We screwed up."

"Like hell *we* screwed up. Tweedle Dee and Tweedle Dum screwed up. They blew it big-time."

"It's our fault."

"Since when do you cover for the CIA?"

"I'm not covering for them."

Dean didn't answer.

"We better tell them what's going on before they freak out," Lia said finally. "Before Mr. Rubens calls on the sat phone."

Dean grabbed her hand before she could switch the com system back on.

"What's with you and Pinyon?"

"Pinchon. Terry."

"Yeah, whatever."

"We worked together on a couple of missions. He was in Delta."

"And?"

"We worked together. I thought he was dead." Lia saw the charred car, the bodies. He *had* to have died. There could be no other explanation.

But he was alive.

"I'm not sure what happened," Lia added.

"He didn't tell you?"

"I didn't ask," she said, turning on the com.

CHAPTER 29

TOMMY KARR FOUND himself zooming up a street narrower than most sidewalks when a pair of headlights turned from a side road and bore down on him. He began to tilt the bike into a skid, then spotted an opening at the right and plunged into an alley just ahead of the headlamps. The alley, barely wider than his shoulders, connected with a second, even narrower one that circled around a large building, spitting him out on another side street. A horn blared in his ears; Karr tucked onto the nearby sidewalk, which quickly turned into a succession of stairs. Karr's teenage summers spent riding dirt bikes through wood trails didn't translate well on the misshapen and slippery steps: after about fifty yards he and the bike went separate ways. The bike spun into a row of discarded boxes and plastic garbage cans, which broke its fall. Karr didn't have nearly as much luck, slamming hard onto the concrete and cracking his head against a metal pole so fiercely that the visor's display died.

Growling, he jumped to his feet and ran to the bike, a flood of adrenaline and anger pushing away the pain of the fall.

Temporarily.

"What's going on?" asked Chafetz.

"I fell. Give me directions."

"Tommy, are you okay?"

"My ego's busted. But I'm fine." He laughed. "Got a headache."

"Mr. Karr, are you all right?" asked Telach.

"Fine, Ma. Sandy, I could use some directions here."

"Take a left at that next block."

"Got it."

Karr wove through a tangled path of streets toward the eastern outskirts of the city, then back toward the center. Karr, chastened by his fall, kept to the main roads, avoiding both steep hills and stairs. He also kept close to the speed limit, for one of the few times in his life.

"They just stopped," Chafetz told him. "There's a hotel on the block—hang on while we see if we can get into its reservation system."

Karr cruised down the block, driving through the neighborhood to get a feel for the area. With adjustments for the profusion of domes belonging to the nearby mosques, the block in western Istanbul would not have been out of place anywhere in Europe, especially Eastern Europe. The buildings were two- and three-story-tall townhouses, the residents prosperous and thoughtful enough to keep the large flowerpots on their stoops watered.

The hotel fit right in, though the flowers in the boxes in front of the over-sized windows on the main floor could have used more attention. It was three stories tall and was perhaps a hundred years newer than its neighbors, which would have meant it was built around 1800.

Karr drove around the block, looking at the houses. The man he was tracking—still unidentified, for all the Art Room's efforts—might be in any one of them.

In that case, though, wouldn't there be more lights on? None of the houses had more than two rooms lit.

Not much of a theory, Karr conceded to himself.

"We have a couple of possibilities in the hotel," said Chafetz.

"What about the houses across the street?"

"We're running the names through watch lists, the whole nine yards. I'll tell you if something comes up. Right now just plant some video bugs around and call it a night."

"Tell you what, first give me the name of somebody who's not in the hotel, but was, say, last week."

"You're going in?"

"Why not? They'll see me planting the bugs from the lobby anyway. I might just as well go right on in. This way we can have a close-up if he's there." Karr laughed. "Besides, maybe they got a restaurant. I'm a little hungry. They wouldn't let me take my fish with me."

"How's your head?"

"Hurts."

"You should get it checked out."

"Will do. Get me that name."

BRIGHT YELLOW WALLS and halogen floodlights gave the hotel lobby a hazy glow. Karr sauntered across the cracked marble floor toward the reception desk, rattled off a greeting in Turkish, then switched to English, asking about a friend he thought was staying there. The man behind the counter jerked his head back, then reached for a small button at the side of his desk.

Not good, thought Karr.

"You sure you don't know him?" he asked.

"Who are you?" said the clerk, a skinny fellow whose face was the color of a Spaldeen after it had survived a dozen stickball games.

"Burt Thompson," said Karr, throwing out the first name that came to him. He stuck out his hand. "I was in town for a conference and hoped to see my friend."

The clerk frowned at his hand. Karr looked at it and realized it was scraped raw. The rough skin on the side was caked with blood.

"Fell down outside," he said. "Don't worry. I won't sue. My friend's name was Sergoni. From Russia."

The clerk shrugged. "Not here."

"Has he been here?"

The clerk shrugged again. A man had come to the curtain behind him, watching.

"Maybe you should check your computer?"

The man shook his head.

"Well, thanks for your help," said Karr. "By the way, you happen to know of a good restaurant around here?"

◆ ◆ ◆

DR. RAMIL SHINED THE light into Karr's eyes, checking his pupils for a sign of concussion. They dilated nicely, very responsive.

"Your head still hurts?" he asked, going into the bathroom for a washcloth and towel.

"Poundin'."

"You don't appear to have a concussion, but of course we'll want to keep a close eye on you. The brain is a delicate instrument, an egg in a basket. We don't want to just toss it around like a baseball."

"Heck, no. A football maybe."

"These are very nasty scrapes," said the doctor, examining Karr's arm and shins. "You must have taken some fall."

"I've had much worse, believe me."

"No doubt."

Ramil cleaned the wounds, then applied an antibacterial agent from his medical kit. He daubed the wound delicately, almost afraid of it. Funny how a surface injury could sometimes seem more daunting than something much more serious well beneath the skin.

"What do you say, Doc? Want to get a drink?" asked Karr when he was finished.

"I don't drink."

"Naw, not *drink* drink. Like tea or something."

Ramil, suddenly glad for the company, found his shoes and followed Karr to the winding spiral staircase at the end of the hall. A blast of warm air hit him in the face when he pushed open the door to the roof terrace; though it was fall, the evening was still very warm.

"Some view," said Karr, pointing toward the Blue Mosque a few blocks up the hill.

Bathed in light, the mosque had an ethereal glow, light flooding upwards around the central dome. Ramil stared at it for a moment, then went over to the table Karr had commandeered. The only other people on the terrace were two older women speaking in hushed tones; Ramil listened for a moment before deciding they were German.

"Are you off for the night?" Ramil asked.

"More or less." Karr gave him a broad smile. The young agent seemed to be the proverbial jolly giant; Ramil couldn't remember ever seeing him frown. "Beer," he told the waiter. "Want one, Doc?"

Though a Muslim, Ramil did occasionally take a drink, but to do so within sight of a mosque felt more than a little sacrilegious. He shook his head brusquely. "Apple tea," he told the waiter.

" 'They ask you about drinking and gambling,' " Ramil told Karr, quoting the passage from the Koran that forbade drinking. " 'Tell them: There is both harm and benefit in them, but the harm is greater.' From the Holy Koran."

Karr nodded thoughtfully. "Maybe that's an argument for moderation, not total abstinence."

"It hasn't been interpreted that way. Are you Christian, Tommy?"

"My mom was Eastern Orthodox, and my dad Catholic."

"Which are you?"

"Both." Karr beamed. "I got baptized twice."

"Is that permissible?"

"Beats me. Couldn't hurt though, right?"

"No," said Ramil. He leaned back in his chair as the waiter set down his tea.

For a Muslim, or at least for Ramil, Karr's easygoing attitude about religion was impossible. Growing up, there weren't many Muslims in America, and his parents had been among the founders of the first mosque in the Washington, D.C., area. Back then, few people outside of the small Egyptian community where he lived—mostly Christian, as a matter of fact—seemed even to have heard of Islam.

Now, of course, everyone in America knew what Islam was—or thought they did. Terrorists like Asad bin Taysr had libeled the religion and its adherents, making it stand for something it wasn't.

"You religious?" Karr asked.

"I wouldn't say so."

What made someone religious? Going to a mosque or church regularly? By that measure, Ramil wasn't; neither were the majority of people he knew. He prayed, but most often in his heart.

"You feel funny talking about it?" Karr asked.

"What?"

"Religion."

He did feel funny, Ramil thought. But he shrugged and smiled, and was glad that the waiter was just arriving with their drinks. Karr was a good kid, but he wasn't the sort of person one discussed religion with.

Charlie Dean, maybe, though Dean was a man of very few words. Dean had a depth born from experience, a weathered pain that could understand something as complicated as religion, or a human soul.

"Pretty mosque. You been in it?" Karr asked.

"No," said Ramil. "If I'm not needed, maybe I'll go visit tomorrow."

"Sounds good."

They sat in silence a while. Then Karr suddenly rose, his beer barely touched. "My head's a lot better, Doc. Thanks for takin' a look."

"I got the impression Ms. Telach wouldn't take no for an answer."

"Yeah, Mom's like that."

"She's not really your mother, is she?"

Karr laughed so hard his face turned red. The waiter ran over.

"Maybe I better finish this," Karr said, sitting back down and picking up the beer. "Some thoughts require alcohol."

CHAPTER 30

AS HE DROVE Lia back to her hotel, Dean waited for her to tell him something more about Pinchon and what had happened. Before training for the Turkey mission, they'd spent nearly two weeks together at a friend's cottage in rural Pennsylvania, wandering through the woods and exploring the nearby villages. Things between them had felt close and easy; they had no walls, secret compartments. But once back at work, all that changed. Lia became a different person, walling off the rest of the world, including him.

Maybe he was that way too, though he didn't do it consciously.

"So you going to tell me about it?" he asked when he pulled up outside her hotel.

"Tell you about what, Charlie Dean?"

"Pinchon. Who was he?"

Lia reached for the door.

"Don't give me the peach pit face," he told her. "What's the deal?"

"There's no deal."

"You told the Art Room that he didn't mess up."

"I said it was a judgment call."

"Sure, if you have the judgment of a five-year-old."

"You don't like him, do you? Was it the crack about your being old?"

"He's not a kid himself."

"There's nothing between us."

Oh, thought Dean to himself. *Oh.*

"All right. I'll see you later," he told her.

"Yup." She slammed the door and walked away.

CHAPTER 31

"THE DRIVER BOLTED as they moved him," Marie Telach told Rubens when he returned to the Art Room. "One of the CIA people shot him."

"He's dead?"

"Very. They took him up the coast to an abandoned dump and tossed him in a swampy area. As of ten minutes ago, the authorities haven't found him. They may not for a while. It's off the beaten trail."

"Why did you tell them to put the body there?"

"I didn't. Lia and Dean had the CIA people dispose of the body. I take it there was a disagreement about how things unfolded."

Rubens had not slept now for more than twenty-four hours. His eyes seemed to be peering at the world through two large tunnels, and the back of his mouth felt like sandpaper.

"Marie—"

"I certainly didn't approve."

This was what came of having to use people from other agencies on a mission. If he had a bigger force, if they had experience with one another and were all under the Art Room's direct control . . .

"We planted a story with a television station that the police ambushed the assailants at the hospital," Telach said. "It's gone out over the air. The police denied it, but it's being repeated by the radio. The rumors that the hit men were part of the Russian mafiya have also been aired. Obviously the reporters didn't see the bodies."

Under other circumstances, Rubens might have had a good chuckle over the media's ability to be misled. But he was hardly in a mood for mirth.

"What does Red Lion think?" he asked Telach.

"His bodyguards haven't woken him up yet."

"Do they know?"

"We can't tell. There are only two in the house with him. My guess is that they know something's wrong, but they're too scared of his reaction to wake him."

No, thought Rubens; they simply haven't figured it out yet. There was a tendency, even among intelligence experts, to see the opposition as omnipotent. More than likely, the men at the house had no contact with the others and weren't monitoring the local media.

"The Turkish authorities are confused themselves," added Telach. "They think the driver shot the three men but was kidnapped by others. From their phone messages, it looks like they believe the men were part of a smuggling operation that went sour. There have been conflicts in the past, so it makes sense from their point of view."

Even so, thought Rubens, the hospital operation had been a fiasco. It was his fault. He could have simply had the driver kidnapped. He'd gotten too greedy, pushed too far.

This was no time to second-guess himself. Leave that to Bing.

"The man who met with Asad?" he asked, changing the subject.

"Still haven't identified him. The images haven't matched anything. Johnny Bib is working with Robert Gallo on a new tool to match up information. Johnny says he should have something by the morning."

"That will give me time to prepare," said Rubens. Sessions with Johnny Bibleria—universally known as Johnny Bib— always tended to be a strain.

Rubens found his concentration slipping as Telach

continued to update him. They had images of this operative; the CIA was complaining that they weren't being given enough access to information; Tommy Karr had fallen off his motorcycle, but Dr. Ramil deemed him fit.

Bing had to be cut off quickly. Rubens had seen enough of these political maneuverings to realize, however, that it would have to be done delicately. The first thing he would have to do was take a sounding.

George Hadash was the person to turn to for advice. Thank God he was back on his game. Surely he'd return to the administration in a few months; he and the president had been close for years and years. They worked well together, Hadash's pragmatism tempering Marcke's enthusiastic idealism.

"You should all go home and get rest," Rubens told Telach when he realized she had finished speaking.

"I've already sent the Art Room team home. They'll be back at midnight."

"I would suggest you go as well."

"You should sleep, too."

"Thank you, Marie. I will try to find space for a nap."

Rubens turned to his e-mail after Telach left, making sure he had nothing major pressing. Then he called over to the hospital, using the direct number to Hadash's room. The phone rang and rang without being picked up.

Thinking Hadash must still be undergoing tests, Rubens turned his attention to other matters. He tried again around six, surely late enough for the tests to be over. But he got the same response. He hung up, worked through some of the memoranda on his desk, then tried again. This time a woman picked up the phone.

"I was looking for George Hadash," he told her. "Have I got the right room?"

The woman hesitated, then said she really didn't know anything. Before Rubens could ask anything else, she hung up. Rubens put the phone down and drummed his fingers on the desk. Then he grabbed the handset and called information for the hospital's general number. He was connected with a rather officious young man who told him that federal law prohibited the hospital from giving out any information about a patient.

"You don't have to give me any information," said Rubens. "Just connect me."

"I'm sorry. That's not possible."

Rubens hung up. Hadash had been divorced for years, but his daughter lived near Washington. Rubens looked the number up in his Rolodex—he hated computerized phonebooks—and called. The answering machine picked up.

"Hello, Irena. This is Bill Rubens. I realize it's rather silly of me, but I seem to have forgotten your father's phone number at the hospital and the boobs there won't give it to me. Would it be possible—"

The phone beeped as Irena picked up on the other end.

"Oh, Bill, it's terrible," she said. "Daddy died of complications a few hours ago. I just got back—I can't believe it."

"No," said Rubens. "Oh, no."

CHAPTER 32

LIA HAD LAST seen Terrence Pinchon three years before. A pair of women who had been working for the International Red Cross had been kidnapped by a group of local thugs. Two separate three-member Delta teams had been tasked to work with the CIA and a Russian intelligence officer to extricate them. Lia, posing as another relief worker, went into the village where the women had last been seen to gather information.

The Russian's intelligence was less than helpful; he hadn't even gotten the names of the local government officials right. Sent on a wild goose chase to locate the kidnappers' hideout, Lia found the real location: two doors down from the aid center.

The local police, with Delta backup, set up a raid. The thieves' lair turned out to have been abandoned about a half hour before they arrived. The local police chief claimed to be amazed by this unlucky coincidence.

It turned out that the women had been handed over—"sold" would be a better description—to a neighboring warlord, who offered them to the local government in exchange for the release of several prisoners. The prisoners were being held for drug trafficking; the locals were willing to let them go but the regional government was not. Lia found out where the women were being held, organized a reconnaissance with the two other members of her team, and suggested an operation to free them—without help from the locals this time. The operation was vetoed by the CIA paramilitary officer.

So Lia and the Delta boys went ahead with it on their own. It wasn't exactly Guadalcanal: they drove up in two cars, overpowered the single guard at the isolated house where the women were kept, and drove off with the two women. Not a single shot, not even a warning round, was fired.

The CIA paramilitary officer was livid and insisted that they go ahead with a plan to pay the warlord ransom money.

Was the para getting a kickback? Lia thought so, and told him that to his face. She could still see the red rings around his eyes—she'd nailed him.

Pinchon, though, didn't think so. With a few months' seniority over Lia, he was in charge of the detachment, and he bought the argument that the warlord would cause trouble if he wasn't paid off properly.

"Two months from now we'll be back to pull out two more people, only they'll be better protected this time," said Pinchon. "And maybe we'll find them dead."

Lia and the Russian intelligence agent handled the payoff. It was a drive-and-drop operation, with Lia and the Russian driving to a deserted curve on a dusty mountain road, dropping the plastic bag of money, and skedaddling—plenty of sweat but no real hassle. Lia thought the hardest part was surviving the Russian's vodka breath, fanned by the finicky heater in the small car.

Mission accomplished, she hooked up with the rest of the team and headed out to the local airport. Three miles away, they were ambushed by a rival warlord's group. Pinchon's vehicle was destroyed by a massive bomb.

There was no question the Land Cruiser was destroyed—even now Lia could see it burning, the stench of flesh in the air. Her vehicle had been more than a hundred yards farther down the road, and by the time she managed to fend off the gunmen and get to the wreck, Pinchon's body had been burned to a shriveled black twist. Still taking fire, she and the others had had to retreat; the body wasn't recovered for two more days.

Lia could still feel the tears from the funeral. And yet it had been a sham.

A sham.

Organized by the CIA, no doubt, since he was working for them now. But why?

LIA COULDN'T SLEEP. She got up and began pacing the hotel room, the adrenaline practically pouring from her sweat glands. She wanted to talk about Pinchon and what had happened—but the person she wanted to talk about it with was Charlie, and he was the last person she could discuss it with. You couldn't talk about an ex-lover with a present lover, no way.

Terry Pinchon was an ex-lover. A brief lover, definitely ex. Even though her heart had jumped at seeing him.

Even though it jumped now, thinking about him.

How could he let her think he was dead?

And what the hell had she seen in him? He was a jerk.

But her heart was racing, even now.

A handsome jerk.

Lia looked out the window. The sky remained dark black, the stars twinkling brightly. She went back to bed, knowing she needed to rest, also knowing she wouldn't get any.

CHAPTER 33

IRENA HADASH MET Rubens at the door to her condominium in her stocking feet.

"Thank you for coming over," she said, reaching to hug him. She smelled of cigarettes—and a little gin, Rubens thought.

Certainly she was entitled to both.

"There's so much—I can't process it all," she said.

Rubens followed her inside to the kitchen. Irena had reclaimed the family name after her divorce a year before, and the condo dated from then as well. It was a small, one-story unit in a development that would not have been considered fancy even outside the Beltway.

"I have to find a funeral home to send him to," said Irena, stacking forms to one side of the table before sitting.

"He's still at the hospital?"

Instead of answering, she told Rubens that her father had begun to bleed uncontrollably during the operation. "That's not supposed to happen, is it? It's not."

"No," said Rubens.

"They want to do an autopsy."

"They should."

"The president—" Irena stopped. "Do you mind, would it be okay if I smoked?"

"Of course not. It's your house." Rubens tried to smile, but even to him his voice sounded awkward and not particularly consoling. He wasn't good at this sort of thing, but he felt as if he had to do something, had to offer some consolation. He owed George Hadash so much, he had to do something, even if it was inept.

Irena got up and went to the counter, grabbing her pocket-book and struggling with a Bic lighter before getting the cigarette to catch. "I'm out of practice."

"What were you saying about the president?"

"He said—he told me he thought . . ."

The phone rang. Irena jerked around to grab it, but then hesitated.

"Do you want me to screen your calls?" Rubens asked.

"Maybe. Yes. Please." Rubens got up and took the phone off the hook on the third ring.

"Ms. Irena Hadash's residence," he said.

"Who the hell are you?" demanded a male voice.

"This is William Rubens. I'm a friend of the family. What can I do for you?"

"Tell Irena her daughter's father wants to know when he can drop her off."

Rubens cleared his throat. "There's been a death in the family."

"Yeah. Put her on."

Rubens cupped his hand over the mouthpiece. "Your ex, I believe."

Irena nodded, took a long puff of the cigarette, then got up again and took the phone, walking with it to the far end of the kitchen before talking. He pretended not to hear her discussing whether or not the kindergartener could stay for a few days; the ex was clearly giving her a hard time. Well, there was no mystery there why she got divorced; the only question was how she could be so even tempered with the jerk.

When she finally hung up, Irena stubbed her cigarette out in the sink and got another.

"I can help arrange for a sitter," said Rubens, though in actual fact he had no idea how this was done.

"No. John will take her. He just wants to make it as miserable an experience as possible, on the theory that I'll be less likely to ask in the future." She smiled faintly. "It's standard operating procedure. Do you want something? A drink?"

Rubens shook his head. "You started to tell me about the president."

"He suggested a state funeral. In the Capitol Rotunda. I— he said it was up to me."

"You don't want him to have one?" Rubens couldn't hide his surprise. "It's an honor due your father."

"I know. But he was such a private—he didn't like the pomp and circumstance. You know that, Bill. He . . ." Her voice faded, but a smile came to her lips. "He didn't live his life in quotes."

She made quotes in the air—just as her father might have.

"Yes," agreed Rubens.

"I remember one time, he'd just come from a meeting with the Senate Foreign Relations Committee, I think, and he had two big stains on his tie." Irena laughed again, this time much more deeply. "And the tie—I swear I gave it to him for Father's Day when I was twelve, so it *had* to be fifteen years old. At least. That was my father."

"He also wrote the definitive book on Asian–American relations in the 1990s," said Rubens. He stopped himself, cutting off what could have been a long list of Hadash's achievements.

The thing was, his daughter was right. George Hadash wouldn't have wanted a state funeral.

They sat silently for a moment, neither one knowing what to say.

"He does deserve to be honored," said Irena finally. She reached her hand toward Rubens. "You'll help figure this out?"

"Of course."

"I remember the first time I met you—Daddy was so careful. Call him Bill, not Billy. Not Billy. But you don't seem like a Billy. More a William, I think."

"I'm used to Bill."

Irena nodded. The truth was, she could call him anything she wanted and he wouldn't have minded.

CHAPTER 34

"FA-*SHONE!*" KARR SPREAD his arms wide as he approached the short man standing in front of the bubble-front helicopter. "Nice cap you got there, dude. Met fan, huh? You got a hangover, right?"

The pilot—his real name was Ray Fashona, though Karr pronounced it right perhaps one time out of ten—grunted and finished his walk around of the helicopter. A rather old though serviceable Bell 47, it had a towline at the rear with a banner advertising "Turkey No. 1 Tours" in Turkish and English.

"This part doesn't say, 'Hey, look at us, we're spies,' does it?" Karr asked, pointing at the banner as he followed Fashona around the rear of the aircraft.

"Wasn't my idea," said Fashona.

"Got a hangover, huh?" said Karr. "You drank that raki stuff, right? What is that, like licorice-flavored white lightning?"

"Make sure your seatbelt's tight. If you fall out, I'm not picking you up."

A pair of laptops were lashed to the dashboard in front of Karr's seat on the right-hand side of the chopper. He opened the top unit and turned it on; ninety seconds later he was greeted by the opening screen of the program controlling a boost unit for the eavesdropping device implanted in Asad's skull. The unit, mounted in the helicopter's boom tail, was considerably more powerful than the ones they had left on the roof yesterday; even so, its range was only about five miles.

"Good to go," Karr told Fashona, pulling on his headset.

"Yeah," said the pilot, cranking his engine to life.

They took a pass about two miles from Asad's house, confirming that the unit was working and allowing the Art Room to run a full set of diagnostics with the master receiving unit, which was a specially equipped 707 flying at forty-five thousand feet over the Sea of Marmara, ostensibly on a NATO training mission.

"Everything looks good, Tommy," said Rockman, who'd just come back on duty in the Art Room. "Unit B is going off duty. You guys are it."

"The A Team is ready," Karr said, his voice booming over the engines.

"It sounds like Red Lion is getting ready to go for a ride. Remind Fashona he doesn't have to get too close. We have plenty of tracking units scattered around the city now."

"Okey-doke."

"Asad has just woken up. We'll keep you up to date."

Karr zoomed the map showing the location of the sending unit.

"Where are we going today, Red Lion?" he said, overlaying a satellite photo on the grid. "What sights will we see?"

ASAD LISTENED AS Katib recounted what had happened at the hospital. It took considerable discipline for Asad not to interrupt; he didn't want to prejudice his chief bodyguard's report by asking questions that might lead Katib to shade what he said.

"The Turks must have set up an ambush," said Katib. "They were waiting in the room. Most likely they had moved the driver already."

The *official* police theory—obtained through a third party Katib knew—was that this was the product of a feud between two dueling smuggling groups, possibly Syrian, who had connections to the Russian mafiya. What the Turks were really up to, however, was difficult to fathom. Their government was not sympathetic to the true cause of Islam, and while the intelligence service was preoccupied with the Kurds in the east, they were not to be taken very lightly. Asad had no doubt that that they had arranged an ambush at the hospital; the question was what the driver, Yorsi al-Haznawi, would have told them.

He didn't know much, not even the location of this safehouse. Still, as a matter of prudence he would have to change locations.

To be truly safe, he would have to leave Istanbul completely. But he couldn't do that; only he could initiate the wave of attacks. If he did not conduct his meetings over the next two days, the entire operation would have to be postponed. Better to move forward and risk failure than flee like a coward and accept defeat.

"I know this is my responsibility," said Katib. "I will make amends, here in Istanbul."

"We will speak of it later. This morning there is much to do."

"We have new vehicles."

"Then let us go to the mosque and pray."

LIA DEFRANCESCA PULLED down the top piece of the religious veil covering her head, adjusting the band so that it covered her eyebrows. The Fiat's air conditioning was at full blast, but she was sweating anyway; she could feel beads of perspiration running down the sides of her neck. She had another full set of clothes on under the long dress and outer jilbab. She also had three pistols, her PDA, two satellite phones, six pin grenades, a dozen video bugs, and two dozen eavesdropping flies. And that didn't begin to count the small booster units disguised as tourist gear and the clothing in the three bags she had in the car, or the extra clothes and gear stashed around the city. Nothing like traveling light.

"Coming in your direction," said Rockman.

Lia reached to start the Fiat, then caught herself; she already had it on. The car was so quiet, it was hard to hear the engine.

"Go down two blocks and turn left," said Rockman.

Lia put the car in gear and followed his directions, moving

mechanically. Ordinarily she would have used the PDA to make her own way, but this morning she simply wanted to do what she was told, a robot moving through the narrow streets.

"They're turning back onto the highway," said Rockman.

Lia got on a few blocks ahead of them, driving slowly so they could catch up. They were in a white Mercedes—the terrorists seemed to have an endless supply of vehicles; no doubt they had a good deal with a used car lot somewhere nearby.

DEAN PARKED A block from the Mercedes in the heart of the Sultanahmet district, the most popular tourist area in Istanbul and the center of the city for more than a thousand years. He could see the walls and minarets of the Blue Mosque just up the hill; beyond it to the right but out of view were the Haghia Sophia and the Sultan's Palace. Literally thousands of people thronged through the area every day; Asad and his al-Qaeda contacts would be just so many needles in a massive haystack, their foreign faces as much a part of the scenery as Dean's.

"Buggee is headed for the Blue Mosque. Must be doing the tourist thing," said Rockman in Dean's head as he pulled on his sunglasses and got out of the car.

Dean climbed up the hill, walking in the middle of the street. A man near the corner asked if he wanted to buy a rug; Dean smiled but said nothing. Yesterday, with thick stubble and slightly rouged face, he and his rumpled coat might have passed for a Turk as well as the Spanish doctor he was portraying. Today, clean-shaven, in a loud tourist shirt, he looked like a very different man. Which of course was the idea.

Built by Sultan Ahmet I, the Blue Mosque had scandalized many of the sultan's subjects because its beauty and size rivaled Mecca's own. The sultan was long gone, but the monument to his devotion and ego remained, drawing a steady stream of tourists as well as worshippers. Dean cut through the garden at the side, ignoring the old ladies hawking scarves and shoeshine men touting for work as he closed the distance between him and Red Lion.

"Just finished washing his feet," said Rockman. "Going up into the courtyard."

Only a few yards away now, Dean slowed down. The enclosed courtyard, constructed of massive marble squares and rounded by a high-columned portico, sat directly in front of the dome-topped prayer hall. Dean took a few steps to the side, as if admiring the cascade of domes while looking for his target.

It'd be so much easier if Asad was just a target and Dean was still a sniper. Set up, spot him, steady the gun.

Bam.

So much easier.

But that was what the idiot CIA jerk Pinchon had done yesterday, wasn't it? Erase the problem. And in the process, lose the chance to find out what these slimes were really up to.

Asad led his three bodyguards to the line reserved for practicing Muslims at the center of the building. Both he and his men wore dark suit jackets; they could easily be visiting businessmen taking the morning off to see the sights.

Dean walked around to the side entrance, joining the line of tourists. He was given a bag for his shoes; slipping them inside, he walked into the cool interior of the mosque, his feet cushioned by thick Turkish rugs.

The massive dome and the high ceilings around it transformed the murmured prayers of the faithful and the hushed awe of the tourists into a low-pitched hum, a sound that harmonized with the blue light from the stained glass windows to create a holy, timeless space. Even Dean, who had not only been inside twice before but was hardly religious, felt the sensation. He stopped for a moment near the door, getting his bearings, then he walked along the rail dividing those praying from those simply admiring, looking for Asad.

The terrorist leader was prostrate near the mihrab, the stone indicating the direction of Mecca. Dean continued across the mosque, drifting in the direction of the modern rooms used for teaching and other mosque activities.

Dean was close enough to Asad's group as he went outside to see that he didn't stop at the table where donations were accepted. Maybe he figured he'd given enough at the office.

"Charlie, you don't have to get too close," said Rockman from the Art Room as Dean tagged along behind Asad, following through the park between the Blue Mosque and Haghia Sophia. "Don't bug the buggee."

You're a barrel of laughs, Dean thought.

Asad walked through the park between the Blue Mosque and Haghia Sophia, then veered to the right, walking toward the entrance to Topkapi, the Sultan's Palace. Dean stayed between fifteen and twenty yards behind, ducking into the middle of a Japanese tour group near the entrance to the palace grounds. Unlike the mosque, where the security people were subtle and largely out of sight, Turkish soldiers with submachine guns clustered around the gates and inner paths.

"He only bought the regular ticket," Rockman told Dean. "Not interested in the harem. Our buggee never was one for the women."

"Rockman, you're starting to bug me," said Dean.

"Hey, that's a good one. I'll have to remember that."

ASAD WALKED QUICKLY through the palace grounds, heading for the chamber of the holy relics. The Ottoman sultans had taken over as caliphs in the sixteenth century after conquering the Middle East. As powerful as their empire was, Asad believed the Turks had encouraged Islam's decline, first by removing Arab wealth for their personal use and then, more fatally, by collaborating with the Crusaders. Decadence and weakness were the inevitable result.

Asad held his breath as he entered the building housing the relics. Unlike much of the palace, the structure was not ostentatious; this, it occurred to Asad, was fitting, as the Prophet, Peace be to Him, was not one for earthly riches or show.

The room containing the Prophet's hair, tooth, and other relics was to the right of the entrance. Bowing his head slightly, Asad walked into the darkened room. The chanted verses of the Koran mesmerized him as he circled the large glass display at the center, awed by the simple display of Mohammed's hair.

A window cut into the wall at the side allowed visitors to catch a glimpse of a cloak once worn by the Prophet. Standing before it, Asad felt faint; he had to put his hand against the glass to steady himself.

Conscious thought slipped away. He felt the touch of an angel on his shoulder, holding him upright.

"Are you all right, sheik?" asked Katib, the head of his bodyguards.

"Yes," Asad whispered. "Filled with joy."

He walked slowly from the room into the reception area, looking at the swords of the Prophet's followers. A short man with Turkish features approached from across the room. Asad saw him out of the corner of his eye, but waited until he was about six feet away to turn toward him. When he did, the man stopped, nodded, and then abruptly left the pavilion.

"Come," Asad told Katib. "They are ready."

"SOMETHING'S UP, CHARLIE," Rockman told Dean as he pretended to read the sign outside the hall with the Islamic relics. "Asad just told his men to follow him. He's moving toward you."

Dean kept his eyes on the sign as Asad passed behind him, walking toward the lower courtyard. Dean let him get about ten yards ahead and then turned to follow as Asad and his men walked through the lower garden.

"Could be headed toward the Circumcision Pavilion," said Rockman. "Yeah, looks like it."

The small building stood at the side of a platform overlooking the nearby park and the Golden Horn, Istanbul's ancient natural harbor. By the time Dean reached the pool next to it, Asad was on the other side, headed toward the Baghdad Pavilion, a large hall perched above a sheer drop at the very edge of the terrace. Dean had to slip through a large group of British tourists to follow; by the time he got through the throng Asad had disappeared.

"Charlie, can you see him?" asked Rockman.

"No," said Dean.

"He's in that big building in front of you, the Baghdad Pavilion. This is it. He just told one of his bodyguards to hang back."

Dean spotted someone watching him from the wall near the building. The most inconspicuous thing to do was to keep walking toward it, going in the same general direction Asad's party had taken. As he approached the steps under the arch, two men in Western-style suits came out from the side, holding up their hands and shaking their heads. He asked in English how he could visit the pavilion, but the men told him it was closed.

"Charlie, what's going on?" Rockman asked.

"Two guys just waved me away from the door Asad used," said Dean as he walked away. "They weren't soldiers."

"He's still in the building," said Rockman. "Set up some video bugs so we can see who comes in."

"On it," said Dean.

CHAPTER 35

MARIE TELACH KNELT down next to the technician's station, looking at his screen.

"See, these sines are diminishing," said the radio expert, pointing at a series of waves on the screen. "It's gotta mean they're going underground. Thing is, we're going to lose him if he goes much deeper."

"Can you boost it?"

"We're at maximum power now. You have to bring the booster units in closer. Your only option."

Telach straightened and walked down to the front of the room, where Rockman was running the mission.

"He's in here somewhere," said Rockman, pointing to the corner where Asad had disappeared. "Below the building with the relics of Prophet Mohammed. That's where we lost the signal. But he came from this direction over here. There must be a set of stairs that aren't on our maps."

"Do we know what's on the basement level of the palace?" she asked.

"Yeah, but if we're not picking him up, he's got to be at least one floor below it, right? Or maybe two or three," said Rockman.

A message appeared on the translation screen: SIGNAL LOST.

"Have Lia go into the palace with the portable booster units," Telach said, stifling a curse. "Put them as close to this area as possible. In the meantime, I'll talk to Mr. Rubens."

◆ ◆ ◆

THE SHRIEK OF the phone woke Rubens with a start and he jerked out of bed. He turned and saw his clock—4:03 A.M. He'd overslept.

He reached over to the side of the bed, picking up the phone that connected to the Art Room.

"Hello, Marie," he said. "What's the situation?"

"It looks like Red Lion is meeting someone in the Topkapi Palace," she told him. "Probably in a basement area. We don't have a definitive map. I'd like to have the U-2 Senior Project overfly the area with its penetrating radar."

"Do it."

"We're having technical difficulties because of the building," Telach continued. "We need to put boosters closer to the source. That may involve going into the palace itself, possibly into the Pavilion of the Holy Mantle where Mohammed's cloak is kept. Charlie's already gone through the security screen and we're confident we can get a unit in without it being detected."

Rubens took a slow breath, contemplating the situation. The president—against Rubens' advice—had already decided against bringing the boosters inside any of the mosques; if the device were discovered, the act would be considered sacrilegious and would have considerable repercussions. The Pavilion of the Holy Mantle was not a mosque—but in some ways it was even more sensitive. The discovery of one of the units in the palace, an official government building, might embarrass an important ally.

Would definitely embarrass them.

"Do what is necessary to accomplish our mission," said Rubens. "But do not leave one of the units unattended in the building with the relics. Have Lia or Dean bring it and stay with it, if needed."

"All right."

"I'm sorry I overslept, Marie. I was up late with George Hadash's daughter last night, helping her make arrangements for her father's funeral. I'll be in shortly."

CHAPTER 36

"ARE YOU SURE you're entitled to wear white?"

Lia spun around, caught off-guard though the Art Room had told her Dean was nearby.

"You'd know," she told him, smoothing the sides of her long outer dress. "And the color is cocoa, not white. Off-white. What's the setup?"

"Asad went into that corner building and they lost the signal. He's downstairs somewhere. They're getting a radar plane to map the basement."

"You sure he hasn't slipped out?"

"Once he's outside they'll hear him."

"Can we get inside?"

"They want to try and map it first." Dean turned toward the building Asad had gone into. "They want to put a booster as close to the building as possible."

"All right. I'll go over to that bench." Lia slipped out one of the pseudo-eyeglass case booster units.

"Give me some," Dean told her. "I'll walk into the Pavilion of the Holy Mantle with them. They don't want us to leave any equipment in there, but I'll find out if there's a signal at least."

Lia gave him the one in her hand and reached into her bag for another.

"Take the fake cameras," she told him. "One for a backup."

The fake camera looked like an early-model digital camera and could actually take two photos. But unlike the eyeglass case, anyone spotting it on the ground would probably take it with them.

"Smile," said Dean, pretending to take her picture. "See you up there."

"NOT GETTING ANYTHING, Charlie. We think now he might have moved to the west toward the water," Telach told him. "Take a turn around the hall and then go back outside."

Dean held the fake camera in his hands, pretending to be angling for a picture of the swords that belonged to Mohammed's followers. A security guard waved frantically at him from the side.

"You're not allowed to use your flash," said the man.

Dean nodded.

"No flash," insisted the man.

"I understand," said Dean, walking away.

"Charlie, the radar plane's above you now," said Rockman. "We found a passage you can use to get into the sub-basement. It's in the second building on your left as you come out. They use it for maintenance. You should be able to slip in."

Dean worked his way toward it, pausing every so often to snap a picture. Finally he backed against the doors, reached his hand around and found that they were locked.

He turned and knelt before it, checking to see how the lock was oriented before reaching behind his belt buckle and pulling out the pick and the tension wrench. He slid the pick all the way to the back of the lock, then began teasing the pressure to undo the lock.

For a split second he thought of Lia, who was so much better at this than he was. He pushed the thought away, concentrated on what he was doing.

When the tumblers clicked into place, Dean pushed down on the handle and the latch moved with a heavy crunch.

"Go to your right," said Rockman. "You should come to a set of stairs on your left."

Dean found the steps and descended to an open landing. Dean paused on the steps, listening. The stone block walls and smooth tile floor meant sound should echo a considerable distance.

"There should be some sort of passage down a few yards to your left," said Rockman.

"Some sort?" whispered Dean.

"We're working with a radar map, Charlie, doing this on the fly. You need to go down at least two levels."

Dean started down the hall, treading as lightly as possible. In contrast to the ornate displays in the buildings above, this section of the palace appeared to be used for nothing more than storage. A pile of cardboard boxes sat in a haphazard pyramid a few paces ahead of him, covered with dust. Just beyond them, Dean found an open door and a set of steps; he listened, then descended slowly, pausing every second or third tread to listen. There were no lights in the passage itself, but a dim yellow haze filtered up from the landing, which Dean estimated was a good thirty feet down.

He stopped at the bottom of the stairs, listening. When he heard nothing he swung out into a large open space lit by a single overhead bulb, forty watts at the most. Stacked cardboard boxes formed a maze of walls about waist high.

"Okay, Charlie. There should be another set of steps about fifty feet in front of you."

Dean threaded his way through the piles of boxes, moving slowly, his eyes not completely adjusted to the dimness.

"Are you going to lose my com system?" he asked.

"If you go down another twenty feet, probably. But we think we can route you through the booster units. We're working on the setup for that. It'll be done soon."

"How close am I to Asad?"

"We're still not sure where he is. You're almost directly under the door where you went into the building. The next passage will take you to a set of stairs for an underground cavern—well, it looks like a cavern—that extends to the west. It may have been a water holding area, or just a big storage hall. It looks like it's the only way Asad could have gone."

Dean walked toward the shadows at the far end of the room. Boxes were stacked along the wall, and it took him a few moments to find the door Rockman had said would be there. He had to move three stacks of boxes before he could open it, the hinges squealing.

A rush of dank, cold air greeted him.

"All right, I have the steps," said Dean. "I'm going down."

"We're with you, Charlie."

Yeah, right behind me, thought Dean.

LIA GAZED OUT over the nearby park toward the city, admiring the view as she waited for a knot of tourists to leave so she could stick the transmitter under the bench without being seen. When they finally left, she slipped the hard case down next to her, pushing on the outside hinge of the hard case to activate it. Then she got up and, as if looking pensively toward the mosaic on the building, prepared to drop it behind the marble bench.

"We're not picking up anything, Lia. Don't bother leaving it," said Rockman about three seconds after she'd dropped it.

"Peachy," she growled, stooping to retrieve it. As she did, she saw a man in a suit watching her a few feet away.

Lia fished out the glass case, patting it against her hand as if it had been bad. Then she walked deliberately away, the bodyguard's stare burning a hole in the back of her head. Lia didn't stop until she reached the restaurant, which was located on the other side of the grounds overlooking the Bosporus. She circled around the outdoor dining area before choosing a table, making sure she wasn't being followed.

"Lia, what's going on?" Telach asked.

"Someone was eyeballing me over near the Baghdad Pavilion," she said. "I don't think he wanted a date."

"Did he follow you?"

"No. I'm having some tea," she added for the approaching waiter. "Just sugar."

Lia leaned back in the chair as the waiter left. "Where's Charlie?"

"He's directly below the palace walls, several levels down. We'd like you to plant some more video bugs," added Telach. "We want to try and catch a glimpse of who's at the meeting as they leave."

"Who's going to back up Charlie?"

"He's fine."

"Someone should be backing him up."

"He's fine, Lia. Mr. Rockman will tell you where to set up the bugs."

ABOUT HALFWAY DOWN the long stone staircase, the light from above faded completely to black. Dean moved down slowly, guided by the light of his keychain flashlight. When he reached the bottom of the steps, he crouched and played the light around the space in front of him. He'd reached another large room, this one with a low ceiling. A forest of thick stone pillars ranged in front of him.

Dean nearly jumped when he heard a light scraping sound to the right. He turned his light but saw nothing.

A rat, probably.

"How we doing, Charlie?" asked Rockman.

"We're doing fine."

"We're just barely reading you, Charlie. Turn on the booster and let's make sure we can get a signal."

Dean took the unit out and activated it.

"Hang on a second," said Rockman.

Dean waited while they dealt with whatever technical issues were involved in switching the communications over the different channels.

"Got it. Okay," said Rockman finally. "But we still don't have Red Lion."

"Charlie, do you have one booster or two?" asked Telach.

"Two."

"Leave one there, and activate the other. It'll act as a relay as you go."

"All right."

Dean put the transmitter down, then walked forward, keeping his light aimed at the floor. After he'd gone sixty paces, he saw a wall ahead. He moved along it to the right, his heart pounding so loudly he could barely hear Rockman when the runner told him to turn right.

"There's another set of steps downward about ten yards away," said Rockman. "That level is a warren of spaces and hallways that extend to the old Byzantine fortress walls by the highway."

"You think he grabbed a car out there?"

"No. He hasn't come aboveground. He's somewhere between you and those old ruins," said Rockman. "There are no other passages that link up to where we lost him. But where, exactly, I don't know."

When he reached the wall, Dean saw a faint light filtering along the floor about twenty yards away. As he approached, he heard the echo of a voice. But the booster still wasn't picking up Asad. Dean flattened himself against the wall, moving slowly toward the opening.

"They're guards," said Rockman when Dean finally drew close enough for his microphone to pick up their echoes. "We're definitely close."

Dean didn't answer. Instead, he started moving back the way he came.

"Where are you going, Charlie?"

Still close to the guards, Dean remained silent. He took another few steps, then froze—a pair of eyes were watching him ten yards away.

Red eyes.

A rat.

But it was at his height. How could that be?

Dean lifted the flashlight and flicked it on and off. The rat scurried to the right, running along a ledge in the wall. To the left of the ledge was a square opening about three feet on each side right above the ledge. The bottom of the opening was covered with a slimy moss.

"Where does this hole go?" Dean whispered.

"Hold on."

Dean climbed up into the hole and shone the flashlight down it. He heard squeals, then the sound of wings. He flattened himself just in time to avoid a pair of bats as they flew over-head, exiting the passage—and then returning, disappearing somewhere beyond the small beam of his light.

Rats, bats, and sewer slime. Clearly Asad was around here somewhere.

CHAPTER 37

DR. RAMIL NODDED AT the desk clerk as he left the hotel, stepping out in the overcast day. He started up the hill toward the Blue Mosque, then turned left and walked through the small array of shops that stood at its base. The open windows of the Mosaic Museum drew his attention; he went through the small alley to the entrance, paying a few lira to walk above the faded stones that had once decorated a Byzantine emperor's palace. The scenes of daily life roughly fifteen hundred years ago didn't hold his interest, however, and he soon found himself back outside, walking in the direction of the Bazaar Quarter. He made his way across Veniçeriler Caddesi, one of the old city's main boulevards crowded with shoe stores and banks. Ducking one of the trams that ran down the wide street, he wandered into the tangle of alleyways near the Grand Bazaar. Everything was for sale here; he passed rows of stores with toys, then a handful of others selling guns, still more with kitchen goods. He'd been in the Bazaar Quarter a week before, while getting oriented to the city, but nothing looked familiar until he reached the Şark Kahvesi, a cafe on the western side of the bazaar, far from where he had started. He stopped and had some Turkish coffee, extra sweet, and listened to the merchants nearby complaining in Turkish that business had fallen off. From there he wandered farther south, passing through the Spice Bazaar and emerging near the New Mosque and the Galata Bridge. A man with a stubble beard waved an array of Turkish flags at him, trying to coax him into buying one before moving on.

The New Mosque stood before him on the right, a towering succession of domes that topped graying concrete. He turned and began walking in the other direction.

He'd been avoiding mosques all day, Ramil thought; he'd walked by not only the Blue Mosque but the majestic Süleymaniye at the heart of the Bazaar Quarter as well.

Just then, the call to prayers sounded. Ashamed, Ramil changed direction and went toward the gate. As he did, a flock of pigeons took flight; the birds were so numerous that they darkened the sky. Surprised, Ramil shielded his head as they flapped by, ducking his head as if afraid they would hit him.

He washed his feet at the fountain, then left his shoes at the door. The air inside the mosque was cool. The air and filtered light cleared his head. He began to pray, holding his hands up and then clasping them, bending and bowing, kneeling and kissing the ground.

"God is Greater," he said in Arabic, using the words inscribed in his memory as a child. "In the Name of God, the Compassionate Source of All Mercy, All Praise be to God."

The words resounded in his head as if his entire body were hollow. At the end of his prayer, turning right and then left to wish peace to those nearby, he felt slightly dizzy. He stayed on his knees, lightheaded.

When he rose, Ramil caught sight of an old man with a prayer cap nearby.

The man eyed him accusingly. Unnerved, Ramil turned and found another man, this one very young, glaring at him as well. There were others back near the door, whispering.

Were they talking about him? He couldn't hear what they said.

Was he just being paranoid? No one could possibly notice him here.

Ramil glanced around. The men he'd thought were watching him before were looking at other parts of the mosque.

It must have been his imagination; the stress of the mission was starting to make him paranoid.

Ramil stepped back, admiring the soaring dome above him. The mosaics made the ceiling seem as if it were floating in air.

A traitor and coward.

Though hushed, the voice he heard was distinct, and nearby. Ramil turned but could not see who had said it.

Traitor? Were they referring to him?

Asad bin Taysr would claim that any Muslim who worked against him was a traitor. He and all of his ilk claimed that any Muslim who collaborated with the "Crusaders" should face death as heretics.

But Ramil was not a traitor. Neither was he a coward. He had not accomplished much in life, perhaps—not in many years—he had no children, or a legacy to speak of, but he was not a bad man. Asad, bin Laden, al-Qaeda and all their filthy, twisted comrades—they were the evil ones.

Traitor! Coward!

By the time Ramil reached his shoes, his heart was thumping fiercely. He started for the nearby tram stop, then, seeing a taxi, ran in front of it to flag it down. The driver jerked his head out of his window, looking at him as if he were a madman.

"I need to go back to my hotel," he told the man in Arabic.

The driver scowled at him.

Was he accusing him as well? Of what? Of being a coward? Of being worthless? A traitor?

No. Few people understood Arabic in Turkey, aside from the prayers they memorized.

"My hotel," Ramil repeated, this time in English.

The driver jerked his thumb toward the back. He had another fare.

Another taxi stopped a few feet away. Ramil stepped back, nodding, bending his head in apology. Panic rose in his chest, but he fought against it, walking to the other car and gently opening the door.

CHAPTER 38

WHEN RUBENS ENTERED the Art Room, he went directly to Rockman's console at the front of the room.

"Where is Mr. Dean now?" Rubens asked the runner.

"He's in a passage under the Topkapi Palace, headed toward the ruins of Constantinople's old sea wall. We're not exactly sure what these passages were. They look like the complex of Byzantine cisterns up near the Hippodrome, or maybe it was a residential district buried by one of the earthquakes. We can't find any documentation."

"Has Dean found Asad?"

"He's close, but we still don't have the signal."

"How can that be?"

"We have a theory," said Telach, coming over. "The room may be shielded. It's probably one of these on the right."

Rubens looked at the schematic sketched from the ground-penetrating radar. While it wasn't technically difficult to shield a room from radio waves, it did require considerable preparation and expense. It was conceivable that Asad or someone in his circles had arranged this, but it seemed out of character.

So perhaps the shielding was already there.

"They're in a mausoleum," said Rubens. "A large bronze tomb. Or a treasury room. Get an opinion from the technical team on whether the radio waves can penetrate them. There's no sense having Mr. Dean prowling old sewers if there's no hope of picking up the signal."

CHAPTER 39

DEAN SQUEEZED FORWARD through the square stone tunnel, try-ing to ignore the dust that was choking him. Every ten feet or so he came to an opening too narrow to crawl into; he shone his light down them but inevitably saw nothing. The tunnel ahead widened; he pushed toward it slowly, listening to the strange echoes. As he neared the passage, the urge to sneeze overwhelmed him. He leaned over and stifled it against his shoulder, but the muffled sound echoed in the stone passage. Something rippled in reaction—an echo, it seemed, and then the space in front of him exploded, black shards flying at him.

Not shards but bats. Thousands of them.

Dean pressed his head against the floor of the passageway, the air vibrating around him as bat after bat flew by. One hit his head and he felt another and another tripping over his back, their cries rattling his ears. Eyes closed, Dean pressed himself against the stone, waiting for the onrush to end.

When the bats were gone, he pushed forward into a large cavern whose floor was covered with mounds of guano. Dean's stomach began to turn. As he clamped his hand against his mouth and nose, he heard the ripple of wings again. He ducked to the right, squatting over a mound of bat turds as the mass of bats came back, circling the interior of the vast chamber before returning to their roosts in the ceiling.

"Where the hell am I, Rockman?"

"We're trying to figure that out, Charlie. Stay where you are."

"There are bats here."

"You're not freaked by bats, are you, Charlie?"

Dean wished nothing less than to have Rockman's neck within reach.

"Mr. Dean, this is Rubens. It would appear that Red Lion and his people are within a complex of Byzantine tombs about a hundred feet from you. It appears that the metal lining the sarcophagi is jamming the transmission. However, the technicians believe that if you set up the booster unit close enough, they will be able to pick up some of the signal."

"You're sure about this?"

"No, I am not. If you believe it's too risky to proceed, please say so."

Dean scanned the bat-filled cavern. How much worse could it be?

"Which way do I go?" he said.

"Straight ahead," said Rockman.

"Figures."

CHAPTER 40

ASAD LEANED BACK, trying to stretch his legs without getting up. Three men had joined the al-Qaeda leader in the small, underground burial chamber; they huddled knee to knee on the rug Katib had set out before going back to join the rest of the bodyguards.

More than a thousand years ago, rich Christians in the Byzantine empire had built this room and the surrounding crypts as a place to remember their dead. The thick bronze and other metals would make it impossible for radio waves to penetrate, lessening the chance that the Turks—or the Americans, who were their masters—would find a way to listen in. This was his only meeting in Istanbul where such precautions were necessary, and in truth Asad realized they were extreme even in this case. But he could not resist the symbolism of meeting here to plan the West's funeral. Nor could he resist the opportunity to lecture his followers.

"The first stage of our war has been largely symbolic," he told the two men who had come to see him. "The martyrs struck at the heart of Western arrogance and power on 9/11. The crusaders struck back in a way that made our battle explicit. Each day, hundreds of brothers join our ranks—in Iraq, Afghanistan, in Egypt, in Spain, in France—in America itself. Now the time has come to move our attacks beyond symbolism. We prepare the war to strike at the economic heart of the corrupt barbarians who enslave us. We will strike at that lifeblood."

"With God's help," said the man on his right, a tall African brother from Somalia.

"And yours, sheik," said the other. Shorter, he was a light-skinned Libyan.

"The ship?" he asked them.

"It will arrive at the rendezvous point within a few hours," said the Somalian. "Everything is prepared. Even the papers, if it is stopped."

Asad nodded. The American project was a complicated plan, involving three different stages; the preparation of the *Aztec Exact* represented only the first. The last would be most difficult and required him to travel to America to initiate it— a task he welcomed with relish. Asad would personally set the keystone attack in motion; the honor was his right as commander.

"We are ready to do more, sheik," said the African. "Say the word, a thousand brothers will join you."

"For now, you have done enough. There will be other chances in the future." He bowed his head. "Let us pray before we go."

CHAPTER 41

DEAN WAS LESS than ten feet from the area with the burial vaults when Rockman told him they had finally picked up the signal. Dean put the booster on the side of the passage and began backing up. He got only a few yards when he heard voices in the space ahead.

"Charlie, they're coming in your direction," said Rockman.

No kidding, thought Dean. He stopped moving, lying silent in the square hole, his chin in the drain inset that ran along the floor. The voices and footsteps echoed wildly, the sounds a bizarre mix of growls. As he lay in the ancient sewer pipe, Dean felt his sweat rolling down from his back. He felt his breath growing short and choppy; his head began to pound.

I'll be out soon, he told himself. Just hang on.

When he didn't hear any more sounds, Dean started to back up again. But he hadn't gone more than three feet when he heard more voices. He stopped, lying flat in his sweat and the dank slime.

"Asad's coming out now," said Rockman. "We think he's the last to leave."

Dean tried to control his breath. His head had begun to pound fiercely.

"He's out," said Rockman. "Give it a minute or two, make sure they're all gone. Then go. Leave the booster unit."

Dean began pushing back immediately, fighting off the dread surging through him.

He'd never been claustrophobic. Neither was he given to

panic attacks. But damn if it didn't seem like he was having one now.

"Mr. Dean, this is Rubens again. Do you think you could scout the mausoleum area? We'd like to get an idea of what's there."

"Sure," said Dean. "Give me a minute."

LIA FOLLOWED SANDY Chafetz's directions, methodically planting video devices along the road that led out of the palace. As she walked out of the main entrance, she spotted two men in black business suits standing next to a brown SUV. She passed them, then stopped to examine some of the evil eye charms being sold by a man with a small table near the Byzantine church's wall.

"I think I found one of the cars of someone at the meeting," said Lia. "Want me to stick a tracker on it?"

"How do you know?"

"Two guards watching it."

"Get the license plate and ID it for Tommy," Chafetz told her. "We'll check it out. We need you to get one more video bug up by the intersection near Haghia Sophia, then go down the hill and get some to cover the lot the tour buses use to leave."

THE WALLS OF the chamber were lined with ornate bronze monuments to the dead, a succession of eagles and marching troops, chariots and masses of soldiers. Long forgotten minor deities shared space with saints and holy figures from the days of the Byzantine emperors. Marble benches lined the walls beneath burial niches. The floor was made of red marble, inlaid with a dull yellow metal Dean thought must be gold.

Dean played his light around the room, looking for a place to put the booster. But there was no place where it couldn't be easily found.

Dean slipped out of the room, leaving the thick vaultlike door exactly two-thirds open as he had found it. Rather than going back in the sewer hole, he walked up the corridor, keeping the beam of his flashlight on the floor directly in front of him. He came to a T; the corridor to the right led back toward the palace. The other looked like it dead-ended in a pile of rubble. Thinking he could put a booster there, Dean went over and saw that two pieces of wood could be moved to open the way into another long corridor.

"Where's this way to the left come out?" Dean asked Rockman.

"On the other side of the train tracks, near the Byzantine sea wall," said the runner. "There's a bunch of ancient ruins there, and on the other side of the highway there's a park. A lot of, uh, hobos hang out down there at night. Homeless people."

"Is it clear?"

"As far as we can see. Cars can stop along the road there any time, though. You want to go out that way?"

"Better there than going up through the palace," said Dean. His clothes were sodden with grime, sweat, and bat droppings. He wasn't going to blend in with the crowd.

"All right. Hang on until Fashona can come back over and we can get another view of the sight."

Dean hid the booster, then walked out through the tunnel, brushing away cobwebs. He had to climb over a small pile of rubble and then crawl on his hands and knees through a small pool of water for about ten yards, but after what he'd been through earlier, this was like a stroll in the park. After crawling thirty or forty yards, he came to a rectangular shaft upwards. Shards of light came through an opening at the top of the shaft, thirty feet above. A wooden ladder ran up the far side about half of the way.

"I found the opening. There's a ladder," Dean told Rockman.

"Fashona and Karr are still on the other side of the city. Give them a minute, okay?"

Dean saw no point in waiting. He climbed to the top of the ladder, then examined the rocks lining the shaft. They fit together so smoothly that Dean couldn't get much of a fingerhold. But the sides were less than three feet apart, and it looked as if he could lever himself upwards, pushing his back and feet up opposite walls.

It *looked* that way. About halfway up his legs started to tire, and Dean found it difficult to continue. He told himself he was too far to go back and pushed on another four or five feet. Then his right knee started to give out. He jabbed his foot against the wall, feeling suddenly old—incredibly old now, in his late eighties rather than his early fifties. He pushed his head against the shaft, looking upwards.

The alternative was crawling through the bat guano. And that was if he survived the fall without breaking a leg.

The notion didn't cure his knee, but it made easier to ignore. He pushed his leg up and shoved himself higher. Just under the planks at the top of the shaft, he wedged himself against the sides so he could push the boards off. As he did, he saw a rope beneath the wood. He tapped at it, then pulled it out, letting it fall into the shaft below. It was a rope ladder, attached to a beam across the top of the hole. Dean pulled at it, not trusting at first though the rope was nylon, and very obviously brand-new. Finally he put his weight on it, standing on one of the rungs as he lifted two boards out of the way and climbed from the hole.

"Charlie, where are you?" asked Rockman in his ear.

"I'm out."

"I thought you were waiting for Karr."

"I didn't."

"All right. The car Lia ID'd looks like it's heading around to pick up Asad and his people. We'd like you to join Lia and tail him. She just finished planting the video bugs."

"I'll have to change first," said Dean. "Tell her I'll meet her at the car."

He rolled over and got up. As he did, he heard something behind him. Dean turned around and saw a pair of eyes staring at him. These weren't rat eyes—they belonged to a man who had a large two-by-four in his hand.

Dean ducked. As the two-by-four sailed past, Dean pitched himself into the man's midsection, tackling him. The other man managed to roll on top of Dean, pushing the side of

Dean's face into the dirt. The other man outweighed him by seventy-five pounds, and all of Dean's fury barely budged him. Finally Dean squirmed to the side and squirted from his grasp. A desperate, unaimed kick caught his attacker in the ribs; it stunned the man, but he remained on his feet. Dean grabbed the two-by-four; it took three shots to the giant's head to drop him.

"What's going on?" Rockman asked. "Charlie?"

"Someone attacked me," said Dean. "He looks like one of the local bums you told me about. But I'm okay now."

Then he looked up and saw that wasn't exactly true—four of the man's friends, some with rocks in their hands, were gathered in a semicircle nearby.

KARR SPOTTED THE white Mercedes just as it pulled into a bus stop along Kennedy Caddesi. Asad and two other men got in and it pulled out quickly.

The helicopter was going in the opposite direction, and by the time they turned around, the vehicles were heading over the Galata Bridge. The Mercedes made a wide circle, came back over the bridge, and headed back in the direction of the palace. It parked on a street only a few blocks north of the Blue Mosque.

"Must've been making sure they weren't followed," Karr said. "Rockman, we're going to fly back over the palace and see if we can find that SUV Lia saw earlier."

"Tommy, don't worry about that now," said Rockman. "Get back over by the water near the mosque—Charlie's in trouble."

"ÇTKIL GIT!" YELLED Dean, waving the wood back and forth in front of him. "Go away! Get out. Go!"

One of the men threw a rock at him. Dean ducked it and feinted toward him, backing the others off. He edged to his left, looking for a path to escape.

"Karr and Fashona are on their way," said Rockman. "They should be there in a couple of minutes."

Another rock flew by, this one much closer. Dean waved his board again; this time, the men didn't retreat more than a step.

"I need the words for I'll kill them," Dean told the translator.

"You sure?"

"They don't speak English."

"*Çtkil git!*" yelled Dean to the nearest man. Then he told the translator, "I need something stronger than 'go away'."

The translator gave him a string of curse words and threats. Dean hurried through them, hoping to make up in ferocity what he lost in pronunciation.

The man closest to him stooped to pick up a rock. Dean leapt forward and whacked him on the side hard enough to knock him down. Then Dean jumped back, squaring to face the attackers again.

The men began jabbering together—complaining, said the translator, about this crazy intruder trying to move into their home.

"I'm going to go," Dean said in English, repeating the Turkish when the translator gave it. "I'm just going to leave. If you don't bother me, I won't bother you."

A path cut through the vines and overgrowth toward a set of stone and dilapidated marble ruins to his left. Dean took a step toward it, then ducked another rock. One of the men let out a blood-curdling yell, apparently their signal to charge— Dean took a swat at the nearest man. Two others lunged at the two-by-four. He poked one in the face, but the other grappled the wood from Dean's hand.

Retreating down the path, Dean scooped up a large stone as a weapon. But when he turned to face his attackers, they had disappeared.

"Charlie, you okay?" asked Rockman. "Charlie?"

"Yeah, I'm here. These guys are hiding somewhere."

"Karr and the helicopter should be there any second. Can you get across the road to the rocks?"

Something moved in the underbrush on Dean's left. He whirled and threw the stone at a thick clump of vines. Whoever or whatever was there yelped and fell over.

Dean scrambled down the path, in the direction of the highway and the coastline beyond. He dashed across to a chorus of horns, then leapt over the guardrail and up onto the rocks at the water's edge. His pursuers followed. As Dean veered along the rocky, debris-ridden shore, he heard the loud drum of the approaching helicopter's rotors.

"THERE—LOOK THERE," Karr told Fashona, pointing at what looked like an overgrown landing near the shoreline. Five men were huddled on the highway side, throwing rocks at another—Dean. "We gotta get him out of there."

"I'm going to buzz them," said the pilot. "Hang on."

The helicopter's nose dropped toward the ground. Something cracked behind them—it was the banner, snapping like the tail end of a whip. One of the men on the ground turned, gestured at the approaching helicopter, and then threw a rock at them.

The rock missed by fifty feet, but it was exactly the wrong tactic for anyone to take with Fashona. The pilot hunched forward, demanding more speed from the throttle and setting his chin in determination.

"I'm going to bomb the bastards," he said.

Before Karr could ask how, Fashona put the chopper nearly on its side, banking sharply toward the cluster of rock-throwers. He reached down and pulled the tow-rope release, shrouding Dean's assailants with the fifty-foot-long banner.

Karr snapped off his seatbelt and leaned out the open door, grabbing hold of Dean as Fashona spun the little helo down. There were only two seats in the helicopter; Karr shoved himself back against the center console, but the best he could do was hold Dean on his lap as they pulled out over the open water.

"We're going back to the airport," Fashona said.

"Yeah," said Karr. "ASAP. Dean smells like a sewer rat. I'm tempted to drop him into the water so he can take a bath."

CHAPTER 42

COLORED DOTS COVERED the computer screen, a seemingly unordered array of Technicolor.

"I fail to see a pattern here," said Rubens, leaning back from the screen.

"*Ha!*" Johnny Bib gave one of his triumphant, semiverbal yelps. "Show him, Gallo."

Robert Gallo, one of Desk Three's computer specialists working for Johnny Bib's analysis team, sheepishly pressed a button on the laptop computer controlling the presentation. The dots began to vibrate, then rearranged themselves on the screen. Three largish circles, one purple, one red, one gold, emerged from the chaos, sliding to the right.

"I hadn't realized we had farmed out our analysis work to Pixar Animation," said Rubens dryly.

"It's not animation," said Gallo. "I mean it is, but it's part of the tool. It's a byproduct, I mean, since, like, the calculation is shown in real time. I didn't do it on purpose is what I mean."

"Big circle—Germany," said Johnny Bib. "Little circle! Qaeda Five!"

Rubens looked at the screen again. The "tool" Gallo referred to was an analysis program that correlated data mined from various sources—e-mail, cell phone transmissions, and the like—with other information about known terrorist groups. It did not directly involve traditional cryptography. Rather it used statistical analysis and inference to make judgments about how data might interrelate.

Say, for example, that the NSA knew that a terrorist organization used a specific class of encryptions. The agency had "tools" that would sift through the mountains of communications it intercepted, looking for such messages. The messages might or might not be selected for decryption. Even the NSA did not have the resources to decrypt every message it intercepted; indeed, only a small portion of those deemed worthwhile were examined in any detail.

But decryption was just only one way of gathering information. Simply knowing that a message was sent and who received it might be infinitely more useful than the text of the message itself, even after it was decrypted. Agency analysts might study the volume of such messages, for example, to determine how many messages the organization had sent within a six-month period leading up to a terror attack. They could build a model based on the message pattern and use it to scan through other data looking for similar patterns—not just in communications, but in other activities, such as money transfers and travel arrangements. Gallo's tool compiled the results from all of *those* tools and showed possible links graphically.

In Rubens' opinion, the results were often merely abstractions of abstractions. But in this case, the analysts had used the tool to identify the man Karr had followed from the meeting with Asad as Marid Dabir, an al-Qaeda member who had disappeared and was thought to have died in Pakistan two years before.

At least that's what Johnny Bib contended the middle circle meant. Rubens himself wasn't entirely convinced. The real problem was that there were no reliable images of Marid Dabir. The NSA—and the rest of the world, for that matter—knew of him only through a variety of assumed names and the tag Qaeda Five, awarded years before because he was the fifth unidentified but high-ranking al-Qaeda operative discovered by the agency.

"We need more data here," Rubens told Bib. "This is provocative, but nothing more."

"Germany," said Bib. "That's where he's been."

"I can see that, Johnny. Mr. Ambassador, any insights?" Rubens turned toward Hernes Jackson, the other member of the analysis section attending the meeting. Jackson, who'd spent more than thirty years in the diplomatic corps, had come out of retirement at Rubens' request. The silver-haired former ambassador had quickly found a place as a voice of reason and historical perspective, tempering the flamboyant imagination of Johnny Bib, who was eccentric even for the NSA.

"Only the obvious one that I doubt Germany would be the sole target of an operation."

"Quite."

"Mr. Gallo neglected to mention one thing significant," said Johnny as Rubens got up to go.

"I did?" blurted Gallo.

"The number of dots on the screen is a prime number," said Rubens, without bothering to look.

"3267000013," said Johnny Bib, pronouncing each digit triumphantly. "What a glorious number."

"Indeed," sighed Rubens as he left the room.

"WE ALWAYS INTENDED to arrest Asad. I'm merely suggesting we move up the time schedule."

"I designed the operation, Dr. Bing. I am fully aware of its outline, as well as its ultimate goal." Rubens pressed his hand around the phone handle. "I see no reason to arrest him yet. The device is working perfectly and he has no idea that it's been inserted. We can track him at will."

"You've gained no new information. The longer you wait, the higher the risk of compromise."

"And the more useful information we will obtain," said Rubens. "We've already found this connection to Germany, which no one has developed until now. If the president has changed his mind—"

"Carry on as you see fit," said Bing, finally retreating. "I will contact the German authorities and have someone get back to you."

Before he could say anything else, Bing hung up the phone. Rubens pushed his chair out from his desk and took off his shoes. He stepped onto the hand-woven silk rug next to his workspace and bent over, arms together, to begin the *Surya Namaskar* or Sun Salutation, a basic but relaxing yoga movement. He turned his body slowly, stretching, trying to find the calm point of contemplation he needed to deal with the present situation.

Bing was going to be an incredible problem, far more difficult to deal with than he had foreseen. He needed to prepare a long-term strategy, but this was not the time.

Rubens continued his yoga routine, sliding his full body to the floor. He spread up into cobra position, pushing his head back. It was too abrupt a move: "too mad Western" in the words of his instructor. Before he could try again, his encrypted phone rang.

"I understand we had a problem yesterday," said Debra Collins, the Central Intelligence Agency's deputy director of operations, when he picked up.

"Debra, good to speak to you."

"I've talked to both of the officers involved," continued Collins. "It won't happen again."

In CIA-speak, that was an abject apology. It was so out of character for Collins, Rubens immediately began wondering what she really wanted.

"For what it's worth," she added, backtracking in a much more familiar tone, "they thought he was going to escape. And they weren't entirely briefed on his importance. The people working on Red Lion have been kept on a strict need-to-know basis, and there are a lot of gaps."

"I wouldn't think any officer needs to be told to avoid using a weapon whenever possible," said Rubens.

"Point taken. But they are good people. They have good track records. It won't happen again."

"I appreciate that," said Rubens, still wondering what she was really after. He gave her a brief update, mentioning the German connection and then saying that Bing had suggested bringing Asad in immediately.

"That makes no sense," said Collins. "I hope you told her that."

She sounded sincere, but Collins was a master at political grappling, and Rubens didn't trust her.

"She made it clear we could proceed," Rubens said, remaining neutral, or at least as neutral as possible. Then he changed the subject. "You've heard what happened to George Hadash?"

"Yes," said Collins. "It was a shock. We knew the operation had risks, but still. It was a shock."

"Yes, it was," said Rubens, though he resented the 'we.' Collins and Hadash had never been close.

"Are they planning a state funeral?"

"Yes, though his daughter would prefer something more private. She called the president last night. It's been arranged for tomorrow already."

"So soon."

"Yes."

"What did the president say?"

It occurred to Rubens that this might be an elaborate plot by Bing to see if Rubens was using his connections to confer privately with the president. The idea galled him, and instantly he decided he was being too paranoid.

And yet, given Collins' history, such a possibility could not be entirely ruled out.

"I don't know," Rubens told her. "Irena spoke to him herself."

"George deserves a state funeral."

"Surely," said Rubens. "Surely."

CHAPTER 43

LIA SPENT THE next two hours tailing Asad as the al-Qaeda leader zigzagged around Istanbul's old city, having lunch in a restaurant a few blocks from the Blue Mosque, then visiting the Tomb of Sultan Ahmet I and the Haghia Sophia. She changed her clothes twice, following along dutifully, making sure that what the Art Room was hearing jibed with what he was doing.

"Don't get too close," her runner Sandy Chafetz told her as she tagged along into the Haghia Sophia. "We have everything under control."

Right, thought Lia. You have everything under control. She liked Chafetz better than Rockman, but even she succumbed to Art Room Ego, thinking she knew all and controlled all just because she had a half-dozen computer screens in front of her.

When the Haghia Sophia—"the church of holy wisdom"—was built in the sixth century as a Christian church, it was one of the wonders of the world, its walls glittering with gold and elaborate mosaics of Christ and the saints. Sacked during the Crusades, it was turned into a mosque during the fifteenth century, and the mosaics and other art were removed or plastered over. Some of the plaster had been removed from the walls in the western gallery, and a mosaic of Christ and the Emperor Constantine IX peeked out from the whitewash. Raised as a Roman Catholic by her parents, the desecration sent a vicious shock through Lia when she walked onto the second floor, and for a few seconds she remained fixed to the spot, absorbed by the image and the violence it implied.

When she lowered her gaze, she realized Asad stood less than ten feet away, a smirk on his face.

Lia was dressed as a tourist now, and Asad had been doped when he saw her yesterday. Still, she had gotten closer than she wanted. She'd let her emotions interfere with her actions.

Slowly, she turned to the side and wandered off to a group of schoolchildren who were inspecting some of the recent restoration work. When she looked back in Asad's direction, she saw that he was heading for the stairway.

"He's outside," said Rockman a few minutes later.

She kept her distance after that.

AROUND FIVE, ASAD went to a house on the northern outskirts of the city, apparently abandoning the one he had used earlier. Lia set up another surveillance net and then moved back, the intercepts indicating that Asad had no plans to go out. The Art Room decided it was a good time for a conference and Lia began trolling the area, looking for a place where she could talk to herself without seeming out of place or being overheard. Finally she settled on a small park, taking out her satphone to pretend to talk to it. Lia had changed again, donning another conservative jilbab. This proved to be out of step with the neighborhood, as she realized when a middle-aged woman passed by and gave her an odd, disapproving glance.

"We're all comfortable?" asked Telach.

"I'm not," said Karr. "I'm starving."

"You're always hungry," said Dean. Lia could hear the helicopter in the background when he spoke; he'd changed places with Karr.

"The operation has been quite successful," said Rubens, coming onto the line. "You've all done very well."

"But," said Lia.

"There is no *but*, Lia."

Baloney, thought Lia. There was *always* a "but" with Rubens. No matter how perfectly a mission went, he found something to object to.

A young woman with a double stroller passed nearby. Lia watched as she stooped to fuss over the two children, lifting one out of the carriage and then the other. Wearing jeans and a blouse, the woman could have been anywhere in Europe, or America for that matter.

"The man Red Lion met with last night is an al-Qaeda operative who was previously believed to be dead," said Rubens. "He took a flight to Germany a few hours ago and we now believe he heads a network of terrorists there. Mr. Karr will travel to Germany to work with German intelligence."

"Bundesnachrichtendienst," said Karr brightly in a mock German accent.

"Thank you, Mr. Karr," said Rubens. "I'm sure we're all well aware of the proper name for German intelligence."

"How's my accent?"

Rubens, who could be very indulgent with Karr, ignored him. "In the meantime, Lia and Mr. Dean will continue tracking Red Lion. The CIA teams will take up any slack—"

"Not either of the clowns who 'helped' us yesterday," said Dean.

"We have to work with the assets available," said Rubens, his voice even more priggish than usual. "Unless, Mr. Dean, you have additional information about what happened."

"I already told Marie what happened."

"Lia?" said Rubens.

"They thought he was escaping," Lia said. "It wasn't the best decision. They did fine in the hospital."

"I don't trust them," said Dean. "They're not under control."

Was Dean right? Or was she?

Why was she defending Pinchon?

Did she still feel something for him?

God help her.

No, she didn't. She couldn't. But she had to be fair. Fair.

"I believe your judgment may be a little harsh, Mr. Dean," said Rubens. "But if you don't believe you can work with them, I will request that they make reassignments."

Dean didn't answer. Lia pictured him in her mind, his jaw set, debating. But instead of his face, she saw Pinchon's.

"Whoever we work with has to understand they work for us, not the other way around," said Dean. "We don't need no cowboys."

"Yee-ha!" shouted Karr. "Not even me, pardner?"

"Not even you, Tommy," snapped Dean. "Just make sure they understand that."

CHAPTER 44

THE GAME WAS a Pac-Man rip-off, a vintage video machine rigged to play without coins. When he first found it in the small lounge at the back of the hotel lobby, Dr. Ramil thought it would relax him. But he soon realized that it was only making him more tense, revving his anxiety. Still, he couldn't seem to push himself away from it, hypnotized by the balls he had to sweep up and the monsters buzzing along behind him. He spent more than an hour pushing the joystick back and forth, convincing himself that he had a strategy to win.

He finally broke away when the call to evening prayers wafted into the back room. For most people in the city—Muslims as well as those of other faiths—the taped broadcasts were background noise; the vast majority went about their business without interrupting what they did. Until today, Ramil had always done the same. But now he left the hotel and walked up the street toward the Blue Mosque, compelled to go there by some force within him.

His heart was jumping in his chest, and his head felt as if he were covered with cushions, constricting his vision and hearing. As a doctor, he knew he must be close to having a panic attack, or even a nervous breakdown. The stress of the mission had unnerved him, but he wasn't sure what to do about it. Praying probably made as much sense as anything.

Even well-trained young men like Tommy Karr reacted to the extreme stress of covert ops. What else was his careless accident and relentless joking but a byproduct of the mission?

How much more fragile was a middle-aged man?

More than middle-aged, to be honest.

Ramil's legs began to slow, his heels scraping on the cobblestones. He was in good health and had completed the most dangerous part of the assignment. To get help, all he had to do was push two buttons on the satphone. Support teams were scattered around the city. He'd been in far more dangerous situations and survived. There was no reason to be nervous, much less panic.

He *had* heard a voice in the New Mosque earlier—a *real* voice, probably from someone who could tell by his clothes that he was American, and disliked Americans. He wasn't losing his mind.

What if it had been God who called him a traitor and coward? What then?

Ramil took a deep breath. He certainly believed in God. But he also knew that God did not talk to people, or at least not to him. He was a doctor and scientist, not a seer.

Was he afraid of the mosque? If not, why was he standing here, glued to the small strip of sidewalk below its grounds?

Ramil crossed the street just ahead of a taxi, then turned the corner and walked up the hill. The outdoor cafe opposite the mosque was packed with tourists. A group of dervish performers were on the stage, spinning and dancing.

The immense mosque felt more like a museum than a house of worship. The vastness of the space, emphasized by the streaks of light flooding down from the windows at the top of the building, calmed him—everyone was insignificant here, not just Dr. Saed Ramil.

Ramil walked past the tourists admiring the blue tiled ceiling that had given the mosque its name, passing into the prayer area reserved for the faithful. The stained glass threw a glorious hue of light all around the interior. Ramil felt as if he were walking into a rose.

He was on his knees in the middle of prayer when he heard the voice in his head again.

They are cowards and traitors to the Word of God. They must be brought to justice. Why have you not done more to stop them?

Hands trembling, Ramil fled back to his hotel.

CHAPTER 45

WITH ASAD APPARENTLY bedded down for the night and electronic sensors in place to keep close track of him, Charlie Dean found himself bored. He went to a restaurant about a mile from the terror leader's safehouse, a fancy place that catered primarily to European tourists and the occasional businessman. The pace was slow, which suited Dean perfectly; he sipped sparkling water while watching the other guests. The wait staff were making a fuss over a six-year-old Italian boy who was sitting with his parents two tables away, treating the boy as if he were the reincarnation of Turkey's national hero and founder, Atatürk. Extra desserts appeared, waitresses and even waiters stole kisses. The father, roughly Dean's age, looked on with a bemused smile, while the mother—closer to Lia's—beamed.

They hadn't talked about kids during their time in Pennsylvania. Maybe they should have.

Funny to be thinking about kids at this point in my life, Dean thought.

"No change, Charlie," said Sandy Chafetz, the runner on duty back in the Art Room.

"Yeah," muttered Dean.

"How's dinner?"

"Not bad," said Dean.

A waiter approached to take his plate. Dean asked to see a dessert menu.

"I feel like I'm living vicariously," said Chafetz. "Try something chocolate."

He ended up with an Italian cheesecake—Lia's favorite.

CHAPTER 46

TOMMY KARR HAD worked with Bundesnachrichtendienst, the German intelligence service also known by the abbreviation BND, in the past, but even if he hadn't, he would have had no trouble spotting the two agents waiting for him near the customs gate when he landed in Munich. In their thirties, they were recruiting-poster types, tall, straight, and impeccable in black suits that looked custom made. They were the best dressed men in the terminal, and probably the city.

"Hey there, guys," said Karr, walking up to them, "lookin' for little ol' me?"

The agents blinked in unison.

"Kjartan Magnor-Karr from America. You can call me Tommy. Do I have to go through these lines or what?"

"No" was the answer, and Karr was whisked through a side door to a Mercedes sedan for the drive to BND headquarters in Pullach. The building was probably the cleanest Karr had ever been in. He could see his reflection in the floor as he walked across the reception area, and the hallways gleamed so brightly he considered putting on his sunglasses.

Waiting in the secure conference room was Heda Hess, an Abteilung 5 supervisor who had investigated al-Qaeda for several years. Accompanying her were half a dozen other officers from Abteilung 5—Section 5 in English, it was the antiterror group. Two men from the Federal Bureau for the Protection of the Constitution (generally known by its German initials, BfV), which also investigated extremist groups, had also been invited and came in a few minutes after Karr.

"Herr Magnor-Karr, welcome," said Hess.

The way she put out her hand made Karr think she expected him to kiss it. He resisted the impulse to click his heels—no German he had ever met had anything approaching a sense of humor—and introduced himself to the others.

Desk Three had forwarded information on Marid Dabir to the Bundesnachrichtendienst already; Karr's job was to put the information into perspective and then help in any way he could. Referring to Red Lion only as an ongoing operation, he told the Germans that Dabir had resurfaced in Turkey. There he had met with another top al-Qaeda official, who had probably ordered Dabir to proceed on a European operation that was part of a planned fall offensive. The targets were believed to be economic, possibly related in some way to petroleum or energy assets, but they had yet to be identified.

Half of the faces in the room dropped when he said that.

"Problem?" Karr asked.

"Marid Dabir took a flight from Berlin to Baden an hour ago," Hess told him. "Baden is about thirty miles from MiRO, the largest petroleum refinery in Western Europe."

CHAPTER 47

DEAN GRABBED A four-hour nap between two and six A.M., then was back on Asad's trail as the terrorist organizer once more played tourist, beginning his day with a visit to the New Mosque near the Eminönü waterfront. From there, Asad walked around the corner to the Spice Market, an indoor bazaar that featured mostly food items, including large bags of piquant-smelling spices.

"Buy something nice for me," Lia told Dean, who was on the far side of the building.

"I'll get you a rug."

"Handwoven."

Asad walked through slowly and came out behind the mosque. Lia took up the tail while Dean doubled back through the bazaar.

"Going underground," said Lia as Asad headed toward a walkway that went under the heavily trafficked highway near the waterfront. The passage was filled with shops and vendors who spread their wares on blankets and rugs, hawking them to the crowds coming off the bridge or the nearby tram station.

"This is probably it," said Rockman. "We have the U2 ready today; if he goes underground, we'll have a map available in seconds."

A gaggle of Japanese tourists pressed into the narrow hallway at the front of the Spice Bazaar as Dean tried to get out. He nudged his way through and began trotting toward the passage. Another flood of people, this one from a tram that had just stopped nearby, clogged the steps as he descended, and he was caught in a steamy mangle of bodies.

"Lia?" he said.

"He's heading for the ferries. Pier Three. He just bought a ticket. I'll stay with him. Relax, Charlie Dean."

ABOUT AN HOUR and a half later, Asad got off the ferry at a small fishing village cum tourist trap called Anadolu Kavaği just south of the Black Sea. Lia watched him go ashore before following herself. When he went into a restaurant just off the pier, she found another nearby. She went up to the second floor, looking down through the open windows at the corner of his table.

"So what's he saying?" she asked the Art Room a half hour later.

"That the red mullet isn't that fresh."

"Pity," said Lia.

An hour passed without anything happening. Finally Asad left the restaurant and headed up the road in the direction of an old fortress. Lia followed, but stayed a half mile back; Fashona was flying above and had the area under surveillance. She found a small grocer and bought a bottle of water, then camped in the shade below the ruins. More than likely, she thought, he'd hold a meeting in some underground cavern like yesterday, but a flyover by the U2 failed to turn up any hidden chambers, and within forty-five minutes Asad was headed back to the village.

"Where are you, Charlie?"

"Still offshore. You want me to come in?"

She *did*, but not for anything work related.

"Asad's going back toward the dock. Thought you'd want to know."

"Thanks."

DEAN WATCHED FROM the small boat as the ferry approached across the strait. It was the last one of the day; if Asad was going to return to Istanbul, he'd have to board it.

Or not. A boat could easily be waiting nearby.

The ferry moved in slow motion toward the dock. Dean, tired from the mission and convinced that Asad wasn't going to do anything important today, pulled his cap down over his eyes; shade was a poor substitute for sleep, but it was the best he could do for now. A faint odor of rotting fish hung over his boat, normally used for fishing; between that and the unsteady rocking of the waves whenever a large tanker passed nearby, Dean's stomach felt queasy.

"Looks like he's going to get on this one," Lia told him. "He's moving toward the dock. I'll get on after him."

"No, go ahead and get aboard first thing," said Marie Telach. "If he stays ashore, Charlie can go in and follow him, and we'll have one of the backup units come closer."

Lia didn't answer, which Dean knew meant she didn't agree but would go along anyway. A few minutes after the ferry docked, she reported that Asad was in the bow with his bodyguard.

"I'm going to plant some video bugs," she added.

Rockman gave her the usual cautions. Dean had his boat's captain—a one-time army special forces soldier who'd retired to Turkey about a decade before—turn the craft toward the opposite shore, where the ferry's next stop would be.

It wasn't until two stops later that a pair of Middle Eastern businessmen drew near Asad. One of them called him *sheik*.

"Hey, here we go," said Rockman. "Oh, yeah. Hang on while we see if we can ID these guys. Charlie, we're going to download the video from the fly to your PDA so you can get a look at them, too."

Dean took out his handheld computer and flipped into the feed from the Art Room. The slightly blotchy picture showed Asad sitting with two bearded men in tan suits.

"The guy on the far left—we've just ID'd him as Tariq Asam," said Rockman. "He's a Saudi. We don't know the other guy, not yet. We want to follow them."

"I'll get on at the next stop."

"We have somebody there already, Charlie. They'll get on and trail the Saudis. You stay with the boat."

◆ ◆ ◆

"NOT YOU AGAIN," said Lia, walking next to Pinchon at the food bar on the ferry.

"Funny. I thought the same thing."

"The two guys with the tan suits in the bow are Saudis. You can't miss them—they're the only ones who have jackets on. They're yours. Don't lose them."

"Where's Grandpa?"

"Pinchon, just do your job, okay?"

"Baby, I thought you'd never ask."

Lia ordered a bottled water, trying hard to ignore Pinchon as he walked away.

CHAPTER 48

"IT LOOKS LIKE the Saudi and his partner are going to get off at Bebek," Telach told Rubens. "Asad is staying put."

Rubens stepped over to one of the consoles and keyed up a map of the greater Istanbul area. Bebek was a small town north of the city on the European side, a relatively well-to-do area that might be compared to some of the Gold Coast towns near Miami. As he had with the others, Asad had spoken sparingly to the men, but it was clear that they were part of the same offensive he was coordinating; he gave them a date only four days away, which Rubens assumed was the date for whatever attack they were planning.

"Should I have Lia get off with them?" asked Telach.

"No. Continue as planned," said Rubens. "Let the CIA people stay with them. She can check in on them later. Have they said anything?"

"Nothing useful, but he did give them a Koran. Maybe it contains a message."

"Tell Mr. Karr about that, in case it's of use to him."

Telach nodded. "What time are you leaving?"

Rubens glanced at his watch. He was supposed to be at the Capitol for George Hadash's lying in state no later than eleven; he should leave within the next half hour.

"As soon as we are sure that Asad is getting off at Eminönü and going back to his safe house," said Rubens, deciding Hadash would have wanted it that way.

◆ ◆ ◆

WHILE HE HAD appeared on his share of news shows, George
Hadash was not a political superstar, and Rubens wondered if
the two hours designated for his lying in state would prove to
be too long. But there was a long queue of people waiting
outside hours before the doors were even opened, and as
Rubens escorted Irena Hadash through the vestibule, he realized that two hours would not be enough. That was as it
should be, he thought: better to have a surplus of grief than
not enough.

Art Blanders, the secretary of defense, was standing nearby;
he caught Rubens' eye and started toward them. Rubens introduced Irena, along with her little girl. The kindergartener
seemed perplexed by everything, but Rubens thought it was
good that she was there; it gave her mother something to focus on besides grief.

"You've heard of Secretary Blanders, I'm sure," said
Rubens. "He's been with the president for years, and was his
chief of staff before going to the Pentagon. Your father often
spoke highly of him."

More than that: Hadash was the reason Blanders had the
job; he'd personally lobbied the president to pick the former
Naval officer, who at forty-five was the youngest cabinet
member by at least a decade.

Still, Rubens worried that he sounded like a flatterer, or
worse. He resolved to say nothing more, to do absolutely
nothing that could be misinterpreted as using the death of his
friend for personal gain. And, he would introduce Donna Bing
in the most positive way; give her no room for complaint.

President Marcke swept in with his characteristic energy, a
controlled firestorm charging up everyone around him. He
wrapped his arm around Irena and led her a few feet away, her
small frame practically disappearing in his. Left alone, Irena's
daughter Julia grabbed for the nearest familiar hand, which
turned out to be Rubens'. Her small fingers gripped his tightly.

By the time Irena was her daughter's age, her father and
President Marcke—probably a congressman then, thought
Rubens—had been friends for many years. How strange it

must be to see a man who bounced you on his knee become president.

"And you, little girl, I hope you are well." The president had returned and now stooped down to one knee, addressing Hadash's granddaughter face-to-face. "Do you remember me?"

"You're Gran'pa's friend," said the girl.

"Absolutely. Your grandpa was an important man. A great man who helped many people, including me. He's with God now."

"Mommy told me we have to share him."

"Yes. Share him with God." Marcke nodded solemnly. "Now he's with all of us."

Rubens felt a twinge of jealousy as the president escorted them inside. Other emotions—grief, mostly, but also concern about the Deep Black operation—mingled with his remembrances of Hadash. There was no man he'd learned more from, no better person to argue with, no one more generous with support and encouragement.

There was a brief ceremony near the casket. When it was done, the president bent over again and told Irena something, then turned and nodded to everyone before leaving. Rubens found himself next to Irena, part of what turned into a kind of reception line as she accepted the condolences of senators, congressmen, foreign dignitaries, and high-ranking administration officials. Some of them, he realized, might think he was more than just a friend.

The idea made him feel guilty, as if he'd intruded on Irena's grief. But when he started to ease away, she reached for him, and so he stayed.

"Mr. Rubens," said Donna Bing, materializing in the line.

"Dr. Bing."

"When you have a moment today, we should speak. I would like an update on the matter we've been discussing."

"Certainly." Braced by the national security advisor's undisguised animosity, Rubens straightened and stared ahead, looking at the long line of people who had come to pay his friend and mentor their last respects.

CHAPTER 49

LIA FOLLOWED ASAD off the ferry, staying close until he got into a taxi near the pier. The taxi was a new development, but it was apparently just a part of Asad's precautions; it took him only a mile away where a new vehicle was waiting. From there, he was driven to a house on the eastern end of town where he hadn't stayed before. She set up a surveillance net, working with Dean but never close enough to see him, before retreating.

When the Art Room decided that Asad was staying in for the night, Lia arranged to meet Charlie in a restaurant nearby, ostensibly to divvy up the overnight duties, though really just because she wanted to see him.

What bothered her even more than finding Terry Pinchon alive was finding that she still felt something for him—that there was emotion there, a real attraction she couldn't deny. It scared her, not just because it cut against any logic—clearly he didn't care for her, clearly he was a jerk, clearly any attraction was a mistake, no more than skin deep—but because it made her unsure what she felt for Dean.

"You're a little late," said Dean when she found him inside the restaurant.

"Sorry."

"You okay?"

"Of course I'm okay."

Dean gave her one of his looks, then turned to the waiter and ordered a bottle of spring water.

"Art Room claims he's in for the night," said Dean when the man left. "Which one of us is going to sleep first?"

"You," she said automatically. Then she regretted it—she wished she'd said they should sleep together. Not that they would have—they had to stay focused on the mission—but she wanted to let him know that she wanted to.

"Fine. You hungry?"

"No." Out of synch now, she felt an urge to get away. She had to—she had to refocus herself, concentrate on the job, not her emotions. "I have to check on the team trailing the Saudis. They're at a hotel on the Asian side. I'll check on them and then turn in."

"Is Pinchon on the team?"

"Does it matter?"

The words came out too quickly for her to take back. Dean raised his eyebrow, but said nothing.

"I'll wake you up with a kiss," she said. Her voice sounded phony in her ears, and she left before he could say anything.

CHAPTER 50

BY THE TIME Marid Dabir arrived in Karlsruhe, Germany, the European al-Qaeda organizer realized that he was being followed by one of the German security forces. He decided he had two alternatives, either to flee or proceed; fleeing was impossible, and so his course was set. To flee meant to fail, and failure meant he would never return to bin Laden's side. Better to die immediately as a martyr than wander in the wilderness any longer.

Who had betrayed him? Logically, it must be someone in his network here, though that seemed beyond belief.

Dabir went to the house he had rented as an adjunct teacher of Middle Eastern history at Karlsruhe University, doing everything one might do after returning from a trip abroad: picking up the mail, checking phone messages, answering the e-mails from university colleagues that had accumulated while he was gone. He then went to his office at the school, checked on his mail there, and while picking up papers from his department chairman's office, pilfered the wireless PDA from his desk. Back in his own office, Dabir retrieved a cell phone hidden behind his bookcase. He connected the chairman's PDA to the telephone, then slipped a small flash memory card into the top of the handheld computer. A screen for an instant message service appeared. Dabir tapped the bottom of the screen and a keyboard appeared; he used it to write seven short messages, which were then sent through the instant message service to the terrorists he had recruited. He wrote in simple German; one of the programs contained on the card he had put into the computer encrypted the messages into a string of letters and numbers that could only be read by someone with the same program. Within a half-hour all of the recipients had sent back a reply: *ja*.

"Yes." They were ready.

Dabir returned the handheld computer to the chairman's office without being noticed, then went back outside to resume his errands. A balding man in a sports coat followed as he walked to his car; clearly he was from one of the intelligence services. Dabir let him tag along for the time being, confident he could get rid of him when the time was right.

CHAPTER 51

THE AFTERNOON SUN turned the Rhine a deep, purplish blue, the German river moving majestically past the hills near Karlsruhe. It looked like a landscape painting come to life.

Aesthetics was never one of Tommy Karr's strong suits, neither could he be called a naturalist. Still, he stared at the river with sharp intensity, his attention focused on the police boats zipping back and forth near the MiRO refinery on the opposite side of the river. Tankers and barges were thoroughly inspected before they were allowed into the lagoon near the refinery's storage tanks at the northern side of the complex; two large tugboats would block the path of any vessel that failed to stop.

"The analysis showed that was the weak point," said Hess, the BND officer Karr had been assigned to help. "Exploding a ship near the tanks—I don't want to think about the effect."

There were other ways to attack MiRO. Crude oil arrived via two different pipelines, one originating in Italy and the other in Bavaria. The large complex was served by several roads and a rail line. These were all being checked with admirable German efficiency. Even Karr and the BND were ordered out of their car at the main gate so it could be closely inspected, and each had to pass through a metal detector to enter the administration building.

"No guns?" Karr asked Hess as they walked down the hallway.

"Why would we need them?"

The guards, at least, had guns. Blaser 93 LRS2s—fancy

tactical weapons popular with police SWAT teams because of their versatility—as well as the ubiquitous Heckler & Koch MP5 submachine gun. The security director was rather proud of his men's marksmanship scores, and Karr got the impression they could have mounted a pretty good rifle team. What they'd do against terrorists remained to be seen.

The massive complex had once been two different refineries; in an emergency, half the plant could be shut off from the other easily, with smaller sections cordoned off and secured piece by piece. The facility's emergency procedures had been tested by a large fire a few years before, and regular drills were now held to deal with terrorist threats.

"We crush them like ants in the house," said the security head as he ended the tour.

As impressive as his accent made that sound, Karr couldn't help thinking that for every ant you saw, there were maybe a hundred more below the floor.

Besides the refinery, a major German nuclear research facility was located in the general area, and security had been tightened there as well. Given a choice between inspecting security there or having dinner in town, Karr went for the Wiener schnitzel.

German law provided no way of arresting Marid Dabir or even holding the suspected al-Qaeda plotter for questioning until either a crime had been committed or the police had overwhelming evidence that one was being planned. Dabir had no known connection to the local terrorist networks or radical groups on any of the various German watch lists. The Germans accepted the American intelligence indicating he was a terrorist, but for the moment the most they could do was place him under surveillance by the state police extraordinary crime unit and wait for him to commit a crime.

Just as Karr was finishing his veal, Hess received a call indicating that Dabir had boarded a train for Frankfurt am Main.

"I'd like to have a look at him," Hess told Karr after she got off the phone. "Do you think you could pick him out at the train station if we flew up there?"

"As long as there's Black Forest cake for dessert," said Karr, "I can do anything."

DABIR CHECKED HIS watch, counting down the seconds as the train approached the stop just over the state border in Hesse. The man who had been trailing him had passed through the coach a few minutes before, undoubtedly to meet the detectives who would take over for him at the state line. As the train pulled to a stop, Dabir pushed the brim of his American-style baseball cap up, then slipped his hand up to prop his head and hunched against the window, feigning sleep. He was careful not to obscure too much of his face.

Having dodged secret police forces in Yemen and Egypt, he found European intelligence services laughingly easy to fool. The German tendency to be precise and punctual made them exceedingly easy to predict, and the raft of laws protecting potential suspects gave plenty of cover.

The train began moving again. Dabir caught a glimpse of two men in brown suits passing through the car—his new shadows, no doubt. He waited four or five minutes, then made a show of rousing and stretching. Precisely three minutes from the next stop, he got up and ambled slowly in the direction of the restroom in the next car. He stood in the aisle, waiting with his back to the train door for the room to clear.

Finally, the man who'd been inside came out. Dabir hesitated for a moment—just long enough for another man to slide in in front of him. Dabir quickly followed.

"The seat is next to the window, in the eighth row. A brown paper bag is in the empty space next to it," Dabir told the man, a second-generation Palestinian who stood exactly as tall as he did. In fact, when Dabir's cap was placed on his head and his jacket around his shoulders, he might have passed for a younger brother or even Dabir himself—exactly the idea.

"The train is entering the station," said Dabir, pulling open the door. "Go quickly."

Dabir untucked his shirt, then left the restroom, walking forward to the next set of doors as the train came to a halt.

◆ ◆ ◆

WHEN THEIR HELICOPTER landed in Frankfurt, Karr excused himself and checked in with the Art Room.

"German intelligence thinks Dabir is using instant messaging to pass communications to his network," Telach told him. "They've detected some encrypted instant messages using PGP originating from Karlsruhe. They haven't been to decrypt them."

"Can we?"

"If they give them to us. We don't have them. The problem is, they don't know we know."

Karr knew better than to ask how "we" knew. "PGP" stood for "Pretty Good Privacy," a commonly available encryption system that, as its name implied, was decently secure as well as being fairly easy to use. Pretty good wasn't good enough as far as the NSA was concerned; most European intelligence services, on the other hand, did not have a good track record with deciphering it quickly.

"So I have to be subtle, huh?" said Karr.

"Remind them that we can help in many ways," said Telach. "We are working on getting the messages through other means."

"They told me to remind you we'll help in any way we can," Karr told Hess as they drove to the train station a few minutes later. "Any sort of resources you need."

"Are you going to send a Stealth Bomber?"

Karr, a firm believer that levity should always be encouraged, especially in a country where it was semilegal, laughed uproariously.

"If you want one," he told her, the car still shaking with his mirth. "And if you need decoding or anything like that, just holler. We're a one-stop service."

Hess frowned. Karr let the matter drop.

They found a parking spot at the train station and joined two police detectives coordinating the surveillance operation from a van parked near the tracks. More than a dozen plainclothes policemen and several cars were standing by, waiting to track Dabir when he arrived. A team of state detectives had gone on board near the state border, taking over from the man who had gotten on with him at Karlsruhe.

A pair of nine-inch black-and-white television cameras sat on a small bench at the side of the van, carrying video feeds from the platform where Dabir's train would arrive. Karr bent down and squinted, examining the pictures.

"Wanna go get some coffee?" he asked Hess, straightening.

She gave him a funny look.

"I'd prefer beer myself, but usually not on duty. We can spot him inside when he gets off the train," Karr added. "Those screens aren't going to give you much of an idea of what he looks like."

"Ah. You were making a joke."

"No, I really did want a coffee. And maybe a chocolate pig's ear if they have any."

Ten minutes later, Karr strolled along the platform as Dabir's train came in, humming a song to himself and finishing the *schweinsoehrchen*—a "little pig's ear" made from serious chocolate—he'd bought from the snack kiosk. Hess stood back by the concourse, trying to look as inconspicuous as possible in her stiff blue suit.

"Gretchen, how are you?" bellowed Karr as the passengers came out. He walked toward a woman in her forties, bent down and kissed her.

The woman stumbled back, blinked her eyes, and unleashed a torrent of abuse. The rest of the passengers hurried by as Karr began to apologize for his mistake. Dabir, followed closely by his two shadows, passed along to the left.

Except it wasn't Dabir.

Karr pulled his satphone out, pretending to use it.

"Hey, Rockman, you there?"

"Always."

"We got a problem. Dabir lost his shadow."

CHAPTER 52

THE SOUND HAD a sharpness he knew wasn't part of a dream, and even as he heard it Dean sprung from the bed, pistol in hand.

"It's me, Charlie," said Lia from across the room. "Relax."

"Lia?"

"Asad's head is bothering him. He thinks it's the wound. We have to go wake up Dr. Ramil."

Dean glanced at the clock. It was a little past three; he'd been sleeping for maybe an hour.

"Charlie?"

"I'm awake," he told Lia, reaching for his shoes.

Asad was concerned enough to have called the number for the doctor he'd been given at the hospital. The Art Room had intercepted the call and arranged for the al-Qaeda leader to go to a clinic near the hospital.

"Dr. Ramil has to be there in an hour," added Lia. "You, too."

"Why didn't the Art Room wake me up?"

"They tried. Besides," she added, coming close and kissing him. "I promised you this."

DEAN WAITED WHILE the overnight desk clerk called upstairs to Ramil's room, his eyes soaking in the bright yellow of the reception lobby. Ramil answered immediately.

"Doctor, an emergency with a patient this morning," said Dean.

"What?" muttered Ramil.

The clerk politely left the room, pretending to be dealing with some business matter.

"It's Dean. We need you."

"Yes, yes. Okay. I'll be right there."

Dean returned the phone to its cradle, then walked up the stairs to Ramil's room. When he knocked on the door, he heard Ramil rushing over, muttering to himself. He was dressed only in his pants and undershirt.

"Let's go, doc," Dean told him. "Asad's complaining about bleeding from the wounds."

"Bleeding? All right. Nothing to worry about—it'll be seepage. Nothing."

"He also has a headache and feels faint, short of breath. He's meeting us at the clinic in forty-five minutes. You need some coffee?"

"Coffee, all right."

"I'll find some. Come on."

The "clinic" was located in a suite of offices two blocks from the hospital where Asad had been bugged. Lia dropped them off around the block so they could go in the back way without being seen. The doctor coughed loudly as they walked up the dimly lit staircase; he was wheezing by the second floor, nearly hyperventilating.

"I'm okay," he said between breaths. "I'm really okay."

"What's wrong with Ramil?" asked Chafetz, the runner on duty in the Art Room. She could see and hear them through a surveillance system installed by Desk Three when they rented the clinic.

"He just needs some water," Dean told her.

Dean left Ramil to catch his breath in the examining room while he made his way to the water cooler in the reception area. He was just filling a cup when Lia warned him that Asad had pulled up outside. A moment later the downstairs buzzer rang.

"There are two bodyguards with him," said Chafetz. "One of them is the one who was in the hospital. Abd Katib is his name. He seems to be the chief bodyguard."

"All right." Dean started back with Ramil's water.

"Charlie, you have to let them in when they ring," added the runner. "You have to buzz from the front room there."

"I'm going to, Sandy. Once I get Ramil ready."

"Charlie—they're forcing the downstairs door open."

CHAPTER 53

TOMMY KARR TOLD the BND agents that Dabir must have figured out he was being shadowed and arranged to trade places with a double; the al-Qaeda organizer almost certainly had planned to take advantage of the jurisdictional hassles that routinely made the police change surveillance teams at the state borders.

He could be anywhere, but the most logical place to look for him was in the Karlsruhe area. Still forbidden to mention the IMs, which might contain useful information, Karr had to settle for reminding his host that he could help in numerous ways, especially by supplying decryption services. The offer was met with a cold stare.

He went back to BND headquarters with Hess, trying not to eavesdrop as she dissed the state police to her boss over her cell phone, using the most colorful German Karr had ever heard. Inside, he hung around just long enough to see that he wasn't wanted, then asked to be driven to the hotel where his bags had been sent when he arrived earlier in the day.

"Call my satphone if you need me," he told Hess as he left. "And don't forget—"

"Yes, you can help in many ways. We'll keep that in mind, Herr Karr."

Karr checked into the hotel, determined that he wasn't being trailed—a nice gesture of trust, he thought—then, without going up to his room, had the front desk call him a taxi. He made the train station just in time for the last train to Karlsruhe.

CHAPTER 54

DR. RAMIL'S CHEST FELT as if it were being poked by a thousand sharp pins. He bent over in the chair, trying to slow his galloping lungs.

The stress was just too much. He couldn't do this. He couldn't. He was losing his mind and all control over his body.

"Come on, doc. Asad's downstairs," said Charles Dean, looming above him.

Ramil forced himself to look at Dean. His head seemed to weigh fifty pounds. "I—I don't know," he stuttered.

"You all right?"

"I—"

Ramil grabbed at his chest, trying to make Dean understand. He couldn't do it. He just couldn't do it.

"Come on, doc. Up," said Dean, taking hold of him. "With me. Come on."

Ramil's legs refused to move. Suddenly he felt himself being lifted.

God has taken pity on me by striking me dead, Ramil thought. But it was just Dean lifting him up, chair and all. He carried him to the back door and slid him into the hallway.

"WHAT'S GOING ON, Charlie?" asked Chafetz.

"Ramil's having some sort of freak-out. He's hyperventilating and paralyzed."

Dean went to the closet and grabbed a white coat.

"Get out of there, Charlie," warned the runner. "They're almost at the door."

"No, it's all right. I'll do it."

"Charlie—"

"Get the translator and a doctor ready. We'll start by talking Turkish."

A stethoscope and a thermal thermometer sat on the desk. Dean grabbed them, stuffing them both in his pocket. He could hear Asad's men pounding on the door.

"Charlie, this is Telli Kabak," said one of the translators. "How do you want to handle this?"

"I'm Ramil's assistant, same deal as the other day. He called me and sent me over here. These guys don't speak Turkish or Spanish. I don't speak Arabic. We use English, like everybody else in Istanbul."

"Okay."

Dean pushed through the door to the reception area without waiting for an answer. A large man stood behind the glass entrance to the clinic, slapping a meaty hand against the door frame.

"*Merhaba,*" muttered Dean as he turned the lock. "Hello."

The man pushed the door open, snapping it out of his hands. Dean hesitated. He didn't want to seem meek, but he also needed to come off like a doctor rather than a fighter. He took one step back, then held his ground as the bodyguard shoved his face into his.

"You are the doctor?" demanded the man in Arabic.

"*Anlamiyorum,*" said Dean in Turkish. "I don't understand."

The man said in Syrian-accented Arabic that he had an important patient with him, and that, with God as his witness, if Dean made the slightest move to harm him, his skin would be slit open and his organs turned inside out. Once again Dean protested that he did not understand, this time adding a stutter to his Turkish.

"You've frightened the doctor," said Asad in Arabic from behind the bodyguard. "Stand away."

Dean held the bodyguard's stare a few moments longer, then turned to Asad. The terror leader looked older than he had the other day. His head was bent slightly; he seemed to be in some pain.

"*Doktor?*" he said, speaking Turkish. "Do I know you?"

"*D-d-dün,*" stuttered Dean, as if he were truly shaken. "*Hasteen.* The other day at the hospital."

The translator caught on, and gave Dean the Turkish phrases to explain that he had treated him yesterday at the hospital. Except that it wasn't yesterday—she added an apology and a correction. Dean rushed through the words, slurring his pronunciation and then switching to English. Asad turned to his bodyguard and berated the man for frightening the doctor, saying he could now barely talk.

"Charlie, you're doing very well," said William Rubens, suddenly coming onto the circuit. "Continue in this vein."

"This way, come on," said Dean, starting toward the examining room.

The bodyguard grabbed his arm. As Dean turned in his direction, the man pushed the nose of his Beretta pistol into his neck.

"We check the other rooms first," said the bodyguard. "If anyone else is here, you are a dead man."

CHAPTER 55

KARR HAD INTENDED on going to the detectives responsible for watching Dabir and pointing out that, while they might not be able to search the places the al-Qaeda organizer had been, he could. He figured he had even odds of being escorted to Dabir's safehouse or the local jail.

He didn't get a chance to test them. Twenty minutes from Karlsruhe, Telach told him that one of the instant messages had been traced to a chemistry teacher in Karlsruhe. The man had come from Pakistan two years before; he had spent time at one of the religious schools there that doubled as terrorist indoctrination centers. His school computer included a satellite picture of the MiRO refinery. The computer also showed that he regularly received IMs—instant messages—from more than a hundred sources, all of which Desk Three was working furiously to track down.

Since German intelligence still had not handed over Dabir's IMs for decrypting, the best Karr could do was call Hess with the information that the U.S. had identified another member of Dabir's terrorist cell. Hess had gone home, and Karr's call went to a night duty officer. By the time Hess got back to him, Karr was sitting in a late-hours bar frequented by students from the local university, listening to a debate about the best way to curb resurgent Nazism among the police.

"How did you get to Karlsruhe so quickly?" she asked.

"Took a train." Karr held a hand over his ear so he could hear the phone better. "There's a chemistry teacher at Karlsruhe you might want to check out. He's sitting across from me in the ratskeller here. Keeps looking at his watch and going out to the john," added Karr. "Which wouldn't be unusual, except that he's not drinking anything."

"Do you have any reason for me to check him out?" Hess asked.

"We've linked him to Dabir."

"Beyond that?"

"Superstitious hunch?" said Karr.

"I need evidence of a crime."

The chemistry teacher got up. Karr watched for a second, making sure he was heading toward the men's room.

"Well, hurry up and get down here, or you may have more than you want."

Karr clicked off the connection, then pretended to redial. As he did, a good-looking blonde, twenty-one or twenty-two, plopped into the chair across from him.

"Hello," he said.

The girl, several shades beyond drunk, smiled.

"You talking to me?" asked Rockman from the Art Room.

"Our friend's headed to his office," Karr told him, returning the blonde's smile.

"Yeah, we're looking at him through the bugs you planted. Hang on."

"You're very intriguing," said the woman, half in English, half in German.

"*Danke*," said Karr.

"*Lass uns einen heben.*"

"I think you've had enough *heben* for the night, don't you?" answered Karr, turning down her offer to "lift one together," slang for "have a drink."

"All right, he called the same number he called before," said Rockman. "He hung up as soon as the answering machine picked up. Didn't listen to a message."

"Well, that's different, isn't it? Last time he hung up after three rings. So that's the message."

"Could be," said Rockman. "But the only message on that machine is 'oops, wrong number'."

"You track the call?"

"Pay phone in a cafe on the other end of town. Called a taxi immediately after it."

"Talk to you outside," said Karr.

He closed the phone and smiled at the girl. She blinked and told him in English with a drunk German accent that not only was he was very handsome but he was very strange.

"Thanks. Let me buy you a drink," said Karr. As he got up, he stumbled and fell flat on his face—right under the table the chemistry professor had returned to. By the time Karr crawled back to his feet, the girl had turned her attentions elsewhere. Sheepishly, he headed for the door.

The taxi driver he'd paid to wait was around the corner, leaning against his cab. Karr dished out a fifty-euro note as a good will gesture, then got in the back.

"Sounds like he's moving," said Rockman. "What'd you do, put the fly on his shoe?"

"It was easier than getting it into his pocket."

The chemist picked out his bicycle from a rack down near the front door and started biking in the general direction of the river. Karr, who'd put a tracking device on the bicycle earlier, directed the cab driver to follow at a safe distance, using the PDA to direct him.

Karr expected that the chemist would take him either to a rendezvous or a safehouse where Dabir was waiting. Instead, he went to a small bait and tackle shop on the waterfront, opened the lock at the gate, and left. Flummoxed, Karr followed him to a second bar.

"Hang for me here," Karr told the driver.

His American slang may have been difficult to decipher, but another fifty-euro note made his meaning clear. Just as he had at the last bar, the chemist was sitting by himself at a table in the middle of the room, drinking a Coke.

"Ack," said Karr, hustling back outside to the cab after he planted a video bug to watch him. "Get me back to the tackle shop—tackle shop—Rockman, how do you say that in German?"

Angelgeräte—"fishing tackle"—was the word Karr was

looking for, and it was featured in very big letters on the fence Karr found had been relocked by the time he arrived.

Had the shop been used to get down to the water?

Perhaps, but there was a landing not fifty feet away.

Then Karr noticed another sign on the building near the door, right under one advertising Purglas casting rods.

OXYGEN TANKS FILLED, it said in German.

Karr went back to the cab. "I'm just about done here," Karr told the driver. "But would you happen to have a crowbar handy?"

"*Nein*," said the driver.

Karr looked back at the fence. "A really strong tire iron will do, then." He took out another hundred euros. "Pop your trunk, close your eyes, and when I say go, take off. I don't have enough money to pay to you be an accessory to a crime."

CHAPTER 56

DR. RAMIL SAT ON the chair in the narrow hallway above the steps, eyes closed. He felt as if he were falling into a narrow well, his body surrounded by thick walls of stone. The earth's surface was many miles above.

You were a brave man once, Ramil. But now you have become a coward. Why? Because God spoke to you.

I'm losing my mind because of the pressure. It's the stress that's making me hear voices, not the other way around.

He'd been under much worse pressure in Vietnam several times. Once he'd come close to being shot by a South Vietnamese soldier gone mad, two or three other times he'd stayed in the operating room while the base was under a mortar attack. Those times were worse than now, far more dangerous.

But he was a kid then, young.

"Up," whispered a voice above him.

Ramil opened his eyes and saw Lia.

"Ssshhh. Come on," she said, taking him by the hand and grabbing the chair. "Down to the first floor. Quickly. They're coming."

"IT'S CLEAR," SAID Asad's bodyguard.

Dean went into the examining room. He gestured for Asad to sit on the table.

"Charlie? This is Dr. Goldstein. We're going to begin with some standard questions. While you're doing that, you should check for pupil reaction, then take his temperature and blood pressure. We're especially interested in the blood pressure, so we'll walk you through that slowly."

Dean followed the doctor's instructions, doing a rudimentary workup before examining the site where the bug had been implanted.

"Charlie, can you put a fly on one of the instruments so the doctors here can get a look at the wound?" asked Rubens.

Good idea, thought Dean—though the bodyguards complicated things. He went to the cabinet at the side of the room and, hands trembling, pulled it out to the stops. Then he dropped the tray on the floor.

"Give him some room," Asad told the men in Arabic. "I don't want him nervous."

Dean knelt and picked up the instruments.

"You want the second drawer from the bottom," said Chafetz. Dean opened it after he picked up the instruments he'd dropped. He took out the light, but there was no way he'd be able to get one of the bugs from his pocket, let alone install it without being noticed.

"I need a drink of water," he told Asad. "Would you like some?"

Asad shook his head. One of the bodyguards followed him through the door, but he stayed near the threshold as Dean went to the cooler. He slipped the bug from his pocket, concealing it in his fingers. Back inside, he attached it and activated it as he pretended to adjust the light.

"The sutures are leaking a tiny, tiny bit," said the doctor in the Art Room. "That's normal. It's not the problem. He doesn't have a fever, so it's unlikely he has an infection. Could you take his blood pressure again? Your last result was low and we just want to confirm it. Then listen to his heartbeat."

Dean took Asad's blood pressure, then used the stethoscope, asking his patient to breathe. He had a little trouble picking up his heart at first, slightly confused, but then he heard it, a dull thump that seemed to race for a few beats and then slow.

"Do you smoke?" he asked his patient, trying to think of a way to communicate the heartbeat to the Art Room. He had audio flies in his pocket, but no way of attaching them to the stethoscope.

"I don't smoke," said Asad. "Nor do I drink."

"When his heart beat," said the Art Room doctor, "did it sound steady, slow, or jump a bit?"

"Your heart sounded a little, what is the word, jumpy," Dean told his patient. "Not a good steady beat. Sometimes weak, even. Different."

Asad shrugged.

"He mentioned feeling faint," said the doctor in the Art Room.

"Have you felt as if you would pass out?" Dean asked.

"Light-headed," said Asad. "Even coming up the stairs."

"Ask him if he has a heart condition," said the doctor in the Art Room.

Dean walked back across the room. "I wonder," he said, playing with his stethoscope. "Have you ever been tested— what are the words in English? Has anyone ever asked if you had a heart condition?"

"I have a headache, Doctor. What does that have to do with my heart?"

"Tell him his heartbeat is irregular, and you're concerned about his health."

Dean repeated what the doctor told him.

"I think these stitches should come out," said Asad. "That's why I have a headache."

"It has nothing to do with that," said the doctor.

"I can take them out if you wish," said Dean. "But they're not the cause of your problem."

CHAPTER 57

"HIS HEARTBEAT IS erratic and he has a low blood pressure," the doctor told Rubens. "He should get a full workup at a hospital."

"I'm afraid that would be very inconvenient," Rubens told him.

"Look, this guy is sick. I'm five thousand miles away, but I'd guess that he has a pretty severe heart condition. That CAT scan from the other day should be reviewed to look for signs of a TIA," said the doctor, using the specialist's abbreviation for transient ischemic attacks. They were precursors to strokes and a sign of heart disease. "I'll bet you'll find plenty."

Rubens looked to the screen at the front of the room, where Dean was preparing to take out Asad's stitches.

"I have a responsibility as a doctor to do something for this man," added the doctor.

Ruben pressed his lips together; this wasn't an argument he cared to get into just now.

"What will a stroke do to your mission?" added the doctor. "Or a coronary?"

"I understand that you have a duty to a person in medical need," said Rubens. "When the subject is taken into custody, we'll have a team address his disease. In the meantime, please continue to work with Mr. Dean."

CHAPTER 58

DEAN'S FINGERS SLIPPED as he tried to cut the end of the stitches.

"Problem?" asked Asad.

"Please don't move," said Dean. He pushed the scissors back and snipped. Then he reached to the nearby tray and took the tweezers, pulling the stitches out.

"Good work," said the doctor coaching him. "From what I can see, frankly, the wound is fine; it's healed quicker than expected. The blood he saw is old, probably from the first few hours and he didn't notice. Clean it a little bit and use one of the suture strips, the butterfly bandages in the top drawer. Honestly, his problems have nothing to do with that."

"You're sweating," said Asad as Dean followed the doctor's directions.

"Am I?"

"You were worried about doing a good job."

Dean shrugged.

"My men are just overzealous," said Asad. "I trusted Allah to guide your hands."

"It's not always easy to follow His guidance," said Dean.

"A very true statement. You are very wise."

"Just experienced."

"Don't push it, Charlie," said Rockman. "Just get him out of there."

Dean went to the sink and washed his hands. Asad was the perfect picture of a wise man, knowledge leavened by the wear on his face, his beard streaked with lines of silver. His soft voice would have been equally at home in a library, or the hushed precincts of a mosque or other holy place. When he spoke of God, he did so not just with confidence but with a touch of humility, the tone of his voice conveying the sense of wonderment that he had been allowed to experience faith and its accompanying grace so completely.

The Devil wears a three-piece suit, his grandmother used to say. And speaks with a silver tongue.

"What happened to the doctor who saw me at the hospital?" said Asad, getting up from the chair. "I was told I would have him."

Dean shrugged, barely understanding the question through Asad's accent.

"He doesn't get out of bed this early?" Asad added.

"Yes. Well, that is the assistant's job."

"I am glad that you could help me. My head feels better already."

"You should try some aspirin."

"Allah is my aspirin. My men will pay you."

"I need no fee."

Asad bowed his head slightly, then left the room. One of his men threw a hundred-lira note on the floor as he left.

WHEN LIA GOT Dr. Ramil into the car, she saw that his hands were trembling. She pulled out of her parking space and drove around the block, anxious about leaving Dean but not wanting to be too close when Asad and his bodyguards came out. The doctor sat like a mannequin in the Renault's passenger seat, staring straight out the front window.

"They're leaving," Rockman told her finally. "Take Ramil back to the hotel."

"No," said Lia. "Get Dr. Ramil a plane ticket. I'll take him to the airport."

"We may still need him."

"He's useless." Lia glanced at her passenger. His eyes were fixed on the windshield. His hands were shaking violently, even though they were resting on his lap.

"Lia, this is Marie. What's the situation with Dr. Ramil?"

"Totally freaked. He's no good, Marie. I'll put him on a plane and you collect him on the other end."

"Get out the satphone and let me talk to him."

"Suit yourself." Lia reached down into her bag and took out the satphone. She hotkeyed to the Art Room, then gave the phone to Ramil. The doctor stared at it a moment, then put it to his ear. He listened without speaking, then handed the phone back.

"Convinced?" Lia asked.

The Art Room supervisor didn't answer. Lia spotted the old city wall ahead; though slightly hazy on where she was, she turned left, knowing the highway out to the airport would be in that direction. She had just found it when Telach got back to her.

"We have him on a plane that leaves at six. It's a direct flight to New York."

"We'll be at the airport in fifteen minutes."

CHAPTER 59

THE OWNER OF the number one bait shop in Karlsruhe, Germany, was not particularly happy about being woken up at two in the morning, especially when he found out why. But he agreed to go immediately to the police station for more details on the break-in at his store. There was a bit of confusion when he arrived, since the police seemed to think that he had reported the break-in, and he thought they had discovered it. This was soon sorted out, however, and a patrolman accompanied him to the shop to identify what was missing. The latch had been pried from the fence, the burglars apparently stymied by the lock; it was a real hack job, in contrast to the rest of the operation, which had been so smooth only the owner would have noticed that anything had been taken—six small oxygen tanks used in scuba setups ordinarily stored around the side.

"There's been a crime, which means you can investigate," said Tommy Karr when he met Hess at the airport in Baden.

"Robbery is not terrorism."

"You should check and see if Dabir took scuba classes. Maybe see who else took them with him."

"As if we don't have anything better to do," said Hess.

"Hey, if you want help, just holler."

"With that, you can help," she said sarcastically.

"Good going, Tommy," Rockman told him. "We're downloading the names and addresses to your PDA right now. Two of them look like real possibilities."

◆ ◆ ◆

FLOODLIGHTS HAD BEEN set up on the land side of the lagoon at the MiRO petroleum plant, covering the large bay ships used to load and unload at the facility. Two helicopters were circling overhead, playing their searchlights on the surface. Sharpshooters were spread out along the shoreline, ready to plaster anything or anyone that came out of the water.

Out on the river, two patrol boats had moved in to close off access to the plant. MiRO 1—the half of the plant near the water—had been shut down; the police were sweeping through to see if the terrorists were already inside. A NATO helicopter was en route from a base on the Baltic with hydrophonic gear sensitive enough to detect the breathing apparatus that would be fitted to the stolen tanks.

"Cripes, there's a creek down there," said Karr, looking out the window from Hess's helicopter as they overflew the massive complex.

"Yes?" said Hess.

The Alb Creek split the plant in two. It fed into a large pond at the north—a pond very close to a road and sheltered from the air by a patch of woods.

"Alert the security people. The terrorists are probably already inside," Karr told Hess. "They'll be in the eastern end of the plant, MiRO 2, not MiRO 1. Have the security teams check that creek."

CHAPTER 60

DEAN WENT THROUGH the clinic carefully after Asad had left, looking for anything the bodyguards might have left behind. All he saw was the money; though it would be difficult at best to get any useful DNA from it, he picked the notes up with a pair of forceps and put them into a plastic bag. Then he shut everything down.

"Charlie, Lia is taking Dr. Ramil out to the airport," Rockman told him when he was ready to leave. "Can you swing by the hotel and pick up his suitcase? We'll send a taxi to meet you out front."

"Who's going to follow Asad?"

"He's heading back toward the safe house. It sounds like he's going back to bed for a while. He told his bodyguards he was tired. Don't worry; we already have one of the CIA backup teams near the house. I'll update you when you have his bag."

The taxi was coming down the block when Dean emerged from the back of the building. He gave the man the address in Turkish—few taxi drivers spoke more English than "hello" and "good-bye"—and sat silently as they drove over to the hotel. With the clerk napping in the small office behind the reception desk, Dean used his duplicate key to get into Dr. Ramil's room. A half hour later, he arrived at the airport.

Lia was waiting in the seats at the far end of the building, across from the rows of check-in windows reserved for Western airlines. Ramil sat next to her, ramrod straight, face pale, hands vibrating.

"Hey, doc." Dean squatted down in front of him. "You all right?"

Ramil turned his head toward him slowly.

"You okay?" repeated Dean.

Ramil shook his head slightly.

"He's useless." Lia scowled derisively.

"Lighten up," Dean told her.

She got up. "I'm going to check in on Tweedle Dee and Tweedle Dum, see if the Saudis have done anything. I'll talk to you later."

"I can do that," said Dean.

"You and Pinchon don't get along too well, Charlie. Better that I go."

Dean, still angry at the way she'd treated Ramil, shrugged and watched her walk away. The sway of her hips made him regret his anger.

"What happened back there, doc?" Dean asked, turning to Ramil. "You okay?"

"I'm—I don't know if I'm having a breakdown or something. I . . ."

His voice trailed off. Dean had seen guys fall apart under pressure before, younger, tougher men than Ramil. It was as if they'd taken some unknown poison that had gutted their intestines, left them hollow inside. Ramil had been a battlefield surgeon and manned aid stations in Vietnam, which you couldn't do if you were a coward. But everyone had secret flaws, and age had a way of wearing down the things that kept them hidden. Wear was in Ramil's face right now: haunted fatigue, not fear.

"You're just tired," Dean told him. "It happens."

"I don't know," mumbled Ramil, so softly that Dean didn't hear the words distinctly. Instead of repeating them, Ramil changed them. "I hope so."

Dean saw a pair of American Airlines employees walking across the concourse toward the row of ticket booths. "Let's go check you in. Get you an aisle seat."

CHAPTER 61

DABIR WATCHED THE German helicopters training their spot-lights on the docking area at the petroleum processing plant. Whoever had tipped the police off had obviously known the general target of his attack, though not the specifics of his plan. The German police were good—but not quite good enough to stop him. In ten minutes, the plant would be in flames.

Who was the traitor?

It couldn't be the men he'd sent inside, who would have been able to identify their targets. It couldn't be the chemist, either—if it had been, the man Dabir sent to get the oxygen tanks would have been arrested, or at least followed.

The only person Dabir could think of who knew the target but not the precise plan to strike it was Asad bin Taysr. As much as Dabir hated him, Asad was a steadfast supporter of the cause and it was inconceivable that he would do anything to betray it.

One of the helicopters passed nearby. Dabir got out of the car and popped the trunk. In his haste earlier he'd forgotten to put out the trunk light; the flood of yellow took him by surprise. He pulled the bicycle out, then slapped the trunk lid closed.

Asad had wanted to watch the refinery burn, but the heli-copters had convinced him that was too much of a risk. With the success of his mission guaranteed despite the odds stacked against him, he began contemplating his next move. He got on the bike; one of the helicopters was swinging in the direction of the creek his men had used to infiltrate the facility.

The Germans were too late. But if it took the rest of his life, Dabir swore as he pedaled down the darkened road, he would find out who had betrayed him.

CHAPTER 62

KARR, FOLLOWING THE chopper's searchlight as it swept along the creekside, spotted a shadow near a complex of buildings used for distilling naphtha, the very volatile lighter components of petroleum used for solvents.

"There!" he yelled to the pilot. "There's someone there. Get your light there!"

Ground units were already scrambling nearby, running toward the pipelines connecting the two portions of the plant. Light erupted near it, so intense that Karr threw his hand up to shield his eyes. The chopper pirouetted away as a ball of fire shot into the air, so high that it exploded over the helicopter, an umbrella of red and yellow.

"Explosions," said Karr, telling the Art Room what was going on. He cursed, angry that he hadn't figured out what was going on sooner. He leaned back toward the window, trying to assess what was going on. The two tall cooling stacks—made of concrete, they looked like smoke stacks but were used to condense gases in the desulphurization unit—stood over the complex, twin sentinels.

A fly was climbing on one.

"That tower there," he told the helicopter pilot. "The smokestack. There's somebody on it. Knock him off."

"*Was?*" sputtered the pilot. "What are you saying?"

"I don't have a gun. Get him off of there. He wants to blow the stack."

Karr reached for the helicopter's controls, threatening to do it if the pilot didn't. It was a bluff—Karr had no idea how to fly the aircraft. But the pilot didn't know that. He pitched the chopper forward, veering as close as he dared to the man climbing up the side of the large stack. The man tottered for a second, then began fiddling with a small pack at his belt. As the helo turned away, the wash knocked the terrorist off balance and sent him tumbling toward the ground.

He exploded about twenty feet from the pavement, obliterating himself, but failing to ignite a fire or destroy the stack, either of which could have touched off a much larger explosion.

"Do not interfere with the controls," said Hess, leaning forward from the back. "You are a very dangerous man, Herr Magnor-Karr."

"Not dangerous enough," said Karr, still mad at himself for being a step behind the terrorists.

CHAPTER 63

AFTER SHE LEFT the airport, Lia drove back toward Istanbul, circling around the roundabouts several times to make sure she wasn't being followed. Even though her back was clear, she took a circuitous route toward the Ceylan Inter-Continental Hotel, where the Saudis who had met with Asad were staying. She tracked through the sleeping business district, once more making sure she wasn't being followed before parking across from the side entrance to the hotel.

The Ceylan Inter-Continental Hotel was one of the fanciest hotels in the world, let alone the city. The Saudis were ensconced in one of its well-appointed executive suites, proof that dedicated jihadists need not take a vow of poverty.

The CIA team had posted two men on the street, watching the main and back entrances, with a third handling communications and coordinating other members. The coordinator was working out of a panel truck around the block from the hotel, using a short-wave radio to talk to the lookouts and a satphone to stay in touch with the Art Room. Desk Three had tapped into the hotel's security system and was monitoring the Ceylan's video cameras.

The panel truck was exactly where Lia had left it several hours before. She went to the passenger side and rapped on the window.

"You should've moved," she said.

"I just got here," said Terrence Pinchon, leaning forward and opening the door for her.

"What happened to Reisler?"

"Went to get some beauty rest. It's a lost cause, don't you think?"

Lia could feel her heart race. It had nothing to do with the mission; she wished it had nothing to do with Pinchon.

"What are the Saudis doing?" she asked, shutting the door behind her.

"Far as we can tell, they're snoozin'. Don't have enough people to put somebody up on the floor."

"You have plenty of people."

"Eight. And some of them have to sleep. But you're here now, right? The rest of us can go home."

Lia reached to the back of her belt and flipped the com system off. Then she turned to Pinchon. His green eyes fixed on her own, boring through the wall that protected her.

He was handsome, there was no question about that; his face had the rugged look of a movie star. But his personality—he hadn't been this much of a jerk when she'd known him. He couldn't have been. And he hadn't been a liar; she didn't fall for liars. Maybe their relationship had been one of convenience and circumstance at the time, but even so, she wouldn't have fallen that badly for an ass.

"What happened to you?" she asked him.

"Took a quick nap."

"In Kyrgyzstan."

"Nothing."

"You were dead."

"Obviously not."

"Are you going to tell me the story?"

"No story to tell."

Someone was talking on the radio. Pinchon pushed the earbud back into place; Lia tapped her com system to life.

"They're in the elevator, coming down," Sandy Chafetz said.

"We got a BMW 740 pulling around," said the CIA agent near the entrance. "Blue. Here's the plate."

"All right. I'll tag along," said Pinchon. "You guys get in your cars." He turned to Lia. "Comin'?"

"For a while."

The BMW collected the Saudis in front of the hotel, then went directly down the hill, swinging toward the Bosporus.

"Probably headed toward the bridge," said Pinchon, directing his team over the radio. "Bobby, get across it. I'll trail. Steve, why don't you jog right and head in the direction of the airport? That's probably where they're going."

"You're getting ahead of yourself," said Lia.

"I was doing just fine before you got here, thanks."

"They're going toward the ferry port," said Lia as the BMW pulled left instead of going over the Galata Bridge as Pinchon had predicted. Reluctant to admit that he had been wrong, Pinchon nonetheless started to reposition his people. Still, they were the closest when the BMW stopped in front of the ferry entrance a few minutes later.

"I'll stay with them until you park the car," Lia told Pinchon, getting out.

The Saudis apparently had already bought tickets; they headed straight for the sea bus that went to the dock at Haydarpaşa, the train station on the Asian side of the city. Lia, just to be sure, bought tickets for all of the destinations. The clerk rolled his eyes and took his time counting the change, shorting her a lira and smirking when she pointed it out. When he finally gave her the coin, Lia flipped it contemptuously into his booth.

She had to run to make the sea bus, hopping aboard as the ropes were tossed and the engines revved the ship from the dock. The boat wasn't quite half full; Lia went forward, spotted the Saudis sitting on the starboard side, and took a seat across from them. The Art Room switched her com unit into the CIA network, and she heard Pinchon shifting his people. There was no quick way to get from Beyoğlu to the Asian side of Istanbul; he sent one of his cars to the vehicle ferry and had another take the long detour to a bridge to the north. He was going to take the next sea bus across, in about twenty minutes.

Lia got up as the vessel neared the pier. One of the Saudis shot her a glance. They made eye contact; she smiled, as if she were a semi-interested tourist reacting to a handsome foreigner. The Saudi was dressed like a businessman on vacation, trim black trousers and a casual shirt; he carried a canvas overnight bag, as did his partner. Lia got off ahead of the two men, but walked slowly so that they could overtake her; they did in short order, striding quickly toward the train station. The man who'd smiled earlier didn't look at her.

"Are there video cameras in that station?" Lia asked Chafetz.

"Negative. You're on your own. First train to leave is the *Süper Ekspresier*—the express Pullman for Ankara. It goes in five minutes. I doubt they're going to take it, though—no way they'd cut it that close."

"Where's that reserve team?" Lia hissed, picking up her pace.

"About ten minutes away."

The Saudis headed directly for the *Süper Ekspresier.* Lia, already guessing that they had timed their arrival so they wouldn't have to wait long, ran to the window and got a ticket for Ankara, the end of the line.

"Lia, what's going on?" asked Pinchon over the radio.

"The platform at the far end, on your left. I have your ticket," she told him. The conductor was starting to shoo people aboard.

"I'm still on the boat," he told her. "I can see the dock."

"Well, get moving," said Lia.

The Saudis weren't on the platform. Lia got on the front car, walking through quickly to make sure they were there.

"Not in the first car," she said.

"Lia—you have less than a minute to get off," said Chafetz.

"Where are you, Pinchon?"

"We're just pulling up to the pier."

"All right. I have the train," Lia told him. "Get somebody to the first stop."

"We can't make the first stop," answered Chafetz. "It's in Sincan, only eighteen minutes by train. There's no way with the traffic."

"Second stop, then."

"That's two and a half hours from now."

"Peachy," said Lia. "Terry, get in the station while I make

sure they haven't slipped off. I haven't spotted them yet. If they're not here, I'll get off at the first stop."

"I may make it," said Pinchon, huffing.

"Relax," said Lia, crossing into the second car.

The conductor yelled "all aboard" in English and Turkish. Stepping into the third car, Lia spotted the two Saudis sitting in a compartment on the right. She walked past, smiling at the man whom she'd seen before—a flirty smile, which she held until she took a seat in a compartment behind them on the opposite side.

"Car three," she told Chafetz, as the train bumped from the platform. She turned and looked out the window, then folded her arms to watch the scenery.

CHAPTER 64

ASAD SLEPT WELL for two hours, then rose, his headache gone and the dizziness completely relieved. Whatever the doctor had done, Allah had surely been with him.

He seemed a thoughtful man, confident of his skills, not easily shaken. This had set the bodyguards on edge—they were used to cowing people, and anyone who did not show abject fear threatened them.

Asad felt just the opposite. He did not want to put himself in the hands of someone with no faith in his abilities. The doctor's insights on human nature and the way of God were small but profound. Under other circumstances, Asad might have arranged for the man to be recruited. But there was much to do this morning.

"Are you ready to leave?" he asked Katib after his morning prayers and tea.

"I am."

Something was wrong with Katib, Asad sensed; the bodyguard was still brooding over the incident at the hospital the other day. Coming on top of the car accident, it had made him doubt his abilities.

"You should not do anything foolish," he told his bodyguard when they were on their way to the airport. "You are needed for the long battle."

Katib said nothing.

Asad stared out the window, thinking of what to tell his follower. So often in the past, words had flowed into his mouth, but today he still had not found any when they arrived at the airport for his flight.

"I will make amends," said Katib, holding the door as he got out of the car. "My mistake will be erased."

"Mistakes are to be expected."

Katib stared at him. Asad considered whether he should order him not to do anything. But he sensed that Katib would not listen to him if he did.

Perhaps this is what I owe the man for his loyalty, Asad thought—approval.

Perhaps it was for the best. He was not taking any bodyguards with him to America, not even Katib. He'd learned that it was far safer to travel alone there, as foreigners in groups tended to attract attention. And action here might add to the crescendo effect of the attacks. Strike here, strike there, continue even as security was increased—the enemy would soon grow disheartened.

But he hated to lose Katib. He had known him since the Syrian since was thirteen, nearly a decade. Though young, he had a sharp mind.

"You have everything arranged?" Asad asked.

"I have friends. It will be done at noon. Taksim will be full then."

His bodyguard's solemn expression tugged at Asad's heart.

"Go with God," he told him. "We will meet in paradise."

Inside, a woman took Asad's bag and set it on the belt to go through the X-ray machine. She was a typical decadent Turk, he could tell, seduced by the West. He moved to the metal detector.

As he stepped through it, a buzzer sounded and the two guards crowded next to him.

"Here," said one of the men harshly. "Spread out your arms."

Asad felt a moment of fear. Stifling it, he raised his hands. The other guard began patting his clothes.

"Your watch," said the first guard.

Asad started to take it off, thinking the guard was asking for a bribe. Then he realized that it was meant as an explanation—the steel band must have set off the alarm.

"Did you want to examine it?" he asked.

"When you go through the next checkpoint, place it in one of these," said the guard, holding up a shallow tub. "Or you will set it off again."

"I'll try to remember that," he said, passing through the gate.

CHAPTER 65

BESIDES HOLDING HIS post as National Security Advisor, George Hadash had served in the U.S. Army as a young man and received both the Purple Heart and Silver Star, making him eligible for burial at Arlington National Cemetery. But his daughter Irena held firm on that issue; her father had always wanted to be buried next to his brother, who had been killed in Vietnam and was interred with other family members at a cemetery in suburban Virginia.

The ceremony was a simple one, with family and close friends only. But as the President of the United States was among Hadash's closest friends, there was no way to make it small, or truly private. The TV people kept a somewhat respectful distance from the gravesite, but their presence hung like a shadow in the distance.

"He was the pragmatist, I was the optimist," said the president, speaking without notes in front of the open grave. "He was the teacher. I the student."

Marcke's modesty touched Rubens, as did his obvious grief; the president looked as pale and drawn as Irena. When he ended his eulogy by simply looking down at the casket and saying, "I'm going to miss you, George," even Rubens felt tears slip from his eyes.

The minister read from the 23rd Psalm, selected by Irena with Rubens' help. Then one by one they threw fistfuls of dirt in the grave—Irena, her daughter, the president, Rubens, the others.

And then it was over.

Rubens watched as President Marcke consoled Irena and her daughter one last time. When the president began walking toward his limo, Rubens went over to her. He had planned to give Irena and her daughter a ride back to their condominium, where she would host a few family members for a light breakfast. He couldn't stay himself.

His phone began to vibrate just as he reached her. He stepped discreetly to the side, activating the phone.

"Red Lion plans to come to the U.S.," Marie Telach told him.

"You're sure?"

"Absolutely. He just checked in for a flight to New York with a connection at Paris."

Rubens clicked off the phone. "I'll be back in a moment," he told Irena. Then he started down the hill toward the president's limo. Marcke was standing next to the open door with a group of aides, including Bing.

"Mr. President," said Rubens as Marcke started to get in the car.

"What's up, Billy?"

"We should talk—perhaps in private."

Marcke slid into the car. Rubens followed.

"Red Lion—Asad bin Taysr, al-Qaeda's number three—he's coming to the U.S. We can arrest him here if you want. You'd spoken of wanting to put a top leader of the organization on trial, if possible."

Marcke said nothing. Rubens guessed he was considering the political ramifications; putting a terrorist on trial was full of pitfalls and could easily backfire.

"We're still not sure what he's planning," added Rubens. "I—we unraveled the plot in Germany as I told you earlier, but obviously there's something here."

"I want him, Billy. I want to put him on trial and show the world what slimes we're dealing with. Can you get him?"

"Yes, sir. First, though—"

"First find out what he's up to, absolutely. You do that. Then we nail him for it. You do it. Whatever it takes. I want that son of a bitch."

There was so much emotion on Marcke's face that Rubens felt his own flush. "I'll get him. I will."

As Rubens reached for the door, the president grabbed him by the shoulder. "George Hadash was a great man. I owe him a lot."

"I do, too," managed Rubens, nodding as the president released him.

BY THE TIME Rubens reached the Art Room, Telach had gotten one of the CIA backup people to the airport and over to the gate area. The flight was overbooked; the Art Room computer wizards were able to change the coding on both tickets to ensure that the men would not be bumped, making it appear that they had not only checked in several hours before anyone else, but that they had both paid the airline's full fare.

"Where are Lia and Dean?" Rubens asked Telach as she pointed out Asad's location on the screen.

"Lia is tracking the Saudis. There's no way she can get there in time. Dean's in the airport, but Asad just saw him. I don't want to risk putting him on the same flight."

"We'll need someone in Paris—a full team in case he gets off there."

"He checked his bag. If he doesn't get on the flight, it'll set off all sorts of alarms."

"I find it interesting, Ms. Telach, that someone like you who regularly finds ways around security systems does not appreciate that someone else might as well."

"I did plan on having someone there," she said defensively. "Should I alert the French interior ministry?"

"The French will merely confuse things. Where is Mr. Karr?"

"He's wrapping up in Germany."

"Have him proceed to the airport."

Rubens turned to go.

"Mr. Rubens, wait," said Telach quickly. "We think there may be some sort of plot involving the Taksim area of Istanbul. Asad's bodyguard mentioned it just outside the airport. We think they're going to strike around noon."

CHAPTER 66

KARR'S TAKE ON the German mission could be summed up in one word: bust.

They'd been consistently one step behind the terrorists, hampered by German laws restricting investigations. Al-Qaeda had succeeded in disrupting operations at Europe's largest refinery, which sent a chill through the commodities market, raising the price of oil twenty dollars a barrel.

The German point of view was considerably more upbeat. The terrorists had detonated their bombs inexpertly, causing far less damage than they intended; the plant kept its vital fuel operations going, and the damage done could be repaired within a few weeks. Meanwhile, a previously unknown al-Qaeda cell had been rolled up. The chemist had been arrested at the bar with the key to the tackle shop gate still in his pocket; he'd gotten it from a girlfriend who'd worked there some weeks before, probably at his urging. The chemist had not manufactured the bomb material—it was a plastic explosive traced to pilfered Czech military stores—but he had raw materials needed to create other explosives, a serious crime under German law. The authorities were confident he would implicate other members of the network in exchange for "consideration" at sentencing.

Six terrorists who had taken part in the operation had died, either by killing themselves or failing to surrender when ordered to. Only two of the men had been identified so far.

Marid Dabir was missing. Fingerprints and hairs matching those in the house the al-Qaeda organizer had rented were found in an abandoned car near the plant. German intelligence was convinced that he had died in the operation and was planning DNA tests to confirm this.

"Except that it's extremely out of character for an important al-Qaeda lieutenant to kill himself," Karr told Hess. "They get other suckers to do the dirty work for them. I'd be searching under every rock and in every sewer for him if I were you."

Hess answered by asking if she could get him a ride to the airport.

HIS MISSION IN Germany over, Karr was due a good hunk of R&R time, and he knew just where and how to spend it—in Paris with his girlfriend, who was going to school there. But the Art Room had other plans.

"Tommy, we need you in Paris," Marie Telach told him when he checked in from the Munich airport. "We're looking for a flight now."

"What a coincidence," he said. "That's why I'm calling."

"Asad is going to de Gaulle Airport. We need you to trail him from there."

"In Paris. Cool."

"No, probably not. He has a connecting flight to the U.S. We're going to get you a seat. In fact, we'll get you a seat on every plane coming out of that airport, just to be sure."

Anyone else would have groused. Karr, being Karr, laughed, then asked if he had time for lunch before making the flight to France.

"Better eat on the plane," Telach told him.

CHAPTER 67

"WE ADMIRE AMERICANS here in Turkey, truly admire them," Istanbul's deputy police chief told Charlie Dean when he showed up to brief the police on the information the Art Room had gleaned from its bug in Asad's skull. "I myself have been to New York and San Francisco several times. And Washington, D.C."

Dean glanced at the head of the Terrorism Section, who was nodding briskly. It was obvious that neither man really believed him.

"My government wouldn't have sent me to talk to you if they didn't think it was a credible threat," Dean said. "I realize that the information is sketchy, but it's derived from a conversation between two al-Qaeda members. Something is going to happen in Istanbul, probably at noon, probably at Taksim Square or nearby."

"And you can't identify the sources?"

"We only have a photo of the person we believe involved. He's a Syrian. He uses the name Abd Katib Muhammad. He may be working with one or two other people whom he knows."

Desk Three had forwarded video captures of Katib, along with other information about him and a transcript of the conversation regarding the attack. While the information had been sent through normal high-level channels, Rubens had ordered Dean to talk to the "people on the frontline" to make sure it arrived in time to do some good.

"How do you even know this man is in Turkey?" asked the deputy chief.

"We believe he is," said Dean, treading carefully because he couldn't acknowledge the Red Lion operation.

"We have been very aggressive against extremists here," said the terror chief. "Even before your 9/11. I myself took part in the raids at Beykoz, striking the heart of the Hezbollah conspiracy."

"I'm sure you do a very good job," said Dean. "That's why I know you'll take this seriously."

"We are always watching Taksim Square," said the deputy police chief. His English had a vaguely American accent. "There are many businesses nearby, and tourists on Istikal Caddesi. A car or truck bomb—it will not get close, I assure you."

"That's a good start."

"We will increase the police presence and take precautions," added the deputy chief, rising to dismiss him. "We appreciate your personal attention. Perhaps tonight you will be my guest for dinner?"

"I'd like that," said Dean. "But I'm supposed to head back."

"You came just to tell us this?"

"It's why I'm here," hedged Dean.

The terrorism supervisor gave him a wry smile, indicating that he suspected there was considerably more to the story but wouldn't press as a matter of professional courtesy.

"I don't think they believe me," Dean told Marie Telach a few minutes later. He'd gotten into a taxi and was pretending to use a cell phone.

"They do believe you, Charlie. The Interior Ministry has issued an alert," she told him. "They're sending more police over to the area and a bomb detection unit from the airport. Your job there is done; we've done all we can. Your plane's waiting—please proceed."

Dean brooded about the situation all the way back to his hotel. There was certainly more that they could do—all of Desk Three's surveillance apparatus could be turned loose on the area. But the Art Room was focused on Asad bin Taysr, tracking him on the flight to America.

It was eleven-thirty when Dean checked out of the hotel and got into the cab for the airport. Taksim Square was about a mile away.

Almost on the way.

He leaned forward from the backseat. "Take me to Taksim Square first, okay?" he said in English.

The driver said something in Turkish. Dean's com system was off, so he didn't have a translation. But he didn't figure he needed one.

"Taksim Square," he said again, dropping a fifty-lira note on the front seat, about twice the normal fare to the airport. "And wait. Keep the meter going. I'll pay two times what it says."

CHAPTER 68

ASAD PUSHED ONTO the bus just as the doors closed. The driver, oblivious, lurched from the terminal exit, pulling into the circular drive that connected the different sections at Paris' Charles de Gaulle Airport. The shuttle bus was crowded with passengers from another flight as well as Asad's, and he found himself squeezed next to a small child and his father. The child, probably American, said hello to him in English. Asad turned away from him without answering.

A bearded man from the Middle East sat a few rows away. He caught Asad's eye, then hurriedly looked away. As the bus pulled into the next terminal, Asad drifted in his direction, until he stood directly in front of him.

"Where are you from?" Asad asked in English.

"Egypt," said the man. "You, brother?"

"Morocco," lied Asad.

"The airport is a confusing place," said the man forlornly. "I think they do it on purpose. All of the West—a devil's paradise."

"The West is a land of opportunity," Asad told the stranger. "You should be thankful you're here."

Rather than answering, the man stared at the floor.

The bus went around a special loop between the de Gaulle international terminals, stopping at each to let passengers on and off. When the crowd eased at the first stop, Asad put his bag on the floor and started to sit, then changed his mind and offered the seat to the little boy who had tried speaking to him earlier. The boy hesitated until, prodded by his father, he sat. He was the child of the enemy, and yet a child was a child, and Asad did not bear him malice. On the contrary, it was good to see how the father and son communicated with gestures and glances, the way Asad had with his father, the way he would have had he had a son.

The bus continued around the outer precincts of the airport, driving through a no-man's-land created so that international travelers could change planes without going through two more layers of passport control and customs.

"Terminal 2B," announced the driver.

Asad turned to join the queue, picking up the nearby carry-on bag.

"Did you take the right bag?" said a small voice in English.

Asad ignored him.

"Say, mister—did you take the right bag?"

"Oh, yes," he told the boy, his earlier impression gone. This child surely was the devil.

"Come on, Bobby, or we'll miss the flight," said the boy's father. He didn't stop to hear the child's explanation, scooping him up and helping him off the bus.

Even so, Asad made sure to give them a good head start before he got off the bus. He waited until they were through the security check before retrieving the new passport and boarding pass his accomplice had slipped him when they swapped bags.

CHAPTER 69

"CHARLIE, THIS IS getting to be a bad habit with you."

"What's that, Marie?"

"You were supposed to go to the airport."

"I'm on my way."

Dean scanned the square. Taksim was a major hub for local bus routes through the Beyoğlu area, traditionally Istanbul's international business district. It was also the end point of a long pedestrian mall extending several blocks that gave the area the character of London's SoHo or New York's East Village. On Saturdays, it was flooded with people, and Dean found himself gazing at a sea of pedestrians walking up from the Galata area. A half dozen large dump trucks had blocked off access to the square from the road; three police buses were parked beyond it.

"Charlie, you're beginning to act a lot like Lia and Tommy, you know that?"

"Thanks."

"I didn't mean that as a compliment. You came to Desk Three as a mature, level-headed op."

Dean smiled to himself. He walked toward the fountain at the center of the square. Two policemen, one handling a German shepherd, walked along the tram tracks. Dean guessed that the dog was a bomb sniffer. Other policemen were stopping pedestrians, asking for identification and looking in bags and backpacks.

The Turks *had* taken the information seriously; there were plenty of policemen here, and undoubtedly more on the side streets just beyond the square. In truth, precautions couldn't have been more thorough in an American city.

It was an inviting area for an attack. Not only were there plenty of people, but there was a multitude of Western symbols, American especially—a huge Levi's billboard flanked one end of the square. Nearby there was a Burger King and a McDonald's, even a Starbucks a small distance down the block.

So if he was going to blow the place up, what would he do? A truck bomb would do the most damage, but there was no way one was running the gamut the police had erected.

Maybe the show of force had already done its job.

Dean started back toward the cab, which he'd left a block away. As he did, he spotted a man in a long gray raincoat—odd on a day when there wasn't a cloud in the sky.

Dean started for him, all instinct, not thinking.

The policemen with the dog got there first. Dean stopped, frozen, sure he that in the next second the young man would explode.

"Charlie, what's going on?" asked Telach.

The boy threw his hands away from his body, holding them out at the policemen's order. Dean stepped back. As he did, he bumped against a short, stout woman in a long, brightly colored dress. He turned quickly to try to grab her but missed; she tottered down to the sidewalk.

"I'm sorry," he told her, bending down.

"I'm all right," insisted the woman with a pronounced British accent. "I can manage on my own."

She refused Dean's outstretched arm, righting herself and walking toward the paved cobblestones of Istikal Caddesi. Dean turned back toward the man in the raincoat; as he did, he spotted a bearded man being chased by two policemen. He was wearing a sweater, and looked like he had a bulletproof vest under it.

His face—it was the bodyguard, Katib.

Dean yelled to the woman to get down. As he did, the man exploded.

CHAPTER 70

KARR HAD NEVER really liked French beer. It seemed to him that it was basically German beer done badly, probably to spite the ancient enemy. But the small refreshment area had a perfect vantage of the gate area where Asad was supposed to catch his plane, and so he decided it was his job to give up his taste buds in the name of an adequate cover.

"Asad should be heading your way," said Sandy Chafetz. "We saw him get off the bus."

"That's nice," said Karr, taking another sip of the beer. In the half hour he'd been there, he'd consumed about a finger's worth from the glass.

He swept his eyes around the nearby gates, looking over the passengers. The Art Room had checked the passenger list; if Asad was meeting anyone here they were unknown to American intelligence agencies. Only European and American nationals had seats on the plane; none had Arabic names, though of course that wasn't a guarantee.

Passengers making connections had to pass through a security gamut on ground level before being allowed into the gate area. Karr had wandered near the stairway earlier, only to be shooed away—though not before he had placed a video bug nearby, supplementing the airport's video surveillance system, which the Art Room had broken into. Asad was also within range of the portable booster in Karr's carry-on bag, and could be tracked to within a meter or so of his actual location.

"Here he comes," said Chafetz finally.

Karr left the unfinished beer on the bar and walked around

the corner to a vendor selling potato chips. He bent to inspect the offerings as Asad approached, shielding his face somewhat from the terrorist's view.

"Definitely our guy," muttered Karr after he passed. Unlike the other ops, Karr tended not to worry if people thought he was a nut who talked to himself out loud. He ambled along ten or fifteen yards behind Asad, watching as he turned toward the restrooms.

"That flight is boarding," Chafetz said. "Maybe you should go over to the gate."

"Uh-huh," said Karr, ambling after Asad. He went into the men's room, making sure there wasn't a door the Art Room didn't know about. Asad was in one of the stalls.

For a guy whose plane was boarding, thought Karr, Asad was sure taking his time. But then, some things couldn't be rushed.

"Tommy, he just checked in at the gate," said Chafetz.

"Uh, no he didn't," said Karr, standing outside the men's room.

"I'm looking at the computer display right now."

"And I'm looking at the door to the men's room. What's the locator say?"

"We're worried it may not be accurate—are you *sure* he's there?"

"Well, I didn't knock on the door," said Karr.

"We're looking at a video from the gate," said Telach. "It looks like him."

Karr sighed. The problem with technology was that sometimes there was just too much of it.

"Tommy, we want you to verify that the man in the restroom is Asad," said Telach.

"You want me to ask him?"

"This isn't a joking matter," she said tersely.

The door to the restroom opened. Karr walked toward it, passing Asad as he came out.

"It's him," said Karr, dawdling at the sink for a moment before going back outside. He could see Asad walking down the hall, past the gate.

"He's not going to that flight," said Chafetz. "There's something wrong."

"Tommy, we're going to attempt to recalibrate the locator gear on the fly," said Telach. "Stand by."

"Relax, Mom," Karr told her. "My eyes are working fine."

Karr quickened his pace until he was just five yards behind Asad. The terror leader walked back to the main area of the terminal, glanced at the board listing flights, then continued toward a nearby gate where a plane for Montreal had just begun to board.

"I'm heading over to Air France 346," Karr told Chafetz.

"Asad isn't on it."

"He will be in about five minutes," Karr said. "Say, am I on the aisle?"

CHAPTER 71

DEAN FOUND HIMSELF on the ground near the garden at the center of Taksim Square. He couldn't hear anything. At first he thought it was because the blow had knocked out his hearing. But in fact silence had descended on the square, a moment of sheer, collective shock.

Then the screaming began. Then the sirens.

Dean jumped to his feet. The woman he'd bumped into a moment earlier lay on the ground ten feet away. He went to her, took her arm and lifted gently, expecting that this time he might get a thank you.

But instead he saw an immense gash where her nose and left eye had been, the center of her face a black knuckle. He set her down, thought of doing first aid, but didn't know where to begin. When he pried open her mouth, two teeth fell out, along with part of gum and bone. He tried CPR anyway, pumping at her chest though it was clearly hopeless.

People were running in every direction around him. Police were moving down from behind the dump trucks. Dean saw a pair of soldiers running up, the first ones he'd seen.

"Charlie? Charlie are you all right?"

"I'm all right, Marie. The suicide bomber. A kid in a big sweater, one of the bodyguards—Katib, I think. The Syrian."

"Are you *all right?*"

Had the woman changed direction because he'd bumped into her? Or had that been her chance to change her fate—if she'd stopped and spoken to him, she'd be alive.

And maybe he'd be dead; whatever had struck her in the face might have hit him instead, smack in the chest.

Even when they knew—*knew*—what was going to happen, sometimes it wasn't enough.

"Charlie?"

Dean stopped pumping and stood up to take stock—to see if he really was all right. His clothes were intact, spotless, aside from the blood and dirt on his knees.

"Yeah, I'm definitely okay," he told Telach. "I'll get to the airport."

As Dean walked toward the dump trucks, he saw an SUV with its doors open across the square; it looked like one of the vehicles Asad's bodyguards had used the first day the terrorist had arrived.

"That truck," he told a nearby policeman. "I think the bomber may have come from there. You better be careful—it may be packed with explosives."

The policeman either couldn't hear him or didn't understand him in the din around them.

"Marie—I need a translator. I think one of the bodyguard's SUV is nearby. It may be booby-trapped."

"I'm here, Charlie," said the translator. She gave Dean the words in Turkish, but the policeman continued to stare, too stunned to act.

Dean caught hold of another policeman nearby. This one understood, immediately calling for backup on his radio and then running toward the truck, waving his arms and shooing people away.

"A suicide bomber," Dean told the cabbie when he reached him. "A crazy man."

The taxi driver nodded sadly.

"Airport?" he asked, his voice cracking.

"Yeah. I gotta get back to work."

CHAPTER 72

SINCE ASAD HAD already left Istanbul, Lia stayed with the Saudis, trailing them as they traveled on the train toward Turkey's capital. A CIA paramilitary undercover officer got on at Eskişehir, the second stop out of Istanbul. He got into the coach directly across from the Saudis, leaving Lia free to stretch her legs and go to the snack car without worrying too much about what her subjects were up to.

The *Süper Ekspresier*, also known as the Blue Train, was considered a luxury express, but that was only in comparison to most Turkish trains. The first-class compartments were on the small side and were almost all empty. The coaches, on the other hand, were packed, with people crowded into the seats. The cars dated from the 1970s, and while they had been refurbished, their dull carpets and poor lighting were a reminder why train travel had flagged in that era.

It took six hours for the train to get to Ankara. Lia spent the time haunted by memories of Pinchon, dozing off once only to wake with a start, convinced that he was leaning next to her in the seat.

"We're pretty sure they're getting off and going to the airport," Marie Telach told Lia as the train neared the Ankara station. "It looks like they're bound for Riyadh."

The Art Room had identified their aliases and booked a pair of the CIA people onto the flight. In the meantime, a trail team was already covering the train station, tasked to stay with the Saudis until they got on the plane.

"Mr. Rubens would like you to go to Riyadh," Telach told

her. "We've alerted the CIA station chief there as well as the Saudis. You'll have plenty of backup."

"What exactly do you want me to do?" Lia asked.

"Continue surveillance. The next move may have to be up to Saudis because of diplomatic considerations," Telach added. "That's still being worked out."

"Goodness knows we wouldn't want to upset the Saudis."

"Heaven forbid," said Telach, for once as cynical and sarcastic as Lia. "We don't want you to take the same plane as your targets. Do you want to catch a nap at a hotel?"

"Not worth it."

"Are you all right, Lia? You haven't slept."

"I don't feel like sleeping. I'll get something to eat at the airport. Book me onto the earliest flight you can."

CHAPTER 73

MARID DABIR STARED at the television screen, watching the report of the deaths in Turkey. The authorities clearly had been tipped off to the pending attack, or otherwise they would not have had so many men in the area when the bomb exploded.

Dabir avoided the obvious conclusion until a photo of the dead attacker flashed on the screen. The European al-Qaeda organizer recognized him immediately: it was one of Asad's bodyguards, the one who stayed closest to him during Dabir's visit to Istanbul.

That made it all too clear who the traitor must be, didn't it?

Asad bin Taysr was the only person outside of Dabir's trusted circle who knew the target in Germany—yet didn't know the plan well enough to allow the police to stop it. The bodyguard who might have implicated him had been eliminated. Most likely the man had been urged to his death by Asad, who would have been sure he would kill himself as soon as the police spotted him.

A traitor to his brothers, to his religion, to God.

There would be more betrayals. Eventually, the traitor would lead the Crusaders to Osama bin Laden himself.

He must be stopped before that happened.

Dabir rose from the table and walked to the counter of the airport lounge. He scratched his chin as he ordered another coffee. He'd shaved off his beard for the first time in more than five years and dyed his hair silver gray, matching the old picture in the Belgian passport in his pocket. He had a flight to Moscow in three hours. Though he hated the city, it was a place where he knew he would be safe.

This was not a time to be safe. It was a time to act. He would have to eliminate Asad bin Taysr now, before it was too late. Only he was in a position to do so.

Asad would go to the U.S. to deliver instructions for the rest of the attacks there. Al-Qaeda protocol decreed that the final orders be delivered in person so there was no chance of interception and no mistake in interpretation. Perhaps he was already there. Perhaps it was too late to stop him.

Dabir refused to consider that possibility. If Asad had gone to the U.S., he would meet with only the most secure and committed cells in the country. Three years ago, that would have meant Detroit, Phoenix, and San Francisco.

Now, though?

Perhaps the same. Dabir had helped build the American network and still had many personal contacts there. He could find out quickly, if he went there.

"Three euros," said the man at the counter.

Dabir reached for his wallet. He could get to Detroit easily enough, and there were brothers there he could count on, brothers whom he had trained and helped plant years ago. They would owe their allegiance to him, not Asad.

He could have them meet him in Ontario, base his operations there. Phoenix would be his next stop, more difficult to deal with than Detroit, though he liked the weather much better.

Dabir took out one of the BlackBerrys he could use to communicate with associates. A set of chips had been added to the guts of the devices, allowing them to encrypt messages. He tapped out a message in English: "Changing plans. Will advise." Then he went to see if he could arrange a flight to Toronto.

CHAPTER 74

RELATIVES AND LIMO drivers crowded the door near the exit from customs at John F. Kennedy Airport, clamoring for loved ones and clients in a patter that mixed New York verve with tender pleading. Dr. Ramil dodged to the left, avoiding a happy young wife as she rushed to greet a husband just back from overseas. Her overflowing emotions encouraged him, as if happiness were not only contagious but a cure for the unsettled panic he'd been fighting against since Istanbul.

It had been some time since he'd been in New York City, and he wasn't quite sure how best to get to Baltimore. He'd decided on the plane that he would call for advice, but now he changed his mind; perhaps staying the night in New York would soothe him further. Besides, he didn't feel like talking to Rubens and the others just yet.

"Doctor. I hope your trip was a good one."

Ramil spun around. Kevin Montblanc was standing at the end of the line, his walruslike moustache twitching as he spoke.

"Come on this way. Is that your only bag?"

"I hadn't expected you," Ramil told Montblanc. Montblanc was Desk Three's operations personnel director, a kind of glorified den mother who looked after the Desk Three operatives. He was a psychologist, overly fond—in Ramil's opinion—of touchy-feely phrases and open-ended questions.

"Thought you could use a lift. And I was in the neighborhood." This was obviously meant as a joke, for Montblanc laughed. He wore a wrinkled linen suit; on the portly side, he waddled just a bit as he led Ramil to the door and then across to the short-term parking garage, pointing him to a green GMC Jimmy.

The car was hot. Ramil lowered the window, as much to stare at the sights as suck in oxygen.

By the time they hit the highway and the local traffic, the air conditioner had lowered the temperature to a comfortable sixty-nine degrees. Montblanc turned off the radio—it had been playing Chopin—and raised the windows.

"Feel like talking?" he asked.

Ramil didn't, but saying that to Montblanc would only make things more difficult later on.

"I was exhausted," Ramil told him, trying to make his voice sound matter-of-fact. "And then, my hands shook. I just froze."

"Ever happen to you before?"

"No."

"How much sleep had you gotten?"

"None."

Montblanc nodded solemnly. Ramil wondered what the psychologist would say if he told him about the voice he'd heard.

He'd nod and say "hmmm." He would ask a few more questions, then give him some "diagnostic tool"—they were never called tests or grillings—when they got back to Fort Meade, or Crypto City as most of the NSA workers called their headquarters. The "tool" would let him slot Ramil into some numbered spot in the manual of mental disorders, a witchcraft's miscellany.

What if God truly had spoken to him? What then?

What then? Where would *that* fit in his manual?

Probably on the page between extreme panic attacks and schizophrenia, which was where Ramil figured he belonged.

"I apologized to Mr. Dean," said Ramil. "I just wasn't myself that day."

"Did you feel palpitations?" asked Montblanc.

"Nothing physical, just—very tired."

"You were breathing pretty heavily."

"Hyperventilating, you mean?"

"Were you?"

"I had to climb several flights of stairs. I'm afraid I'm no longer in great shape."

Montblanc began asking a series of questions that Ramil realized were designed to see if he was suffering post-traumatic stress—as if one could figure that out from a few questions asked in a car. Ramil answered them honestly—except for the one about whether he'd ever had an auditory hallucination.

"I don't believe I'm Joan of Arc," Ramil replied sharply.

"That would be interesting," said Montblanc, his tone light. "A Muslim thinking he was a Christian saint."

Even though he knew he should just keep quiet, there was something about the other man's flipness that annoyed Ramil. And so he asked, "Do you think God talks to people?"

Montblanc, clearly disturbed by the question, took his eyes off the road to look at him.

"Not to me," said Ramil, his voice steady. "To people like Joan of Arc."

"I would think she displayed the classic signs of schizophrenia," said Montblanc, returning his attention to the road. "Onset of adolescence, stress, and all that."

"God spoke to the Prophet Muhammad, may peace be unto him," said Ramil.

"Well, yes. To some people, God must speak," said Montblanc, obviously not wanting to contradict one of the main tenets of Ramil's religion. "It must be quite a burden for them. I'm sure others would think they were crazy."

"They'd probably think so themselves," said Ramil, reaching to turn the music back on.

CHAPTER 75

KENAN CONKEL SLID back in his seat in the upper New York state diner, refolding the map he had spread out on the table. He had the route completely memorized now and would refer to the map only if absolutely necessary.

He would get up from the booth, leave a tip, go to the cash register, pay, go down the five steps to the lot in front, get into the car. He would drive down the highway for two miles, find the first right easily. He would take the second left, go until he came to a T, turn right, make a quick left, drive for exactly 3.3 miles, find the county highway, take the first right. The lake would be to his left. There was a place to park exactly a half mile from the landing where Sheik Asad would arrive.

And if a policeman stopped him?

He wouldn't drive above the speed limit, so there would be no reason for a policeman to stop him.

But if he was stopped, he would pull over and take out his license, a perfect New York forgery that matched the ID of a real person. The digitized photo even looked like Kenan would have had he shaved. The cop would have no reason to check further.

And if he asked why a resident of Long Island was this far north?

He was driving out here because he was . . . visiting his mother, who lived near the lake. He had the address.

But he wasn't going there because sometimes a guy needed breathing room.

That part he'd have no trouble with. He knew that part by heart—had lived that part, was still living it.

He would not stare at the officer, but he wouldn't avoid eye contact either. He would force himself to smile.

That would be the most difficult thing. Kenan knew that he was not, by nature, someone who smiled easily. The reflection he saw in the diner window when he turned to it was that of a serious man—not sad, certainly, but not carefree either. He tried to smile, but it looked more like a smirk.

The image itself seemed slightly foreign. He'd trimmed his beard earlier in the day and wore a collared shirt with nice dress slacks and freshly shined shoes. The imam had advised him to look like a man on his way home from work, above suspicion. He was not to carry a bag or backpack, or do anything that would draw a second glance.

Kenan smiled again. This time it was a goofy, scared smile. Better than a smirk, but far from adequate.

He tried again. Better. A little better.

Smile as if you're happy, he told himself. He thought of his trip to Pakistan two summers before, his time at the madrasah. The religious school had filled him with a special peace, and understanding for the first time of why he was alive. Kenan had found Allah, and himself, two years before attending the school; there, listening to the teachers and living among the other committed Muslims, he finally felt at home. He understood the dichotomy of the world, how there were Followers of God and those who had given themselves to the Devil. And he realized that a believer such as himself would never be happy until the jihad was complete and the Followers of God had triumphed. To be involved in the struggle was a great honor, a blessing beyond blessings.

Kenan glanced at his watch. There were still four hours before Sheik Asad would arrive. The drive would take only two hours and he did not want to be too early; a car in that isolated area might arouse suspicion. He must stay here at least another half hour.

Kenan had met the sheik four times. Each was a riveting experience; angels walked with him for days afterward, filling him with confidence. Simply being in Asad's presence allowed Kenan to understand things he had never known, from passages of the Koran he hadn't studied to the tricks of the Crusaders and the Devil People, who lured the innocent with sex and drugs and money.

His heart was already pounding. Kenan turned his attention back to his tea, taking a small sip as he silently prayed he would be worthy of the great tasks that lay ahead.

CHAPTER 76

A CHARTERED GULFSTREAM took Dean from Istanbul to Canada, crossing Europe and the Atlantic in roughly twelve hours. Tommy Karr met him at Montréal-Trudeau airport, laughing and grabbing his luggage to lead him to the small customs area where he had to show his diplomatic passport.

"What's up?" asked Dean.

"Nothin'."

"Why are you laughing?"

"Beats bawlin', don't ya think? How was the flight?"

"Long."

"You shoulda tried my flight. I'm on this 777, right? *Coach.* Got this seven-year-old sitting next to me doing his math homework. I helped him most of the flight."

"Where's Asad?"

"House outside Montreal couple of miles from here. Lia's there. We got a pack of *federales* riding shotgun, too. FBI," added Karr, just in case Dean didn't pick up the slang. "And we got two Mounties who don't know the whole score, just that we're kinda sorta maybe interested in this guy, who maybe sorta is somebody, except we're not sayin' who. They're pretty good sports about it. Rubens sent your ol' friend Hernes Jackson up to hold their hands."

"Good choice," said Dean.

"Better him than me," said Karr, and he laughed again.

As usual, Asad had said very little, but his comments seemed to indicate he wasn't planning on staying here very long. The plan was to follow him as long as possible, hoping to get more information about whatever plans he had for an American operation. A large posse had been assembled and was waiting to swoop in when the time was right.

"The more people who know about this, the more chances something'll go wrong," said Dean.

"Agree with you there, partner. But it ain't my call."

DEAN AND KARR were just getting out of the airport parking lot when the Art Room told them that Asad had started to move. An army Super King Air electronic surveillance plane was circling nearby, so there was no need to hurry—a fact Dean emphasized as Karr mashed the gas pedal.

Dean also cinched his seatbelt. He'd driven with Karr enough to know that, whether he was rushing or not, the younger man looked at speed limits with a mathematician's eye—he doubled them, then used the result as a minimum speed.

Asad took Highway 10 heading east, backtracked around some local roads, then got back on the highway and drove for about fifteen minutes before getting off again. Finally he stopped at a small family restaurant in Bedford, within spitting distance of the U.S. border.

"Looks like he'll head for the border when it gets dark," predicted their runner, Sandy Chafetz, filling them in. "Don't get too close. Mr. Rubens doesn't want any pressure on him."

Karr turned to Dean and winked. "I'm kind of hungry," he said. "What do you think about us grabbing a bite in Bedford?"

"Tommy, you can't do that. He saw you on the plane, and even though Dean's changed his appearance back to normal—"

"Relax, Sandy, he's pulling your leg," Dean told her. "We'll keep our distance unless absolutely necessary."

Karr really was hungry, so they got some sandwiches from a deli, gassed up, and drove around the area trying to psych out where Asad would go. For the most part, the border between the two countries was invisible, as abstract as the line between close neighbors in a suburban subdivision.

Asad took his time having dinner, and when he finally moved out, it wasn't south as they'd expected but north, back in the direction of the highway. A series of feints across back roads followed before he got onto Route 401, the Canadian highway that ran along the northern shore of Lake Ontario. Dean admired Asad's caution and discipline—and was glad that it did him no good.

Asad got off the highway near Belleville and headed south, driving through tiny hamlets that had rolled up their sidewalks and gone to bed as soon as the sun set. By now they had realized he must be planning on getting into a boat, and the Art Room marshaled its task force resources, ever hopeful that Asad would meet with his American compatriots and discuss what he had in mind. Once they knew the target of the attack, they could move in.

Dean hoped that was soon. He wanted the operation to be over already. He'd slept on the plane, but still he was tired, and he missed Lia, who at last report was headed for Saudi Arabia.

Asad finally got into a small open boat on the Canadian shore of Lake Ontario; five minutes later he transferred to a slightly bigger but considerably faster speedboat and headed south. A Canadian police boat met Dean at a pier about a mile away. By then Asad was moving east, crossing the lake in the direction of Sackets Harbor south of Watertown, New York.

The Canadian and American police forces as well as customs and border patrols had a lot of experience with smugglers in the area, who used the lake to transport everything from marijuana to Cuban cigars to prescription drugs. Under other circumstances, the Canadian boat captain assured Dean, the small speedboat would have been stopped and inspected before it reached American waters.

Dean wasn't so sure. The radar aboard the Canadian vessel lost the speedboat within a few minutes and Dean had to guide them using information from the aircraft above.

THE YOUNG MAN who met Asad on the pier looked as if he'd been constructed of paper and wood. The strings of tiny white lights strung across the dock made his skin seem nearly translucent. It would not take much to knock him over.

Asad had not been told who would meet him, and it was not until he was only a few feet from the young man that he saw who it was. He had met Kenan Conkel three years before on his first trip to Detroit and immediately recognized his value as a "clearskin": a dedicated Muslim who could pass through any screening without attracting attention. Recruits such as Kenan were rare jewels, to be hoarded until the proper moment. The boy had been given a progression of tasks to prove his loyalty, and yet at the same time great pains had been taken to keep him unknown, not only to law enforcement agencies, but to the sort of databases that the American CIA could tap for information. He had no credit card, no bank account; his license was supplied by the network. He was a ghost—almost literally, Asad thought, looking at the boy's thin frame. Asad had met him a total of four times, and each time he seemed more frail than before. But God's will would make him strong.

Kenan had been chosen for this mission not for his strength, or even his appearance, but for his intelligence. He had done well in the training, both at the holy school in Pakistan and with the seamen, who had no reason to be easy on him. A mujahideen need not be big in stature, so long as he was strong in spirit.

"Sheik?"

"So good to see you again," said Asad.

The young man bowed his head as if he were a servant, then reached to take Asad's bag with his change of clothes and Koran. Asad turned and signaled to the boatman who had taken him here that he could go.

"I am tired and would like to rest before we set out," Asad told Kenan. "My head aches. Is there a place we can rest?"

"I could find a motel."

"Please."

BY THE TIME Dean and Karr landed on shore, Asad had been taken to a motel several miles up the highway, apparently for the night. The Art Room directed them to a car rental place about a mile up the highway, where a grumpy night clerk rented them the largest car on the lot—a two-door Ford Focus. The car seemed to shudder as Karr got into the driver's seat—not that Dean would have blamed it if it did. They drove in a circle around the lot of the motel where Asad was staying, planting two video bugs before heading to a nearby Red Roof Inn. There they flipped a coin to see who got to sleep first; Karr won and was snoring in less than ten minutes.

CHAPTER 77

THE SAUDI CUSTOMS officer flipped through Lia's official passport briskly, his face tight with disapproval. Lia kept her mouth shut; the subjects she was trailing had arrived more than four hours earlier, and she didn't want to give the man any excuse to turn his dislike for Americans into active though unknowing obstruction.

Finally the man handed her passport back, waving her through with a frown.

Terrence Pinchon waited for her in a white Mercedes just outside the airport building. Lia pulled open the car door and slid in without saying a word.

"How you doing, soldier?" said Pinchon.

"Been a long time since I was a soldier."

"Time just flies when you're having fun, huh?"

"I guess."

"What do you think of the NSA, anyway? All that high-tech geewhiz crap get in the way of what's real?"

"What's real?"

Pinchon thought her remark was a joke and laughed. Lia, not in the mood to make small talk—or, more importantly, to press him on Kyrgyzstan—changed the subject.

"Where are the Saudis?"

"Al and Amin are five miles out of town, in a fancy compound with all the forbidden amenities of the West," said Pinchon. "You sure these guys are al-Qaeda?"

"I'm sure they met with Asad."

"Saudi intelligence claims they're not on any watch list. And they watch everybody."

"I'll bet."

"You ever been in Saudi Arabia before? Interesting place. A lot of fanatics. And half of them are in the government. Everybody's got—what's the old expression? bucoo bucks?"

"Money interest you?"

"Of course."

"I didn't think it did."

While Pinchon laughed, Lia thought back to their days together. He wasn't one of the people who groused about how much more "contractors" were being paid for doing next to nothing, or who talked about tripling his pay when his enlistment ended. Nor had he seemed interested in expensive things.

He did like cars and having a good time—those things *were* expensive. They'd spent a few days together in a nice hotel in Puerto Rico . . . a very nice hotel.

Where had he gotten the money for that?

Maybe he hadn't changed—maybe he'd been a slime and a jerk all along and she'd missed it, fooled by lust into seeing what she wanted to see.

"Here we go," Pinchon said, pulling off the road. The headlights reflected off painted stones; if it weren't for them, the driveway would have been impossible to see, since it was nearly the same color as the surrounding desert in the dark. An Arab-looking man stood in front of large iron gates that barred the way into a walled compound. Pinchon had to show his credentials before the man would open the gates.

"Locals. Very suspicious," he said as he pulled up in front of the low-slung house.

"How close are we?" Lia asked.

"We can see the house from the roof," said Pinchon. "Embassy rents the place, just happened to be close by. One of the deputy secretaries in charge of serving tea or some such BS lives here. Nice spread, huh? Wait until you see the pool."

Lia followed him inside. There were three Saudi intelligence agents and four CIA people sitting in the living room. The TV had been pulled away from the wall; wires snaked from it to a control box on the coffee table, and from there down the hall. An infrared video of the compound they were watching was on the television screen, the green shadows casting an eerie hue around the room.

"How do I get on the roof?" Lia asked.

"Down the hall, hang a right, go out the door. There's a ladder outside. If Reisler's snoring, give him a kick in the ribs. It always makes him turn over."

Lia found Reisler at the eyepiece of a 1200mm Zhumell-Kepher telescope, panning it slowly across the compound where the two Saudis had gone.

"Hello," he said, not looking over.

"What are they doing?"

"Looks like they're in the second room from the right in the back. Can't really tell what they're doing. At least two other people are in there with them." He pointed to a parabolic microphone mounted on a large stand nearby. The microphone picked up vibrations from surfaces such as windows. "Haven't gotten much."

"Why don't we get closer?"

"Saudis won't let us."

"They're in charge?"

"Yes and no. It's their country." Reisler finally looked up. "Want a peek?"

Lia bent over the eyepiece. She could see the window of the room clearly; the shades were drawn but two heads were near the bottom of the frame, bobbing every so often.

"Why can't we hear anything?" Lia asked. "Are we too far?"

"I think they may have something against the windows, muffling any possible vibrations. And between you and me, these mikes never work as good as they do in the movies, you know?"

Lia swung the telescope down and started examining the house. In order to bug it, she'd have to get inside.

The old deliveryman ruse?

Too obvious. And she couldn't do it; they'd seen her in Turkey.

Maybe Desk Three could cause a blackout, or mess up their phone.

Lia stood up. She pulled the satphone from her pocket with one hand and turned the com system on with the other. As she did, a pair of helicopters passed overhead from the south. They were only about fifty feet off the ground, still descending; the vibrations shook the roof. Lia turned and saw them descending toward the compound. Meanwhile, several white and light blue Saudi police cars were charging up the road in the other direction.

"The Saudis are raiding the compound," yelled Lia as she ran to the ladder. Pinchon, cursing, met her in the backyard; they ran to the car, trailed by two of the other agents.

They were just pulling up to the roadblock when the rear of the house burst into flames. Lia stared at the red ribbon of light encircling the roof; a moment later a tremendous boom shook the air.

CHAPTER 78

ASAD BIN TAYSR and his driver got up before dawn to say their prayers and were on the road a short time later. Dean and Karr followed along, their distance varying from a quarter mile to nearly two, depending on the road. The driver had not been identified; his picture and voice patterns had been compared to files of known operatives, but there were no matches. Working on the premise that he would be from the state where the car was registered, the NSA had used an administrative subpoena to access New York State driver's license images, but the image captured on the video bugs matched more than five thousand drivers, and winnowing the list had failed to produce a solid ID. It wasn't clear whether the car had been stolen or its plates simply switched from a similar vehicle in Long Island; that lead was being followed up gingerly, so as not to tip off whoever was helping Asad that they were on to him.

If it became necessary to grab Asad, Dean and Karr would be the tip of the spear in the snatch plan, backed by several dozen federal agents shadowing Asad in helicopters and vans. In the meantime, their main job was to stay awake.

Which wasn't difficult in their less than comfortable Ford Focus, especially with someone like Tommy Karr at the wheel, who managed to find every pothole in the pavement. By nine A.M., they were on the New York State Thruway, heading westward toward Rochester a half mile behind Asad's light blue Buick Regal. The posted speed limit was 65 miles per hour. Most vehicles did about 80. Asad's driver was going a steady 56.

"He's gonna get pulled over for obstructing traffic," Karr complained. "Ten bucks."

The Regal pulled off at a rest area just beyond Batavia. Dean and Karr followed, taking a spot near the very end of the lot. Both Asad and his driver got out.

"I hope he's changing cars," said Karr. "Or at least drivers. Want to get something to eat?"

"I'm not hungry," Dean told him.

"Hey, suit yourself," said Karr.

Karr trotted in the direction of the snack building. Dean got out and stretched his legs, walking toward the grass beyond the lot. This part of New York was farmland; ignore the cars and squint into the distance, and it looked much as it had nearly two hundred years before, after pioneers had cut back the trees to plant corn and let their cows graze.

Dean turned around slowly, pretending to be absorbed in the view, though he was really trying to spot a substitute car. There were about thirty other vehicles here, and more on the other side of the building where the gas pumps were. Any one of them could be waiting for Asad. Any one of them could be filled with explosives, ready to be detonated at Asad's whim.

He folded his arms, waiting.

"Charlie, Asad is coming out of the building now," said Rockman. "All right, we have a good view of the driver. Same guy."

Dean walked slowly back to the car. He was surprised to find Karr already inside, a McDonald's super-size box of french fries in his hand. The small Focus smelled like the kitchen of a fast-food restaurant. "Big Mac?"

"No thanks."

"He's moving," said Rockman. "Sounds like they're going to Detroit. The driver mentioned the interchange there."

"You ID the driver yet?" Dean asked.

"Negative. The closest match is a Jewish guy in Hempstead; funny how computers work, huh?"

"Yeah," said Dean. He'd have to remember Rockman's re-mark; the runner generally put a nearly blind trust in the high-tech gadgets he controlled from his bunker.

"They're on the highway. You guys should get going, right?"

"We're on it, Rockman," said Karr, chugging the french fries and then backing out of the parking space. "Detroit or bust."

CHAPTER 79

"YOU DIDN'T EXPECT Saudi intelligence to apologize, did you?" Pinchon plopped down in the sofa of the borrowed embassy house and threw his head back on the cushion. "Being Arab means never having to say you're sorry."

Lia pursed her lips. She didn't want the Saudis to apologize; she wanted them to turn back the clock and not have tried the raid in the first place.

"I don't blame them," continued Pinchon. "They figured their oil fields were threatened and they dealt with it."

"Oh, yeah, like they had enough information to go on." Lia stalked back and forth across the empty living room. She'd turned her communication system off so the Art Room wouldn't hear her venting. An embassy driver was due to pick her up and take her to the airport at any minute.

The house they'd been watching had been leveled by the explosion, which had undoubtedly been rigged beforehand to prevent capture. Besides the al-Qaeda operatives, three women and two servants who'd been inside at the time, as well as two Saudi policemen, had been killed; another cop had been seriously wounded. The house was a charred mess of rubble and ash.

The Saudi intelligence officer in charge of the raid claimed that one of the suspects had sent a message to a worker at the state oil agency implying that there was a plan to detonate the doomsday device protecting Saudi oil fields from foreign attack. The device, a network of explosives rigged across the wellheads and pipeline systems, would have been a major terrorist prize.

The NSA had also intercepted the message. It was far from clear that the doomsday safeguard had been the target. If it was, there must be at least a dozen more al-Qaeda operatives in place to carry it out. It seemed unlikely now that they would be caught.

"The Saudis blew it," said Lia. "They should have known the house would be rigged to explode. They went in there without even talking to us. Your boss—"

"My boss?"

"The station chief was supposed to get them to cooperate, not play cowboys. We could have gone in there ourselves."

"Then we would have been the ones blown up," said Pinchon. "And I don't work for Riyadh, thank you very much."

"Whatever."

"You're just mad because they didn't ask us. Come on, Lia, what'd you expect them to do? Wait around until it's too late to act? Besides, the world's better off—two pests have been exterminated. Good riddance."

Pinchon got up from the couch. "You're pretty when you're pissed off, you know that? But then again, you're always pissed off."

He put his hands on her hips. Lia tensed but didn't push him away.

"Miss me?" he asked.

"No."

He leaned to kiss her. She moved away.

"Hey, hey, I'm not going to bite," he told her.

"What happened to you, Terry?"

"Come on, Lia. Obviously I can't talk about it, right?"

"That's bull."

He smirked and held up his hands.

"I don't mean just on the mission," said Lia. "You changed."

"Changed?"

"You couldn't have let me know somehow that you were alive."

Pinchon shrugged. That was all the explanation she was ever going to get. But it said it all, didn't it?

No, the killer was that she had felt something for him, and that even now her heart was pounding—if he stopped smirking, if he came clean, if he said he loved her, what would she do?

Pinchon reached for her, but she backed away.

"This isn't the place," she told him.

"Where, then?"

"Nowhere." Lia turned on her com system. "Where the hell's that car to the airport?"

CHAPTER 80

"I THINK DR. RAMIL could certainly use some rest," Kevin Montblanc told Rubens after he returned from the White House. "On the other hand, I think he feels embarrassed by what happened and wants to make amends. He asked about his patient—he still calls him his patient."

"Was the incident in Istanbul an anomaly, or can he no longer take the pressure?" Rubens asked Montblanc.

"I don't know. I'd recommend giving him a few weeks off. When he comes back, I could reinterview, observe him for a while. We might even send him on a training exercise to see how he holds up."

The problem was, Rubens needed him right now. The doctor who had been standing by with the team in Detroit had come down with the flu and had a 104° fever. The Art Room had two military doctors available as backups, but Rubens much preferred using one of his own people for security reasons.

Still, if Ramil wasn't up to it, there was nothing he could do.

"What if I needed to use him right away?" said Rubens.

"Well, in that case I'd keep an eye on him. If you really needed him."

"Where is he?"

"Downstairs in the squad room. I said you wanted to talk to him."

"Very good."

* * *

RAMIL SIPPED THE iced tea, letting the cold liquid fill his mouth before swallowing. The squad room—the ops' nickname for the large lounge where Desk Three missions were debriefed—had the air of an English country club, with thick leather furniture and a variety of amusements. It was also quiet, off-limits except to Deep Black ops and the few people who worked directly with them. Ramil felt quite comfortable here, calm and alone. Safe.

What would a mental breakdown feel like? Something similar to what he had experienced in Istanbul, he thought, but it would last much longer. His was only temporary, a burp—he'd been tired.

"Doctor, I'm glad to see you made it back," said William Rubens, striding into the room. He pulled a leather club chair over and sat on the edge, pitched forward like a dentist on a stool about to examine his teeth. "How are you feeling?"

"More relaxed. I think I was overstressed by the heat and the jet lag."

"It was considerable stress." Rubens nodded. "Perhaps you'd like a long vacation."

"No." Ramil felt his heart begin to race. "I'm fine. Where do you need me to be?"

"I don't want to push you beyond your means."

Ramil felt angry, as if Rubens had called him a coward.

"I'm quite capable," he said. "It was a temporary glitch. You know the brain is a sensitive organ. Too much stimulation—too much adrenaline, a change in the blood flow—we react. We have to react. I'm over it."

Rubens stared at him.

"I've been through much worse situations," Ramil told him, striving to make his voice as conversational as possible. "I can't tell you how many times I had to operate while we were being shelled."

Actually, he could—fifteen in total, though only two had been truly scary.

"Morris is sick, I heard," added Ramil. "So I should be there, in the background, in case anything goes wrong. I'm familiar with the patient. He has a heart condition. We don't want to lose him."

Rubens frowned, ever so slightly, but Ramil had seen that frown before; it meant he agreed, though with reservations. Desk Three did not have unlimited resources; it carried as many doctors as Art Room supervisors, and the latter were considerably more important to the success of any given mission. If Ramil didn't go, Rubens would have to bring in a doctor who, even if he was on active military service—not likely in the States—would not have passed the rigorous security and background checks the NSA routinely required of even contract employees. Worse, Rubens would have no direct control over the doctor, since he would answer to a military commander. And Rubens was nothing if not a control freak.

"Ms. Telach will make the arrangements," said Rubens finally. "If possible, I'd like you to leave within the hour."

"Where am I going?"

"Detroit. Asad bin Taysr arrived there an hour ago."

CHAPTER 81

"THE BROTHER SAYS the imam requested a special meeting after Friday prayers."

Marid Dabir nodded, carefully controlling the expression on his face. While he trusted his informant, prudence required that he not give any sign of emotion. And besides, the fact that there was a special meeting did not necessarily mean Asad was in Detroit. Dabir would have to continue methodically, discovering where the traitor was and then delivering justice.

Dabir had arrived in the city from Ontario the night before, riding the bus through the tunnel between the two cities. The passport formalities were trivial. His prematurely gray hair made him appear too old to be a threat; the al-Qaeda organizer did not fit the profile of a terrorist.

Nor did Asad.

So how would Dabir find the so-called Red Lion of Mohammed, Islam's most perfidious traitor?

Dabir could not confront the imam, who owed his allegiance to Asad and would surely believe him rather than a man known to have fallen from favor before being banished to Germany. Nor could he send one of his people to the mosque; with the exception of his informer, they were unknown to the imam and would not be trusted with important information.

He would have the mosque watched from a distance. Sooner or later, Asad would show himself.

And if he didn't?

Then it would mean that he wasn't here. At that point he would formulate a new plan.

"Brother, have I done well?" asked his informant, snapping Dabir from his contemplative daze.

"Extremely," Dabir told him. "Extremely."

CHAPTER 82

THE AIR CONDITIONING in the secure conference room in the White House basement was on the fritz, and Rubens estimated that the temperature was no higher than sixty-five degrees. CIA Director Louis Zackart and Debra Collins huddled around a carafe of coffee for warmth. Even Secretary of Defense Art Blanders, who made a habit of attending even the most formal cabinet meeting in shirt sleeves, had left his suit jacket on.

Bing entered the room with the president. Rubens reminded himself not to read anything into that; the national security advisor might very well have been stalking him in the hall.

"Gentlemen, ladies, good morning," said Marcke, his tone as brisk as the air in the room, "thank you for getting up early for me. Let's get going. Where are we, Billy?"

"The Saudi situation is stable," said Rubens.

He ran over the highlights quickly, indicating that the Saudis had moved after tentatively linking the two al-Qaeda contacts to the oil fields; more arrests were expected and the entire military was on alert. He then moved on to Asad—identified even here only as Red Lion—noting that he had spent the night in Detroit.

"The operation is proceeding, but it is at a difficult stage," said Rubens. "We still do not know what the American target is."

"An attack on the Alaskan pipeline would be on par with an attack against the Saudi oil fields," said Defense Secretary Blanders. "It'll be on that sort of scale."

Rubens listened as other possible targets were named: natural gas pipelines, large oil fields in Texas and the Gulf of Mexico. But the target did not have to be bigger than the Saudi oil fields to have a large impact on the U.S. Striking even a small American facility would send tremors through the commodities market. Hurricane Katrina had proven how sensitive the system was to disruption, and while that disaster had by now been accommodated, the market was still shaky. The price of oil had jumped twenty dollars a barrel following the attack in Germany. A successful strike in the U.S. might be triple that, at least in the short term. The successive attacks, fully successful or not, would make it seem as if al-Qaeda was gaining momentum in its war on the West. Within weeks it would cost over two hundred dollars to fill an economy car with gas.

"Rather than guessing or waiting for Red Lion to tell us what he has in mind," said Bing, "we should arrest him now and find out what the target is."

"I doubt we could break him in time," said Rubens. "I doubt we can break him at all."

"Maybe arresting him will stop the operation altogether," she said.

"Arresting al-Qaeda's number three man last year didn't stop the attack on our embassy in Pakistan. I doubt it would work now."

"These points were discussed during the planning stage," said Blanders. "I seriously doubt any interrogation will be as effective as the implanted bug. And if we want to put him on trial—"

"We can't put him on trial," said Bing. "If it comes out that we implanted a bug in him, we're finished."

Rubens didn't particularly relish the idea of a trial; too much could go wrong, and inevitably some information about the operation would slip out. Still, he resented Bing's implication that Desk Three was operating illegally, and her insistence on revisiting decisions that had been made before she was appointed.

He resented Bing, period.

"The legal issues were thoroughly researched beforehand," said Rubens. "This is just another instance of electronic information gathering."

"I've read the background legal papers, thank you, Mr. Rubens," said Bing. "And in no case do they mention what would happen in a U.S. court. The idea was *always* to render Red Lion to Yemen for justice. Assuming he was alive."

"We'll have the lawyers work this bullshit out," said the president angrily. "I want the bastard to pay for what he's done, and I want him to do it here. I want a trial—I want to show the world exactly what kind of slime advocates killing innocent women and children. Billy—have your people stay on him until they know exactly what the target is, then I want him in custody. The bug won't be used to make the case. The attorney general assures me we'll have plenty of evidence without it."

"Yes, sir, Mr. President," said Rubens as Marcke rose and abruptly left the room.

CHAPTER 83

FRIDAY AFTERNOON PRAYERS were held in a storefront mosque, a humble, shabby building at the outer edge of Detroit. The brothers, about two dozen in all, were mostly young men whose fathers had immigrated; to a man they were struggling to find their way in their ancestors' faith.

Asad, who had passed through a similar challenge himself, noted how carefully the imam answered their questions. The man was not the most eloquent—he rambled and at times lost the thread of his thoughts—but he had studied with the right teachers and lived in Afghanistan for a time, before the triumph of 9/11 had brought the struggle to the next phase. His message to the small congregation was a strong one, even if his sentences were not: the Followers of God must do all that they could to survive the Devil's onslaught.

A call to arms, yet one that could not be faulted by the most severe police spy.

"This way, sheik," Kenan told Asad as the others began filing out.

Asad followed him to a back room and then down a set of creaking steps to a dank basement populated with cobwebs. For a moment his faith deserted him. Asad worried that he had been betrayed, brought here to die. He tensed, waiting for the inevitable blow even as he followed Kenan into a pitch-black room.

The young man retrieved a small flashlight from his pocket. Its dim beacon fluttered across a floor of bare dirt, picking its way across cement blocks and an assortment of dilapidated pieces of wood.

I am walking through the outer precincts of hell, Asad thought. The devil will tempt me and test my courage, but I will not fail.

Kenan stopped before a large metal door. He held up his hand to Asad, gesturing that he should be silent. Then he knocked twice. The door swung open; light flooded into Asad's eyes. When he blinked, a man with an M16 stood in front of him.

"Muhammad's Lion is here to join us," Kenan told the man with the gun, his hushed voice full of reverence.

The man stepped back.

The room looked like the inside of an expensive coffeehouse in Egypt. It smelled of sweet tobacco, though none of the dozen occupants were smoking. As Asad entered, all of the men rose quickly, bowing their heads and even closing their eyes in respect. Asad had personally chosen only Kenan and Nathan Green; the others had been selected by the imam, with some additional vetting by another al-Qaeda operative.

"Sheik, we have waited night and day for your return!" thundered Nathan. A short and stocky man whose light-skinned face had the look of a jester, Nathan was given to overblown rhetoric and superlatives. But he was dependable, and as far as Asad could tell from their encounters, sincere though emotional.

They embraced.

"We are safe here," said Nathan. "Let me show you."

He gestured at one of the brothers nearby, who produced a small radiolike device and began waving it around the air. "For bugs," added Nathan.

Asad, appreciating that his host was attempting to be discreet, smiled and held out his hands. "You must check me like you check everyone. There should be no margin for error."

CHAPTER 84

"CHECKING HIM FOR bugs," Karr told Dean. "Think they'll find any?"

Dean ignored his partner's laugh, studying the satellite locator map on the PDA. The meeting was being held two blocks away in the subbasement of a building across from the mosque Asad had gone into for services earlier.

The Art Room was feeding the intercepted conversations back to them; it played like a low, slightly off-tune radio station in the background.

"Ranting about oil again," said Karr. "At least it's in English."

"Tell me if he explains why he murdered people."

"You think he's got a good explanation?"

"It's not something to joke about, Tommy."

"I'm not joking," said Karr—but he laughed anyway, a habit he couldn't avoid, Dean realized. "He's a psycho. He doesn't have an explanation. Not one that makes sense."

"I guess," said Dean. "The problem is he feels compelled to share his insanity with the rest of the world."

CHAPTER 85

THE MESSAGE ON Rubens' secure BlackBerry consisted of two words: "Call me."

Not unusual in the least, except that it had come from Debra Collins at the CIA. Collins almost never used the secure instant messaging system to contact Rubens.

Rubens went to one of the consoles at the back of the Art Room with a secure phone. To his surprise, Collins picked up right away.

"That was quick," she said.

"I gathered it was important."

"Lahore Two says the network's target is Houston. Al-Qaeda has purchased somewhere over a hundred tons of commercial-grade explosives and can use them in the operation."

Lahore Two was a CIA source in Pakistan who had an enviable track record predicting al-Qaeda moves. While his identity was a secret to Rubens, the pattern of his revelations made it obvious he was a triple agent in the Pakistan intelligence service—probably a Pak "turned" by al-Qaeda and then turned again by the CIA. Rubens did not concern himself with the details; the source's true allegiance would be to himself in any event.

"Nothing more specific?" asked Rubens.

"He's promised a diagram or a map. I'll have a copy sent to you as soon we get it. Assuming he carries through," added Collins, her voice making it clear that the source didn't always deliver on such promises. "They've been planning this for some time. No target date. Oil or energy is somehow involved. I gather that meshes with what you've already heard from Red Lion. I'll send you a copy of the officer's report, if you'd like."

"I would. Do you see a link?"

"Don't you?"

Rubens saw many; that was the problem. Raw intelligence was a Rorschach test, subject to the preconceived notions of the tester as well as the viewer.

"We're of course passing this along to the National Security Council. I thought you'd appreciate knowing before they did," added Collins. In effect, she was telling him that she would have to pass the information on to Bing—and more importantly, that she didn't want Rubens blindsided by that.

Collins an ally? It hardly secmed believable. But perhaps Bing was moving against her as well.

"Thank you," said Rubens. "I appreciate it."

CHAPTER 86

AS ASAD FINISHED his speech, he turned and looked at each of the men in the room, holding their gaze for a few seconds before turning to the next. Two blinked and looked to the ground when he made eye contact. He decided they couldn't be trusted and would be removed from the operation. That left him four to choose from for the assignment.

Kenan had to go. Only he or Nathan could work on the bridge, and the charismatic Nathan would be more valuable recruiting more brothers and organizing cells; the man was clearly a leader. Kenan wasn't, but he would be working under the guidance of another brother who was already in place.

So one from the other three. The short one seemed a good match, bulky where Kenan was thin. But no, there was something weak in his face.

None of them, then. He would send Kenan, and another brother from New Mexico, his next stop.

Yes, that was the way to proceed.

"A message will be sent if you are needed," he said. "If you are not called today, you will be called tomorrow or the next day, or the next. May Allah guide your steps."

The men nodded. Asad turned to Kenan, whose round blue eyes locked onto his. "Let's go."

"Yes, sheik."

The youth remained fixed in place, still under the spell of Asad's speech, possibly even awed by his presence. It struck Asad that such devotion in one so young was dangerous; it meant that his judgment was impaired by emotion. Such a person's faith, seemingly rock solid, could be shaken by events. Better that one come to believe through a long, difficult process, wrestling with his faith so that his will was tempered and strong.

Finally Kenan snapped out of it.

"This way," he said. "Come."

They walked back into the dank basement. To Asad, the route seemed the same, but instead of the mosque they emerged on the first floor of an apartment building. He smelled something frying as they left the building. A sharp pang of hunger followed.

"Could we get something to eat before you take me to the airport?" he asked Kenan.

"Yes. Yes. I know a very good restaurant, owned by an Egyptian. A reliable man. He is not a brother," added Kenan quickly. "But very religious. Four or five blocks away."

"Let's go."

The day had begun dark and threatening, but the sun had gradually chased all of the clouds away. They turned the corner onto a wider avenue, filled with people. The facades were noticeably brighter, the area more prosperous than the one they had just walked from.

It had always been a mystery to Asad why the Lord had allowed the infidels to become so powerful and prosperous. Asad had been fortunate in his life to meet many devoted brothers, men of devotion and good will. What plan did Allah have for them? Where was the suffering to lead?

The thought occurred to him as he saw the shiny stone facade of a Christian church across the street, its bell tower rising high above the main building. It was a sharp contrast to the dilapidated mosque where he had just been. He was not jealous, and he did not curse or berate God as a sinner might. But he wondered why the Lord allowed the nonbelievers this moment of prosperity.

Perhaps to provide the proper challenge to people like Asad himself, the chosen ones who would establish the new order. The idea was heady and full of conceit, and yet it was only logical.

Asad began to smile. As he did, pain seized his chest, powerful pain that dashed him to the pavement and pinned him against the concrete.

Kenan stared down at him. Asad struggled to get up, but all he could do was ask, "Why?"

CHAPTER 87

DEAN SAW THE commotion a few seconds after the Art Room told him that Asad had collapsed.

"We have an ambulance on the way," said Rockman. "There's an emergency trauma center three blocks away."

"Do you have somebody there?"

"Ambassador Jackson and Dr. Ramil are on their way. Tommy's coming up behind you on foot."

Dean stayed on the edge of the crowd, eying the young man kneeling next to Asad. While he'd seen the kid's face in the video captures plenty of times by now, it was shocking to see how young he looked in person—seventeen or eighteen at most, as young as he'd been when he'd gone into the marines.

"All right, let me see if I can help," yelled Tommy Karr, pushing through the crowd from the opposite direction. "Back up—let's give the man some air."

"You a doctor?" asked the young man with Asad.

"Paramedic." Karr flashed a quick smile and dropped to his knee. The op wasn't lying—he'd had to take advanced medical training to join Deep Black's operations team. Tommy being Tommy, he'd gone beyond the basic requirements and was fully qualified as a paramedic.

"First thing we want to do here," Karr bellowed, "is everybody move back. Three steps. Anybody got any water?"

"How bad does he look, Mr. Dean?" said Rubens in Dean's ear.

Dean edged away from the others. "Pretty pale."

"If there is any way to obtain information about the young man who is accompanying him, that would be most useful."

"Just what I was thinking."

HERNES JACKSON HAD set up a liaison office at a building used by the Treasury Department; this happened to be only a few blocks from the emergency trauma center. As soon as the Art Room alerted him to Asad's "episode," he went down the hall to fetch Dr. Ramil.

"There's been an unexpected problem," said Jackson, quickly explaining the situation. Ramil rose from his seat without saying anything, following Jackson out to the front of the building where a driver had been stationed to wait for him.

In the car, Jackson put on a faux hearing aid, which used a short-distance radio signal to connect to the satellite communications unit in his jacket pocket. The unit would allow him to get updates from the Art Room without attracting suspicion at the trauma center.

"Tommy Karr will be with him," said Marie Telach. "You'll have a little time. If it becomes necessary for Dr. Ramil to treat him while he's conscious, we'll have to roll up the operation and arrest him; we don't want to take the chance of tipping him off at this point."

"Understood," said Jackson, who also understood that the preferred option was to continue things as they were.

The trauma clinic—essentially a hospital emergency room without the hospital—was located in a shopping mall at the edge of a residential area, a kind of no-man's-land between a row of dilapidated four-room tract houses and a parcel of condominiums converted from an old factory complex. While the staff was expert in dealing with extreme cases like gunshot wounds, the overwhelming majority of their time was spent on things like the flu and sprains. The waiting area was full to overflowing when Jackson and Ramil arrived, and even Jackson's untrained eye discerned that there were few if any extreme medical emergencies among the patients. That was good, he thought; it made him less of an intruder.

Jackson walked to the receptionist's glass window, rapping on it to get the woman's attention.

"I'm Hernes Jackson and this is Dr. Ramil," he said through the glass. "I believe you're expecting a patient of Dr. Ramil's, a Mr. Rahman," added Jackson, giving the pseudonym Asad had been using.

The receptionist frowned at him, and for a moment Jackson wondered if she was going to hand him a clipboard and ask that he fill out his medical history. But another woman in the office had overheard him and got up from her desk.

"Oh, yes, your office just called. The patient hasn't arrived."

"Is there a place where we could wash up?"

"This way," she said, going over to the door.

RAMIL'S TENUOUS CONFIDENCE vanished when he walked down the clinic's white hall toward the staff area at the back. His legs wobbled so badly that twice he had to put his hand out against the wall to keep himself upright.

He is evil. He has gone against the faith and should be punished.

I am not a murderer, Ramil thought to himself.

It is not murder if it is the will of God.

I'm cracking up. The stress has sent me over the edge.

Oh, God, why are you making me crazy? How can you let me lose my mind?

You are as sane as everyone around you. The Deep Black people are seeking the same goal, but they are weak and will let him escape. You must act. Do not be afraid.

"Dr. Ramil?"

Ramil pushed himself away from the wall as Hernes Jackson turned the corner.

"Are you all right?" asked Jackson.

"I just stopped for a drink of water." Ramil pointed to the fountain. "I felt a little thirsty."

"Nervous?"

"Of course not."

Ramil didn't want to admit he was losing his mind. He couldn't.

"Stay in the background as we discussed," said Jackson. "There's no need for you to see him; the doctor here is competent. If it gets to the point where he suspects the implant, then we'll give him the story. But not until. Understood?"

"Of course."

Ramil had shaved his beard, dyed his hair, and donned glasses—he could not look more different than he had in Istanbul. Asad was his patient; he felt he should be the one to examine him, rather than hovering in the background in case something went wrong. But he nodded.

A man in his late twenties strode toward them down the hall. A black man with large, round glasses and a small, star-shaped scar at the top of his forehead, he wore a white lab coat and the slightly overconfident air of a doctor about a year removed from his training.

"Doctors. I'm Dr. Joshua Penney. Can you fill me in on what's going on?"

Jackson introduced himself and Ramil, then gave the cover story that they had prepared, saying that he had received a call a short while ago that one of his patients had an apparent heart attack on the street.

"Must have some clout," said Penney.

"Doctor, perhaps we could discuss this in a place that's more private," said Jackson.

"All right," said Penney, puzzled. He led them to a small office at the back and shut the door.

"We're with the government. I am not a doctor, but Dr. Ramil is. This is not time for a vita, but I assure you he is quite distinguished. The patient who's coming in is a very important man who has to be handled very carefully."

"Uh-huh," said Penney. "You don't think I can do the job?"

Why would Allah not talk to you? You either believe in God, or you don't. If you believe in God, why would He not talk to you?

"I'm sure you can do a fine job," said Jackson. "We're not here to interfere. If there's a crisis or you require assistance, then Dr. Ramil can help."

Ramil heard the ambulance siren outside.

"You don't think an inner-city doctor can handle a heart attack?"

"On the contrary," said Jackson. "We have every confidence."

"Until something goes wrong, is that it?" Penney turned to Ramil. "Let's see what's wrong with him. Doctor, this way, please."

CHAPTER 88

KENAN STOOD LOST on the sidewalk as the door to the ambulance closed. Two policemen were pushing him back, saying something to him he couldn't understand.

"Do you want to go with your friend?" asked a man behind him.

Kenan turned around. The man who had spoken was about his father's age, perhaps even a little older, but in much better shape. His beefy arms flexed as he pointed down the street.

"I have a car," said the man. "Come on."

Kenan started to follow, then stopped. Would Asad have wanted this?

"They won't let you in the ambulance unless you're related to him," said the man. "I'll take you to the clinic."

"He's not my friend—he's my teacher," said Kenan.

"Come on."

CHARLIE DEAN LED the boy to a Toyota they'd left in the area earlier as a backup. Dean found himself snarled in traffic after half a block, but that was fine—he wanted to prolong the drive as long as possible.

"Is he a good teacher?" Dean asked the young man.

"The best."

"You in high school?"

"College."

"Which one?" Dean said nonchalantly.

"College? Uh, Upper Michigan."

"Good school?"

"Uh-huh."

"What are you studying?"

"Like, uh, engineering."

"Good career."

The kid shrugged.

"Probably make a lot of money when you graduate, huh?" suggested Dean.

"Money's not everything."

"Hell of a traffic jam, huh?" said Dean, unable to think of anything else to get the kid talking. He stuck out his hand. "My name's Charlie Dyson."

The kid took Dean's hand. His nails were long, his grip weak.

"I'm Kenan."

"Kenan?"

"Louis Kenan."

"You from Detroit?"

"Uh-huh."

"I'm from California," said Dean. "Moved around a bit. Spent time in Arizona, back East north of Philadelphia."

"Uh-huh."

Dean thought of telling the kid he'd been in the marines but decided against it; that wasn't the sort of thing that would interest a terrorist wannabe.

What would? He couldn't think of anything to say to get him talking.

What he wanted to say was simple:

Listen, jackass, do you know what you're involved in? Are you insane? You got about three seconds to straighten yourself out.

That would work real, real well. Dean even had the perfect model—his old man, telling him not to join the U.S. Marine Corps.

"So where in Detroit are you from?" Dean asked.

Kenan didn't answer. The urge to take him and shake some sense into him almost overwhelmed Dean. He considered driving the kid to the police station, having him locked up, saving him, maybe saving some victim down the line.

But he didn't.

"I'm just visiting Detroit," Dean told him instead. "Any good places to eat around here?"

"Turn over there," said Kenan. "My car is right there."

"I can take you to the hospital," said Dean.

"No. That's okay." Whatever daze Kenan had been in had lifted. "Thank you."

"It's okay, Charlie," said Rockman from the Art Room. "Get the license plate. We'll get more from him when he goes into the clinic. Good work."

Dean, frustrated at how little Kenan had really told him, pulled to a stop and let the kid out.

The kid turned back to look at him, and it was all Dean could do to stop himself from grabbing him and shaking him until he came to his senses.

"God be with you, all praise be to him," said Kenan.

"Yeah," muttered Dean as the young man slammed the door. "Same to you."

He shook his head, then read the plate number aloud for the Art Room.

CHAPTER 89

TOMMY KARR'S FAMILIAR grin shocked Dr. Ramil, not because he didn't expect the blond-haired Desk Three op to be here, but because his manner was as casual as it had been in the after-hours bull sessions they'd had during training. It seemed almost obscene to smile in an emergency room, at least before the patient had been examined.

"Condition is stable," said Karr, walking along with the two ambulance attendants. "Vitals are all good, except his blood pressure is slightly low. He might just have fainted."

Ramil stood behind Dr. Penney, careful to stay out of Asad's line of sight.

How would he kill him? There were countless ways—a scalpel was nearby. He could take it, make two quick cuts; Asad would quickly bleed to death.

But he couldn't. He wouldn't. And even if he had decided to do that—even if he thought it wasn't insane to even think of doing it—there were too many people here. They would stop him, or save Asad.

Take a knife, and slit his neck. A quick cut and it is done.

Too many people. He'd never get away with it.

I'm a lousy coward, Ramil thought to himself. A failure in the eyes of God, and in mine as well.

"IS IT A heart attack?" Jackson asked.

"No," said Dr. Penney. He glanced back at Ramil, who shook his head as well. "His blood pressure is low and his heart is somewhat erratic. He fainted. Could be a precursor for a stroke, could be heart disease, could be diabetes, or even that he's just exhausted. We'd have to do some tests to be sure."

"He does have a heart condition," said Ramil.

"Ah." Penney continued his examination. He ran his fingers over the back of his skull, where the device had been implanted. "This wound hasn't healed right. There may be something still in there."

"There was surgery in that area recently to remove a small tumor," said Jackson. "The scar tissue you feel is the unfortunate result."

Jackson could tell that Penney wasn't buying this.

"Please check for oxygen saturation," said Ramil. "And of course, you'll want to look at blood sug—"

"You don't have to tell me my job," said Penney. He nodded at the nurse, who was placing a fingertip monitor on Asad's hand. Before she could secure it, however, Asad stirred on the table. Dr. Penney put a hand on his chest, keeping him down.

"You're all right," said Penney. "You fainted. I want to run some tests."

Asad blinked at him but said nothing.

"Doctor, can I talk to you for a second?" asked Penney, gesturing them outside.

PENNEY'S ANTAGONISM ANGERED Ramil, and he felt his own animosity rising. He was glad for it, in a way; it was something to focus on.

"It's not an aneurysm," Ramil told Penney. "Obviously he has a heart condition, and that's why he fainted. His head is fine."

"How can you rule anything out without taking a CAT scan?"

"It's unnecessary," said Ramil.

"You don't want me to take one, right? That's what the problem is."

"Do whatever tests you want," said Ramil.

"What is that scar tissue all about?"

"I told you."

"And I don't believe you, doctor."

Ambassador Jackson stepped between them. "Dr. Penney, the lump you noted has to do with the matter we discussed earlier. The patient is not aware of it at this time, and that must continue. If you want to proceed with any tests or procedures you feel are necessary to ensure his health, by all means, proceed."

Ramil saw the distrust in Penney's eyes. The fool was going to betray them—he was going to help the devil.

They'd take Asad into custody if they had to. They could always do that; it was the plan. But it felt like a defeat somehow.

"You can perform whatever tests you feel are necessary," Jackson repeated. "But call this number first."

He slipped a business card into the doctor's hand. Penney looked at it and frowned.

If you're not brave, evil will prevail.

Ramil struggled to ignore the voice. The lump *could* be scar tissue; his explanation was not so far-fetched that he deserved to be insulted.

"Go ahead and call the number," said Ramil.

Penney frowned, then went to find a phone.

ASAD HEARD A hum in his ears, the sound of a loud motor idling. People were moving around him, but they were shadows of people, indistinct blurs. He pushed to get up but he could not.

He struggled to focus his eyes. Finally one of the blurs congealed into the face of an old man hovering above his.

"Can you hear me?" asked the man.

"Yes," said Asad.

"You seem to have fainted. Can you tell me what happened?"

"I passed out." Asad's instincts said that he must escape.

"Did you have heart palpitations? Pains?"

"Pains? Maybe."

"Are you on medication?"

"I want to leave."

He pushed to get up. This time, someone helped him—a large man with blond hair standing next to him.

What had happened to Kenan?

"I was with a friend," said Asad. "Is he here?"

"We can check for you."

"I'll check myself," said Asad.

"You're still too weak," said another man, stepping forward. He was a young black man, obviously a doctor.

"No, I can go."

"Mr. Rahman, I'm Dr. Penney," said the man. "You may have a heart condition. There are a series of tests we can do, all quite painless, that can determine exactly what the problem is."

He started to slide off the table. The large blond man grabbed him. Asad braced himself for a struggle, then realized that the man was helping him to his feet.

RAMIL FELT JACKSON's light touch on his back, a signal to stay back, to keep his face turned away and out of sight. Asad had not seen him, and there was no sense blowing it now.

Do it! He is an enemy to the faith and must be destroyed.

The knife was out of reach, but there was a pair of scissors on the table nearby.

"Are you sure you want to leave? I can't stress how serious this may be," Penney said to Asad, helping him toward the hall.

Do it!

Whether it was the word of God or some internal conscience, it was speaking the truth—Asad was a demon, a threat to all. He must be destroyed.

But it was too late. The al-Qaeda leader was gone.

Realizing his hand was wet, Ramil looked down at his fist. He'd squeezed the scissors so tightly that he'd cut a gash in his forefinger, and blood was dripping onto the floor. He dropped the scissors with a shudder, then went to wash his hand in the nearby sink.

CHAPTER 90

"THE CAR IS registered to a seventy-year-old in Almont, Michigan," Rockman told Dean. "It's not reported stolen. Ambassador Jackson will send someone over there to see what they can find out."

"What about Kenan?"

"The FBI people are trailing him," said Rockman. "By the way, that must be some sort of fake name. Doesn't exist in Detroit. We're just finished another run of his face through an ID matching program for a Michigan license. No match."

"He said he was a student at Upper Michigan," Dean said.

"Yeah, we're working on that. He doesn't exist, and neither does the program he claimed to be in. We ran first names, last names, all sorts of variations. He draws a total blank so far."

Rockman only meant that the name was probably an alias, but for Dean, the comment summed up his take on the kid: a blank looking for something to fill him up. What a waste.

"The FBI people will stay with him," Rockman added. "You and Tommy remain in the background from here on out."

"When are we pulling Asad in?"

"Not my department. All right. They're leaving the clinic. Stay with them until they settle down, all right?"

Kenan drove Asad to a motel outside the city and got a room for the night. The one-story motel's rooms opened onto a sidewalk in front of the parking lot; Dean had no trouble placing video bugs to cover the room and building front and back. When he was done, Rockman told him that the backup surveillance team was in place, and Dean went up the road to find a place to eat. His best choice seemed to be McDonald's; he was halfway through a quarter-pounder when Karr came in a short time later.

"About time you found a good restaurant," said Karr. He plopped down across from him. "Real high-class place our friend is staying in. I heard it got three stars in the *Terrorist Guide*." Karr pointed at his french fries. "You eating all of those?"

"Help yourself."

"How long before we bring him in?"

"Maybe pretty soon. The kid who's with Asad was on the phone confirming a flight out at the airport tomorrow morning." Karr finished Dean's fries. "Going to New Orleans, then on to Phoenix. They're tracking the credit card and that stuff now. No word on the other people at the meeting."

"How'd Ramil look?"

"The doc?" Karr laughed. "Shaved and dyed his hair. Hardly recognized him."

"He had a panic attack in Istanbul."

"Really? Seemed pretty cool when I saw him. You want anything? Your fries got me hungry."

"No, thanks." Dean got up. "I'm going to go check on the surveillance team."

"Suit yourself," said Karr. "But those guys got to pay for their own food."

THE TWO FBI agents tasked to watch the motel were parked in an unmarked car that practically shouted POLICE; it had spotlights under the mirrors, big brake lights on the rear deck, and a set of aerials off the bumper so large they'd need red warning lights if the car drove within ten miles of an airport. They were in a lot diagonally across the street from the motel. While they weren't visible from the small window at the front of the unit, it wouldn't take much for someone to spot them.

Dean rapped on the side window twice before the occupants lowered it.

"Guys, your car is a little too obvious," he told them. "We have to do something about it."

"This is the car we got," said the man in the passenger seat.

"Yeah, I can see that. So will our friends. One of you come with me. You can take one of our rentals, and I'll get this out of here."

"Charlie, your friend Kenan is moving," said Rockman.

Dean, unsure exactly how much information about Desk Three's technology the immigration people had been given, pulled his cell phone from his pocket and started talking to the runner. "Where's he going?"

"He's going shopping. He said he'd be back in an hour or two. One of the FBI teams is going to stay with him. We'll have them stay pretty far back."

"You need these guys here for a backup?"

"Other team should be able to handle it."

"All right." Dean leaned back into the car and told them that Kenan was coming out. "I'll be down the street."

"We can handle it," snapped the man in the passenger seat, raising the window.

There was a deli nearby; Dean went in and got himself a coffee, then went back to his car. Flipping through the radio he heard an old Hank Williams song and settled back to listen.

Just then, a police cruiser came down the street. Dean sat up, watching as it pulled into the motel lot and stopped in front of Asad's room.

"Damn," yelled Dean, grabbing for the car door.

CHAPTER 91

ASAD HEARD THE call to prayers far in the distance, the eloquent reminder of his faith waking him. He shook off his slumber and started to push himself off the bed, determined to make his devotions to God. As he did, he realized that he wasn't alone in the room, and that he hadn't heard the call to prayers at all—that had come from a dream, or a snatch of memory. Three men were coming through the door. They had guns.

The room exploded with light. Asad thought of his trip to Medina two years before, the glory he experienced when he understood the full meaning of the words that had been spoken to the Prophet: *You are a mercy to all creation of the world.*

Then Asad thought of nothing and felt nothing, and experienced nothing more of this world.

CHAPTER 92

THE SHOTS SOUNDED as Dean bolted across the highway. He jumped up the embankment from the road, sprinting between the parked cars as the two fake policemen came out of the room.

"Federal agent!" he yelled, dropping to his knee. He braced the Beretta in his hands.

One of the men spotted him and raised his arm to fire. Dean squeezed off two shots, striking the man in the jaw and temple. His companion threw himself back into the room.

"Get the backup people in—Red Lion is down!" Dean yelled to Rockman, as if the runner would only be able to hear him if he shouted. Dean scrambled to the front wall of the building, half crawling as he made his way toward the door. The man he had shot lay a few feet away, sprawled on the pavement, blackish red blood pooling around him.

There was a siren in the distance. The two FBI agents who'd been watching from the car had taken positions a short distance away, their faces ashen.

"Give yourself up!" Dean yelled to the man inside.

The answer was a muffled gunshot.

Dean rose slowly, knowing exactly what the sound meant.

CHAPTER 93

RUBENS LISTENED IMPASSIVELY as Telach told him what had happened. Asad's death was bad enough, but in the confusion that had followed, the FBI agents who'd been trailing Kenan had lost the youth somewhere in northern Detroit after he had abandoned his car.

"Since he was coming back, we told them not to get too close," said Telach. "It really wasn't their fault. We've given the local police a description of him, saying a witness saw him at the motel right before the shooting. They're scouring the city," she added.

"No doubt," said Rubens dryly. "We have an ID?"

"No."

"Asad's murderers?"

"So far, no IDs. The shooting only took place an hour ago. The police car was stolen from the police garage. It's likely that whoever killed Asad had contacts on the force, or at least there. The uniforms weren't legitimate, but they were close, about what you could get at a good costume shop."

Rubens rose from his desk. Desk Three's powers might be prodigious, but they were not omniscient, and until now they had proceeded carefully for fear of tipping off Asad or his accomplices. Rubens was confident that Kenan, or whatever his real name was, would eventually be IDed, but the delay was frustrating. The same went for the killers. A trail would be found, tracing the men back to whoever had ordered the murder. Inexorably, the murder plot would be revealed.

The problem was, that wouldn't necessarily help them determine where Asad had been planning to attack.

"Dean's taking it pretty hard," said Telach.

"Understandable."

"It wasn't his fault."

"I didn't imply it was, Marie." Rubens walked over to the middle of his small office, rubbing his temples with his fingers.

"The FBI people want to arrest the head of the mosque," Telach told him. "What do you think?"

"I think that it is unlikely to yield any useful information."

The Art Room supervisor frowned.

"I will raise the issue with the National Security Advisor," Rubens said. "As well as Homeland Security. However, technically, the case will be under their jurisdiction."

"Should I pull Dean and Tommy in? I don't think they'll be of much use in Detroit. Ambassador Jackson can work with the police. He and Dr. Ramil are going to retrieve the bug as soon as possible."

"Have Mr. Dean stay in Detroit to see if he can help locate the young man. Send Tommy—have him take the flight the young man was interested in," said Rubens. "Have him fly armed, as an air marshal."

"You don't think Asad was thinking of hijacking it, do you?"

"At this point, Marie, I'm afraid I have no theories at all."

CHAPTER 94

THE SCENT OF the disinfectant stung Ramil's nose and sinuses as he walked with Jackson and the pathologist down the hallway toward the morgue. His eyes felt as if they were being squeezed, and he could already taste the dry heave that waited at the pit of his stomach.

As a medical student, Ramil had worked on or seen literally hundreds of cadavers; he had also served a very short stint with a military morgue when the unit was understaffed. But plunging among the dead always unsettled him. Damage to a living body was one thing; even in the most desperate situation he could focus on the mechanics of the parts, know precisely what must be done, even if in realistic terms it could never succeed. Coming into a morgue was different. It was the enemy's empire, and entering meant admitting impotence and worthlessness beyond measure.

In this case, the corpse he was to view would rebuke him even more strongly, for it was evidence not only of his limitations as a doctor, but of his failure as a man and as a Muslim. Asad lay dead, but not by his hand; Allah had found another more worthy to purge the sinner.

"I've only been in a morgue once," Ambassador Jackson told their guide.

"I would say once is usually enough for most people," replied the pathologist. He had the light, ironic chuckle common to his profession.

The NSA had arranged for Asad to be taken here, a breach of normal protocol that would allow for the removal of the bug without prying eyes or embarrassing records. The body had not yet been identified—it would never be, Ramil suspected—and their host referred to it as John Doe 347. It lay on a table almost exactly in the center of a room large enough to hold perhaps another twenty or thirty gurneys. Ramil, his eyes glued to the floor, noted that there was a large drain a few feet away.

A rack with gowns stood near a sink at the far end of the room; the three men dressed quietly, though this was probably unnecessary. Ramil washed his hands, fastidiously scrubbing as if he were going into regular surgery. The cut on his finger he had made earlier with the scissors became a white bead at the center of a thick red line.

Hands dry, Ramil worked the latex gloves down between the grooves of his fingers, snugging them tight. Then he joined the others at the head of the steel table. The dead man stared at the ceiling, his face marked with astonishment.

The assassins had shot Asad in the chest, not only making Ramil's job easier, but avoiding any conflicts between it and the forensic investigation.

He remained evil and ignorant to the end, as misguided as anyone who ever lived. He will be tormented in Hell.

But what of you, Saed Ramil? Now that you have failed to do God's will, what will become of you?

Ramil turned to the rolling tray, selecting a scalpel handle and matching it to the proper blade. He pushed Asad's head gently to the side. Ramil's hands, still surgeon's hands, did not betray him, and the bug was quickly removed. Ramil had brought thread to resuture the wound. This he did more slowly and with a good deal of attention, working so carefully that he almost tricked himself into believing that the patient was not dead.

But a good doctor could not be fooled so very easily, and whatever else had happened to him, Ramil was still a good doctor. When he straightened, the room had become very large and sweat was pouring down his temples.

Hearing the voice now, here in the morgue—that did mean he was insane, didn't it?

Or that God had truly spoken to him.

"Almost done," said Ramil, ostensibly to the others, but really to himself.

You'll have another chance.

"I don't want one."

The two other men looked up at him. Rather than explaining—what explanation could he possibly give?—Ramil smiled uneasily.

"We need a sample," said Jackson, reminding him. "For DNA identification."

Surely that was unnecessary, thought Ramil. But he snatched the kit from Jackson's hand and collected the material from inside the dead man's cheek. He managed to complete his work and get nearly to the door before doubling over, a stream of green bile pouring from his mouth.

CHAPTER 95

WHEN KENAN SAW the three blue sedans and four or five squad cars blocking the street in front of the mosque, his heart began pumping like an out-of-control machine. He turned quickly into the small delicatessen at the end of the street, nearly knocking over an old black woman as he entered. He circled around the lone set of shelves at the front of the store, so panicked he couldn't think.

He grabbed for something to buy, an excuse to be here; he'd buy something, then walk out in the other direction, turn the corner before running.

He grabbed what he thought was a can of soup and started for the cash register. As he did, he turned the label and saw it was a can of pork and beans, not soup. Kenan saw the word "pork" on the label and dropped it to the floor. In his panic he had grabbed a forbidden meat, nearly blaspheming against God.

The motor that had replaced his heart spun even faster. He lowered himself to his knees, hands shaking as he retrieved the can and returned it to the shelf. He took a Campbell's Tomato Soup can from the row above it and walked to the counter, where the owner eyed him suspiciously. Kenan dug into his pocket, fishing out dimes and nickels to pay. He had plenty of bills in his wallet—too many, for the sheik had given him a supply to run errands with, and he didn't want to flash them.

"You owe me another ten cents," said the man at the counter after Kenan finished sliding out the coins.

Kenan began to protest. The man put his hands on the edge of the counter and leaned toward him.

"Give me a dime or get out of here," said the store owner.

Kenan fled without the soup or his money.

KENAN KNEW THAT he must not use a phone under any circumstance. He guessed that his car would be watched as well. This was easily abandoned; the imam had arranged for him to use it and Kenan had no idea who owned it.

Gathering his wits, Kenan walked a few blocks to calm his heart, then took a bus in the general direction of the motel. The closest he could get was two miles away; he walked so quickly that he could feel stitches at the top of his thighs by the time the motel sign came in sight.

His heart began pounding again when he saw the van and police cars in the lot. He got close enough to make sure they were directly in front of the room Asad had taken, then, as calmly as he could, turned and walked in the opposite direction. His heart thumped crazily, and his head floated in the disturbed ocean above it, bobbing with the rush of the cars as they sped by.

The imam had warned that the crusaders would attack when he least expected it. Those who were complacent would find themselves upturned and in misery. Kenan did not believe that he had been complacent, but surely his world had been turned upside down.

He walked down the road until he came to a diner. The smell of the fried food in the vestibule sickened him, but he forced himself to take a place at the counter and ordered a Coke, fearing that tea would make him stand out and give him away.

As he drank the soda, he worked out what to do. If the police had arrested the imam and the sheik, then it was very likely that they would come looking for him. Most likely they were looking for him now.

When Asad had given him the shopping list, he had pressed a small Koran into his hand as well. Kenan had felt tremendous joy; he realized that it meant he had been chosen for the mission, though of course the sheik had said nothing.

Kenan took the small book from his pocket and began leafing through the pages. There was no message in the Koran, per se; rather, the book was a sign that he should proceed with a plan that had been told to him several weeks before: board a bus for Indianapolis in the morning. There he was to make his way to the airport, board a plane for St. Louis and finally catch a flight to Mexico, where he would receive further instructions.

But surely the police would be watching the bus station. They were probably already doing so.

Kenan ordered another cola, stirring the ice with his straw and thinking of what to do. Finally he decided that he would go to Indianapolis, but by car, not bus. The only problem was getting one.

THREE HOURS LATER, Kenan trudged down a deserted suburban street roughly ten miles from the diner where he had started. There were no streetlights, but he could have found the house with his eyes closed. His family had lived in the raised ranch his entire life.

Kenan didn't have his key with him, but he knew from experience that the door at the back of the house could be jimmied open with a thin card. After carefully checking the neighborhood to make sure there were no police cars staking it out, he went to the backyard and used one of his false identity cards to slip open the lock.

Kenan's chest tightened as he walked inside. Everything was his enemy here, familiar and yet foreign at the same time.

In the first days after he had heard the Prophet's word, Kenan had foolishly tried to share his joy with his parents and younger sister. But they had been incapable of understanding, and after a few arguments he realized they were hopelessly enmeshed in the Devil's world, beyond salvation. He walled them off, seeing them only when absolutely necessary; he had not made the mistake of talking to them about God and the need to live according to the fullness of the Koran for more than three years. Returning now, he felt like a ghost, visiting not his parents but his old self; he half expected not his father to loom from the shadows but the boy he had been, the wannabe baseball player and nerdy geek who'd taken top honors in math at high school graduation. A thousand memories flooded back, the stale taste of beer mingling with the smell of warm cookies his mother baked every Saturday morning, her own form of religion. Kenan dodged them as surely as he dodged the rack of freshly laundered white shirts in the hallway, passing stealthily through the den as if he were five again, playing hide-and-seek on a rainy afternoon with his mother and sister.

The house was silent. His parents' room was directly above him, but he heard nothing, not a snore or the creak of the bedsprings.

Kenan slinked up the stairs to the kitchen. The car keys were sitting on the counter in the kitchen; the cars had changed over the years, but the keys were always there, along with his father's wallet.

The wallet tempted him. Kenan had plenty of cash, but he didn't have a credit card, and a credit card could be very useful.

He wasn't sure how long it would take for his father to realize the card was stolen. A great deal of time, he thought—his father noticed very little, either about himself or the world around him. But surely, sooner or later, he would find that it was gone, and then it would be a liability, telling the enemy where he was. Kenan left the wallet and took the key ring, patiently removing the key for the Malibu and leaving the rest.

At the hallway he listened to the sounds of the house at rest: a clock ticking, someone's soft wheeze—his mother, he thought.

It was a shame that he couldn't save her. But Allah had a plan, and he must trust it.

Outside in the driveway, the radio blared on as soon as he started the car. Kenan fumbled before finding the switch to kill the sound. Then he backed out of the driveway and drove off as quickly as he could without screeching the tires.

CHAPTER 96

WHEN THE MEN he had sent to assassinate Asad failed to meet him near the grocery store as planned, Marid Dabir took a bus to the downtown bus station they had set as a backup. But as he neared it, the al-Qaeda organizer began to consider the possibility that Asad had somehow managed to turn the men against him. If that were the case, it was very likely that the police would be waiting to arrest him. He got off as soon as he could, walking down several blocks until he found a coffee shop where he could consider the situation.

Dabir had personally recruited the brother who had met him in Ontario some years before; the man was a mechanic working for the city police, a valuable source of information who had also been able to supply an old police car for the project. The other two men had left the mosque a year ago in a dispute with the imam; while the mechanic vouched for them, Dabir did not know them personally. They said the right things, however, proclaiming allegiance to the cause and hatred for puerile traitors like Asad.

Unable to locate Asad, he'd had to resort to having the brothers watch the mosque. They'd seen him enter but not leave and had almost given up when Allah struck him down on the pavement a few blocks away. When Dabir heard the news, he thought that God truly had marked Asad bin Taysr as the traitor and had chosen Dabir as his executioner.

Now he was not so sure. It was possible that the incident on the sidewalk was merely a ruse to get Asad safely away.

Perhaps his men had been ambushed at the hotel. Or perhaps they were involved in a plot to trap him.

The latter, it seemed, was much more likely. Asad knew he was the only one dangerous enough to expose him and bring him to justice.

It came down to a matter of trust. Did Dabir trust the men he had sent well enough to believe that they would not betray him? When he found he couldn't easily answer the question, he realized that he must not, and therefore had to assume the worst.

Dabir placed the cup of tepid tea gently on the table, trying to remain outwardly calm, though his insides raged. Asad was not merely a traitor, he was a cancer, spreading throughout the movement.

The first thing to do was to find a new place to stay.

Pulling three dollars from his wallet to cover the bill and a modest tip, Dabir quickly counted the rest of his money. He had six twenties in the wallet and a pair of hundred-dollar bills in each sock, more than enough to find a room for the night. The thing he could not do was pay with a credit card, which would limit his choices.

When he asked if there was an inexpensive hotel nearby, the cashier stuck a finger into her hair and twirled it around, as if she were winding up her brain for the answer.

"Not reeeallly," she said, drawing out her words in a way that made it hard for Dabir to decipher. "You could go down to Stephenson Street that way and see."

Outside, Dabir walked in the direction she'd indicated. But there didn't appear to be a Stephenson Street nearby. One-story houses the size of cottages sat among wide open lots, with an occasional two- or three-story brown brick building in between. After several blocks, Dabir turned around; two black youths who'd been behind him gave him a caustic glance as he passed. He quickened his pace, suspecting that they would follow him.

Two blocks later, he turned to the right. Now completely lost, he found a small greengrocer on the corner and went inside to ask for directions.

The store had been a house not too long ago, and it still had family quarters up the steps that sat behind a partially open curtain at the right. A familiar smell wafted down the stairs—Middle Eastern–style lamb.

"Can I help you?" asked the man behind the cash register. Short and thin, he had a narrow, Egyptian face and a heavy accent.

"The lamb smells good," said Dabir, using his Yemen-flavored Arabic.

"We are in America now," said the man.

"You're Egyptian?" Dabir guessed.

The man frowned. "I'm American. What can I get you?"

"I'm visiting a friend and I want to stay somewhere for the night," Dabir said. "I was wondering if there was an inexpensive motel somewhere. So I'm not a burden for him."

The man studied him for a moment. Then he yelled, "Robert! Robert, come here."

A twelve- or thirteen-year-old boy bounded down the steps, parted the curtain, and ran into the middle of the store.

"Take this man over to Michigan Avenue," the shopkeeper told the boy. "He's looking for a place to stay."

"Yes, Papa."

"*Barakallah*," said Dabir. "May God bless you."

The man frowned at him, then nodded and went back to his business.

CHAPTER 97

CHARLIE DEAN SPENT most of the night listening to the police interview the imam and several of his followers. Immigration had found that two of the mosque's members had overstayed their visas, but this failed to supply much leverage, either with the men or the imam. The mosque's spiritual leader was a naturalized citizen, with no police record and an unshakably placid demeanor. He listened politely to the questions about Asad, gave a few meaningless answers and insisted, in a logical and very calm voice, that he had never seen the man before afternoon prayers. The imam volunteered that he had spoken on the need for a believer to help others in his community, an imperative which all people of the Book, Jews and Christians as well as Muslims, surely shared. He wasn't lying; a transcript of the talk had been forwarded to Dean by the Art Room.

But of course his very existence was a lie, created to facilitate the terrorist network Asad and others had assembled. How much easier it was to be a sniper than a policeman, Dean thought. You didn't have to listen to other people's falsehoods, let alone pretend you believed them.

The U.S. attorney had obtained a warrant to search the mosque and its records, but Telach told Dean to stay away, just in case the area was being watched by Asad's associates or whoever had ordered the murder. Even though he'd already blown his cover at the motel, Dean didn't argue; he doubted the search was going to come up with anything very useful.

Around four A.M., Dean finally left the interrogation area to check on the progress of the search for Kenan, which was going about as well as most missing persons investigations, which was to say not very. The FBI forensics team had taken the car to one of the city garages to examine the interior of the vehicle; since it was only down the block, Dean went there to have a look himself. When he arrived, he met one of the police detectives assigned to find Kenan: a short, Hispanic black woman around thirty years old who introduced herself as Elsa Williams.

"Guy did some grocery shopping this afternoon," she told Dean, pointing to a table where the items in the car had been bagged and tagged after being checked for fingerprints. There were bottles of water, shoe polish, disposable razors, Post-It Notes, and a large collection of snacks. There were also two pair of sandals in different sizes. Kenan seemed to have stopped at six different stores in all; the receipts were laid out in plastic bags next to the items.

Dean slipped the camera attachment onto his PDA and beamed copies of the receipts to the Art Room. At best, he expected an exotic analysis of Kenan's eating habits. What he got was a lead.

"We were able to get into three security systems at the stores Kenan was at," Rockman told him twenty minutes later, while he was walking back to the police station. "He spoke to a clerk at this Rite Aid for a while. It looked like he knew him."

"Where?"

"Clerk's gone home," Rockman said. "I've sent an instant message with his name and address to your handheld. It's, um, a kind of grotty end of town."

FROM ROCKMAN'S DESCRIPTION, Dean expected to find the clerk in the heart of a burned-out battle zone. Instead, he found him on the top floor of a three-family house converted into student apartments. Discarded mail sat stacked on the radiator just inside the door. Bicycles lined the downstairs hall and the second-floor landing. The place smelled like a gym locker.

After eying the lock, he took out a pick and small torsion wrench from beneath his belt and worked over the tumblers. Like any skill, lock picking required considerable practice to master, and while the lock on the clerk's room wasn't complicated, it took Dean almost ten minutes to get it open. When it finally gave way he nudged the door slightly, returning the tools to his pocket and taking out his gun. Then he eased the door open, expecting but not finding a chain lock.

The door opened into a small kitchen; beyond it to the left was a large room that served as combination bedroom, dining room, study, and living room. Textbooks were piled neatly in the middle of the floor, making an irregular wall about knee high.

A student. The books covered a variety of subjects—chemistry, literature, Plato.

Plato. Maybe the kid was a philosophy major, thought Dean.

The textbooks' owner lay sprawled on the bed under a mountain of covers. Dean looked over the room quickly, making sure that Kenan wasn't there. Then he retreated, checked the bathroom just off the kitchen, and went back to the door.

"Rockman, call the room here."

"You sure?"

"Yeah. I want to wake this guy up without waking everyone else in the house up."

The clerk was either very tired or a very sound sleeper; it took six rings before he reached for the phone. Dean waited a second, then knocked.

"Now what?" asked a sleepy voice inside.

"Martin, I need to talk to you."

"What?"

"There's been a murder and we're afraid there's another victim. Please."

Dean went to the stairs and gestured to the cop to stay put. There was no sense coming on too strong.

"What the hell is going on?" mumbled the clerk from behind the door.

"There's someone we can't find. We're afraid he's dead."

"You're going to have to show me a badge or something."

Dean took a business card with a generic U.S. Marshal logo from his wallet and slid it under the door.

"How do I know this is real?"

"Call the number. But do it quick, all right? I'm not exactly sure if we have tons of time here," said Dean.

The door opened. Bare chested and skinny, the clerk frowned up at Dean and asked what the U.S. Marshals were doing in Detroit.

"Do you know this kid?" Dean unfolded a print of Kenan made from one of the video bugs.

"Kenan's dead?"

"No. At least I hope not," said Dean. Something in his voice must have tipped the clerk off—Dean had never been a very good liar—and the boy immediately stiffened, suspicious.

"We think he may have been targeted by the person who murdered this man." Dean gave him a picture of Asad, dead in the room, lying in a pool of blood.

"God," said the clerk, his resistance gone.

"When did you last see Kenan?"

"I didn't."

Dean pulled out the print of the surveillance photo from the store where the kid worked, which had a time stamp on the bottom from that afternoon.

"Did you see him after this?" he said, trying to sound as diplomatic as he could.

"Jesus."

"You're not in any trouble, Martin. I just want to prevent another murder if I can. How do you know Louis?"

"Louis? This is Kenan Conkel."

"Kenan. Yeah, I'm sorry, that's what I meant. It's been a long night. You know him well?"

"We were freshman."

"At Upper Michigan?"

"No. Wayne State. I didn't know he went to Upper Michigan."

"You went to Wayne State with him," said Dean, realizing why they hadn't found Kenan. "When was this?"

"Three years ago, when I was a freshman."

"Kenan Conkel, Wayne State."

"Working on it," said Rockman in his head.

CHAPTER 98

THOUGH HE ROSE just before dawn, Marid Dabir felt as if he'd overslept. He said his prayers, then went to find some place to eat and consider his next move.

The small hotel had three dozen rooms, arranged in two stories around a parking lot. The steps down from the second story went through a small building next to the entrance to the lot. As Dabir passed through, he noticed the night clerk sleeping on a couch behind the reservation desk.

Dabir walked over to him, looking to see if he'd left his wallet anywhere nearby—the man's credit card number would be handy for making a plane reservation. But Dabir didn't see it and decided it wasn't worth trying to sneak it from his pocket.

His search had disturbed the mouse for the hotel computer, waking the unit from sleep mode. The program for handling reservations flashed on the screen; as Dabir looked at it, he wondered if he might be able to get a credit card number from that. Backing through the records could be done easily with the mouse, and within seconds Dabir had not one but three different credit card accounts with their owners' information, including the supposedly secret printed IDs on the cards.

There was a bagel shop across the street from the hotel, but the idea of having breakfast with Jews nauseated him. Dabir walked two blocks until he found a silver-walled diner. On the way in he picked up a copy of the local paper, having learned from experience that even the nosiest American tended to leave a reader in peace.

He was halfway through his tea and toast when he found the story about the murder of an unknown man in a city suburb. Barely six paragraphs long, the story said that the man seemed to have been killed by three gunmen, who were then caught in a shootout with police who responded to a 911 call.

Unsure how much if any of the story was true, Dabir turned the page.

CHAPTER 99

"THIS IS ALL your fault," Bing told Rubens. Her ears were tinged red and seemed to stick straight out from the sides of her head. "You bypassed all of the controls, all of the processes—"

"I bypassed nothing," said Rubens. He tried to continue toward the conference room, but Bing put out her hand, blocking his way.

"You used a personal relationship with the president—you used George Hadash's death to get around me."

"I did nothing of the kind," said Rubens sharply.

"If you had taken him when I suggested, he'd be alive and we'd know where the target was. You put your ego above what was best for the country."

Second-guessing was standard Washington procedure, and Rubens had fully expected it. The accusation that he had used Hadash's death, however, angered him greatly. Rubens pressed his teeth together to keep from saying anything. His silence did the trick—the red tinge on Bing's ears spread to the rest of her face, and she swirled around and headed down the hallway.

"I see you're warming up to Ms. Bing," said Defense Secretary Blanders behind him.

Rubens managed a wan smile before continuing to the briefing room. The head of the NSA, Admiral Devlin Brown, had arrived earlier and was sitting on the far side of the room. Bing was stooped down behind him, whispering something in his ear; she saw Rubens come in and rose abruptly, moving over toward her spot at the head of the four-sided table.

Rubens pretended he hadn't seen her and took his seat next to Brown. He poured himself a cup of coffee from the nearby carafe, even though he'd already had two that morning.

"Anything new?" Brown asked.

"We've identified the man who was with Asad and we're looking for him. We're looking for patterns in airplane flights and one of our people will be on the flight that we think Asad was to take from Detroit. Outside of that, we have nothing."

More precisely, they had quite a lot: intercepts of possible messages, money transactions, telephone conversations, a vast file of rumors and innuendo compiled by the different agencies now involved in trying to determine the plot's target. What Rubens meant was, they had so much information that they had nothing.

President Marcke burst into the room, moving as briskly as Rubens had ever seen him walk. At most sessions with his aides, the president assumed the role of a listener, waiting until all sides of the issue were raised. He'd sit back in his seat, often unconsciously twisting a paperclip, not quite Buddha-like, but generally impassive and as unemotional as a judge as his advisors debated an issue. It was only in one-on-one or very small meetings that he put the true Marcke on display, thumping his desk and occasionally jabbing his companion's chest to make a point.

But today was different. Today he spoke as soon as he came through the door, his voice sharp, as if he were a football coach at halftime with his team down by a touchdown.

"Gentlemen, ladies. One thing I want to make clear from the start," he said, walking to his usual spot at the table but not sitting down. "Some of you believe this crisis is a byproduct of my decision to allow Asad into the country rather than having him arrested in Turkey. I believe it was the best and most logical decision at the time. Some of you may disagree. Those disagreements are with me, and you may take them up at the proper time. That time is not now. Billy, what do you have for us?"

Rubens, cheered by what he interpreted as a not-so-subtle slap at Bing, began his briefing.

CHAPTER 100

EVEN FOR A U.S. Marshal—or an ersatz one, such as Tommy Karr—carrying a pistol on an aircraft involved major bureaucratic hassle. Forms had to be filled out, identities checked, authorizations reviewed. Karr didn't mind, however—someone had left two boxes of Krispy Kreme doughnuts in the security office where they parked him. He was just debating the relative merits of powdered versus granulated sugar coverings when the head of airport security arrived to take him to the plane.

Carefully finessing the detector at the gate so he would appear to be just a regular passenger, Karr boarded with the first-class passengers, taking a seat not far from the pilot's cabin. The passenger list had already been thoroughly vetted, but Asad's organization had demonstrated that they were adept at operating under the radar, and Karr eyed each passenger carefully. The people boarding, carry-ons pushed against their knees to squeeze down the aisles, were mostly business types bound for the Gulf Coast area, where construction was booming more than a year after Hurricane Katrina had laid New Orleans low. Only two were of obvious Middle Eastern descent.

"How you doing, Tommy?" asked Chafetz from the Art Room as the plane backed from the gate.

"Fine."

"Lia's going to meet you at the airport."

"Can't wait."

"The ten or fifteen minutes after takeoff is the most crucial. Statistically."

"I guess I better not take a nap then, huh?" Karr laughed.

The man in the seat next to him had overheard him talking to himself and eyed Karr as if he were a nutcase. Karr gave him a bright "How ya doin'?" and pushed back in his seat, all smiles.

As the plane taxied, a large black man walked up into first class from the rear cabin. He walked slowly, obviously looking for someone he thought was a passenger on the plane.

"I'm sorry, sir," said a stewardess, chasing him from behind. "You have to remain seated until the plane is in the air."

The man ignored her. Karr watched as he went around the front of the first-class area, turning slowly and walking down the other aisle. The stewardess shook her head and repeated her admonitions without visible effect.

"Sit down, bub," said Karr's neighbor. "Give the lady a break."

"Mind your business."

"I said sit down."

"Stuff it," said the other man, disappearing into coach.

"Nice, real nice," said Karr's neighbor, turning to him. "That's supposed to pass for clever, right? You believe that?"

"No manners. Young people," added Karr's neighbor— even though he and the person he was criticizing were both about thirty.

Fifteen minutes after they'd taken off, the black man returned again, once more moving slowly and looking at passengers' faces.

"What are you, the grim reaper?" asked the man sitting next to Karr.

"Just shut up."

"You're telling me to shut up?"

"You see any other jerk with a garage door for a mouth?"

"Federal agent, buddy. Sit down," said the man, rising. "FBI."

"Air marshal," said the other man. "You sit down."

Karr buried his face in his hand, trying to keep his laughter to a level that wouldn't cause the plane to shake. As he did, he noticed a passenger one row ahead shielding his face and making a very serious effort to count the clouds outside.

"HE'S IN SEAT 2B," Karr told the Art Room from the restroom a few minutes later. "About five-eight, light-skinned black, close-cropped dark brown hair, maybe twenty-five. New suit jacket. Nice. No puckering at the shoulders. White T-shirt. Gold chain. Generic sneakers."

"Are the sneakers significant?" asked Chafetz.

"They're the whole thing," said Karr. "They're not Nike. Get it? See if he was a rap star or something like that, he'd pay attention to his footwear. Here—"

"It's kind of thin, Tommy."

"Maybe. But I say we check him out anyway."

CHAPTER 101

DEAN LOOKED AT the Conkel house while the marshals circled around the block, cutting off possible escape routes on the chance that Kenan Conkel had decided to hide out in his parents' house. The raised ranch looked almost exactly like its neighbors, any eccentricities carefully hidden behind the dented aluminum siding. A basketball hoop hung down above the single-bay garage; the rim was bent slightly to one side, though not quite enough to prevent play. The grass had been mowed recently but the edges left untrimmed.

"Units are in place," said Chris Sabot, the marshal next to him in the car.

Dean cracked open the car door and got out. They'd decided against asking the local police to come for backup. The Art Room thought it unlikely that Conkel was here, and they needed to walk a delicate line, gathering information without inadvertently giving any away. Besides, half a dozen police cars weren't going to make Conkel or his parents any more likely to talk.

Dean scanned the house and yard as he went up the driveway. His right hand stayed near his hip, ready to grab the Beretta from its holster beneath his jacket if necessary. He jogged up the three steps to the stoop and tapped the buzzer.

The curtain behind the row of windows next to the door moved. A face appeared about chest high. Though beardless, it was so much like Kenan's that Dean froze. Then he realized it was a girl's.

"Can I help you?" she asked through the glass.

"I'm here from the U.S. Marshals Service," Dean said. He

held a business card to the window. "I'd like to talk to your parents."

The girl drew back. A minute later, a woman in her early forties answered the door. Short and slightly stocky, the woman wore thick glasses that emphasized the roundness of her face. She didn't look like Kenan at all—except for the color of her hair, an almost foxlike shade of golden red.

Dean introduced himself and gave her the card.

"I'd like to come in. I have some questions about your son, Kenan. Is he here?"

"Kenan? Is he in trouble?"

"I'm not sure," said Dean. "We're afraid he may have witnessed a murder and gone into hiding. We're worried about him."

"Oh, God. Oh, my God. Come in. Frank? Frank!"

Dean nodded to Sabot, and they went inside the house. Sabot went downstairs to check the basement rooms; Dean followed Mrs. Conkel upstairs. The dining room, kitchen, and living room were clustered on his left. The rooms were small and a quick glance showed Kenan wasn't there.

Mrs. Conkel had gone down the hall to the right. There were two rooms on the right; a bathroom and another room lay on the left. Dean took a few steps down the hall, far enough to see into the first room on the right; there was a sewing machine set up in it, and an exercise bike.

"My husband will be right out. He's just taking a shower," said Mrs. Conkel, emerging from the room at the end of the hall on the left. Dean guessed it was the master bedroom.

"Your son isn't here?" asked Dean.

"No, he's at school in Detroit."

"Have you spoken to him today?"

"No."

"Recently?"

"Well, no. Not very recently. He doesn't talk much. You know at that age, they don't." She smiled awkwardly. "Would you like some coffee?"

Mrs. Conkel started past him toward the kitchen. Dean took a step down the hall, glancing into the room on the left;

it was the sister's, and from the hall looked empty, though of course Kenan could be hiding in the closet. The master bedroom door was closed. Dean turned back and went into the kitchen, temporarily putting off a more thorough search.

The family had only just finished breakfast; a bowl of cereal and a half-eaten piece of toast sat on the table. Dean looked at the glasses and counted three places.

"How do you like your coffee?" asked Mrs. Conkel.

"Black," he told her.

Sabot came up and stood in the doorway, shaking his head ever so slightly to indicate Kenan hadn't been downstairs.

"So, you haven't heard from Kenan recently," said Dean.

"No."

"And that's not unusual."

"Not with Kenan. God, I do wish he'd call more." Her voice trembled slightly at the word "God."

Frank Conkel came into the kitchen wearing a blue work uniform. The logo on the pocket said he worked for Cole Heating & Cooling. He was taller than his son, with dark, ruddy cheeks that hung away from his face, but he had the same overall build, thin and narrow. His hair was still wet from the shower.

"What's going on?" he asked Dean.

"I'm wondering when the last time was that you saw your son Kenan."

"Why?"

"He may have seen a murder, Frank," said his wife.

"Detroit is a cesspool," said Mr. Conkel. And with that he collapsed into a seat, as if the supports had been knocked out from under him.

"We shouldn't have let him go to school there." Mrs. Conkel put the coffee down on the table. "We shouldn't have."

"Is he here?" Dean asked Mr. Conkel.

"Here? Look around. Do you see him?" His voice was pained, not angry.

"Have you checked his dorm?" asked Mrs. Conkel.

"He doesn't seem to be at school a whole lot," Dean told her. "He hasn't shown up for his classes all semester."

"What do you mean?" said Mr. Conkel.

"Daddy, where did you park the car?" asked Kenan's sister, coming down the hall. "It's not in the driveway."

Mr. Conkel went down the steps to the front door, pushing open the screen and stepping onto the stoop in his socks. Mrs. Conkel followed. If they were acting, thought Dean, it was an Academy Award performance.

KENAN GOT TO Indianapolis a little after nine A.M. and managed to find the airport without having to ask directions. Worried that his parents might report the car stolen, he decided it was better not to park it at the airport, since if it were found there it might help them trace him. So he got back on the highway and drove east a few miles. He found an apartment complex, left the car in an open slot marked "guests," then trudged back in the direction he'd come. He was way ahead of schedule—the bus wasn't supposed to arrive until three in the afternoon—but he kept as brisk a pace as he could, constantly shifting his small suitcase back and forth. The bag had only a pair of pants and a sweater in it, but grew heavier and heavier as he walked.

There'd been nothing on the radio about the mosque or the sheik. The more time passed, the more it seemed as if it hadn't really happened—as if all the police cars were just part of his imagination. Kenan almost believed that if he drove back to Detroit, he'd find the sheik waiting for him at the motel, probably concerned that he had missed praying with him before sunrise.

A car buzzed by the shoulder of the highway, so close that the wind spun Kenan off his feet. Fear seized him; he did not want to die before he fulfilled his God-given mission. But it was hard to get up. He hadn't eaten since last night, nor had he slept. Finally, he managed to push himself upright and, watching the traffic more closely, walked the rest of the way to the airport.

CHARLIE DEAN SAT on the narrow bed, staring at the posters of players from the Detroit Tigers and Red Wings, interspersed with smaller pictures of rap stars and musical groups. Change the uniforms and faces, and Kenan's room would look like a lot of boys' bedrooms across the U.S.

Date the posters a bit, replace the rap stars with Hendrix, and maybe it would have looked like the one Dean shared with his brother when he was a kid.

"He was always a good student," Mrs. Conkel told him, continuing to describe her only son. "But he drifted. It was like he wasn't challenged much in school. Things came too easy at first, and then when they didn't, he didn't want to bother. You know what I mean?"

"Sure," said Dean.

He and Sabot had searched the house; Kenan wasn't there. He wasn't here in a larger sense, either—everything in his room appeared to date from high school.

His parents bounced back and forth between denial and an almost unworldly numbness. Mrs. Conkel had mentioned twice that Kenan didn't have a license and therefore couldn't have taken the family car. Her husband wondered aloud whether he should find a lawyer, but made no move to do so.

"Are either of you Muslim?" Dean asked Kenan's parents.

"Of course not," said Mr. Conkel.

"Were you surprised that Kenan converted?"

"He didn't convert. That nonsense ended two or three years ago."

"Why do you say that?" Dean asked.

"Because Kenan stopped talking about it, that's why. We're Catholic, not Muslim."

"What does being Muslim have to do with anything?" asked Mrs. Conkel.

"The man who was killed was Muslim, and he had been at a mosque just before the murder," said Dean. "Kenan seems to have been there, too."

"I doubt it," said Mr. Conkel.

"Kenan went through a phase," said Mrs. Conkel. "He was looking for something."

"We go to church every Sunday," said Mr. Conkel, his voice insistent. "When he's home, he comes with us."

Mrs. Conkel nodded. There was no point arguing with them, so Dean changed the subject.

"Why do you think he would take the car without telling you?" asked Dean.

"He wouldn't. He doesn't have a license." Mrs. Conkel turned away, but not before Dean saw the tears she was trying to hide.

"Do you know where he would go?"

She shook her head. Her husband shrugged.

"Relatives?"

"We don't have any nearby, and Kenan wasn't close to any of them," said Mr. Conkel. "These people—would they threaten my son?"

"It could be," said Dean. "We don't know who they are."

"Is this some sort of radical group?"

"Possibly," said Dean.

That wasn't the answer Mr. Conkel had hoped for. The expression on his face, which had mixed anger and pain and disbelief in roughly equal portions, turned entirely to anguish.

"Kenan would never hurt someone. Never," said his mother, tears flowing from her reddened eyes. "He wouldn't kill this man. He's not a murderer. He's not."

"All right, calm down, Vic. Let's just calm down." Mr. Conkel glanced at his watch. "How long is this going to be?" he asked Dean. "I gotta get to work. I work six days a week, just to send him to college. You know? It ain't easy."

Dean took another of the Marshals Service cards from his pocket. The number would be answered by the Art Room.

"If you remember anything, please let me know," he said, handing it to Mr. Conkel. "You should report the car stolen with the local police department."

"It's not stolen if my son has it," said Mr. Conkel. "Right?"

"It is if you didn't tell him he could take it."

"They'll arrest him and throw him in jail," said Mrs. Conkel between sobs.

"That may be best thing that ever happened to him," said Dean.

CHAPTER 102

DR. SAED RAMIL LAY on the bed in his suburban Baltimore home, staring at the ceiling fan as it spun in an endless circle. He'd been married for a few years after Vietnam, but the marriage had fallen apart for numerous reasons, and ever since then he'd lived alone, without even a pet to keep him company. He was used to silence, long ago realizing that it was composed of many sounds: the slow swish of a fan, a distant car door slamming, the flutter of a bird hunting for food before dawn.

The voice had not returned since he left Detroit. He was glad—he didn't want to be insane.

If he'd had a blow to his head, a shock to his brain stem, he could understand it. Pulmonary disease, anemia, a central nervous system disorder—a wide range of conditions could cause auditory hallucinations. Unfortunately, none applied.

Lack of sleep, food or water deprivation—these *might* explain it. Yet they did not seem satisfactory excuses, either.

Psychological stress. Well, he couldn't argue against that. But if it was stress, did it mean he'd never be able to do his job? Would he have to give up being a doctor entirely?

And if it was stress, why didn't he hear the voice now?

He couldn't argue that what the voice said was false. Asad bin Taysr *was* an enemy of Islam, and the world was surely better that he was no longer here to spread his hate. Ramil knew this in his heart.

God spoke to the Prophet, Peace Be Unto Him. So why did Ramil dismiss the possibility that Allah was speaking to him? If he believed in God—and he did—should he not accept the possibility that this was God talking to him, not stress, not something caused by a random bump on the head?

Ramil was a good Muslim, but he was not a prophet. What he had heard must be the result of stress and perhaps his own wishful thinking.

He continued to stare at the fan, not quite sure what to believe.

CHAPTER 103

BY THE TIME the plane landed in New Orleans, the Art Room had IDed the passenger in Seat 2B as Joseph Roberts. According to his ticket and the Department of Motor Vehicles, he lived in a large Detroit apartment building; a crosscheck showed that there were at least four other adults with addresses there. He had no credit card, didn't own anything that had to be registered, and did not appear to have had any brushes with the law.

Lia, who had plenty of experience with Karr's "hunches," scowled as the plane rolled up to the gate. Picking at straws was not one of her favorite pastimes.

"Comin' at ya," said Karr as the plane started to unload.

"Peachy."

Lia drifted back toward the middle of the small knot of people waiting for relatives and friends, sipping her coffee to ward off her nagging jet lag. Like most of the Gulf Coast area, the airport still bore the mark of Katrina's ravages. Though it had been well over a year since the hurricane struck, debris still littered the highway and edge of the parking areas. On the other hand, the rebuilding effort was everywhere in evidence, with cranes rising above new steel skeletons as the nation worked strenuously to erase the horror of the storm and shame of its aftermath.

Karr's blond head loomed over the crowd; Lia sidled to the right to get a better view of the young man directly in front of him. The kid looked like a well-dressed toothpick, nervous and jumpy, eyes darting back and forth. She started paralleling him as he walked, her focus not on Roberts but on anyone who might be trying to spot someone tailing him. She turned sharply on her heel, gesturing as if she'd forgotten something; no one seemed to notice. Now at the back of the crowd, she swung around a few yards behind Karr, who was still a few feet in back of Roberts.

"Any time," muttered Lia, indicating to Karr that he could peel off whenever he wanted.

A man in a black suit stood about thirty yards from the flow of passengers from the plane, arms at his side. Robert approached him tentatively; the man tilted his head slightly, then whirled around and walked in the direction of the doors.

One of the FBI agents assigned to help them was sitting in a car ready to pick Lia up and follow Roberts. But Lia had also left two cars outside, and so she followed Roberts to the open-air parking lot, where he and the other man got into a Chevy Impala. Though it dated from the 1960s, the car had been restored and its paint gleamed in the sun. Lia got into her rental and pulled out behind it; a small video bug on her bumper gave the Art Room the license plate number.

"Nice car," said Rockman. "Sixty-eight Impala. Bet it's got a short block, four on the floor, headers. Doesn't handle, but it can haul."

"If I want *Car Talk*, I'll turn on the radio," Lia told him.

They drove west and then north, weaving through the highway work and escaping the built city area and suburbs. Within an hour they had left the interstates, following a succession of state and then parish highways; a half hour after that they were on local roads, only some of which were paved. Swamp and more solid land alternated in an intricate patchwork arranged by man and nature according to a logic so tangled it was indecipherable. Reminders of the hurricane were everywhere: trees that had been pushed off the road and then forgotten, flattened and roofless houses. But nature as well as man had started a recovery—the vegetation was lush, with new growth springing up to replace what had been lost.

"I'm going to lose him soon," said Lia, who had to keep slowing down to avoid being spotted. "These roads are empty. Where's that plane?"

"We're still working on it," Rockman told her. "The plane we've borrowed from customs had engine problems and we've gone to a backup."

A plane might not have helped; the canopy was so thick it looked like early evening rather than noon, and in some places the trees hung so low over the road that they swatted Lia's windshield. Fortunately, the old Chevy kicked up rocks and dust as it went, making it easier to track. Then suddenly the road turned back to macadam. Lia sped up, realizing she was probably going to lose them.

"I see where you are," Rockman told her. "There's a farm just to the west, some sort of fields that are cut out of the jungle there."

A dirt road swung off to Lia's right. By the time she saw the dust hovering in the air near the intersection, she was by it. She hit the brakes and threw the car into reverse.

"I have a turnoff here," she told Rockman.

"You sure he took it?"

"Somebody did."

"I don't see it on the map," said Rockman. "You sure it's there?"

"No, Rockman. I like to share my hallucinations." Was it all men she had a problem with, or just the dumb ones? Lia braced herself as the car bumped off the pavement. "I'm going up it. Where's Tommy?"

"About five minutes behind you."

"Have him stay on the macadam."

After about fifty yards the trail narrowed and then swung hard to the left, then widened and zigzagged through a grove of thick trees. The road dipped downwards and straightened, a swampy ditch on either side. A tangle of fallen trees sat on the right; Lia noticed a clearing beyond them. There was a trail there.

Two men in dark green clothes appeared from behind the tangle. Both men had shotguns.

Lia continued past, her eyes riveted on the road.

"I think I found out where they went," she told Rockman, slowing to take the next curve.

CHAPTER 104

KENAN HAD NEVER been in the St. Louis airport before. Not sure where he had to go to catch the connecting flight to Mexico, he stopped to read the signs. As he did, someone bumped into him from behind. Caught by surprise, Kenan flew to the ground. Unable to get his hands up in time to break his fall, he took most of the blow on his chin. The pain blinded him, a searing shock he felt in his back and skull as well as his face. Tears welled in his eyes, not merely from the pain of the fall but from the last twenty-four hours.

God had forsaken him. He was alone among the People of Hell, without friends, without hope.

A strong hand gripped his arm.

"Let me help you up," said a calm voice.

Fighting back tears, Kenan struggled to his feet.

"Are you all right?" asked a man with yellowish skin. He was roughly Kenan's age, but built like a football lineman.

Kenan managed to nod.

"You dropped this," said the man, scooping up a book from the floor. He placed it in Kenan's hand, then started away.

Kenan, dazed from the floor, stared at the book, a cheap paperback thriller.

It wasn't his.

The man was gone. Kenan tucked the book under his arm and stepped to the side. He moved his jaw up and down, pushing against the pain.

Kenan glanced at the cover of the book. It showed a nondescript skyline framed by a red explosion in the background.

Not only wasn't it his, but it wasn't the sort of thing he would read. Kenan glanced around, looking to see where it had come from. There were no bookstores nearby, no magazine stands. Obviously the man who'd bumped into him hadn't had it.

Unless he was a messenger, sent to encourage him.

That wasn't part of the plan. And the man didn't use any of the words the mujahideen used to identify themselves to others.

But the book must be a message, Kenan thought. Nothing happened randomly—all was part of God's plan, waiting to be revealed. It was meant to encourage him, to keep him from giving up.

Kenan's hand trembled as he looked at the cover again. It showed an explosion deep in a city—God's wrath, surely.

He took a deep breath, then began looking for the flight board, book in hand.

CHAPTER 105

THE BUS STOPPED in front of a store that sold tractor parts. Marid Dabir descended the steps confidently, pretending he came to the small northern Ohio town once or twice a week and knew exactly where he was going.

In truth, it looked as foreign as the moon. He began walking back in the direction of the cluster of businesses they had just passed a half mile away. Small houses bunched together on both sides of the highway, their roofs shimmering in the afternoon sun. Dabir reached a gas station which doubled as a convenience mart and went inside. Thirsty, he took a bottle of water from the cooler and brought it to the counter.

"How do I get to the town library?" he asked the clerk as he paid.

"Black Mountain Highway, next to the town hall," said the girl.

"How do I get there?"

"Well, um, let me see. Chris?" she yelled to one of her co-workers near the back of the store. "Library. How do you get there?"

The clerk, a woman in her mid-thirties who stood about five foot, came up the aisle. "Go up 55, take a left and a quick right, two miles to Black Mountain Highway, make a right, three miles on your left."

"Is there a bus there?"

"Bus?"

"I don't have a car."

The clerk gave him a suspicious look. "There's a taxi service in Redstone. The number's on the phone outside."

"You need to go to the library?" asked a woman in her mid-thirties. She slid a bag of potato chips onto the counter.

"I'm supposed to meet a friend there," said Dabir.

"We're on our way there. We'll give you a ride."

"Thank you," said Dabir. He took a step back, making way for the woman's child, a four- or five-year-old who leaned up against the counter and retrieved the bag of potato chips.

"Let me pay for that before you take it," the woman told the child.

Dabir followed them outside to a small red SUV. The woman strapped the boy into a car seat in the back.

"Go ahead, get in," she told Dabir. She held out her hand. "My name's Debra."

"Thank you. I'm Robert," he added, using a name from one of the credit cards.

"Really? That's my son's name."

"A good name."

"You don't live around here."

"My father did. I'm visiting an old school friend."

The woman's cotton dress rode up on her thigh as she backed out of the parking space. Dabir wondered if the Lord had put her here to tempt him, or to help him.

Perhaps both.

"I thought you were from overseas," said the woman. "Because of your accent. Somewhere in the Middle East. We visited Egypt last year."

"My family was from Egypt," lied Dabir. He knew it was his dusky face that had tipped her off as much as his accent. "We moved here when I was eight."

He thought of killing her and taking her car. He would have to use his bare hands, but it was not difficult; he had killed two men that way, and both were twice her size.

"Where do you live now?" asked the woman.

"Detroit," said Dabir.

"You took the bus?"

"Yes," said Dabir.

The boy in the back dropped his bag of potato chips and began crying. As the woman reached across the seat to retrieve it, she brushed against Dabir's shoulder.

The Devil is tempting me, he thought, holding his breath.

They turned down an empty rural road. Dabir decided that he would kill her here. But as he turned to grab her neck, a siren sounded behind them.

He jerked back in his seat, absolutely still. Debra slowed and pulled toward the shoulder. The police car closed in behind them, then passed, lights flashing.

"Probably just going to lunch," muttered the woman, pulling back onto the highway. "He startled me."

"Yes," said Dabir. He said nothing the rest of the way to the library.

A STORY ON a Detroit newspaper's website that Dabir read at the town library said the police had no new leads in the murder and suicide in the city two days before. While Dabir still did not entirely trust the American media, these reports gave him hope that the brothers had in fact accomplished their mission and then were caught by the police and either forced to kill themselves or did the honorable thing. In any event, Asad bin Taysr had been killed. Dabir could go back now, not to Europe but to Pakistan, and take his rightful place at the Sheik's side.

Dabir booked a flight from Cleveland to Boston in three days; he couldn't find a direct flight with open seats and opted for a connection at an airport in New York state. Using a different card, he booked a flight two days after that from Boston to Dublin, Ireland. He had friends there who could ferry him the rest of the way.

The breaks between the flights were partly to throw off anyone looking for him. But he also needed time to obtain IDs to match the credit cards.

When he was finished, Dabir deleted the history file in the web browser, then went to the desk to find out how to get a bus for Cleveland.

CHAPTER 106

JOSEPH ROBERTS, THE young man Tommy Karr and Lia De-Francesca had followed, was really Jamari Dicoda, a twenty-three-year-old Detroit resident who had spent two years in a medium security prison, but had no known connection to any terrorist organization. According to his prison records, he was a Christian; however, the same records indicated that about midway through his prison stretch he asked to be placed on a pork-free diet. The Desk Three analysts took that to mean that he had converted to Islam, a not uncommon occurrence in prison.

"Or maybe he just doesn't like pork," said Rubens.

"I didn't say it was a lot to go on," admitted Telach.

"Is he still on parole?"

"Ended a few months ago. Johnny Bib hasn't been able to dig up anything more recent. He doesn't have a driver's license or credit cards."

Rubens nodded. Legally, there was no reason to search the compound where he had gone. Common sense, on the other hand, argued that it should be checked out. Not only was the compound protected by armed guards, Desk Three had traced the limited liability company on the tax rolls to a nonexistent address in Baton Rouge. There was no other listing of the company anywhere.

If they were operating overseas, Rubens could have relied merely on common sense to approve the operation. On American soil, however, he had to take legalities into account—the form of them, if not the substance.

"Is there anything we can connect here to Asad's murder?" Rubens asked.

Telach shook her head. "They haven't paid their property taxes in two years," she said.

"I hardly think that would justify a raid. We'll have to use the imminent danger clause in our finding," Rubens told Telach. "I will handle the legal end. Get a force in place."

"Right away."

When Telach had gone, Rubens picked up the phone to tell Bing and, through her, the president. Using the finding—the formal document authorizing the Deep Black mission—as the legal authority for the search was not a panacea. It greatly complicated the prosecution of anyone who might be apprehended at the site, since citing it at trial might open a legal Pandora's Box exposing covert operations around the world. It was one thing to do so in the case of someone like Asad bin Taysr, one of al-Qaeda's most important leaders. Here, they were likely to capture mere foot soldiers, if they captured anyone at all.

On the other hand, Rubens couldn't allow whatever Asad had been planning to proceed. If he had a chance to stop it, he had to take it.

He used that exact phrase to explain his reasoning to Bing. Uncharacteristically, she didn't criticize his decision—in fact, she was so quiet that he almost asked if she was still on the line when he finished.

"You're proceeding on your own authority, then," she said finally.

In other words, if something goes wrong, I'll hang you out to dry.

"Yes," he told her. "That's right. We're following the finding and I'm proceeding as I see fit."

"Very well," she said, promptly hanging up.

CHAPTER 107

CHARLIE DEAN MET Elsa Williams, the detective from the murder investigation assigned to dig up information on Kenan, at the college dormitory building where Kenan had supposedly lived. Elsa's loud voice boomed in the small dorm suite, and even Dean felt a little intimidated as she pressed the roommate for information.

"You didn't think it was *strange* that he disappeared?" Williams demanded.

"He was kind of a strange guy. Disappearing is like, his M.O. I roomed with him a couple of semesters ago. Kind of, you know, cool to have a roommate who's never around."

"Strange how?" asked Dean.

"Just, you know. Strange."

"Who were his friends?" asked Williams.

"Didn't have any."

Williams reared her head, as if she had to move it to process what the roommate said. "Now I find that *hard* to believe. No friends? None?"

"Well, I was kind of a friend."

"Were you a good enough friend to lend him your credit card?" asked Dean.

Williams gave him a sidelong glance, but said nothing.

"No," said the roommate.

"You think he might have used it?"

"No."

"You sure about that?"

The kid gave him a shrug.

"I'd like to check it," said Dean.

"Well, like, um, my mom gets the statements."

"So you don't really know if he used it," said Williams.

"I mean—"

"It's okay," Dean told him. "Give me the number and I'll do it for you."

The young man dug the card out of his wallet and Dean read it as he wrote it down on a piece of paper, allowing the Art Room to hear.

"Just one?" Dean asked.

"All I need. We pay it off every month."

Williams went back to asking about possible friends. Dean looked again at Kenan's things, collected in a small pile on his bed. There were no books and only a few clothes; no papers, no pens.

"This is all he had here, huh?" Dean asked the roommate.

"He had more, books and stuff, but he took it with him."

"And you don't know where."

"Nope."

"You got a lot of stuff," said Williams, taking a long glance around the room. "Computer, books—what's your major?"

"It's chemistry."

"Tough subject."

"You bet."

"He ever borrow money?" asked Dean.

"A couple of bucks, maybe."

"He pay you back?" asked Williams.

The roommate shrugged. "I guess."

"You're a Tiger fan?" Williams picked up a coffee mug with the baseball team's logo.

"Nah. That's just for loose change. Half of it's pennies. And change for the laundry. That's what Kenan mostly borrowed for. Quarters. Half dollars."

Williams shook the cup. "You use slugs, huh?"

"No way."

She picked out something and flipped it at the roommate.

The roommate looked at it. "Well, it's like Mexican. Pesos."

"Isn't worth a dime, I'll bet. But it fits right where a quarter would."

"I didn't use it."

"Relax," said Williams, putting the cup back. "We're not going to bust you for putting slugs in the condom machine."

"I THINK I'D LIKE to call it a night," said Williams after they finished. It was a little after five.

Dean shrugged.

"You disagree."

"I want to talk to his professors," said Dean.

"The religion one especially."

"Him especially." Since it was Saturday, the teachers weren't on campus, but the police had obtained a list from the school, along with home addresses and phone numbers.

"Suit yourself," said Williams.

The religion professor was just leaving his house for dinner. Williams told him they were investigating a murder; he shrugged, but still seemed reluctant to answer their questions.

The man was more than a little full of himself and somewhat contemptuous of his students. He had had Kenan Conkel in two classes: Comparative Religion, an introductory class where "he didn't rise above the herd," and Christianity and Western History this semester.

"How's he doing?" Dean asked.

"Not particularly well, I don't think. I can't recall the specifics, which leads to my conclusion."

"Does he attend class regularly?" asked Williams.

"I don't bother taking attendance. I'd rather that someone not interested in learning stay away."

"Does he ever argue with you in class?" Dean asked.

"How so?"

"He's a Muslim. He must have disagreed with some of what you said."

"This is a history class and my approach is neutral," snapped the professor. But then, in a less confrontational voice, he added, "Why do you think he's Muslim?"

"He is."

"He never identified himself as one. I do have Muslims in my class," the professor added.

"Can you tell me who they are?" Dean asked.

"Really, I can't believe you're asking me to discuss my students' private religious beliefs like this."

"Who did he hang out with?" Williams asked.

"I wouldn't know."

"Kareem Muhammad," said Rockman from the Art Room. "There were only twenty kids in the class. That's *got* to be one of the Muslims."

"What about Kareem Muhammad?" asked Dean.

The professor made a face. "An African-American Muslim with, I must say, many misconceptions."

"Adam Binte," said Rockman.

"What about Adam Binte?"

"I'm not going to discuss my students' religions with you," said the professor. "I really must be going."

"Binte was a friend of his?" Williams asked.

"For your information, Mr. Binte is a Syrian Christian," said the teacher.

"Mr. Dean, please ask the professor if he ever arranged for Asad bin Taysr to talk to a class," said Rubens, suddenly popping onto the line.

When Dean did, the teacher frowned, though Dean couldn't tell if it was because he recognized the name or not.

"Three years ago," said Rubens. "When Mr. Conkel was a freshman."

"Asad bin Taysr was on campus three years ago, wasn't he?" said Dean.

"I often have guest speakers, and I encourage students to seek out other points of view."

"Even al-Qaeda's?"

"I won't dignify that with an answer," said the man. "It's time for you to leave."

"Thank you, Charlie," said Rubens. "Most likely the professor is just an idiot, but we'll look into it further."

"How'd you do that?" asked Williams as they walked back to her car.

"Do what?" said Dean.

"The friends' names. Did you come here with them?"

Dean shrugged.

"Why didn't you tell me about them before? We could've checked on them in the dorms."

"It just kind of came to me," said Dean.

"The speaker he had here—he was from al-Qaeda?"

"Yeah."

"What a jackass."

"You think we can track down some of the kids in his classes? College hangout or something?"

"Sure. But first, we eat," said Williams. "My stomach's startin' to rumble. And you don't want to be in the car with me while that's happening."

CHAPTER 108

"SOMEBODY WHO'S SPENDING that much money subscribing to sports websites is probably betting online," said Robert Gallo, squatting next to Angela DiGiacomo as the Desk Three analyst double-checked the charges on Kenan's roommate's credit card.

"He may have another card to bet," said DiGiacomo. "Check for other accounts while I finish going through these."

"Yeah, sure."

Gallo got up and went to the computer station next to her, bringing up a tool that allowed the NSA to access credit reports with similar characteristics to any known account. The results were presented on tabbed pages behind the main screen, with different tiers of matches represented by each tab. The top tab showed all accounts tied to the same social security number; the next one down matched addresses, then came names. The matches quickly became esoteric and the results more extensive. Gallo could see, for example, the account numbers of every card used to subscribe to MLB.TV the same day that Kenan's roommate did.

He didn't have to go that far, however.

"Look at this—same social number, different spelling of the last name," Kenan said over his shoulder to DiGiacomo.

"Good."

"And ten bucks says that address isn't his, either."

It wasn't, but finding the phony credit card turned out to be only the first step. The card had been used only once, to buy an unrestricted round-trip ticket to Los Angeles a month before. The ticket had never been used—instead it had been exchanged for two other flights, with the difference made up in cash.

Gallo and DiGiacomo discovered that both of those plane tickets had also been exchanged, this time for round-trip tickets between Chicago and Houston. One of these had been used two weeks before.

Tracking down the user was more detective work than computer hacking, and Gallo let his workmate handle that part of the job. Intrigued by the pattern of ticket exchanges, he sifted through airline records to see if he could find other flights that had resulted from a similar series of exchanges. He found several, and once more handed off the information for DiGiacomo to develop while he examined the transactions that had started the trains, trying to find a pattern that he could use to develop more information.

An hour later, Gallo got up from his computer station and lay down on the floor, flooding his bloodshot eyes with eyewash. The only thing the transactions had in common was that they were made with someone else's money.

"WE THINK THIS is Kenan Conkel," Marie Telach told Rubens, pointing at the monitor. "The computer matched it against the feeds from Detroit and the parents' photo."

Rubens leaned close to the machine, studying the slightly blurred video. It had come from a security network used at an airport in St. Louis. The researchers had taken Gallo's information about airplane tickets, coordinating the flights with their arrival times and accessing the airport records, trying to match the flights with information about Asad, al-Qaeda, and other known terrorists. Not all of the airports had computerized video surveillance available, but for those that did, a face recognition tool was used to try to find matches. The tool had found Keenan near the gate where the plane landed four hours ago.

Or maybe not. The face had been caught at an extreme angle, and even the computer had its doubts.

"The computer says it has only a seventy-six percent confidence that this is Kenan Conkel's face," said Rubens.

Johnny Bib began bouncing behind him. "Seventy-six percent confidence is a *significant* level. The formula is based on the standard deviation between the overall match points. More than twenty percent are obscured and therefore the computer scores the points based on a formula developed by—"

Sensing a complicated mathematic dissertation looming, Rubens cut Johnny off.

"It's a guess, whether the computer does it or not. But assuming this is him," Rubens said quickly, "what did he do next?"

"His face doesn't show up on the surveillance tapes at the exits, so it's likely he took a flight out," she said. "Eliminating the gates we have good views of, there are nine flights he could have taken over the next four hours. Passengers on the planes were eliminated for various reasons, if someone was making a connection with the same name, if someone used a credit card, wrong gender, known age—"

"We've narrowed it to thirteen people," said Johnny Bib, for once cutting to the chase. "Thirteen—*thirteen.*"

Thirteen, of course, was a prime.

"There are four flights I think we should concentrate on," continued Telach, doing her best to ignore Johnny Bib. "Houston, two to New York, and one to Mexico City."

"Mexico," said Johnny Bib.

Telach, probably nearing the end of her patience with the eccentric analyst, sighed. "Mexico *was* mentioned in several of the intercepts relating to al-Qaeda two months ago, and there have been a number of money transfers routed there. But—"

"And the flight number is 7-3-3," added Bib.

More prime numbers. Rubens shuddered to think what Bing would say if she thought he committed Desk Three resources based on a crazy mathematician's mystical appreciation of numbers.

"We need something better than that," Rubens told Johnny Bib. "Keep working on it."

ORDINARILY, RUBENS DIDN'T answer his personal phone when it was forwarded down to the Art Room, which it was programmed to do automatically when he was there. But it happened that he was near the phone set when it rang; glancing at the caller ID panel, he saw that the caller was Irena Hadash.

"William Rubens."

"Oh, Bill, thank God. I didn't know who to call. There are two FBI agents here and someone from the NSC. They're telling me I have to surrender my computer."

"Your computer?"

"I need it for work. I come home at three to make sure I'm home in time for Stacie; without the computer I can't work."

"Why are they taking your computer?"

"They're looking for government property. I don't understand."

"Irena, I can't leave where I am now," Rubens told her. "But I'm sending my personal attorney there, James Darcey. Do absolutely nothing until he arrives. You can trust him, I assure you."

"But—"

"Don't worry about the expense."

"Are they going to take my computer?"

Very possibly, Rubens thought; he would have Darcey find her a replacement if that happened. Searching for something reassuring to say, Rubens told Irena that it was common for classified documents and papers to be secured after a top official's death.

"But they did that already," objected Irena.

"Yes. Darcey will straighten this out."

"Will I see you later?"

"Yes." Belatedly, he realized he had misinterpreted the question. "I'll get there as soon as I can, but it will be hours. Unfortunately. I'm in the middle of something difficult to leave. Trust James. I'm calling him now."

◆ ◆ ◆

BING HAD ONE of her aides return Rubens' call, but this was just as well; Maria Mahon had worked with Hadash and Rubens knew her well. When he told her why he had called, Mahon's voice dropped to a whisper.

"There are several sets of documents missing, code-word classified. They're numbered PDF documents."

"Surely no one thinks George's daughter took them."

"I don't think that's the point."

No, of course not. Investigations such as this had been used in the past to throw a little mud on national security figures. It didn't matter what the documents were. Hadash would look bad—as would those who were associated with him.

But this sort of play could easily backfire in this case, given how close the president and Hadash had been. Bing would pretend to steer clear of it, while encouraging it behind the scenes.

"What does the new director think?" Rubens tried to make his voice as neutral as possible, but evidently it didn't work; Mahon didn't answer right away. That told him she was, at best, neutral. He'd hoped for an ally on the inside.

"I don't think she has an opinion. We're supposed to cooperate, if requested."

"I would appreciate knowing if I can do anything to assist," said Rubens.

"I'll keep you updated," she said, her voice still soft. So perhaps there was hope yet.

"I'm sure George would have appreciated that," said Rubens as he hung up. Sometimes it paid to make a direct play at emotions.

CHAPTER 109

DUSK CAME EARLY to the thickly treed plantation about an hour and a half north of New Orleans. By then, four dozen federal officers—mostly from the Bureau of Alcohol, Tobacco, and Firearms, but with a smattering from Customs and the Marshals Service, and led by a core team of FBI Hostage Rescue Team (HRT) agents—were aligned within striking distance of the compound. Another two dozen state police officers were preparing to shut down traffic on the nearby roads. An army reconnaissance aircraft—officially, an RC-7B four-engined Bombardier/de Havilland DHC-7 equipped with an integrated surveillance package, referred to as a "Crazy Hawk"—had flown over from Biggs Army Airfield in Texas and was circling overhead. Had there been time, the aircraft's optical and infrared video information would have been sent to the equivalent of a small workstation on the ground; in this case, Desk Three had fashioned an uplink to the Art Room, which then radioed information not only to Lia and Karr but to the head of the HRT team and three other FBI agents selected as team leaders. Satellite communications systems allowed everyone to talk to each other. A Coast Guard Dauphin helicopter and a small Bell chopper belonging to the state police rounded out the armada.

The question was, would the force be anywhere near enough? Peering through a pair of night glasses from the front of the state police helicopter, Lia couldn't even see the road she'd taken past the compound because of the thick vegetation shielding it. Of the three large buildings where the terrorists might be gathered, only one could be seen from the air. At least the grounds of the abandoned plantation were dry; had the terrorists located a little farther south or to the west, the swamp alone would have protected them.

"What do you say, princess?" snapped Karr over the Deep Black com system. "Ready to rock?"

Lia swept the glasses to the west, eying the clearing where Karr and four members of an FBI Hostage Rescue Team—a cross between SEAL Team 6 and a SWAT team—were to land.

"Your landing zone is clear," she told him.

"Get those ground boys moving," said Karr, practically singing. "We're zero-five from touchdown."

Karr's intense enthusiasm irked her. Most people got dead serious before an action; Karr seemed to get jollier.

Lia gave the go-ahead to the ground units, beginning the complicated ballet. As the state police cut off access on the roads, four different teams would move toward the compound. A fifth team would arrest the two guards who were stationed near the main entrance.

"We're moving," Lia told Rockman in the Art Room.

"We see. Situation is the same as it was," he told her. "Just the two guards near the road. We haven't seen anyone else."

"That's one of the things that bothers me," she told him.

KARR GRIPPED THE handhold at the side of the Dauphin, waiting to jump off. Since the primary goal was to obtain information from the people here, the shotgun he gripped in his right hand was filled with nonlethal shells. Instead of buckshot, shells were filled with a mixture of hard plastic balls and pellets filled with cayenne pepper, which would explode and send a disabling spray over whomever they hit. The modified Pancor Jackhammer could fire all ten of its rounds within a few seconds; Karr had two more of the canisterlike cassettes hanging off the tactical vest he wore over his body armor. His lower pants pockets held two stun grenades apiece. He also had an Uzi submachine gun, borrowed from the marshals, strapped between the two vests to use if things got very ugly, and a pair of pistols, one a .45 at his belt and the other a small Ruger strapped to his right calf. Two of the FBI agents behind him in the helicopter were also armed with nonlethal shotguns; the other two had standard assault rifles. Besides the guns and armor, Karr was wearing a lightweight set of night glasses so that he could see in the dark.

"We're ready, Tommy," said Art Koch, the head of the HRT team. He and his men had participated in several antiterror operations in the past, though never directly with Desk Three.

"Do it!" said Karr, leaping from the aircraft as it landed thirty yards from the largest of the three buildings on the property.

He got about ten yards before two men came around the side of the building holding rifles. Karr swung the Jackhammer level and fired three times. One of the men crumpled, screaming in agony; the other disappeared around the side.

"We are federal agents making an inspection for the Bureau of Alcohol, Tobacco, and Firearms," barked Lia's voice through a loudspeaker projected from her helicopter. "We are serving a warrant under the U.S. Patriot Act. Anything you say can and will be used against you. Do not resist the officers. Do as you are instructed and no harm will come to you. Lay down your weapons and stand with your hands raised high in the air."

The man Karr had shot howled, his eyes streaming with tears. Karr spun him down, then left him as one of the trailing FBI agents came up with his plastic handcuffs ready. He sprinted for the barn, some twenty yards away; when he got there Karr threw himself against the side of the building, caught his breath, then rolled around the corner, gun poised to fire.

There was no one there. He scanned the vegetation to the left, making sure the man hadn't hidden himself there, then began crawling forward, looking for a spot ahead he might use for cover.

"DRIVEWAY IS SECURE. Two men under arrest," reported Team Five.

"Good," Lia told them. "How are we doing on the buildings, Tommy?"

Karr didn't answer. Rockman started to tell her something about the barn, but the head of the team tasked to take the building they called the Cottage reported that it had been secured; two prisoners had been taken. The transmission was so loud she couldn't understand what Rockman said.

"All right, Cottage. Good. Hold on. Rockman, what are you telling me?"

"You have three individuals going toward the barn from the shed."

"Did you hear that, Tommy?"

"I'm not only hearing it, I'm living it," said Karr, huffing as he spoke.

He'll be joking in his grave, Lia thought, picking up the microphone to repeat her warning speech.

KARR SAW THE three men Rockman had warned him about run down the slope toward the barn. When they got about thirty feet from him, he fired at the lead man. The shell popped him in the side and the man slid down, tripping both of his comrades like a scene from a slapstick comedy. But all three jumped right back up. Karr yelled at them to stop, then fired again, this time nailing the closest man in the head. A cloud of pepper spray descended on his as he fell to the ground. The others escaped unscathed: Karr's next shot sailed to the side, missing by a good margin. Frustrated, he started to aim again when a barrage of gunfire sent him to the ground. The bullets missed, but he bashed his knee on a jagged rock so hard that he felt blood rush to his head.

"There! On the roof!" yelled one of the FBI agents.

A barrage of automatic rifle fire followed. By the time Karr got up, the gunman on the roof had tumbled to the ground, dead.

"You all right?" asked Koch, running up to him.

Karr growled. "Let's get into the barn," he told the FBI agent, ignoring his torn pants and bloody knee. "This is getting old."

CHAPTER 110

HERNES JACKSON SORTED the yellow pads one more time, making sure not only that their pages were blank but that there were no impressions left on the underlying pages. He hated the idea of throwing out perfectly good paper; once he was sure there was no vestige of even a stray doodle, he would bequeath them to one of the investigators working on discovering the man or men behind Asad's murder.

Asad's death ended the Deep Black bugging and snatch operation known as Red Lion. While Desk Three was still trying to find out what Asad's target had been, Jackson's job in Detroit was over. Some of the members of the task force were staying on to investigate the murder, under the Department of Justice's direction. A senior FBI agent had flown in that afternoon from Washington to take over. Jackson had written an eyes-only memo for him and then, following Rubens' instructions, dismantled his temporary office. Dean would stay to work with the task force; Jackson was to return to Fort Meade.

Rather than staying overnight, Jackson had booked a late flight back to Baltimore. If he left tonight he would be home in time to honor his weekly Meals On Wheels commitment at lunchtime the next day.

Jackson took one last look around the small office, making sure he had everything. Then, briefcase in one hand and pads in the other, he left the office, walking down the hall and around the corner to the large room that many of the agents and detectives working on the murder were using as a workspace. Jackson looked around the tables and finally spotted Dallas Coombs, an FBI agent who had helped him coordinate the backup teams. The FBI agent was on the phone, so Jackson set the notepads down at the corner of the table he was using as a desk and left.

It had started to mist outside. Jackson tucked up his coat collar as he walked to the car.

"Say, Mr. Jackson. Ambassador?"

Jackson turned around and saw Coombs trotting toward him.

"Glad I caught you," said the agent, winded from the short run.

"I hope you can use the pads of paper," said Jackson.

"Oh, yeah, thanks. Listen—I have to check out some surveillance videos that the Detroit police think may have been Asad bin Fayser."

"Bin *Taysr.*"

"Yeah, I'm sorry. Asad bin Taysr. I was wondering if you could help, because I haven't seen anything except for those still photos, and I don't even have them. I gave my set to the secretaries to get copied."

"I've shredded mine, I'm afraid."

"You think you could check the video for me? Otherwise I'm going to have to go over to the Justice Building and try and find someone to get me into the right office. The secretaries have gone home."

"They left without making the copies?"

"This is Detroit," said Coombs.

"I have a plane at midnight," said Jackson. "And I was going to get something to eat."

"Great. Where did you want to eat? I saw a pizza joint up the block."

"Let's look at the video, and then we'll discuss dinner," said Jackson, opening his car door. "I'll drive."

CHAPTER III

KARR SIDLED UP next to the door of the barn, the shotgun in his hand. The pungent odor of manure mixed with the smell of gas, diesel, and fertilizer, though the nearby fields had not been plowed in at least a year. Two of the ground teams had joined Karr's group, surrounding the barn. The FBI's Hostage Rescue Team was poised near the door, ready to enter.

Koch, the HRT leader, adjusted his radio to act as a public address system and broadcast a warning, telling the people inside the barn to come out with their hands up. Karr tensed, expecting the answer would be gunfire.

They waited a minute, then Karr motioned for the agent to make the call again.

"You have a chance to come out peacefully," said Koch. "This is your last warning."

The large door had a chain that pulled down to release it; once released, the door would swing outwards. The HRT members had rigged a rope so they could open the door from the distance.

"We can toss flash-bangs in through the windows on the side," said Koch. "Pull the door open when they pop, throw more flash-bangs, secure the interior."

"I'd like to get them out alive," said Karr. "That's kind of a high priority."

"We can try tear gas. Barn this old, there's a good chance of a fire, especially with that gasoline I smell."

"Maybe we can get a better idea of where they are inside." Karr rubbed his chin, examining the side of the building.

There were no windows or other openings, just the main door and a closed hayloft door on the second floor. When he was eight or nine, he'd spent weekends at his Uncle James' house, playing hide-and-seek with his cousins. They had an old barn just like this. Once used to store onions, it was slowly disintegrating; one winter holiday they'd taken some boards off it and used them as snowboards. He walked around the side of the barn, looking at the boards, but none seemed loose enough to pull off.

Then he got another idea.

"Start haranguing them on the loudspeaker," he told Koch. Then he grabbed hold of a nearby tree and shimmied up the trunk. Koch, realizing the loudspeaker was supposed to cover any noise Karr might make, explained in loud detail that there was simply no hope of escape and that it was possible and even very likely that the judge and jury would go easy on whoever was inside if they surrendered peacefully.

Karr stepped onto the roof as gently as he could, then climbed up to the top, where a large, louvered cupola provided ventilation to the antique structure. Handmade, the cupola measured at roughly four feet by four feet square. Karr slipped the barrel of his shotgun into the top slot and pried; rather than pulling off the roof of the cupola as he thought, he lifted the entire structure.

"Give me some noise," Karr told Koch. "Couple of flash-bangs. Don't go in yet though."

The grenades, designed to produce a very loud boom and flash of light but not harm anyone, went off in quick succession near the barn door. As they did, Karr yanked the cupola off the roof and threw it to the ground. Then he peered in over the side.

He couldn't see anyone. The problem was, the floor was a good nine or ten feet below the opening; if he jumped, the people downstairs would hear him. He put a pair of video bugs on the rafter and sat back.

"Anyone stirring?" Karr asked Koch.

"Not that we've seen or heard," said Koch from the ground.

"Put two ropes together and toss one end up to me. Then anchor it against a tree."

"You're going inside?"

"Nah. Just playin' Tarzan."

LIA CHECKED ON the state police units, making sure they were in position as the helicopter circled above the plantation. She hated the fact that she was up here, useless.

Not useless, exactly, but up here, away from what was going on. She heard Karr and his plan to climb onto the barn roof and thought *That should be me.*

"Rockman, how does the video from the surveillance plane look?"

"Clean. All the action's at the barn."

"Yeah."

BY THE TIME the rope had been tossed to him, Karr had swapped his shotgun for the submachine gun. He wanted the people inside alive, but not at the expense of his life.

"You watching that top floor for me, Rockman?"

"No one came up."

"All right, FBI, here's the story," Karr told Koch, testing the rope. "Give them one more chance again, as loud as you can. Toss some feedback screeches in, sirens, anything you got. I'll climb down, get near the stairs at the far end, have a look at the interior. I say *go*, hit the flash-bangs and come on in. Don't fire too high, all right? I'm the only guy who's going to be on the top floor."

"Are we still trying to take them alive?"

"Not if it means our guys get hurt."

"Thanks."

"Lia, have the chopper make a couple of passes near the field to add to the noise level. Starting now."

"Roger that."

Karr eased himself into the barn as the helicopter came overhead. Landing a little heavier than he wanted, he opted for speed rather than stealth, sprinting to the open landing.

He pushed back against the nearby wall, then slid around so he could cover the stairway.

Empty.

He bent down and leaned forward, looking first in the direction of the door to the left of the stairs. There was no one near it. A sheetrocked wall separated the barn interior in two.

"There's a wall on your right as you come in," Karr whispered to the FBI team. "I'm at the top of the steps on your left. There's no one in the middle of the barn but I can't see below me. Go! *Go!*"

The interior flashed bright white and the air snapped as the door to the barn flew open. In seconds, the team was inside the barn. No shots had been fired.

No terrorists had been spotted either.

So where were they?

The logical explanation was behind the metal door in the sheetrocked wall. The HRT lined up, ready for the next phase.

"Door opens out," said Koch. "We can blow off the hinges and go in."

"You're assuming it's locked," said Karr. He went to the wall and nudged one of the agents aside. Then he got down on his hands and knees as he crawled next to the door opening. There was about a half-inch clearing between the door and floor, just enough for a video fly to peer through. He took one out, activated it, and held it between his thumb and forefinger, sliding it across the opening.

"Whatchya seein', Rockman? Besides my thumb?"

"Nothing. Shadows."

Karr put the fly level on the floor and then tapped it through the opening with his finger.

"Anything?"

"I can see a table. There's no one by the door."

The stench of manure practically choked him as he got back to his knees. Karr remembered the downside of visiting his uncle's farm—mucking the horse stall.

Though it had never smelled quite this bad.

"Give 'em more of the spiel before we get asphyxiated,"

he told Koch. The FBI agent gave the Miranda warning yet again, this time adding a Spanish translation.

"Movement?" Karr asked Rockman.

"Negative."

"You see a booby trap on the door?"

"I would've told you if I did."

Karr slid out his PDA and did a scan anyway, looking for a magnetic field that would indicate an electric current. Then he tried the knob. It was indeed locked.

"You want us to force the door?" asked Koch.

"Just a second. I need some air," said Karr.

He slipped back and went outside the barn. "Lia—start looking around the perimeter for a tunnel or something like that. I think these guys have flown the coop."

LIA RADIOED THE state police backup units in, spreading them out along a road that ran along the southern and eastern perimeters of the plantation property. In the meantime, her helicopter pilot spun toward the west, giving her a better view of that side of the target area. The Dauphin hovered to the north.

"I think we have some movement fifty yards west of the small house," said Rockman, examining the infrared from the overhead army plane. "Yeah—two figures running through the woods there, in the direction of that creek."

Lia sent a police unit up the road to a bridge over the water. She scanned the area near the creek without seeing anything.

"You see them, Lia?" asked Rockman. "They're cutting across the creek. Three of them."

Lia caught one shadow as it slipped up the embankment. By now men from the assault team were in pursuit, moving toward the water.

"That field over there," Lia told the pilot, pointing to an open area beyond the woods. "We'll let them get into that about halfway, then buzz down in front of them and tell them to surrender. If we can slow them down, our people on the ground can surround them."

The shadows popped from the woods sooner than she expected; the troopers hadn't gotten up to the road yet.

"Get down there," Lia told the pilot.

"What are we going to do if they shoot?"

"I'll take care of that," said Lia, taking out the two pin grenades she had in her belt. "Get us between them and the road."

The pilot pitched the Bell practically onto its side, skidding in the direction of the road. Lia cracked open the door, pulled the pins on the grenades, and dropped them into the field. Then she picked up the mike for the PA system.

"The next grenades will be high explosives," she said. "Throw down your weapons and put your hands up."

Two of the men complied. The third began running toward the road.

A contingent of troopers reached the side of the field and began approaching the two men who'd stopped. But they were too far to catch the third man, who continued across the field toward the road. A thick patch of junglelike woods sat on the other side. The vegetation was thick enough that even their infrared vision gear would have a hard time picking him up.

"Put me down on that road," Lia told the pilot.

"What?"

"Go. I have to get that guy," she said.

Not designed for quick exits, the helicopter door slapped against Lia's arm as she pushed out, throwing off her balance just enough that she fell to the ground. As she rolled to her feet, she saw the man cutting toward the road about twenty yards away. Lia scrambled after him, guided by the spotlight from the helicopter. The ground was uneven and the brush seemed to bite at her as she ran. She barely gained ground, but just as he was about to reach the road, the helicopter descended in front of them, sending a spray of dirt and herding him back to her right. The man seemed to have forgotten her, or at least lost track of where she was, and within a few seconds she was close enough to hear his huffing breaths. Just as she reached out to grab him, he cut back toward the road. Lia lunged; she got hold of his pant leg and shoe, tripping him up. He tumbled free, but as he rose she leapt onto his back, her forearm smacking his head.

To Lia's surprise, the man not only managed to get to his feet but continued running. He flailed his elbows as she tried pulling him down; finally he tripped over something and they both sprawled to the ground.

Lia had had enough of this. She pulled her pistol from its holster near her ribs as she got to her feet.

"I'll blow your ankles apart if you move," she warned the man.

Either he got the message or was too exhausted to run any more.

THE FBI TEAM used a shotgun with special metal slugs to blow off the hinges and lock; three quick blows and they were inside.

The room was empty, a trapdoor open on the right. Three of the walls were filled by large shelves stocked with boxes and large bottles; the fourth was bare, with a padlocked door at the center. The smell here was more chemical than barnyard, and Karr finally realized what they'd found.

The HRT men scrambled downward and began working their way through the passage out to the plantation's southern field.

"Big-time drug factory," said Koch. "Methamphetamine. That's sulfuric acid, rock salt—that's probably the lab room in there."

He pointed at the padlocked door. Karr went over and examined the lock.

"We don't want to blow that door down," the FBI agent added. "We're going to have to call a hazardous materials team. We'll probably need a new warrant, given that the door there is locked and this doesn't look like a terrorist setup, at least not—"

"Well, look at this," said Karr loudly, slipping his lockpick back under his belt, "the door is unlocked."

He bumped his shoulder against the jamb and the door swung wide open.

The room was better stocked than most high school chemistry labs and could have given a few college classes a run for the money as well. Rather than simply extracting ephedrine from over-the-counter cold medicine and making methamphetamine from it as most meth labs did, this operation apparently produced the illegal drug using raw ingredients obtained from Mexico. Sometimes called crank or speed as well as meth, methamphetamine was an illegal stimulant popular with bored suburban youth, rural yahoos, and people seeking a high to accompany sex.

The lab also had the ingredients needed to made ecstasy and mescaline as well.

"This is a huge haul," said Koch. "Might be a record, at least for this area. Congratulations."

"Somehow I don't think that's going to be much consolation for the folks back home," said Karr.

CHAPTER 112

"I WASN'T REALLY a friend, not really," Muna Lufti told Dean. "Kenan—he was kind of strange, you know?"

"Did you ever go to a mosque with him?"

The girl made a face, then glanced at Elsa Williams before turning back to Dean, as if she thought the black police detective was somehow on her side. "First of all, women and men are usually, you know, separate. Right? And second, it's *masjid*. Mosque is a Western word. It comes from mosquito. It's like, a slur."

"Which masjid did he belong to?"

"I don't know."

"When did he become a Muslim?" Detective Williams asked.

The girl shrugged. "I don't know. He wasn't born one?"

"A white boy like that?" said Williams. "No way."

The girl, a very light-skinned Arab-American, looked at the FBI agent as if she had used a four-letter word.

"How often did he go to class?" asked Dean.

"Couple of times. Kenan kind of blows in and out. You wouldn't see him for weeks, then all of a sudden he'd be there. Like a ghost. He always aces tests. He's like a genius nerd."

"When did you last see him?" asked Dean.

Muna shrugged. "First or second week in September, around there. In class. We talked about my trip."

"Where'd you go?" asked Dean.

"Mexico City. I'd been, like, planning it for years. Months. He was pretty interested—we probably talked about it for two or three hours. Longest I ever talked to him about anything."

"Was he trying to hit on you?" asked Williams.

"Kenan? Are you kidding? Like, *me* and Kenan?"

"What interested him about Mexico City?" said Dean.

"I don't know. How I got there. What the taxis are like, the airport, hotels, buses."

"Not the mosques?" asked Williams.

The girl made a face and rolled her eyes. "It was just—it was stuff like how to get around, did I have to talk in Spanish, that kind of stuff."

"Did you give Kenan any Mexican money?" Dean asked.

"Why would I do that?"

"CHARLIE, WE NEED you to go to the airport," said Marie Telach as Dean and Williams got into the detective's car a short time later.

"Excuse me just a second," Dean told Williams, taking out his cell phone. He pretended to punch the buttons, then held it up to his ear. "Hi, it's Charlie. You have any news for me?"

"Muna gave us some good leads," said Telach in his implant. "We're pretty sure Kenan took a flight to Mexico City earlier today."

"He had a Mexican coin in his room."

"Oh? So he'd been there before?"

"I don't know. Maybe in September."

"Okay, we're going to check into that. In the meantime, I have a Gulfstream that should land at the airport in about an hour. Can you get there?"

"Yeah." He snapped the phone closed and found Williams staring at him.

"I have to go to the airport," he told the detective.

"Why?"

"Catch a plane."

"Where to?"

"I don't think I can say."

"*No,*" said Telach.

Williams shook her head. "Which agency are you working for again?"

"Marshals Service."

"Right. And I'm the Queen of Sheba."

CHAPTER 113

JACKSON KNEW AS SOON as he saw the video from the Detroit area convenience store that it wasn't Asad bin Taysr. He zoomed in on the side of his head, where he'd been bandaged in Istanbul; there was neither a bandage nor a healing wound there.

But his profile was very familiar, and not simply because his close-cropped grayish beard and sideburns mimicked Asad's. In height, build, and approximate age, he looked very much like the subject of the German operation: Marid Dabir.

Jackson was tired, and the video, shot by a convenience store security camera, was hardly the best quality. Most likely it wasn't Marid—the Germans had concluded he was dead—but it was something that should be checked out. Very possibly it was another member of Asad's circle who had not been previously identified.

"Are there other images?" Jackson asked the city detective who'd shown him and Dallas Coombs the tape.

"Not from this store. There are other cameras in the area. We haven't checked them yet. We just weren't sure it was worth it. I mean, the clerk in the store gave us almost nothing. The guy seemed suspicious, that's all."

"I'd like to take these to a lab that can analyze them," said Jackson. "And we should look at other cameras in the area, especially around the same time. Ten in the morning?"

"No. A.M. and P.M. are flipped on the tape. That was shot at night. You can see the darkness at the very edge of the frame there, from outside. It's nighttime."

"There's someone standing watching from outside," said the FBI agent who'd accompanied Jackson.

"Face is too fuzzy to see," said the policeman.

"My lab may be able to check that as well. I'd need the original."

"Not a problem."

Jackson looked at his watch. "Do you think the clerk at the store would be working tonight?"

YASIF RAMADAN WAS a thirty-year-old father of two who lived on Detroit's south side. The nightshift gig was his night job; during the day he was a plumber's helper for a small company in the city. He volunteered his background without prompting as soon as Jackson and Coombs showed him the print from the surveillance tape. Ramadan remembered the man not because he was Arab but because he had stared accusingly at Ramadan through the whole transaction.

"Like I was a bug," said Ramadan. "I could tell he was a slime."

"Did you think he was trying to steal from you?" asked the FBI agent.

"No. I watched him—I watch everyone at night. Of course I watch them." He pointed to the side below the counter, where a split television screen carried feeds from four video cameras stationed in the store. "I saw that he was not stealing. You could tell he wasn't from around here, because of the way he looked at things in the store. He couldn't read English very well, if at all."

Jackson surveyed the store. The surveillance cameras were so well hidden that he couldn't spot them, even though he knew from the screen where they must be stationed.

"Was he with anyone?" Coombs asked.

"Guy stood in the door the whole time," Ramadan told the FBI agent. "That was creepy. Was he the victim?"

"We're not sure," said the FBI agent.

"Why did you think he was?" asked Jackson.

"I heard that it was an Arab," said Ramadan. "There are rumors he was a terrorist."

Word spreads quickly, Jackson thought.

"We really don't know," said Coombs.

"We should hang all of them," said the clerk.

"Where did you hear the rumors?" Jackson asked.

The clerk shrugged. "Everyone is saying it. Maybe because he's a Muslim."

Jackson saw the pain on Ramadan's face, as if the accusation against someone who used the same words to pray as he did implicated him as well.

"If you think of anything else," Jackson told him, "please call Agent Coombs."

CHAPTER 114

AN OPTIMIST MIGHT have pointed out that the Louisiana raid had not been a complete fiasco, given that it had broken up a major drug lab; indeed, it was very likely that the illegal drugs manufactured there had already ruined a hundred times more lives than terrorists ever could.

William Rubens had never been accused of being an optimist, and so he described the operation without making any note of a positive side. Neither did anyone else who was listening in on the late-night conference call with the president.

"This puts us back at square one," said Bing. "Worse— we've lost twelve hours."

"Maybe the attack died with him," suggested the vice president.

No one wanted to state the obvious—they couldn't count on that—and after a few moments of dead air, the head of Homeland Security gave a report on different preparations around the country, ending by recommending that the security status be raised from orange to red. Rubens had never liked the color codes and had little use for the system in general, but this was neither the time nor place to voice his objections. In the end, the president vetoed the change, noting that the guidelines called for such an alert to be given only if a "site specific" threat had been clearly identified.

"Well, hopefully we get that intelligence before it's not too late," said Bing, characteristically driving a knife into Rubens' ribs as the phone conference ended.

Tired, Rubens rose from his desk and kicked off his shoes,

beginning a Yoga routine to stretch his tight muscles. He leaned back, breathing from the pit of his stomach. The yogis who'd taught him as a boy had said that the exercise emptied the bad energy from his body, replacing it with fresh strength. Rubens had stopped believing most of the spiritual mumbo-jumbo that accompanied yoga when he was fourteen or fifteen, but he welcomed that particular idea now.

He remembered his promise to Irena Hadash. It was far too late to call her; he'd do so tomorrow, first thing.

Perhaps he should call now anyway.

No. It was too late. Better to let her sleep.

The Art Room phone rang as he started another stretch. Rubens exhaled slowly, then picked up the receiver.

"Rubens."

"Mr. Rubens, Ambassador Jackson has something you ought to know about," said Chris Farlekas, who had relieved Telach as Art Room supervisor for the night. "I have him on the line right here."

"Let me speak to him."

"I think Marid Dabir was in Detroit the night before Asad was murdered," Jackson told him when he came on the line. "I have a video surveillance tape of him, or what might be him, in a convenience store near where the murder took place. It looks very much like the video from Istanbul."

"How soon can you get the tape to us?"

"My flight leaves in two hours."

"I will have Mr. Farlekas see if he can arrange a courier to take the tape," Rubens told him. "I'd prefer you to stay and help the task force. Mr. Dean is investigating another lead."

"I did have a commitment back home."

"Meals On Wheels," said Rubens, remembering Jackson's weekly charity, delivering food to shut-ins. "We'll arrange for someone to cover that for you. Don't worry."

"Thank you," said Jackson. He sounded disappointed.

"If Dabir is in Detroit," Rubens continued, "it's possible he helped set up the mission. He met Asad bin Taysr in Istanbul and was involved in the German operation."

"I seem to recall from the background paper that they

didn't get along. Even in the transcript of their meeting, they seemed restrained."

"Yes." Rubens knew from personal experience that it wasn't necessary for people who worked together to get along. Besides, the information on the inner workings of the al-Qaeda leadership was so thin that any account of friction had to be regarded skeptically.

"The reason I brought it up," continued Jackson, "is that maybe he was involved in the murder. Maybe he thinks Asad set him up in Germany, and he wanted revenge."

A possibility, agreed Rubens, though it was more likely that Marid Dabir was some sort of accomplice.

"Whatever his motivations," said Rubens, "finding him will be a priority, if this does turn out to be him."

"Understood."

"I was wondering, Mr. Ambassador," added Rubens, "what you thought of Dr. Ramil's performance in Detroit."

"He was very good," said Jackson. "I sensed he bristled at being forced to stay in the background, however. The other doctor was somewhat aggressive, and I believe they clashed. Doctors, in my experience, never like to play second fiddle, especially to other doctors."

"Very well," said Rubens. "I'm going to hand you over to Mr. Farlekas. Please stay on the line."

CHAPTER 115

KENAN GOT TO the Mexico City bus station with only ten minutes to spare. But that was enough—he already had a ticket
and remembered the way to the boarding area quite clearly.
He joined the queue and got a seat about halfway down the
aisle.

Kenan still held the paperback he'd found at the St. Louis
airport in his hand. He was convinced that the book was a
sign that God was watching him.

Just as the bus driver started to close the door, another passenger ran up. The man boarded the bus; though there were
plenty of empty seats, he sat next to Kenan.

For a moment, Kenan bristled. Then the man took a small
Koran from his pocket.

With trembling fingers, Kenan took out his own and showed
it to his guide.

CHAPTER 116

BY THE TIME Dean landed in Mexico City Sunday morning, the Art Room had found the alias Kenan Conkel had used during his September visit and connected it with a pair of stolen credit cards used for a cash advance and meal in Mexico City, as well as an airline ticket to Veracruz, a city on Mexico's Gulf Coast.

"I doubt he was there on vacation," said Telach sarcastically as she briefed Dean, "but we haven't figured out what he was doing. If he was setting up a safe house or some sort of network, that may be why he's there."

The fact that it might be part of whatever attack Asad was planning was left unsaid. The Mexican police had been told that Kenan was wanted in connection with the murder in Detroit; Dean was to talk to them first thing Monday. He would also check in with the CIA, which had an extensive file on al-Qaeda dealings in Mexico.

"First, get some sleep," Telach told him. "I know you haven't had much the last week."

Dean grunted. He took a cab to the hotel the Art Room had booked, then went out again to check the area where the cash advance had been made, a business district largely deserted on Sunday. The restaurant, by contrast, was in a bustling neighborhood, the street choked with locals and a smattering of tourists. Dean wandered through the nearby streets as if he were a jet-lagged, awestruck tourist, sizing up the area. After about five minutes he realized it was useless to look for Kenan here, but he kept walking anyway, hoping for a lucky break that would snag the kid. When he finally gave up, he had an impossible time getting a taxi and ended up walking nearly three miles back to the hotel.

Worn out, Dean collapsed on his bed as soon he got into the room. Within moments, he was sound asleep.

He woke at three A.M. the next day. Dim yellow light filled the room, as if it were encased in amber. Smog had descended on the city, filtering the bright lights of the hotel and nearby buildings. Outside, the city was cast in a sinister sepia, the color something stolen from a 1930s gangster movie. It would be the scene right before the good guy was shot, thought Dean, the setup for the big tearjerker at the end.

He closed the curtains and went back to the bed, but couldn't sleep. He thought of Kenan Conkel and then his parents, clueless and confused back home.

Dean thought of his own father, stubborn—twenty times more stubborn than Kenan's for sure—and ornery. He'd have come after Dean if he heard he'd been mixed up in something like this.

Or maybe not. Maybe he'd been in denial as well. Dean had expected him to make trouble with the marines, but he hadn't. He'd just treated Dean as if he didn't exist, which at the time was all right with Dean.

If he saw Conkel now, Dean wasn't going to bother shadowing him. He'd grab the kid and get him locked up. It was the best thing for him, and his family, to say nothing of the innocent people he might end up helping to murder.

Assuming Dean caught up with him.

Dean closed his eyes, but he couldn't turn off his brain. After an hour more of fitful tossing and turning, he got up and took a shower, then went to look for something to eat.

CHAPTER 117

"IT'S A CHEMICAL plant in Galveston, not Houston," said Johnny Bib, pointing at the diagram. "Not Houston. Close, but no banana."

Rubens ignored the non sequitur, looking over to the analyst he'd brought along with him, Mark Nemo.

"So it's legitimate?" Rubens asked.

"Yes, but." Nemo opened the folder on his lap and slipped out a piece of paper with a photo on it; it was an exterior shot of the site. "This file is based on the company's own website. Someone cut and pasted a few bits into the file."

Lahore Two, the CIA source purporting to know al-Qaeda's U.S. target, had finally delivered his promised information. The file consisted of several bills of sale concerning the purchase of explosives from a Chinese company, supposedly for resale, by a commercial supplier in Turkey. Normally used in construction, the explosives totaled several tons. The Turkish company did exist, but the computer geeks working for Desk Three could find no trace of the purchases in the company's records—which might or might not prove that they were diverted to al-Qaeda. The Chinese company's records were in such disorder that anything was possible.

The file also contained a diagram of a chemical plant, along with a crude map of the area showing the nearby Houston Ship Canal, which connected the two cities. The diagram didn't show where a bomb would be detonated, but any reasonably intelligent psychopath would be able to pick out half a dozen places where the explosion would do decent damage.

Rubens put the printouts of the file and the website side by side on his desk. The similarities were obvious; whoever had put the file together had used the website to gather data.

"What's the 'but'?" asked Rubens.

"Well, the thing is—someone from Pakistani intelligence accessed that website the same day this file was created," said Nemo. "They have a pretty good system for checking page downloads and hits. And, this is a chemical company. They go weeks without anyone looking at their pages."

The file could be a preliminary mission brief, rough instructions delivered to a field commander, who would then conduct an on-site reconnaissance before formulating the real plan. Or it could be something someone put together to justify a decent payday from the CIA.

Rubens leafed through the web pages of the real plant. According to the information, Galveston PC was the biggest maker of plastics on the Gulf Coast.

A decent target, but big enough? Asad's other targets had been larger.

If it were one of several targets, it would certainly be big enough. Disrupt the plastics industry, and the effects would be far reaching. Asad had made it clear that the aim of his campaign was economic damage.

Even so . . .

"You did good work," said Rubens, handing back the files. "Keep at it."

"SO YOU THINK Lahore Two's information is bad?" said Collins when Rubens told her what they had found. She had only the slightest defensiveness in her voice, and Rubens couldn't decide whether she was sincere or had simply become better at hiding her animosity.

"It's really something you will have to make the call on," Rubens said. "The file with the diagram could have been put together in about ten minutes by anyone with access to a computer. And if your source is in Pakistani intelligence, the timing seems provocative at best."

Collins would not identify her source, and Rubens didn't

expect her to. But her silence tended to confirm that he was, in fact, with Pakistani intelligence.

"Are you going to bring this up at the conference call this morning?"

"I thought it would be proper for you to do so," said Rubens. "Unless you want me to."

"Thanks." Collin's relief was obvious. "I'll do it."

CHAPTER 118

ON HIS WAY over to interview the owner of the Mexico City restaurant where Kenan had apparently eaten during his first visit, a thug sidled up next to Charlie Dean and tried to steal his wallet. The would-be thief made the mistake of grabbing Dean's arm and twisting it behind him; Dean promptly threw the man to the ground, then swung back in time to land a haymaker on the jaw of an accomplice. The plainclothes Mexican detective accompanying Dean grabbed both, offering Dean a chance at "instant justice" as he called it: five minutes in the alley with each of them, and they'd call it even. Dean passed.

It was the highlight of his day. The restaurant owner didn't remember Kenan, nor did any of the staff; they seemed so harried that Dean didn't doubt they wouldn't remember his face in five minutes. Everything the Mexican police knew about al-Qaeda came from reports Dean had read on the way down. Though the deputy chief in charge of terrorism matters was exceedingly polite, Dean could tell that looking for Kenan would have about the same priority for the overworked department as rescuing a cat stuck in a tree.

As for the CIA—the officer who was supposed to pick up Dean at the hotel got stuck in traffic and never showed up. Dean finally found his own ride to the embassy, where he got a half-hour lecture on the problems of dealing with the Mexican authorities from the deputy station chief.

The FBI agents assigned to the city to assist in terrorism investigations were more receptive—not to mention punctual—but they didn't have much useful information either. Most of what they knew about related to guerilla groups and drug smugglers far outside the city; Kenan's name and face drew shrugs. But at least they offered to take him to dinner.

"Try Veracruz tomorrow," Telach told Dean when he checked in. "If we come up with anything for you to check out in the meantime, we'll let you know."

CHAPTER 119

A NEW DETROIT was rising from the ruins of the old near the river and the old downtown; one could look through the shell of the abandoned 1250 Fort Street Building and see the luxurious Riverfront Apartments in the background, or view the Renaissance Tower above the pockmarked hulk of the Highland Park Ford Plant, where the assembly line had changed America and the world forever. The juxtaposition of old and new reminded Hernes Jackson of Kosovo and Bosnia, war zones he'd toured while in the State Department. But here ruin and rebirth were on a larger scale, the decay more widespread, the optimism more promising. If every boarded-up window and gleaming new brick represented a family, millions must be scrambling.

Ambassadors looked at the world from the macro level—whole cities or nations on the move. Now that he was retired, Jackson thought of the individuals. What did the gross national product measure if you lost your home, or just bought a new one?

"Penny for your thoughts," said Dallas Coombs as he and Jackson drove to a raid on a house where one of the suspects might have stayed. Coombs had been assigned by the clearly skeptical head of the task force to work with Jackson on "the Dabir angle," trying to locate the al-Qaeda terrorist in the Detroit area. Neither he nor Jackson believed that Marid Dabir was still in the city, but finding traces of him might prove useful in unraveling whatever the terrorists had planned.

"I doubt my thoughts are worth even a farthing," Jackson told Coombs.

"How much is a farthing?"

"A quarter of a penny."

Coombs laughed, but only for a second. They turned the corner and saw a Detroit patrol car ahead, blocking off traffic for the raid. Coombs got out his ID and showed it to one of the officers, who had to move his vehicle to let them through.

The target of the raid was a small bungalow on the southwestern side of the city. Built in the early 1900s, the two-room cottage stood alone in a sea of empty lots, its faded asbestos siding and ripped fabric awning rising above waves of weeds and crumbled concrete. Jackson followed Coombs through the side door into the kitchen, where a confused young man in his underwear stood next to the table, his hands outstretched as if begging for an explanation. With none to offer, Jackson continued into the front room, whose floor was covered with mattresses. A pair of detectives were standing to one side while a forensics team surveyed the room.

"We're checking on the rest of the occupants now," one of the detectives told Coombs. "We'll have them picked up for questioning by four, no later."

Plastic boxes sat next to most of the beds; shirts and underwear were neatly folded inside, with a few personal items like radios and books.

It was obvious that Marid Dabir would not hide in this sort of place unless he was truly desperate, and Jackson had no reason to suspect he was. The men who had committed the murder might be a different story. All three had phony drivers' licenses and so far had not been identified.

Jackson went back to the young man in the kitchen. Two plainclothes officers were asking him questions about the others who lived here.

"So everybody here works at the same place?" asked one of the policemen.

"Two different restaurants, during the day. At night, some as watchmen," said the young man. He had a pronounced accent; Jackson, no expert, guessed it was Egyptian.

"Everyone works?" asked Jackson. The policeman who had been asking the questions deferred to Jackson—a benefit, one of the very few, of thinning silver hair.

The young man nodded.

"And how long has each one lived here?"

The youth began calculating.

None of the occupants had been in the house more than ten months, according to the young man, nor less than three. He himself had been there the longest and had, it appeared, the best-paying jobs; most of the others worked three to his two.

"I wonder if this man looked familiar," said Jackson, taking two pictures of Dabir from his pocket. The man studied it, then shook his head.

"Thank you." Jackson extended his hand; the young man hesitated, then pumped it profusely.

"He recognized him. I'd bet my life on it," said Coombs outside. "You see how he hesitated?"

"On the contrary," said Jackson. "He was tempted to lie because he thought it might help him, but decided against it."

"Nah."

"Perhaps I am wrong," admitted Jackson. "But I have a great deal of experience with lies."

JACKSON AND COOMBS had spent Sunday giving pictures of Marid Dabir to mosques and stores in the ethnic areas of Detroit and its suburbs, saying that the man was possibly involved in Asad bin Taysr's murder. The fliers produced a number of calls to a toll-free number set up by the task force; the majority accused the police of stereotyping Arab-Americans and appeared to have been made by a woman calling from one of the well-to-do—and predominantly white—suburbs outside the city. But several appeared to be legitimate and worth checking into. About halfway down the list was a call from an imam at a mosque near Dearborn who said one of the mosque's members thought he recognized the picture of Dabir and had helped him find a hotel a few hours after the murder.

"That would be the one we should check first," said Jackson.

Located about two miles from the towering Islamic Center of America, the mosque was modest in size; the house Coombs had just been in was only slightly smaller. A group of children were lined up on the sidewalk outside when they arrived, waiting to go to an after-school day care program. The imam, a tall man with a booming voice and a jutting chin, met them as they walked toward the entrance, undoubtedly tipped off to their identity by the large aerial antennas on the rear of Coombs' car. He gave them directions to a small store in Detroit and promised that he would call ahead.

"Terror is the enemy of us all," he said as they left.

His tone was the sort a preacher might use; Jackson discounted it. The man at the convenience store, however, was as sincere as he was taciturn, identifying the man as someone who had appeared in his shop and asked for an inexpensive hotel. His son had taken him to a motel three blocks away.

"See, those are the guys these people hurt," said Coombs as they drove to the motel. "Guy struggling to make a living. Turn a lot of people against Muslims."

"That's part of the goal. The extremists don't want Muslims to integrate into Western society," explained Jackson. "Their vision of Islam doesn't allow it."

"Yeah. Well, they'd have trouble anyway. I felt bad for the guy. I was going to buy something, just to help him out."

The motel clerk remembered that someone had come in with a young man "a day or three ago," but he didn't recognize the picture.

"Could be, might not be. Guy kind of looked Egyptian, but you know," said the clerk, who was an African-American. "Paid cash." He shrugged, as if the money settled any and all questions.

"Is he still here?" asked Coombs.

"No, sir. Room's vacant, if you'd like to look at it."

"I would. Do I need a search warrant?"

"Nah. We're friends, right?" The young man laughed nervously. Jackson wondered if he would have said the same thing to Coombs if the FBI agent had been white. "Besides, if you was staying the night, you wouldn't need a piece of paper to do that, right? So where's the harm?"

"That's right," said Coombs.

The room had obviously been cleaned. While Coombs debated whether it was worth calling in the forensics unit or not, Jackson asked the clerk if the motel had a computer system.

"We have a computer," said the clerk. "Just the one. For reservations."

"I wonder if it would be possible to look at the computer."

"Look at it? It's right on the desk."

"I meant, look at what's on it."

"I guess so. How long will it take?"

"Are you connected to the Internet?"

"DSL," said the man proudly, as if the high-speed connection were a status symbol.

"It won't take very long, I suspect," said Jackson taking out his satellite phone.

CHAPTER 120

KENAN STOOD UP as the boat approached the tanker. From the distance, the ship's sides seemed very low in the water. But now that they were close, it loomed above them, larger even than the vessel he had crewed on the year before, let alone the ships he'd trained on as part of the advanced bridge management classes this past summer. It was a modern ship, with a long red hull and a bright white superstructure several stories high. The controls he expected to find on the bridge would allow it to sail with a normal complement of fourteen, and in fact it could be sailed with far less—and would be.

The *Aztec Exact* had been built in 1996 for a Dutch concern that had gone bankrupt; bought by the Iranian state petroleum company, it had been sold to two businessmen fronting for al-Qaeda. The plan to convert it into a floating bomb had been conceived more than two years before, but logistics—and money—had prevented its use until now.

Kenan braced himself, preparing to reach for the boarding ladder that hung over the side. Suddenly the boat seemed to lurch backwards. Kenan recoiled against the thin metal rail, barely keeping himself from falling into the water.

"There is the matter of my pay, *señors,*" said the boat captain, his English considerably better than when they started out.

Kenan looked at him, then at the mujahideen who had come in the bus with him from Mexico City.

"You were paid," said the other man.

"Not enough," said the captain. "If another hundred dollars

cannot be found, perhaps I will forget my promise not to tell others what I have seen. A large boat like this, anchored out here for days—why would that be? Smuggling, perhaps?"

The captain grinned.

Kenan controlled his anger as the other mujahideen took the small shortwave radio from his belt. The greed of Devil People was almost incomprehensible.

"We have no money," the mujahideen told the captain. "But I will see what I can arrange."

The captain smiled. Kenan heard the mujahideen say something in a language he guessed was Arabic. Before he could try and puzzle out their meaning, shots rained down from the ship above, and the boat captain had fallen to the deck.

CHAPTER 121

IT TOOK ROBERT Gallo about two hours to download a full copy of the computer drive from the hotel Ambassador Jackson had found. By the time he was done, Angela DiGiacomo had already determined that the man believed to be Marid Dabir had used a fake name and address to register at the hotel. The name—Burkha Akhtar—didn't correspond to any known alias used by al-Qaeda, let alone Marid Dabir. It did, however, match a name that had been cited by German intelligence in reports two years before of possible al-Qaeda activity in Germany. It was another coincidence, tantalizing but not quite conclusive.

"Kinda like my mom's meatballs," said Gallo as he discussed it with DiGiacomo.

"What do you mean?"

"They're kinda like my grandma's, but not quite."

"Any time you want good meatballs, just let know."

"Maybe I'm overinterpreting this, but did you just invite me to dinner?"

DiGiacomo flushed, but then shrugged. "Maybe."

That "maybe" powered Gallo for the rest of the day.

"SEE, THEY'D BE in two different places at the same time," Gallo told Johnny Bib, showing the credit card charges for the flights. "Why would you be making reservations to fly from Cleveland to Boston when you're in Des Moines?"

"You're sure he's in Des Moines?"

"Angie checked it out. She called his hotel."

Johnny Bib turned to DiGiacomo. "True?"

She nodded.

"Maybe it's his wife or another relative."

"No wife," said Gallo. "And his relatives are all back in Texas."

"We think he gained access to the motel's computer and took the credit card numbers from there," Gallo said.

A grin came to Johnny Bib's face. He snatched the memory stick with the data on it and was about to bolt from the room, probably to tell Rubens, when Gallo stopped him.

"Wait, we're not done. See, I checked out where the reservation was made from. Turned out to be a computer in a library in Ohio."

"Good."

"Another reservation came from there that same day, almost at the same time. This one's for a flight from Boston to Ireland."

"Better!" chirped Johnny Bib.

"It's on there," said Gallo as his boss flew from the room.

"Do you think he was always strange?" asked DiGiacomo.

"I don't think he's that strange," said Gallo. "Comparatively."

CHAPTER 122

THE NOISE IN the engine room was deafening, but Kenan nodded as the senior engineer showed him and the man who had
accompanied him from Mexico City around. The man's name
was Razaq Khan, and he was their leader.

The two engine experts had stayed with the ship when it
was left here two weeks before. Kenan could tell from the
rush of words leaving the engineer's mouth that he was starved
for company.

"The engines perfect in order," said the man with his less
than perfect English. "They are soldiers of God."

"*Mujahideen,*" said Kenan.

The engineer smiled and nodded enthusiastically. Kenan
turned and looked at his assistant, a young man no older than
he was. The youth had a slightly dazed look on his face, as if
he were drugged. Kenan guessed it was the result of the foul
air in the engine compartment, which smelled of sea water,
fuel, and stale cigarettes.

The ship had been prepared in an Algerian dry dock several
months before crossing the Atlantic. The tanks were filled with
a liquid explosive derived from rocket fuel, primed to be ig-
nited by a web of plastic explosives surrounding the tanks. The
detonator wires ran through the ship to a pair of large control
boxes connecting them to a control panel on the bridge. The
bomb would be detonated by turning a simple key on the box
and moving four levers one by one from neutral to the top position before plunging them together to the bottom. Khan kept
the key on a chain around his neck.

"We will join together on the deck for evening prayers," Khan told the men, using his Punjabi-flavored English. "Come."

The senior engineer seemed reluctant to leave his engines. He took a rag from his back pocket and wiped his hands, even though they were as clean as Kenan's. Then he threw down the rag and started for the door.

Besides Kenan, Khan, and the two engineers, two African brothers were aboard. The men had been chosen probably as much for their ability with rifles as their experience as seamen; it had been one of them who had shot the Mexican fishing captain. They understood very little English; Khan used Arabic to speak with them, though it was not his native language.

"We have begun well," said Khan when they reached the bridge. "We will do even better. It will take two days and nights for us to find our destiny."

Kenan listened carefully as Razaq Khan laid out the plan. There had been some complications—at least one other brother was supposed to be with them—but they would leave immediately, for the plan required them to follow a strict timetable. This presented some difficulties, but Allah would help them overcome them.

Yes, thought Kenan; surely God would allow them to fulfill His plan. No job was too difficult if Allah willed it.

"We will live a glorious life in Paradise," said Khan. He pointed to the east. "Mecca is that direction. We should all pray and rededicate ourselves to the glory of the one, true God, the God who brings His enemies to justice."

CHAPTER 123

"YOU'RE CONSISTENT, BILLY, I'll give you that." The president leaned back in the chair behind his Oval Office desk. He'd been twiddling an oversized paperclip in his fingers since the briefing began; the wire was now a perfect circle.

"We don't know where the target is. If we bug Marid Dabir, we may be able to find out."

"Been there, done that," said Bing. "Our best chance of getting information is to grab him as soon as we can."

"He's not planning on leaving the country for another three days," said Rubens. "Why not? The most logical conclusion is that he has to meet with someone else."

"All the more reason to grab him now, before he can do so," countered Bing. Rubens knew she was still smarting from the fact that he had called on the president personally, bypassing not only her but the president's chief of staff. Marcke had called her in, but only after Rubens had already told him what they'd found.

"What information do we have on a target?" Marcke asked.

"Nothing new," said Rubens.

"Houston remains the best guess," said Bing. "Despite the question raised about the CIA's source."

"Nothing new on that, Billy?" Marcke asked.

"I'm afraid not. We are working on it. I hope to have additional information by the evening phone conference with Homeland Security."

Marcke got up and walked around the perimeter of his

desk, thinking as much as stretching his legs. Word of the thwarted al-Qaeda plot in Saudi Arabia had leaked out over the weekend; the effect was another run up in oil prices. A successful attack on American soil, even one that was only partly successful, would push prices through the roof.

"The CIA has information that the attack may come from the sea," said Bing.

"Based on what?" said Rubens.

"Humint. It's being evaluated." Bing rattled off the slang term for human intelligence—spies—with phony casualness. "There are also tons of Chinese explosives in the mix, remember," said Bing. "It would be easiest to move those by ship."

Rubens hadn't forgotten about the explosives at all, but once again, the information was so vague that it was in effect useless. The Chinese had sold explosives to a company that maybe was helping al-Qaeda, or that al-Qaeda operatives had pretended to represent—of course, it could be true. Until they were able to actually trace the explosives—they'd tried without success, as had the CIA—the information wasn't worth the status of rumor.

"You're not positive this is Dabir who's going to Boston?" said Marcke, returning to a point Rubens had made earlier.

"We'll know tomorrow in Cleveland," said Rubens. "We know someone is using those cards other than their legitimate owners, and that the tickets were bought from a small town accessible to Detroit by bus. It may not be Dabir, but the circumstantial evidence is tantalizing."

"Where would you mount the operation?" asked the president.

"The airport in Cleveland is a little difficult to control," said Rubens. "I've spoken with the FBI people about this extensively, and we think it would be easier to get him when he changes planes at Stewart Airport in Newburgh, N.Y. We could stage an incident that would look entirely natural, and insert the bug there."

Located about seventy miles north of New York City, the airport was much smaller than Cleveland's and the layout made grabbing Dabir simpler; he could be isolated when coming off the plane without tipping off any of the other passengers, or even anyone at the airport. Stewart also had Air National Guard and Marine Corps facilities that could be used.

"The old Stewart Air Force Base," said Marcke. "Ham Fish Jr. used to fly a puddle jumper to D.C. from there. Back when I was knee high to a grasshopper." Fish had been a prominent Republican congressman when Marcke served one of his two terms in the House. "I wonder what Ham would think of this mess." He smiled wanly, as if remembering the old congressman.

"We can't run the risk of losing a second source," said Bing. "It's too much. At least if he were in custody, we'd have a chance of getting information. And politically, it would at least be defendable."

That was the sort of argument that George Hadash had *never* made—basing a national security issue on how it would benefit or hurt the president. Rubens waited for the president to rebuke her. Instead, Marcke merely frowned.

"Time's running out here, Billy," said the president. "Let's arrest him and interrogate him. Take him in Cleveland, as soon as he shows up for the flight."

"It's possible that Dabir's arrest may move up the timetable for an attack," said Rubens. "The quieter the operation, the better. The FBI preferred Stewart because it would be easier to control. It's a little more than an hour away."

"Very well. Do it there," said Marcke. "But get it done."

CHAPTER 124

LIA DEFRANCESCA PUSHED the cleaning cart slowly across the floor, eying the line of food shops at the Cleveland Airport Terminal as she continued on her quest to get a good idea of the place before the mission tomorrow evening. There wasn't all that much different about this terminal than most others in America, or across the world for that matter, but sometimes the subtle things made a difference; knowing to turn left rather than right out of the bookshop to get to the gate, for example.

She stepped over to a waste can that had a view of the concourse and put down the video bug she was using to check positions for the surveillance tomorrow.

"If you could go six inches to the right, that would be perfect," said Claudell Greenstreet, the runner. Greenstreet was new, which was why he drew the comparatively unimportant task of helping her prep for the mission.

The fly blended perfectly with its surroundings, and rather than move it Lia pushed the waste can itself over.

"Lookin' good," said Greenstreet.

As Lia returned to her cart, a middle-aged woman wearing a dark blue business suit and a touch too much makeup walked up and waved her hand in Lia's face.

"Yo, Miss. Miss?"

"Yeah?"

"That little brat over there spilled his soda all over the floor." The woman pointed in the direction of the food concessions, where a three-year-old was using the tables as a jungle gym.

"And?"

"You're going to clean it up, aren't you?"

"What do I look like? A janitor?" asked Lia, pushing the cart down the aisle.

CHAPTER 125

EVEN THOUGH HE had performed well in Detroit, Rubens would have preferred giving Dr. Ramil a few days off. But his other doctor was still sick, and it made more sense to have Ramil standing by for the operation than to bring in an unvetted replacement. Still, Rubens reserved the option and his decision until Dr. Ramil reported to his office that afternoon.

"I have another assignment for you, if you're up to it," he told Ramil.

"Of course."

"Rather easier than the others. I'd like you to stand by in Newburgh during an operation there. On the off chance that something goes wrong."

"Another bugging operation?"

"No," said Rubens. He would not give Ramil any more information than necessary, which meant it was unlikely Ramil would get *any* information.

"Marie Telach will pick out a place for you to stay that's convenient. You'll want a car. The usual arrangements will be made."

"Sure."

"I'm assuming that you don't have any prior connections to Newburgh?"

"Never even heard of it," said Ramil.

"Good." He started to dismiss him, then thought better of it. "Doctor—now that you've had some time to reflect—"

"I was just tired in Istanbul."

"You threw up at the morgue in Detroit."

"Morgues." Ramil looked down, embarrassed. "It's been a while. Morgues are a certain specialty."

"If there comes a time when things are overwhelming, you will let me know," said Rubens.

"Yes."

"SOMEONE WITH A Dutch passport took a flight to Turkey connecting from Detroit last year," Mark Nemo told Rubens, briefing him in one of the analysis section's conference rooms on the floor above the Art Room. "They landed in Istanbul and then flew to Karachi a few hours later. They stayed for two months."

"Why do you think that's significant?" asked Rubens.

"Kenan was absent from class during that period. And we have this photo from Pakistani intelligence on the students at the Lahore Madrasah at roughly that time."

Nemo clicked the scroll button on his laptop. A fuzzy picture of a young man with pale skin and reddish facial hair appeared on the screen next to a recent picture of Kenan. Beneath it, the computer declared it was a match "with some certainty"—sixty percent on its one-hundred-point scale.

"The Dutch passport?" Rubens asked.

"Probably a fake. We're still waiting for definitive word."

"But the *real* significance," said Johnny Bib.

"After the person using the passport returned to the U.S.," continued Nemo, "he went from New York to Houston. He rented a car for three days. The same credit card was used at a motel in Galveston."

So was Lahore Two right, then? Was the Galveston chemical plant really the target?

Rubens closed his eyes. It was the classic intelligence conundrum, with evidence supporting mutually exclusive conclusions.

The interesting thing was that neither Johnny Bib nor Nemo seemed to appreciate the fact that they were contradicting their earlier information.

"Has the card been used anywhere else?" Rubens asked, opening his eyes.

"No. No links or parallels that I can find," said Nemo.

Was he resisting because he didn't want Bing to be right? If so, that was a very childish reason, far beneath him.

"Very well," said Rubens. "Johnny, what about the claims that al-Qaeda was trying to obtain a ship?"

"CIA."

"Yes, I *know* where the claims came from," said Rubens, struggling to remain patient. "What about them?"

"No intercepts."

"Nothing to back it up at all?"

Johnny Bib shrugged.

"Would it be possible to check ship registrations and somehow coordinate them with legitimate companies?" Rubens asked.

"Many gaps."

"Try it anyway."

Johnny Bib's face contorted in a way that warned Rubens he was about to launch into a whining speech about not having enough people, the people he had were doing jobs far out of their classifications, were working insane hours, and on and on.

All legitimate points, but Rubens had no time to deal with them.

"Keep me informed," he said, cutting off the tirade by getting up. Sometimes strategic retreat was the only way to handle a bad situation. "If you'll excuse me, I have business upstairs."

CHAPTER 126

DEAN GOT THE same shrugs in Veracruz that he'd gotten in Mexico City. The police in the port city on Mexico's eastern coast were considerably more concerned with sailors from the local navy school than possible al-Qaeda terrorists. A few thousand tourists stopped in the city's hotels every week, but the vast majority of them were middle American gringos and their families—"People like you," the police chief told him, "looking for bargains."

Dean figured it was supposed to be a compliment and nodded.

The chief gave Dean a few recommendations for dinner.

"Mention my name," he explained, "they take care of you, no charge. You see."

"Thanks," said Dean, making it a point not to remember the restaurants' names.

Dean took a walk through the city, trying to imagine what he would do if he were Kenan. But that was a lost cause; it had been a long time since he was in his early twenties. He fell back on the obvious, stopping into hotels too small and cheap to have computer reservation systems; no one recognized the photos he showed.

He worked his way down toward the sea. Ships lined up in the distance, heading toward the port; it reminded him of Istanbul's procession of tankers up the Bosporus.

"You think there's any possibility that Kenan Conkel hooked up with a ship out of here?" Dean asked Sandy Chafetz when he checked in with her a half hour later.

"I can't rule it out," she told him. "But we can't rule it in, either. Boats and ships leave there all the time."

"I can spread some photos around by the docks," said Dean. "It'll be a long shot."

"Before you do that, I have something for you to check out. It's a long shot, too, but it's much more interesting," Chafetz said. "A boat and its captain have been missing from a town north of Catemaco called Negro Olmec since the day before yesterday. The police there say that the captain was seen with a young white male and someone who was possibly Arab."

"How do I get there?"

IT TOOK TWO and a half hours to drive to Negro Olmec from Veracruz. The sun had set a half hour before Dean started out, depriving him of what would have been a gorgeous view of the ocean for much of the drive. But he didn't mind; he found a station that played American country-western, alternating between the likes of Dwight Yoakam and the Judds, with the occasional Hank Williams tune thrown in.

"Hey, Hey, Good Lookin' " came on, a gringo request according to the deejay. Dean sang along. Hank Williams was one of the few things he and his father agreed on, even to this day.

Negro Olmec had only three full-time police officers, and none were on duty when Dean arrived a little past nine P.M. But the man at the station was the cousin of the chief, and when Dean explained in Spanish that he was an American investigator who might have some information about the missing boat captain, he picked up his phone and told the chief that the case was solved.

The police chief walked through the door before Dean could finish telling his cousin that he had only a possible lead, not a solution. The cousin waved the picture of Kenan at the chief, telling him the murderer of boat captain Oscar Nunez had been discovered.

"You're sure this is the man?" the chief asked Dean.

"No. I want to know if it is. I've been looking for him. He

came to Veracruz about two months back. I'm wondering if he came back in the past few days."

The chief picked up the phone, dialed a number, and began shouting into it, speaking so quickly that Dean couldn't decipher his Spanish.

"Come," demanded the chief. He put down the phone and marched out the front door, down the short flight of creaking wooden steps and across the street to a small stucco house where a battered Volkswagen with bubblegum lights sat in the driveway. By the time Dean got into the car, the chief was drumming his fingers impatiently on the steering wheel. Dean had barely closed the door when the policeman threw the car into reverse, skidding onto the road with a screech of tires that would have impressed Tommy Karr. Fifty yards down the road he jammed on the brakes, sending Dean against the dashboard.

An elderly woman was waiting at the door of the house. Before Dean could take the photo out of his pocket, she was proclaiming that Kenan had murdered her son, the most dedicated son in all of Mexico.

"How do you know he's dead?" Dean asked. "I thought he was only missing."

The chief nudged him aside. "We find the body today," he said in English. "And the boat. Fifty miles offshore."

"Fifty miles?"

"Maybe it drift, maybe not. The ocean is like a wandering woman. The captain—shot through the head."

"I'd like to see the body," Dean told him.

NEGRO OLMEC'S MORGUE was not only a funeral home but a restaurant and travel agency. The police chief assured Dean that this was the village's best restaurant and most likely the best on the coast.

"Julio will show you when we are done," he said, as the funeral home director and restaurateur led them down the hall to the funeral parlor. "Yes, Julio?"

"Anything you want," said Julio. He took out his keys and unlocked the door. "I have to go back now. The customers come on nights when we have shark. We've been so busy. You stop by; you'll see."

The smell of fish stew flowed into the large viewing room with Dean and the chief, staying with them right up to the door to the back room. There a new odor took over, the scent of decay and the chemicals meant to arrest it.

The body had been brought in just before dinnertime at the restaurant and had not been worked on yet. Sea birds had picked at the dead man, and there were gouges on his face, chest, and hands. Dean took out his PDA and placed the camera attachment on it to beam images back to the Art Room.

"A good hunk of the jaw is gone," Dean said, ostensibly talking to the police chief but really passing the information along to Chafetz and a pathologist.

"A big wound, yes," said the chief.

"See if there are any shots to the chest," Chafetz told him. "Examine the clothes carefully."

Dean glanced at the side table, looking for gloves. He didn't see any. Gingerly, he picked at the dead man's shirt, moving the handheld computer across it slowly.

"I don't see any bullet wounds, do you?" he asked the police chief.

The chief didn't answer. He was standing across the room, face toward the door.

The pathologist directed Dean to scan the skull slowly, then had him turn his attention to the jaw.

"Shot him in the face?" Dean asked.

"No, that's probably an exit wound," said the pathologist. "There is a smaller hole toward the top that would line up almost exactly. I can't be sure, but it looks to me like he was shot from above at an angle. Definitely from above."

Dean couldn't find any other wounds and bruises, aside from the damage done by the birds. When he was done, neither he nor the police chief were in any mood to eat. They went back to the police station and looked at the bullet that had been recovered from the boat; Dean could tell from a glance that it had come from a rifle.

"One other went through the side of the boat, making a

hole," said the chief. "But it was high enough that only a little water came in."

"Can we take a look at it?"

"Yes, come."

Dean braced himself for another car, but the dock turned out to be across the beach directly behind the police station. The chief showed the way with a large flashlight whose light conked out every ten steps or so; he would tap it and the light would flash back on.

"What sort of customers did Señor Nunez get?" Dean asked as they walked out onto the pier.

"Some scuba, sport fishermen."

"He ever take drug dealers or smugglers anywhere?"

"I've never heard that he did," said the police chief. "And now that he is dead, who would speak ill of him?"

Even in the dark, Dean could tell the boat wouldn't be a smuggler's first choice. Twenty-nine feet long, it was thirty years old at least, with a stubby, low-slung cabin and a single Mercury at the rear—the sort of boat you might call dependable, but never fast. It would be cheap to rent and inconspicuous—the sort of thing a terrorist might prefer when rendezvousing with someone else.

If the blood was any indication, the boat's captain had been standing near the wheel when he'd been shot. Dean climbed up onto the cabin deck and had the police chief stand at the wheel. His head came to Dean's waist.

"How tall are you?" Dean asked him.

"Five foot nine, señor."

"How tall was the captain?"

The chief shook his head.

"Six-three," said Chafetz.

Dean adjusted his arms, figuring where he would have to hold a rifle to shoot someone at the wheel to hit him in the middle of the head. It was *possible,* but far from likely.

"You'd have to hold the gun way up here," said Dean, acting it out for the police chief. "Be a very unnatural shot. Easier to shoot him like this, in the face."

"Assuming the bullets came from a rifle," said the chief.

"True," said Dean. "Where's the hole?"

The police chief pointed it out on the starboard side of the vessel.

"I'd say he had to have been shot from another boat," said Dean. "Something higher to get that angle."

"Or a ship," said Chafetz. "Much more likely. We're sending a pathology team down there to check out the dead man and the boat. Good work, Charlie."

CHAPTER 127

TOMMY KARR PUSHED the baseball cap back on his hat and surveyed the tarmac next to the terminal at Stewart International Airport. Small planes generally lined up along the terminal's eastern end, filling a small number of slots. Marid Dabir's plane would be directed to the slot at the extreme south. Ordinarily passengers disembarked into a large room where they could pick up their baggage. Special dividers had been brought in, creating a narrow hallway to control the traffic. Dabir would be seized in the hallway after he was surrounded by FBI agents dressed as airline and airport workers. Lia would be on the flight with him and would make sure they got the right man.

Assuming, of course, they had the right man to begin with.

Karr wanted to see where Dabir would end up if he managed to slip out of the plane somehow. A parking lot for rental cars was just around the corner from the gate area where they were going to bring Dabir's plane. Hopping the fence would take all of five seconds; he'd have to put two guys on the plane side of the fence to forestall that possibility. That was in addition to the people they'd have disguised as ground crew on both sides of the plane.

A hangar across the way that was used by U.S. Marine reserve units to maintain some of their aircraft had been vacated a few hours before. Right after the plane carrying Dabir landed, a CIA Gulfstream would taxi over to the area in front of the hangar; the jet would take off a short time later—a ruse to make anyone watching think Dabir had been taken away. In fact, he would be moved to a trailer set up in one of the large C-5A hangars on the Air National Guard side of the complex, guarded by a team of FBI agents and federal marshals as well as U.S. Air Force security. Several members of the Justice Department and FBI interrogators were already there, preparing for their interrogation.

Karr checked the truck that would be used to ferry him across the base, then looked at the two vans which would carry the federal agents. The trucks were guarded by a pair of U.S. Air Force security men, who were trying to look nonchalant while holding M-16s at the ready.

"Lookin' good," Karr told them after circling the trucks. "Now tell me, no bullshit: Where's the best pizza place in town?"

CHAPTER 128

BETWEEN FATIGUE AND his concerns about the operation set to grab Marid Dabir, Rubens found his patience in short supply from the very start of the evening conference call updating possible al-Qaeda targets. He tried to explain how circumstantial the evidence his people had found that the Galveston–Houston area might be a target was, but the others clearly didn't hear the nuances. As soon as he mentioned that one of the terrorists had possibly met a boat or ship off Mexico—information that the Art Room had given him only a few minutes before—they put two and two together and came up with forty-four.

"Sink a ship in the Houston Ship Channel and it would be even more devastating than blowing up the chemical plant," said Cynthia Marshall, second-in-command at Homeland Security. "We'll need National Guard troops. I'll move the Coast Guard over and blockade the port. The Navy will have to help as well."

"There's no evidence the channel is being targeted," said Rubens. "And from what I understand about the threat coming from the sea, there's no evidence there either."

"We have one source saying al-Qaeda may be interested in ships," said Collins from the CIA. "That's the extent of the intelligence."

"Can we really take a chance?" asked FBI Director Griffin Bolso, who until now had been a voice of reason and an ally. "Blow up something there, and it'll be worse than 9/11."

"We have to be prudent in using our resources," said Rubens.

He might just as well have read the horoscope, for all the good it did. Bing ended the meeting by saying that the Houston and Galveston area would be put under a virtual lockdown, with the navy and coast guard tasked to search every ship in the vicinity. Searching the ships would take weeks, not days, but the general representing the Department of Defense on the conference call was from the air force and clearly didn't understand the logistics involved.

A few minutes after Rubens hung up, Collins from the CIA called him back. He'd promised to update her on the Dabir operation.

"They're overreacting on Houston," she said without prompting. "But you can't blame them. We've given them bits and pieces of possible conspiracies, and they put them together in the worst way."

"Concentrating on the wrong target may be worse than concentrating on none," said Rubens.

Collins didn't answer. Rubens told her about Dabir; when he was done, she asked if she could send a CIA interrogation team there as well.

Even though he'd expected the question, he wasn't sure how exactly to answer it. The Justice Department had been adamant that the CIA people not take part; truth be told, they would have greatly preferred it if Desk Three wasn't even involved in the operation, since the intelligence agencies would inevitably complicate any prosecution. But Collins was a potential ally against Bing, and Rubens knew that telling her no wasn't going to go over well.

What else could he do, though? Base his decision on politics?

"Justice wants to handle the interrogation itself," said Rubens, hoping that would end the conversation.

It didn't.

"Justice wants a lot of things. The FBI has a terrible track record on interrogations. We don't."

"I can't argue with you, Debra, but it's not my call."

"If you said the team was from Desk Three, no one would question it."

"Well, I can't lie," blurted Rubens.

A moment of awkward silence followed.

"Bill, sometimes it would be helpful to remember the old adage, 'one hand washes the other'," said Collins before she hung up.

CHAPTER 129

THE BIG HELICOPTER shook the shoreline as it approached, but the night had turned overcast, and Dean couldn't even make out its running lights.

"They want you to fire a flare, Charlie," Chafetz told him. "To make sure they're in the right place."

Dean didn't have any flares. This was just like the navy: always asking a marine to do the impossible.

And being a marine, though a retired one, he came up with a way to do it.

"Turn on your lights," Dean yelled to the Mexican police chief a few yards away. "The helicopter needs something to guide it."

The chief reached into his Volkswagen and red and blue beacons split the darkness.

"All right. They got you," said Chafetz.

A spotlight searched the beach as the helo, a large CH-53E Super Stallion from the *USS Wasp*, settled over the beach in a hover, descending to about eight feet above the ground, whipping grit and a fine spray of water in every direction.

"Charlie, they're waiting," said Chafetz.

"For what?"

"Aren't you getting in?"

"Aren't they landing?"

"Beach is too narrow and sloped," said the runner.

Dean saw a crewman in the surf, trotting toward him.

"Sergeant Dean?"

"Nobody's called me that in about a million years," Dean said.

"I was told you were a marine, sir. Once a marine sergeant, always a marine sergeant. I should know," added the man, who was wearing marine combat fatigues. Though it had taken off from a navy ship, the helicopter was actually a marine aircraft.

"Gunny, you're just trying to butter me up so I won't complain about having to climb up the rope, right?"

"I hope it worked," cracked the marine. "Otherwise I'm going to have to throw you to the crew chief."

CHAPTER 130

LIA PULLED THE covers around her neck, pushing onto her side and trying to find a comfortable position in the hotel bed. She'd jacked the AC to full, chilling the room so she could bundle up. Covers always made her feel drowsy, and helped her to sleep.

So did cuddling next to Charlie. She'd slept like a baby during the two weeks she'd spent with him in Pennsylvania.

She missed him badly. She felt—not that she'd betrayed him, exactly, with Pinchon, because she hadn't, not at all. But she hadn't given him the attention he deserved.

Or the explanation. Something of an explanation.

He was just a guy I fell in lust with, that's all. Doesn't mean anything, Charlie.

He wasn't as big a jerk then, either.

Lia could almost see Dean squinting at her. Then he'd say, "Okay." In a while, if she didn't add any more, he'd drop it completely.

That was the way he was.

She, on the other hand, would brood and think and scheme, try and figure it out. Attack it.

Dean thought they were good together because they were alike in a lot of ways, but she knew they were different, different on this.

She curled the covers tighter, missing Dean more than she ever had before.

CHAPTER 131

DR. SAED RAMIL TOOK a train from Baltimore to New York City's Penn Station, then made his way to Grand Central, where he caught a commuter train north to a burp of a city named Beacon. There a limo met him and took him across the river to Newburgh, where he'd been booked into a small hotel not far from the airport. The driver gave him a brief history lesson on the area along the way, telling him how Newburgh had once been voted the best city to raise kids in the U.S. and was now among the worst.

"Because nobody believes in nothin' no more," railed the driver. "They got their rap, their MTV, video games. Don't go to church. No morals. No beliefs."

Ramil didn't know what to say, but the man didn't really want answers; he wanted to rant. Ramil gave him a tip, even though the Art Room had said he'd already been tipped, then ensconced himself in his room at the Holiday Inn.

This was an easy gig, merely standing by in case something happened. Inevitably, nothing did. Ramil could stay in his hotel room the entire time if he wanted. Or he could go and explore the local area, as long as he kept the Art Room aware of where he was.

The last time he heard the voice, it had told him he would have another chance. Was this what it had meant?

No. The voice was simply a result of stress and fear—a perfectly logical explanation.

Unless it had predicted the future.

Lying awake well past midnight, he thought of the limo

driver's rant. The problem with the world wasn't that no one believed in anything anymore, but that they believed in the wrong things. And the line between wrong and right was more difficult to discern than one could ever imagine.

CHAPTER 132

THE U.S. NAVY'S LHD-1 *Wasp* was an amphibious assault ship, designed to deliver roughly two thousand marines to a beachhead or an inland battle zone. To Dean, it looked like an aircraft carrier, albeit one with a straight landing deck. The ship sat high above the water, which made it easy for it to deploy its air-cushioned landing craft sitting at a sea-level "garage" below the flight deck.

This type of ship had not existed in Dean's day, and under other circumstances he might have enjoyed an early-morning tour after his "rack time"—which was actually a decent snooze in an honest-to-God bed. But both Dean and the ship's company had better things to do. The *Wasp* had been tasked to join a sea armada checking vessels approaching Galveston from the south. Her helicopters were assisting ships to the north and west. Dean, meanwhile, had been told by the Art Room to get up to Houston to check over the chemical plant that the terrorists might be targeting. First thing after breakfast, a UH-1N Huey—a Vietnam-era helicopter retained as a utility craft—was gassed up and readied for him.

"We are *just* going to make it fuel-wise," the pilot warned Dean as he strapped himself into the copilot's seat. "Ready?"

"Sure." Dean adjusted the headset. "Sorry to put you out."

"Hey, no way. I get to spend two days in Houston thanks to you. Got a whole bunch of friends there. We'll be golfin' and shootin'. I should be thanking you."

The helicopter leaned forward and rose, skipping away from the deck of its mothership like a young bird anxious to leave the nest. The sun had just broken through the low-lying clouds at the horizon, coloring the distance a reddish pink.

"You want some joe?" asked the pilot, handing him a thermos.

"I'll take some coffee, sure."

"All I got is that one cup. Don't worry. I don't have AIDS."

Dean poured about half a cup's worth of coffee into the cup. It had far too much sugar in it for him, but he drank it anyway.

"Heard you were a marine," said the pilot.

"Ancient history."

"Once a marine always a marine."

"True enough."

"What were you?"

"I did a lot of things. I was sniper in Vietnam."

"No kidding? You're that old?"

"Older," said Dean. He laughed. "I bet this chopper's as old as I am."

"Probably flew you around in Vietnam." The pilot reached over and took the coffee from him. "You liked being a sniper?"

"It was a job."

The pilot had to answer a radio call. Dean tightened his arms around his chest. He had liked being a sniper. He liked the simplicity of it. Not like now.

"I have a sharpshooter's badge myself," said the pilot. "I'm pretty good. Every marine, a rifleman."

"That's right," said Dean. But inside he was thinking that there was a world of difference between doing some shooting and being a sniper. Shooting was the least of it.

"We practice insertions, do a lot of work with some recon guys," continued the pilot. "It's good work."

"Yeah?" said Dean, feigning interest, thinking about Kenan and how he hoped he was wrong that he'd met a ship.

CHAPTER 133

UNABLE TO SEE the O's for the 0's, Gallo had printed a dump of the storage files on the drive belonging to Kenan Conkel's college roommate. He hoped that looking at the data on paper might put it into a new light, but all it did was cover the lab with paper. He had piles and piles of printouts, showing files in every conceivable format.

Most had to do with chemistry and hockey. The roommate seemed to have a perverse need to follow the Red Wings; the remains of web pages pertaining to the hockey team were strewn across the drive.

"Paper, Mr. Gallo?" Johnny Bib was standing in the doorway.

"You told me to go back to the roommate's drive to look for clues."

"Paper?" said Johnny Bib again, as if it were a foreign substance.

"I thought it would, like, let me see things more clearly. I was here all night, and I figured, you know, get a different look at things."

"Did it?"

"Not yet."

"Mmmmmmmm," said Johnny Bib. He walked into the room, surveying the different piles. "Chemistry?"

"Organics."

"Mmmmmmmmm." Johnny Bib leaned down and picked a solitary piece of paper from the floor. "Why the boat?"

"Um, like, got me. It's the only one on the drive." Gallo turned to his computer and pulled up the file, displaying the contents in HTML, a common web page language, as well as in the machine language. "Looked odd, you know, the only one there, so I checked it for encryptions, odd fractals, the works."

"Coast guard," said Johnny Bib.

"Well, yeah, it's a cutter or something."

"Coast guard."

Gallo stared at Bib, trying to puzzle out exactly what he was saying.

"Coast guard," repeated Bib.

"You think it's important?"

"It's different! Different!" Johnny Bib practically screamed. "We like different! We *love* different!"

"I'll see what I can figure out."

RUBENS HAD JUST arrived at Crypto City after two hours of fitful sleep when Johnny Bib flew at him in the main hallway.

Literally flew at him, his hands spread wide.

"*Sturgeon,*" said the head of the Desk Three research team. "*Sturgeon!*"

"Are you planning on catching some?" asked Rubens.

Johnny slid to a halt, arms still extended. "It's a ship. A U.S. Coast Guard *cutter.*"

"Actually, they call it a coastal patrol boat, officially," said Robert Gallo, coming up behind Johnny Bib.

"I trust this is significant?"

"I think Kenan Conkel was interested in this ship," said Gallo. "There was this picture on his friend's hard drive, and I've recovered bits of queries about its capability and where it berths, coast guard routines I think. The queries were all right before he went to Mexico in September—and according to the time stamp, his roommate would have been in organic chemistry class."

"It guards the Louisiana Offshore Oil Port," said Johnny Bib. "The biggest port of entry for oil in the United States."

"Come down to the Art Room with me," said Rubens.

IT MADE MUCH more sense. He should have realized it from the start.

Rubens stared at the screen at the front of the Art Room. A picture of the Louisiana Offshore Oil Port, better known as LOOP, was displayed as one of the analysts quickly summarized the port's assets and importance. All of Asad's major targets had been aimed at the energy infrastructure—the Saudi oil fields, the major refinery in Germany. LOOP was their equivalent, much more important than a single chemical plant.

The Louisiana Offshore Oil Port had been built because many supertankers couldn't get close enough to U.S. ports to unload. The process was fairly simple—a tanker would moor at an oversized floating gas pump called a single-point mooring base, referred to as an SPM. Raw petroleum was pumped through LOOP into a massive pipeline that brought it to Port Fourchon onshore. There it was stored in underground salt caverns before being shipped to refineries. Besides the mooring base and the onshore facilities, there were several vulnerable points—most notably the pumping and control platform, eighteen miles from shore.

LOOP had survived Hurricane Katrina when the worst part of the hurricane veered eastward; it was back in operation within a week. But drive a ship with several hundred or more tons of explosives into it, and the pumps, pipes, and mechanisms that had withstood the wind and waves would be shattered. Given the already fragile state of the Gulf Coast oil infrastructure, the result would be catastrophic—worse than the immediate aftermath of Hurricane Katrina. The U.S. would lose between a third and half of its oil for years, not months.

That *had* to be their target.

It was a guess—but one with evidence.

"Tell the coast guard to shut LOOP down," Rubens said. "Order all ships out of the area. Evacuate the control platform. Keep working on that list of ships coming up from Mexico, validating them—expand it to include the area near LOOP."

Telach frowned. "All we have is Johnny Bib's hunch on this cutter."

"That's enough for me. Where's Charlie Dean?"

CHAPTER 134

"CHARLIE, CAN YOU change course and get north to Port Fourchon?"

Marie Telach's voice over the Deep Black communications system felt like a spike in Dean's brain. He pulled his
headset off of his right ear and reached into his pocket and
pulled out his satphone, pretending to use it.

"This is Dean," he said.

"We need you to go to Port Fourchon," repeated Telach.
"It's south of New Orleans."

"How far from New Orleans are we?" Dean asked the
pilot.

"Twenty minutes. Maybe fifteen. Why?"

"There's a deep-water port called LOOP out there, south
of Port Fourchon," Telach told Dean. "Johnny Bib has a theory Kenan may be heading there."

"What's a deep-water port?" Dean asked.

"You talking to me?" said the pilot.

"If you know the answer."

"Port ships use them because they draw too much water to
get into a regular harbor," said the pilot. "Like LOOP, up near
New Orleans, and that gas port they're talking about building
near Houston."

"We need to get to LOOP if you know where it is," Dean
told the pilot.

"I don't know if we have enough fuel."

"Push it," said Dean.

CHAPTER 135

WHEN THEY WERE twenty miles away, Razaq Khan told Kenan to go and prepare. Kenan went to the small shower in the captain's compartment and cleansed himself, scrubbing deliberately and praying that he would be worthy of the task ahead. When he was done, he pulled on a fresh white shirt, leaving its tails untucked. It was as close as his mission allowed to the pilgrim's shroud one wore to Mecca.

Kenan took over at the wheel while the helmsman went to change. They were moving steadily now; he could see a supertanker just leaving the LOOP moorings far off to starboard. In fifteen minutes, he would be challenged; he could answer in his sleep. Just in case the monitors aboard LOOP became suspicious, Kenan would push a button that would broadcast the distress call of one of the work ships that operated out of Port Fourchon. The coast guard patrol craft would investigate, leaving the way to LOOP free for the *Aztec Exact*.

"I am ready," said the helmsman, returning.

Kenan stepped to the radio. Khan took the key from his neck and placed it into the control panel.

"Do not leave the bridge for anything," Khan told Kenan. "If I am gone, you are in charge. Complete our mission."

Kenan, awed by the trust Khan showed in him, nodded.

"May God grant us our moment," said Khan, going to check on the others.

CHAPTER 136

THERE WERE SEVEN large ships within three miles of LOOP, and another dozen or so within an hour's sailing time. And that didn't count another dozen or so merchant ships near Port Fourchon, let alone the myriad of small vessels scattered offshore.

"All right. The coast guard is working from the west," Dean told the pilot, relaying what Telach had told him. "There are two ships coming up from the southeast we want to check on."

The pilot stared at him. Dean realized that he had forgotten to pretend to use his phone.

"I can't explain the communications system. It's classified, all right?"

"Yeah, not a problem. We have enough fuel to buzz one or two, but then we absolutely have to head inland to land."

Dean spotted a helicopter on the LOOP platform.

"There's a helipad on the LOOP platform," said Dean. "You think you can refuel there?"

"If they let me, sure."

"They'll let you," said Dean. "Don't sweat it."

CHAPTER 137

KENAN FELT HIS pulse rise as the radio call came in. He answered smoothly, exactly as he had practiced a million times.

The response he got was one he hadn't expected.

"LOOP is being closed," replied the voice.

"Closed? But—"

"You'll have to talk to the coast guard," replied the man on the other side of the radio. "We've been ordered to return to shore. You're to stop where you are and await further instructions. Other arrangements will be made."

They were roughly seven minutes from the tie-up point, and another five from the control rig where they were to detonate the explosives. Could they be stopped in twelve minutes?

No, thought Kenan. No. Allah had brought them close enough to succeed.

They were expecting a response. Should he continue to protest? What would a "normal" ship do?

They would comply—there really was no choice, was there?—then the captain would contact his shipping company for directions, or perhaps make other arrangements to offload his crude.

"Roger, we copy," said Kenan. "*Aztec Exact* is changing course and will await further instructions."

He debated whether to use the radio distress call that was planned as a distraction. Perhaps he should save it until later.

No. Best to follow the plan as closely as possible. He pressed the button, jamming the radio frequencies with the bogus calls of a pleasure boat sinking miles away.

Twelve minutes. All he had to do was press the ignition button as the ship drew close to the platform. The explosion would rupture the pipeline and destroy the platform in one swoop.

"Helicopter," said the helmsman.

Kenan looked toward the control platform. A helicopter had just taken off.

"They're evacuating," Kenan told him. "Just hold our course."

Then he heard the sound of a rotor nearby and realized the helmsman had been talking about different craft completely.

CHAPTER 138

DEAN COULD SEE two people on the bridge. He swept his binoculars around, trying to find someone else.

"I see only two people," he told Rockman. "How many would it take it to run the ship?"

"More than that. Are they answering your hails?"

"They were just talking to LOOP control. There's a distress call blocking the channels."

"We're working on that," said Rockman. "We haven't been able to locate the boat that's sending it."

There hadn't been time to send a plane overhead to provide video from the scene. The Art Room was tracking vessels by compiling data from the coast guard cutter and navy ships well offshore, along with satellite images a few minutes old. But there was no way to easily pinpoint the locations of all the small vessels in the area.

"He's not changing course or stopping," said Dean, studying the *Aztec Exact*.

"Tell them to leave the area."

"Stand by."

Dean leaned over to the radio to make sure he had the proper channel.

"Fuel's getting low," said the pilot. "We only have a couple of minutes."

"Let's talk to this ship and see what they're up to. Then we can go over to the platform and gas up."

Dean broadcast on the channel LOOP had used earlier, warning the *Aztec Exact* to stop. It didn't acknowledge. He broadcast again, this time using the emergency bands; still no answer.

"The radio works, right?" he asked the pilot, picking up his binoculars.

"Yeah, it works," said the pilot testily.

Something moved near the superstructure, something white.

A man with a white shirt.

"Somebody else on deck. Two people," said Dean. He pulled the binoculars back up and focused—right on the barrel of an AK-47.

"Duck!" Dean yelled as bullets began cracking against the side of the Huey.

"DEAN IS UNDER fire!" said Rockman.

"Ms. Telach, please tell the coast guard the *Aztec Exact* is to be stopped," said Rubens.

"They're more than three miles away. They won't get there in time," said Rockman.

"Have them target it with their deck gun and sink it," Rubens said.

"COAST GUARD'S POSITIONING to open fire," the pilot told Dean. "They're going to try to sink it before it gets to the platform—they're too far away to cut them off in time."

"Let's get out of the way."

"I gotta land on the platform," said the pilot. "We're too far from shore."

He was already a few hundred yards from it.

"They're wasting their time from that distance," added the pilot.

"Why?" said Dean.

"Their deckgun is a twenty-five-millimeter Bushmaster. It can fire about three and three-quarter miles, but its effective range is less than half that."

"You're sure?"

"I help with target spotting, remember? That's all I do for weeks on end."

"Rockman, are there weapons on that platform?" Dean asked.

"Uh, I'm not sure. There's one guy standing by to help you refuel. He has to come out with you."

"Find out about the weapons," said Dean. "Go!"

"DEAN WANTS TO know if there are weapons on the platform," Rockman told Rubens. "I think he's going to try and shoot the people on the bridge of the tanker."

Rubens rubbed his eyes. It was already clear that the coast guard patrol craft wasn't going to be able to stop the tanker. Two marine Harriers from the *Wasp* were about five minutes away, also too far.

"If there are weapons, tell him where they are. Tell him to make sure he's off that platform before the ship gets there."

SMALL-ARMS LOCKERS HAD been posted around the platform. Aimed at assisting the crewmen in the case of a terrorist boarding, each waterproof locker had two M4 carbines with grenade launcher attachments, along with two dozen magazine boxes of ammunition and twelve grenades.

"There's a locker back by the railing there," yelled the crewman who met them on the helipad to refuel the chopper. "Guns and grenades."

Dean ran to the locker, bolted to the side of the catwalk twenty yards from the helipad. He grabbed one of the M4 automatic rifles and a Beretta pistol, then stuffed four grenades into his pants pockets. Pulling his shirt out of his pants, he piled seven or eight magazines into it, using it as a crude basket to carry the ammo back to the helo.

"How close?" yelled the pilot, who'd opened the rear side door while waiting for Dean.

"Drop me on the deck above the bridge house," Dean shouted.

"Drop you?"

"We're not going to sink him with a rifle."

"I can't drop you on the ship."

"Go in front of the bridge. I'll dump a grenade into it. Then drop me on the deck," said Dean, pushing into the back. "Listen to me!"

"Do it," said Dean. "Now."

CHAPTER 139

KENAN WRAPPED HIS hand around the wire behind the speaker and yanked, ending the radio's incessant drone.

"They're firing at us!" said the helmsman at the wheel.

Kenan saw a black bird arc toward the water off the starboard bow. Only when it plunged below the ship's waistline into the water did he realize it was a shell, undoubtedly fired by the cutter.

"God will protect us," Kenan told the helmsman. "Stay on course."

The yellow girders of their target loomed ahead. A helicopter peeled off the top—the last of the demons running for cover.

The Devil People were all cowards. That was why the mujahideen would triumph, even though they were outnumbered.

"The only god is God," said Kenan loudly as he stepped to the auxiliary control board, waiting to detonate the bomb. He looked at the laptop, which had a global positioning indicator plugged into it; the program calculated that they were four and a half minutes from the detonation point.

The seconds were dragging, as if God had slowed time so He could savor their victory. A phalanx of angels must be hovering over the ship, waiting to lead the warriors to Paradise.

Razaq Khan burst onto the bridge, an AK-47 in his hand.

"Stay on course!" yelled Khan. "God is delivering our enemy to us."

The helmsman yelled something, and Kenan looked up in time to see a helicopter swooping so close he was sure it was going to crash into them.

CHAPTER 140

THE HELICOPTER SWEPT across the port side of the *Aztec Exact*, slowing as it drew even with the white superstructure. Dean, poised against the side of the door, leaned his knee against the metal and steadied the rifle against his body.

"Closer!" he yelled, but the chopper bumped unsteadily away, its tail bucking back and forth so hard Dean was thrown against and then away from the door. As he scrambled back, the helo dipped again, this time no more than ten feet from the large glass windows at the front of the ship's bridge. Dean pumped a grenade toward one of the panes near the center; the grenade shattered the glass but deflected onto the deck in front of the bridge.

Once more the Huey veered upwards.

"Get me down—get me down!" Dean yelled.

He pushed another grenade into the launcher. As the helicopter stuttered above the thick plume of smoke erupting beneath it, Dean put the fresh grenade into the bridge and then sprayed the remaining windows with bullets, running through the magazine. He dumped the box, but as he reached for a fresh mag, he saw the fence ringing the roof of the bridge before him. Dean pushed himself forward and leapt, curling the rifle under him as he rolled onto the metal deck. He tumbled against one of the radio masts, stopping with a hard smash to his ribs that took his breath away.

KENAN FOUND HIMSELF on the floor, choking. Smoke and glass whirled around the bridge.

Had the bomb already exploded?

Impossible—he would be in heaven.

He had to detonate the bomb. Kenan pushed to get to his feet.

"Stay down for a moment," barked Khan in his Pakistani-accented English. Then he leapt up with his AK-47 and began to fire.

DEAN STARTED TO get up, then remembered that he hadn't reloaded. He grabbed one of the magazines from his pocket, fumbling as he tried to slam it into the gun. A broken cloud of smoke drifted over him, knots of gray interspersed with light. He heard a loud pop and *crack-crack-crack*; instinctively he dropped flat, realizing he must be under fire though he couldn't locate the gunman or the weapon.

Or, thankfully, the enemy's bullets.

Finally he saw something moving to his right, near the large radar mast that dominated the roof area. Dean fired a burst toward the shadow, and the gunfire stopped.

He crawled forward a few feet; not drawing any fire, he scrambled for the railing on the side, hoping to climb over and down to the deck next to the bridge. But as he started over the rail, the roof near him seemed to explode, bullets smashing all around him. Dean pushed himself over the side headfirst, losing the gun but grabbing at one of the fence posts on the way down to break his fall. He twisted around enough to land on his feet, though the impact knocked him backwards. The M4 bounced once on the deck, then bounded off the side, clattering somewhere below.

Dean pulled the pistol from his belt as he rolled upright. The door to the bridge was a few feet away.

Dean didn't even bother trying the handle. He put a slug through the knob; the sudden release of the lock sent the door bounding toward him. Surprised, Dean grabbed the edge and threw it open, leveling the pistol at the thick haze inside.

Something moved at the right of the cloud. Dean fired twice; only as the body fell was he sure it was a man. Before he could step inside, the far side of the bridge sparked with gunfire. He threw himself inside as the fat bullets of an AK-47 pummeled the nearby glass and metal.

KENAN WATCHED AS Khan started past him, his rifle shaking as bullets spewed from the barrel. He disappeared for a moment in the smoke, and then Kenan saw him again, his head thrown back, covered by a black hand—blood, blood pouring from two holes above his eyes.

Kenan got up to go to him, but as he reached his feet something slammed against him and threw him back to the deck. He rolled on his back, freeing himself, only to find the eyes of Wasim, the helmsman, staring at him. Wasim blinked, then gulped at the air. In the next second he bent his head to the deck, eyes gaping, his life gone.

Why was God allowing this to happen now? Where was His hand when it was needed?

DEAN AIMED THE Beretta at the muzzle flash on the other side of the bridge and fired twice. The shots roared in his head, the sound more like a freight train than a gun. The smoke stung his eyes. Choking, he propelled himself forward with his left hand, getting to his feet only to trip over a body on the floor. As he fell, he saw someone entering the bridge through the door on the far side; Dean fired and the man ducked away.

"Charlie? Are you on the bridge?" said Rockman.

Dean ignored the runner. The barrel of an AK-47 appeared in the doorway. Dean raised his pistol and fired. The rifle disappeared, though he couldn't tell whether he'd hit it or not. As he crawled toward the door, he saw a man edging around the side of the opening. Dean waited until he had a good aim, then put a bullet through the man's forehead.

"Steer the ship away from the connecting pipeline," said Rockman. "Get it out of there."

KENAN WAS OVERCOME by a sense of shame and failure, then revulsion. He had become his old self, the useless and faithless drone he had been for his first eighteen years, before the voice of God had touched his ears and led him from the wilderness.

Should he die like this, a failure, a coward, with Paradise so close?

God had not abandoned him. He had only set a final test.

They were surely close enough to detonate the bomb. He must do so now.

Tears streamed from his eyes, blurring his vision. With a roar that came from the depths of his soul, Kenan leapt to his feet and threw himself at the control panel.

DEAN TURNED BACK to the bridge, heart racing. Some of the smoke had cleared, but a gray haze hung over the space, as if it belonged to the outer precincts of hell rather than earth.

One of the men he'd tripped over earlier rose from the deck. For a second, Dean thought he was running from the bridge and decided to let him go, concentrating instead on finding the wheel and getting the ship away from the platform. But as he grabbed the spoke and pushed downward, he realized that the man had remained, working over a control panel at the side of the bridge.

"Get away from that!" yelled Dean. "Away!"

The man's hand reached toward the panel.

Dean raised his gun.

"No!" he yelled.

Even as the word left his lips, Dean fired. His bullet shattered the man's head and threw him against the side of the bridge.

Dean turned his attention back to the wheel. Only when he was sure that the ship had responded did he glance back over, confirming that he'd just killed Kenan Conkel.

CHAPTER 141

RUBENS SAW THE ship in the long-range video camera of the Harrier jump jet; it had turned away from the platform and the nearby pipeline.

"Marine helicopter is three minutes away," Rockman said. "Coast guard cutter has stopped firing. I think we're going to be okay."

"Yes," Rubens said softly. "On this one."

CHAPTER 142

BY THE TIME the marine assault team fast-roped down from their helicopter, the ship was nearly two miles from the LOOP platforms. The men swept into the bridge, then continued down the superstructure toward the engine compartment and the crew spaces to make sure there were no more terrorists aboard. A total of four men had been found dead and two more severely wounded on the bridge and the deck; Dean had shot all of them.

He turned over the wheel to one of the marines and went down with them to the main deck, giving them advice based on Rockman's reading of the ship's blueprint. But when the troops got ready to go into the space below, the gunnery sergeant in charge put up his hand and told Dean he should stay above; they were going to use tear gas and didn't have a mask for him.

"No offense, old-timer," said the sergeant, before disappearing through the hatchway.

Dean was too tired to take offense. Then as he walked back up the ladder toward the bridge, he started to laugh at the absurdity of the sergeant's remark. Age wasn't *just* in your head—his throbbing ribs and aching back attested to that—but it wasn't a handicap either. The only way to pile up the experience other people called instincts was over time.

When he came into the bridge, the navy corpsman who'd accompanied the team onto the boat was just getting up from Kenan's body. He shook his head, but Dean already knew the boy was dead.

"This guy was going to blow himself and the ship up?" asked the corpsman.

"Yeah," said Dean.

"Why? Why the hell would he do that?"

Dean glanced at the deck, splattered with Kenan's blood. "You really think an answer would make a difference?" he said, more to himself than the sailor.

"Maybe."

"Yeah," said Dean, knowing nothing he could say really would. "Too bad there isn't one."

CHAPTER 143

SOMEONE HAD GOTTEN Rubens a sandwich while he waited for the president to come to the phone. Without thinking—and famished—he took a bite, and so his mouth was full of bacon and tomato when Marcke's voice boomed into his ear.

"Billy, what's the situation?"

"We've diverted the ship," Rubens told him, swallowing his food. "LOOP is safe. Marines are searching the vessel now."

"LOOP?" said Bing.

"The deep-water port south of New Orleans," said Rubens.

"I know what you're talking about," said the national security advisor.

"Have you arrested Dabir?" asked Marcke.

"He should be arriving at Cleveland airport any moment now," said Rubens. "I'd like to change the mission, given the circumstances."

CHAPTER 144

"OH YEAH, OH yeah," said Rockman. "It's Dabir. Coming through the front door like he doesn't have a care in the world. Alone."

Lia checked her watch, then went to the counter of the Great American Bagel to order a coffee. The flight was in an hour. So far, neither she, nor the FBI agents working with her, nor Rockman, monitoring the video bugs from the Art Room, had seen anyone who might be backing up Dabir. They must be somewhere, though; she doubted he'd be traveling alone.

"Comin' at you, Lia," said Rockman. "We have a positive match. That is our man."

She dug into her jeans to find the right change for the coffee, then dawdled to give Dabir time to pass her.

"He's passing C-11," said Rockman, referring to the gate just beyond the bagel place. Lia took her coffee and walked down the hall, heading toward the cluster of gates at the far end of the concourse, a beehive where passengers waited for their aircraft to board. Lia drifted toward the Burger King, turning back in the direction she'd come as she tried to spot anyone who might be trailing Dabir to see if he was being followed.

A middle-aged man in a worn leather jacket, the kind its owner thinks screams "I'm cool," smiled at her. Lia frowned back.

Jerk.

"How we doing?" asked Rockman.

"Fine," said Lia into her coffee cup. "See anyone?"

"Negative. Keep looking."

She found a seat near the fast food restaurant where she could see Dabir and sat down. Dabir was standing in front of Gate 20 near the corner of the terminal—a problem, Lia thought, since his flight was to take off at Gate 27.

If he didn't take the plane here—if he was simply meeting someone— the FBI agents in the terminal would nab him as he left; more than two dozen men were waiting in case something went wrong. More complicated was the contingency if he took another plane; the aircraft would be ordered back to the gate, with the pilot feigning a mechanical problem necessitating a plane change. Dabir would then be arrested as he came off.

The problem with either scenario was that there'd be people around, and while he didn't have a weapon—he'd already passed through one detection system—Lia worried that he might figure out what was going on and try something desperate. Small kids were all over the place; he might try and grab one as a hostage.

She'd kick his head off his shoulders if he tried it.

"They're about to announce boarding," said Rockman.

Lia turned and looked at the gate. A boarding agent had just stepped to the podium.

"First-class passengers are encouraged to board at this time," said the woman, launching into her spiel.

Dabir's ticket was in coach; Lia's was two rows behind his.

"Here we go," said Rockman, his relief evident. "He's coming over."

Lia waited until Dabir was nearly to the boarding area before getting up. She removed the ticket from her purse and pulled it out, walking to the end of the line. The ticket agents checked each stub, then shooed the people through quickly; within thirty seconds of arriving, Dabir was the third in line.

Then he abruptly turned and walked away.

◆ ◆ ◆

"WHAT IS HE doing?" demanded Rockman.

"Relax," Telach told him. "Lia, stay in line. He may be trying to flush you out."

Only Lia could have sighed in a way that seemed obscene.

Telach heard her ask the boarding agent if the flight was overbooked. Dabir, meanwhile, had walked toward the long hallway that led back to the terminal.

"Should I bring the FBI people in?" asked Rockman.

Telach turned to Rubens, standing next to her.

"Do we grab him?"

Rubens pointed at the screen at the front of the room, which was split into five panels, each covering the concourse area near the gate. Dabir had circled around the Burger King and gone into the men's restroom.

"Think he's lost?"

"Doubtful," said Rubens. "Watch for anyone who may be meeting him in there. Have Lia get on the plane."

"But what if he doesn't board?" asked Rockman.

"He will," said Rubens. "But if he doesn't, tell her Boston is very nice this time of year."

CHAPTER 145

DABIR STARED AT his face in the mirror. His cheeks looked very pale, paler than he had noticed this morning at the hotel.

The people at the gate bothered him, asking questions as they double-checked tickets. And one of the passengers—a tall man, well built, with a ruddy complexion—had eyed him surreptitiously as he joined the line. Were they FBI agents? CIA? Did they suspect something?

There was nothing tangible to indicate something was amiss, just his apprehensions. But Dabir had survived many years thanks to his instincts, and he would rather rearrange his plans than run the risk of being caught.

He stared again at the mirror, then slowly ran his forefinger over his left cheekbone.

Just tired, he thought. It would pass.

There was no reason to fear. He had killed the traitor. If he did not board now, it would be difficult to obtain another ticket. Besides, since he'd already checked in, his absence might raise alarms.

Dabir stared into the face of his reflection, noticing the blood at the corner of his left eye for the first time.

He held his hands out to pray.

"Take away my fear," he said softly. Then he started for the door.

CHAPTER 146

"LIA, HE'S COMIN' at ya," said Rockman.

She was too busy trying to make herself comfortable in the narrow seat to even grunt an answer. But sure enough, when she looked up Dabir was walking down the aisle. She rolled her head back, disguising the glimpse as a yawn.

"Ms. DeFrancesca, this is Mr. Rubens. There'll be a slight change in plans when you reach Newburgh. Mr. Rockman will explain everything before you land. We are still working on the details."

"Peachy," she said aloud.

CHAPTER 147

DR. SAED RAMIL STARED at the sheen of water, hypnotized by the gentle ripples and the soft glitter of the light. God was ever present in the universe, so why couldn't he talk to someone? Not Ramil, necessarily, but someone else, someone worthy of hearing God's voice directly?

Because modern man didn't believe in such things. Some did, certainly, but men like Ramil—students of science—didn't. Allah might guide them, influence them, push or pull them in the right direction, but speech was something that happened in the past, not now. Even someone like Asad bin Taysr, a devil incarnate, didn't claim God spoke to him, not in words.

Had religion changed, or man?

Man, Ramil decided. Man always changed.

And therefore religion changed. Not God, not the core of belief, but the manmade world around it.

That was what this struggle was really about. Asad bin Taysr and his ilk didn't like the way Muslims had changed. They didn't understand that someone like Ramil could be at home in the West, could be a contributing member to its society, could save lives.

Not many, but enough. In his small way, Ramil had made a difference. Asad could not fathom that.

Nor could he fathom that someone like Ramil could hear God's voice—not in his head, but in the slow roll of the river as it rolled endlessly past.

And that was at the root of his sin, was it not?

◆ ◆ ◆

TOMMY KARR AMBLED down the rocks, easing his way toward the river line. The Hudson sent a gentle surge against the shore, a kiss belying its awesome power.

"Nice view, huh?"

Dr. Ramil turned around with a start.

"Hey, Doc," said Karr, sliding down next to him on the big rock. "Long time no see."

"How'd you know where I was?"

Karr gave him a smirk.

"Oh, the chip in the phone," said Ramil after a second. "I'd forgotten."

"Kind of slips out of your mind, huh?"

"The technology—does it bother you ever?"

"Ah. Just gizmos. Tools of the trade." Karr shrugged. "How ya feelin'?"

"Not bad. The river is very peaceful."

"Not the best neighborhood up there," said Karr, thumbing past the railroad trestle.

"I hadn't noticed."

The waterfront park was an oasis of upscale development, with restaurants, parking lots, and a marina; above it lay a pot-holed stretch of city even Karr might not have walked through alone at night.

"There's been a change in plans," Karr told the doctor. "You up for implanting another bug?"

Ramil's eyes seemed to catch fire. "On Dabir?"

"Advance to Go. Collect two hundred dollars. Art Room says it's a K-three-point-two bug. That's supposed to mean something to you."

"Yes," said Ramil. "It has more range but is a little bigger. The procedure is the same."

"Good," said Karr. "Come on. We've got a lot to do."

CHAPTER 148

LIA PULLED THE small carry-on bag up from the floor in front of her seat, holding it close to her chest as the plane began to empty. She could see the back of Dabir's head. He was still seated despite the fact that the line was nearly to his row. She thought of waiting as well but decided not to; the airport was well covered, and there was no need to call attention to herself. She pushed past him, walking swiftly through the plane and even smiling for the stewardess, who thought the fact that she had given her an extra bottle of water earlier had made them best friends for life.

Passengers were disgorged down a long hallway. Lia tensed as she turned the corner where the arrest had been planned; two FBI agents dressed as airline employees were standing there, exactly as if the original plan were still in place.

She continued into a large, auditorium-like room with a baggage carousel. Lia managed to get herself in a tangle of travelers, allowing her to stand off to the side as Dabir walked into the hall, the last passenger to get off the plane.

"Coming at you and past," said Rockman in her ear. "You swing to your left, go through security again, and go up the escalators. Gate will be to your left."

Lia started walking in that direction. Dabir had stopped to get his bearings. Lia passed him, then feigned interest in a newsstand.

"Heading toward the door," Rockman told her. "Stand by."

Was he leaving rather than taking the connecting flight?

While they had prepared for that contingency, it would require them to fall back on the arrest rather than implanting the bug.

Lia picked up the latest Dale Brown thriller from the newsstand, flipping through it while she waited. She got four pages deep before Rockman told her Dabir was coming back. She bought the book; by the time she got to the security checkpoint, Dabir was on the escalator.

CHAPTER 149

SMALL AIRPORTS SEEMED to confuse Dabir more than large ones, possibly because the people who used them tended to do so a lot and there were fewer explanatory signs. But he found the gate for the aircraft to Boston with more than twenty minutes to spare. The plane, a small two-engined turboprop, sat below on the runway, being inspected by a pair of technicians.

Dabir turned his gaze from the window to its reflections, examining the area behind him. Five people were scattered around the seats, each in a different state of boredom. Dabir turned abruptly and began walking back toward the coffee kiosk; no one seemed to notice.

He bought a cup of tea, ordering two tea bags to make the taste tolerable.

"Have to charge ya for both. Sorry, hon," said the woman. Her thick Hispanic accent was difficult to untangle, and he simply nodded and handed her a five.

The group waiting for the plane had swelled to eleven. All of the newcomers were people he recognized from the plane. Six were women. Two of the men were bald, well into their fifties. Only one had the look of a possible intelligence agent, a young black man in his early twenties.

A policeman walked down the aisle and turned around, circulating through the terminal to make passengers feel more secure. In truth, there were plenty of flaws that could be exploited, a multitude of gaps and loopholes waiting until it suited al-Qaeda's agenda to do so.

Dabir would help set that agenda from now on. Asad's death—and Dabir's role in discovering that he was a traitor and carrying out the execution—would greatly enhance his position and prestige.

I must be humble, Dabir reminded himself.

The attendant stepped to the podium and picked up the microphone as another went to the door behind her. Dabir picked up his bag and joined the others.

As he did, the lights in the terminal died.

CHAPTER 150

LIA WATCHED THE gate attendant as she furiously clicked her microphone button, not quite comprehending the fact that power in the entire terminal had died.

"I've never had this happen," said the attendant.

"Power failure," said the other gate person, coming back from the door.

Some of the passengers began grumbling.

"Hold on, folks. This will be straightened out in a minute."

Lia knew it wouldn't. And while some emergency power would be resupplied, a Desk Three-engineered glitch would prevent any flights from taking off for several hours—or until Dabir was safely out of the terminal.

DABIR REMAINED SILENT as the passengers around him complained and cursed the idiots running the airport.

Was this just a freak event? Or was it somehow aimed at him?

If it was aimed at him, if the American intelligence services had somehow found him, what would they expect him to do?

Run.

He went and sat in a seat, watching as people knotted around the other gates. Dim yellow lights were on along the walls, and there was enough of the fading sunlight coming through the windows for people to see where they were going. There wasn't panic, but there were plenty of complaints.

If the American CIA or FBI did know he was here, they

would have arrested him when he came off the plane. Turning off the power was too much trouble.

No, it was just the West's typical incompetence, relying too much on computers and technology, rather than people. In refusing the one true God, they had rejected the value of people as well.

"I've been flying for twenty years and I've never seen anything like this," said a short, balding man plopping down in the seat next to him. "Ridiculous."

"Ridiculous," said Dabir.

"I have a meeting in Boston first thing in the morning. This is crazy."

"They said the planes will be taking off pretty soon," said a woman sitting across from them. She was in her early thirties, slim, with an Asian face. Like many American women, she seemed to naturally assume that men would be interested in talking to her. Dabir tried to hide his disdain.

"I shoulda gone to LaGuardia," said the short man. "I saved a hundred bucks. Big deal now, right?"

"A hundred bucks is a hundred bucks," said the woman.

Dabir rose.

"You leaving?" asked the man.

"Just stretching my legs."

"I'm going to get some coffee," said the Asian-American woman, getting up. "You guys want anything?"

"Nah," said the man.

"You?" She looked at Dabir.

"No."

"Do I know you?" asked the woman.

"I don't believe so."

"You were on the plane out of Cleveland, right?"

Dabir nodded. The woman stuck out her hand. "Li."

He took her hand and bowed his head ever so slightly, barely remembering to use the name he had used for the plane tickets.

Her warm hand reminded Dabir of the deprivations he'd faced over the past two years. He steeled himself; it was not a time for pleasure.

"So you want something or not?" the woman asked.

"No. Thank you."

"Sure."

LIA WALKED SLOWLY to the coffee bar. The next step was up to Dabir. She hoped he would decide to rent a car and drive to Boston, not because that particular contingency was the easiest for her—it wasn't—but because it involved the least amount of hanging around. She hated hanging around.

But that was her job. She got the coffee and walked back to the gate area. Having made contact with Dabir, she found a seat in the next row. Making idle chitchat with mass murderers was not her forte.

CHAPTER 151

"YOU CAN SKIP the taxi routine, Tommy—he took the hotel vouchers and the minibus," said Rockman.

Karr yawned and glanced at his watch. It was five minutes to nine; he'd been sitting outside the airport terminal since five-twenty. He turned the ignition and eased the taxi out of its spot at the side of the terminal.

"Lia's with him. Four other passengers as well," said Rockman.

"She invite him up to her room for a drink?"

"Very funny. All right, he's coming out of the terminal. Now what? He's not going for the bus."

"Relax partner. I got it covered." Karr angled the taxi around the parked minibus. Dabir had split from the main group and was walking along the sidewalk. He put up his hand, flagging down the cab.

"Hey, now," said Karr cheerfully as he hopped from the taxi. The trunk popped open. "Take that for you, sir?"

"It stays with me," said Dabir.

"Hey. *No problemo.*"

Karr tapped the trunk shut after Dabir got into the cab. He winked at Lia, who was in the line for the bus.

"Where we headin', boss?" Karr asked as he got in the cab.

"I need a good hotel."

"Not a problem. Holiday Inn?"

"That'll do."

Karr saw Dabir looking at the voucher in his hand. The

hotel he'd been given a voucher for was the Minerva, located several miles from the Holiday Inn.

"Holiday Inn comin' up. So what's goin' on in there? Heard they lost their power."

"I don't know."

"Really puttin' you out. Kind of a rip-off, huh?" said Karr, glancing back. "Did they at least offer to put you up or buy dinner?"

"They canceled our flights and told us to come back tomorrow."

"Where ya goin'?" asked Karr. He jerked his head around. Dabir's face, tired, seemed pale.

"To the hotel?"

"No, I mean flyin'. Maybe I could drive you."

"No, thank you."

"You're the boss. Holiday Inn's our next stop."

Karr pulled around Route 300, driving toward the hotel and humming the *Star Wars* theme song as he did.

"Uh-oh," said Karr as he pulled into the driveway. "Homecoming week."

"What does that mean?" asked Dabir, digging into his wallet to pay him.

"It's a college thing. Graduates come back. The hotel may be booked. Want me to wait?"

"That won't be necessary."

"No problem for me. The night is dead. You want change?"

"Keep it," said Dabir, getting out.

"Good tipper," Karr told Rockman as he pulled ahead. "He's at the desk. Not too happy."

Karr put the taxi in gear and drove to the end of the driveway. As Dabir came through the front door, he pulled out, then pretended to spot him, and veered back into the lot through the other entrance, narrowly missing a pickup truck.

"Problem?" he asked Dabir, rolling down the window.

"Take me to the Minerva."

"You got an address on that?"

"You never heard of it?"

"It's near the river somewhere. I can find it, but, uh, if you have the address it'll kind of save a little time, you know? Most people come here."

Dabir gave him the voucher.

"Be there in two shakes," said Karr, handing the slip back.

CHAPTER 152

DABIR GOT OUT of the taxi and walked into the hotel, trying not to let fatigue lower his guard. The clerk at the Holiday Inn had been a snotty kid, full of American arrogance toward strangers, taking glee in predicting that he would not find a hotel with a free room until next Monday. That behavior would never be tolerated in Europe, thought Dabir, let alone in an Arab country, where guests were to be treated with honor and respect.

He would remember the kid when he coordinated his first attack here. It would inspire him.

"Oh, there you are," said one of the passengers from the plane, passing him in the lobby. It was the Asian-American woman named Li. "We wondered what had happened to you."

"I decided to see if a friend was home," lied Dabir. "But he wasn't."

"Oh, too bad. Well, listen. There's a restaurant up the street. Some of us are checking it out."

"No, thank you."

"There's no room service," she added. "But they do have a little coffee shop around the back through that door. You can take the steps. See you on the plane in the morning."

Dabir presented his voucher to the clerk, who immediately punched it into his computer and retrieved a key for him.

"You can leave your bag, sir," added the man. "We'll bring it right up to you."

"No, that's all right," said Dabir, who was nonetheless pleased to see that at least some employees here had manners. "Thank you, though."

"Elevator right there. I'm sorry that you were inconvenienced at the airport. It's really unusual."

The room was good sized. The desk clerk's polite manner had mollified Dabir somewhat and he found himself actually regretting that he hadn't gone to dinner.

The woman was attractive. It might have been enjoyable to spend a few hours with her.

Dangerous, though. It would mean lowering his guard, something he must not, could not do. Besides, she was an American, a nonbeliever who, at heart, was his enemy.

Dabir decided he was feeling hungry rather than lonely, and after washing up went to find the hotel cafe she had mentioned. The stairs were at the end of the hall; he pushed open the door, took a step, then felt himself falling backwards. The back of his head seemed to pop, and everything went black.

CHAPTER 153

"HEAVIER THAN HE looks," grunted Tommy Karr as he hauled Dabir over his shoulder. "How we lookin', Rockman?"

"Coast is clear. I thought you were going to wait until he'd eaten?"

"I sees my chances and I takes 'em, boss," said Karr, still talking like the cab driver he'd pretended to be. He slid open the door and hustled into the hallway.

The door to room 213 opened and Hernes Jackson's face appeared.

"Here we go, Ambassador," said Karr, striding into the room. "One patient, prepped and ready to go under the knife."

SWEAT ROLLED DOWN Dr. Ramil's fingers as well as his brow. His first thought was that Dabir was dead. He felt for a pulse at the neck.

It wouldn't be a great loss if he were dead, Ramil thought. But the thump beneath his fingers was strong and steady.

"Did you give him the drugs?" Ramil asked Karr.

"Popped him on the head, poked him with the tack," said Karr. The "tack" was a hypodermic needle designed to be concealed in a fist. It looked like a rubber ball with a metal snout and needle.

"Is there a problem, doctor?" asked Jackson.

Ramil looked across the bed at him. "No, I—I just want to make sure we're ready."

"Looks gone to me," said Karr.

Ramil turned around to the second bed and opened the two attaché cases. He pulled on the gloves, aware that he was breathing deeply.

This is your chance. Cut the veins in the neck. It will take only a minute.

Ramil looked at the knife, then went to Dabir. The new device was designed to be inserted at the back of the skull. Its design made it harder to detect, and it had a range nearly twice that of the one he had implanted in Asad.

Do it, Ramil. Rid the world of the vermin.

The knife felt heavy in his hand. Ramil looked across the room at Jackson, who stared back at him.

Was this really what God wanted? Murder? It was not murder to kill an enemy of the faith. And Dabir clearly was an enemy.

But Allah would not command him to make such a judgment. The voice was not God's, it was his—a product of stress.

Yes. Every time he'd heard it he had been under heavy stress.

Take revenge for the people he has murdered.

And if it weren't stress, surely it came from the Devil, not Allah. For wasn't what it commanded him to do not only a sin, but one that would harm many others? It would stop the operation, depriving Desk Three of the chance to save others.

Karr's heavy hand clamped on Ramil's shoulder. "Don't cut the wrong place, right?"

Ramil turned and looked at Karr. The op grinned, then took his hand off his shoulder.

Ramil made the cut. His hands took over, moving swiftly, expertly. The device was a little more difficult to handle, but he got it in, checking twice to make sure it was oriented properly. The shape and location of the incision allowed them to use surgical glue rather than stitches; with a bandage in place, Dabir would never know he'd been slit open.

A tear slid down Ramil's cheek as he finished. He felt his shoulders sag.

Done.

He would never hear the voice again. But God's true voice—in the flow of the river, in the wind, in the science that saved lives and made men whole—that voice Ramil was only beginning to hear.

JACKSON WATCHED RAMIL finish. The doctor's hands were shaking, but he had held up.

"Maybe we should get a drink," Jackson suggested as the doctor cleaned up. "Then bring something back for Mr. Karr."

"Sounds good," Karr said. "Two Italian heroes, the works. I saw a sub place up the block."

"I don't drink," said Ramil. He smiled weakly. "It's against my religion."

"Sorry," said Jackson. "I didn't mean to offend you."

"No offense," said Ramil.

"Doc doesn't drink," said Karr. "I've tempted him myself."

"Sometimes we all give in to temptation," said Ramil. "We all occasionally slip."

"It's difficult to do the right thing," said Jackson.

"Very," agreed the doctor, closing his medical case.

CHAPTER 154

"DONE. DOWNHILL FROM here," said Telach. "Bug is working perfectly."

"Yes," said Rubens. He walked over to the console and picked up the phone.

"Calling the president?"

"No. Ms. Collins, actually."

IT DIDN'T SURPRISE Rubens at all that Collins was suspicious when he proposed that the CIA take over the "handling" of the bugging operation.

"Since when does Desk Three turn over any operation it starts?" she asked.

"It's not a trick, Debra. Desk Three is designed for short operations, not keeping someone under surveillance for weeks or even months at a time. We simply don't have the personnel to devote to an extended mission. As this one has shown."

"You've done pretty well until now."

"I appreciate the compliment."

Collins was silent, but it was obvious what she was thinking: *What is he up to?*

"I believe you yourself said that we're not enemies," Rubens told her. "Your people were supporting the operation overseas anyway."

"It's Bing, isn't it? You figure she'll hound you until you make a mistake, and you don't want to take a chance."

Rubens sighed. He did hate Bing. He suspected Collins

did as well. But that wasn't it. On the contrary, he was sure that Bing would use this against him somehow. It was all grist for the mill.

If there were a way to store the information and occasionally download it or pick it up, like some of the NSA's other programs, his feeling might have been different. But politics aside, having the CIA take over was the best strategy.

"Desk Three is not designed for long-term missions," he said. "It's simply not what we do. You are positioned much better. But if you want—"

"No. No, you're right," said Collins. "When do you propose we switch?"

"As soon as you want," said Rubens. "There are FBI agents standing by in Boston. They can back your people up as easily as they can back up mine. Assuming the president agrees."

"And Bing."

"Yes. And Bing."

"Bill?" she added as he was about to hang up.

"We shouldn't be enemies."

"I hope we're not."

"I didn't mean what I said the other day."

"About?"

"One hand washing the other."

"Well, it does, doesn't it?" said Rubens. "We just can't make decisions on that basis, can we?"

CHAPTER 155

THE LIGHT POUNDED through his skull, pushing its way past his heading, pushing and diving into his skull, pounding him.

"Oh, thank God. I was beginning to worry that you'd never wake up."

Dabir started to rise but the pain pushed him back down.

"Where am I?"

"St. Theresa's," said a woman's voice on the far side of the room.

"I found you on the steps when I went down for breakfast. You seem to have passed out," said another voice. It seemed familiar. "Are you okay?"

"Li?"

"Yes. Listen. The plane for Boston leaves in an hour. Um, I hate to leave you here, but I kind of have to make it. I'm late already. Is there anyone you want me to call?"

"No. I—I have to make the plane." Dabir started to get up.

A woman in a white dress—a nun or a nurse, he couldn't tell which—came to his side. "Are you sure you're okay to leave?"

"What happened to me?"

"You bashed the back of your head on some steps. We took X-rays. They're negative. You don't have a concussion, but I would imagine it hurts a great deal."

That much was true. Dabir touched the back of his head gingerly.

"There was a small cut and some abrasions. We cut off

some of your hair to clean it. I think it will heal fine," added the nurse. "You didn't even need stitches."

"That's all that's wrong with me?"

"Yes."

"I have to go." Dabir placed his feet on the floor. His head hurt, but he wasn't dizzy.

"You should leave the bandage on for a few days," said the nurse.

"Are you going to try and make the plane?" asked Li.

"Can we?"

"If we hurry. I'll call a taxi."

Dabir gazed at her as she left the room. She had a small, compact body—an attractive one. Had circumstances only been different, he might have found it too tempting to resist . . .

CHAPTER 156

DEAN FLEW INTO Boston to back up Lia, even though the Art Room told him it wasn't necessary. He'd learned from experience that he was one who had to make that call as far as Lia was concerned, or he wouldn't be able to live with himself.

Waiting for her flight to come in, Dean found himself with time on his hands. After scoping out the terminal for the third time, he wandered over to the payphones. As he stared at them, he realized he hadn't wandered here at all. He went to one, punched in a credit card number, then told the Art Room he'd be off-line for a few minutes.

"Hello." The word sounded more like a demand than a greeting.

"Hey, Dad," said Dean.

"Who is this?"

"It's Charlie. Who'd you think it was?"

"Why are you calling?"

"I felt like it."

The answer seemed to stump his old man. Dean imagined him scowling at the phone. He half expected him to hang up.

"Good," said his father finally. "I'm glad."

To Dean's great surprise, he actually sounded as if he meant it.

LIA TOOK A taxi from Logan Airport in Boston, checked into a hotel, and waited for the Art Room to tell her Dabir had gotten a room before leaving. A pair of CIA agents had trailed him from the airport; Desk Three was feeding them intercepts from the implanted bug and would continue to do so until he arrived in Ireland, where the CIA was installing gear to take over the rest of the job.

As far as she was concerned, they could have the creep. Every minute she spent near him, the temptation to shoot him increased tenfold.

Charlie Dean was waiting for Lia when she got out of the taxi.

"Hey, good looking," he said, grabbing her by the waist. She started to resist—reflex only—then gave in, wrapping her body around him in a long kiss.

"I missed you," she whispered. "Bad."

"Yeah? Even though I'm over the hill?"

"Oh, stop."

"How's Terry?"

Lia felt her face warm. She bit down on her lower lip. "Stop that," she told him.

"You gonna tell me about Pinchon sometime?" asked Dean, taking her bag.

"Sometime. Maybe," said Lia. "Where's our flight?"

"I DON'T LIKE the insinuations that my father was a criminal," said Irena when Rubens met her for lunch. With the bugging operation now in the CIA's hands, he'd rewarded himself with a few hours off. "The Justice Department people were quite nasty."

"You mustn't take it personally. It's part of Washington politics."

"I hate it. They're implying that he had the documents simply because they can't locate them. He must *not* have had them, or they would have found them. Right?"

"No, not exactly," said Rubens. He patted her hand. A warm wave—of what? electricity? emotion?—ran through him. "Your father is not the real target here."

"Who is?"

"Me. Among others."

Rubens explained that an investigation, even one that began innocently, could be used to damage reputations by casting doubt indirectly. Clearly that was what was going on here.

The papers that were missing had to do with Asian trade matters, and while they had been code-word classified, the information in them would hardly bring down the republic if revealed. They had been prepared in conjunction with Hadash's recent mission to China, which accounted for their secret classification. It was possible that Hadash had inadvertently shredded them without recording that fact (or returning them to their electronic "locker," which would have been the correct procedure). It was also possible—and more likely, Rubens thought—that one of his aides had taken the copies under his authority while preparing for the mission and now felt there was too much heat to own up to the mistake.

"Is this going to hurt you?" Irena asked.

"I wouldn't think so. On the contrary, it's so transparent— I would think it might help in some quarters."

This was a lie. Every bump and bruise, no matter how slight, took its toll. The slate would eventually grow crowded, and sooner or later the tipping point would be reached. The criticisms, spoken and unspoken, would coalesce; one's star would sink. That was the Washington way. But Rubens wasn't thinking about that eventuality now. He wasn't thinking about politics at all. He was staring into Irena's eyes, lost in them.

"I'm not so naive as that," said Irena. She lifted her hand. Rubens began to draw his back reluctantly, but stopped as she caught his fingertips. "You've been a real friend. More."

"Of course."

"I would like to see you. Under—other circumstances. I would like that. If it's possible," she said.

For the first time, he noticed a tremor in her voice. His own throat suddenly dry, Rubens nodded, then moved his hand to hold hers properly.